Photo: Antonia Hayes

Drusil[...]
most [...]
Engla[...]
before arriving in Australia in [...]
books include *Exiles at Home*; the NSW
Premier's Award winner *Poppy*; *Sisters*,
which she co-edited; the Nita B. Kibble,
NSW Premier's Award and Australian
Bookseller's Book of the Year Award
winner *The Orchard*; *Timepieces*; and
Secrets with Robert Dessaix and Amanda
Lohrey. She is also the author of the
bestselling *Stravinsky's Lunch*, winner of
the Nita B. Kibble and the NSW Premier's Award. *The Mountain* is her
first novel.

Praise for *The Mountain*

'A wonderful achievement. It is moving and panoramic. It takes us into the
heart of our near neighbour Papua New Guinea in a way that's never been
done before, through the point of view of the founders of independence,
their friends and lovers. At the same time, it's a sweeping story of love and
friendship, of hope and regret, and of the generational loyalties we inherit,
as well as the ones we create for ourselves. *The Mountain* is a novel as intricate and powerful as the bark-cloth paintings at its heart.' Anna Funder

Praise for *The Orchard*

'Modjeska is accessible and entertaining, a good story-teller . . . Her dexter-
ity at interlacing . . . assorted skeins without unravelling or entanglement is
to be marvelled at' *Canberra Times*

'A beautifully written narrative . . . *The Orchard* is written with style and
complexity' *Melbourne Times*

'A book brimful with ideas, informed by a wide-ranging imagination, and
certain to inspire those who read it to act upon their dreams . . . As enrich-
ing a book as you're likely to read this year' *Herald Sun*

Also by Drusilla Modjeska

Non-fiction

Women Writers: a study in Australian cultural history 1920–39
Exiles at Home: Australian women writers 1925–45
Inner Cities: Australian women's memory of place
Poppy
The Orchard
Secrets (with Robert Dessaix and Amanda Lohrey)
Stravinsky's Lunch
Timepieces

Edited

The Poems of Lesbia Harford
Sisters
The Best Australian Essays 2006
The Best Australian Essays 2007

THE
MOUNTAIN

DRUSILLA
MODJESKA

VINTAGE BOOKS
Australia

A Vintage book
Published by Random House Australia Pty Ltd
Level 3, 100 Pacific Highway, North Sydney NSW 2060
www.randomhouse.com.au

First published by Vintage in 2012

Addresses for companies within the Random House Group can be found at
www.randomhouse.com.au/offices

National Library of Australia
Cataloguing-in-Publication Entry

Modjeska, Drusilla
The mountain / Drusilla Modjeska

ISBN 978 1 74166 650 2 (pbk.)

A823.4

Cover photograph by Jason Isley, Scubazoo/Getty Images
Cover design by Sandy Cull, gogokingko
Map on p. v by Ice Cold Publishing
Internal design by Midland Typesetters
Typeset in 12/15.5pt Adobe Garamond by Midland Typesetters, Australia
Printed in Australia by Griffin Press, an accredited ISO AS/NZS 14001:2004
Environmental Management System printer

Random House Australia uses papers that are natural, renewable and recyclable products and made from wood grown in sustainable forests. The logging and manufacturing processes are expected to conform to the environmental regulations of the country of origin.

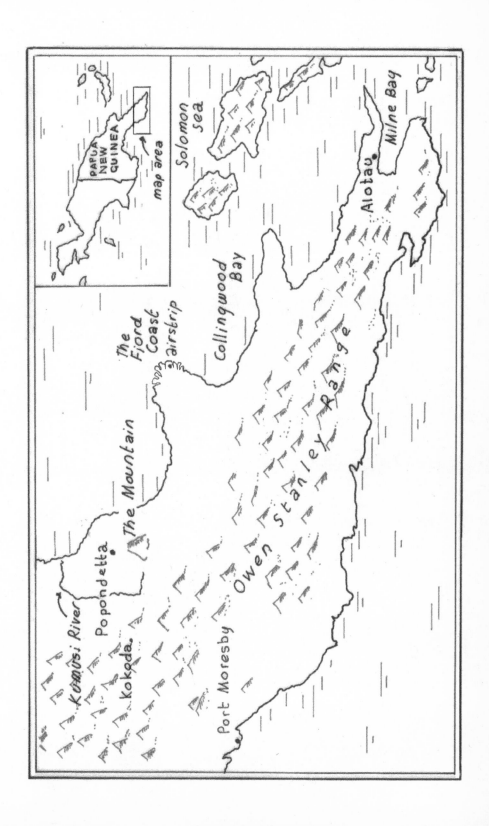

PROLOGUE

Lunch with Jericho, 2005

FROM HIS TABLE ON THE TERRACE OF THE MUSEUM, JERICHO SEES Martha coming through the crowds on the Quay. She's walking fast and takes off her dark glasses to scan the tables. Her hair is short, well cut. The odd thing is that she looks like Rika. Rika's clothes are more expensive, of course, but Martha has the same style and form. Well, there was a time when they were friends. Like sisters, Leonard said. For thirty years they haven't spoken, and still they look the same.

Martha spots him at a table towards the end of the terrace, and waves. He's chosen a good position, under a heater, with a view across the water to the Opera House. It's June, the beginning of winter in Sydney, and out of the sun the air is chill.

'How good you look,' Martha says as they embrace, and Jericho sees the pleasure in her face. When he first came down from the mountain to Rika, barely five years old, she was the other mother. Rika and Martha. They were younger then than he is now, and he thinks again of how it must have been for them, in a country that wasn't theirs, suddenly presented with a small child to raise.

'So, Jericho,' Martha says when they're settled at the table with the menus. 'You're going back.'

He nods, a quizzical expression that says, *Yes, he's going back, but he's not at all sure.*

'A big decision.'

'It's thirty years now,' he says. 'A good round number.' Not much of an answer, but it's a start.

'Thirty years,' Martha says. 'I suppose it is.' Thirty years since independence. She remembers the celebrations, the dancing and the music. And the rain, the mud. Independence. What a fine word

that is, and something stirs in a dark region of her memory, something sad and raw. She doesn't expect the raw, not after all this
time.

'I've got leave from the gallery,' Jericho says. 'A year away from
London.' He makes a face that says, *Help! A year! Will I last that
long?* 'Did you know,' he says, 'that they've closed the airstrip on the
mountain? I'll have to walk in.'

'Where from?'

'The road that goes up to Kokoda. I've looked it up on the map.
There's a side road part of the way, but it's still a long walk just to
get to the river.' The river at the base of the mountain.

Martha knows that road. Dust when it's dry, cut by flooding
gullies when it's wet. 'How fit are you?' she asks. He's not tall, but
his legs are well muscled. Legs born for a mountain that is steep and
ridged, with many peaks.

'I've been training at the gym,' he says. 'And at weekends I walk
for hours. London's so flat, it's probably been a complete waste of
time.' He laughs. 'At Easter I went to Wales with Leonard. We did a
lot of walking, but nothing compared to the mountain. His advice
is not to think about it too much and when the time comes to just
do it!'

'I don't know about that,' Martha says. She never went up, but
everyone who did came back without an ounce of fat, and Jericho
doesn't look as if he has much to spare. He's lean, small-boned, with
the soft, coppery skin of his Papuan mother and the long face of his
English father. The black curls of his hair are as thick as they were
when he was a child.

The food arrives. Small portions on large plates. They should
have crossed the road at the back of the museum and gone to a café.
She knows he's been with the curators all morning, as his gallery in
London is borrowing from their holdings for a show in two years'
time. Even so.

'How's Rika?' she asks. It's a question she can't not ask, and fears
will take her where she doesn't want to go.

'She's in New York.'

'I know. But that's about all I know.'

Jericho takes a photo from the satchel of papers he has with him. 'I'm taking it up to the mountain,' he says. 'To show them.'

As he hands it across, Martha feels a sharp stab of betrayal. Rika is standing against a white wall beside the ground-spider bark-cloth. Its many legs stretch above her, white on a dark background, long and thin, like the rays of the moon.

'So she still has it.' Martha keeps her voice even, not letting him see how angry she is. Rika keeps the cloth, lets herself be photographed beside it, and yet for thirty years has ignored letters, closing off the past as if it can be banished by the force of her refusal. 'When was it taken?' she asks.

'Recently. For an exhibition.'

'Does she talk to you about what happened?'

'No. Never.' He shakes his head, sighs. 'Leonard tells me what he knows, but he wasn't there for most of it. And she won't talk about any of it. Nothing.'

He thinks of the row they had before he left London. Not a row exactly, Rika is too controlled for that. Better if it had been. She said she'd never interfere with him returning, but it didn't mean she should dredge up a past long gone.

'She gives me access to the archive,' he says. 'It's all there, all the photos, but she won't tell me what they mean. She seems to think they're enough on their own. But they're not.'

Martha hears the frustration in his voice and she leans across, puts her hand on his. 'What is it you want to know?'

'Everything. What burst you all apart.'

'It's thirty years ago,' Martha says. Her heart feels tight. There's a part of her that wants to say to Jericho, *Let us bear the burden of the past, it should not be yours.* He may be thirty-six and think of himself as getting old, but she knows he's too young to realise how fast the rest will go, the accelerating decades, and she wants to say to him, *Don't look back. Be brave, go up there, do what you must, but when you leave, be sure you're poised for the future.* Then she thinks of her own departure, remembers the faces of her Papuan friends. *It's all very well for you guys. You can leave.* That's the least that was said. She should remember, betrayal cuts many ways.

She sits there, silent, looking at Jericho, remembering. *The gift child*, they called him on the mountain.

A waiter comes, clears their plates. They smile at him, turn their faces into those of people enjoying the pleasures of Sydney. Over at the Quay, ferries are easing in and out; the life of the city goes on, as it does, every day. The man sprayed silver continues to stand like a statue, the jugglers continue to juggle, and the didgeridoo plays to the tourists.

Martha looks at Jericho and understands it will be a hard return.

BOOK ONE

1968–73

Should we have stayed at home and thought of here?
...
Is it right to be watching strangers in a play
In this strangest of theatres?

Elizabeth Bishop,
'Questions of Travel', 1956

BIRDS OF THE SUN

 RIKA FIRST HEARD OF THE MOUNTAIN IN the flat country of her birth. It was a November day when Leonard, visiting Leiden from Oxford, told her the story of the old woman who carried the sun and the moon in her string bag. They were walking back to the house on the canal after Leonard had given a lecture at the museum. He was a house guest, the first since her mother had died, and to welcome him, her father had let her open the curtains of the old dining room, let in the fresh air. That was Leonard's first gift, freeing Rika from the tight corner of the kitchen where she and her father had been cramped for a long, bleak year. She had much to thank Leonard for, and she went with him to the museum, where her father was curator and host to his lecture. She sat at the back and while Leonard spoke of the value of ethnographic film, her mind drifted. It was a habit she'd learned while her mother was ill, letting the drift take her elsewhere, into another world, of blue water and blue skies. Sun. She often dreamed of sun. Did Leonard ever think it odd, she asked him after the lecture, that so many of the things in the museum, the masks and

carvings he was speaking of, had come from places in the sun, yet were marooned here in the gloom? They were walking along the canal and a soft rain was falling. Leonard took her arm as they crossed a bridge.

In Papua, he told her, deep in the ancestor past, an old woman had carried the sun and the moon in her string bag. Each morning, she climbed the great mountain in the dark, and when she reached the top she took the sun from her bag and hung it in the sky. Its light fell in glorious rays, shining through the trees, so that her daughters could see the abundance of the world around them. Amazed at its beauty, they painted all that they saw in its clear, bright light. They painted leaves and fruit and spider webs, the bones of river fish and the markings of caterpillars. And they painted the mountain with its many peaks. When they were tired and had worked enough for one day, the old woman climbed back to the peak of the mountain, took the sun down from the sky, returned it to her string bag, and in its place hung the moon. Then her daughters could rest, and she could rest with them.

Though Rika was schooled in Holland, that land of reason, there was a part of her that believed that a place which bred such people, such imagination, must be a place of redemption. So when, on a later visit, Leonard said he was going there, to that very mountain, to film its people who still painted the world around them, she said, yes, she'd marry him and go too.

In fact, marrying Leonard had meant a year in Oxford, which in terms of sun wasn't an improvement, but the year had passed and now, at last, here they were in Papua, at the end of a long journey. But instead of a mountain covered in rainforest and inhabited by artists, they were in a dry valley outside an awkward house in a row of awkward houses, expected to climb the steps and into a party of people gathered in welcome. Red-faced men were calling out from the veranda with beer bottles in their hands. They were wearing beige shorts, garments Rika had never before seen on grown men. The women, all but the youngest, were dressed in the slacks of Australian fashion. *Slacks*, in this heat. Rika was in an indigo shift, and her fringe fell over her eyes as she looked down at her own pale legs. Leonard put an encouraging hand on her shoulder and again she hesitated, turning to look into the dark.

It was a still night. The moon, just past the full, gave the hills a silvery quality. She'd seen them from the plane; they'd looked like waves coming into shore. Behind them lay the dark bulk of mountains; beyond that, on the other side of the island – Leonard had shown her on the map – was the mountain she'd come to think of as theirs.

From the plane she'd also seen villages curved along beaches, canoes pulled up on the sand; blue water, blue skies, just as she'd imagined. Beside the houses were trees with spreading branches, and along a sandy track a line of trees with flame-red leaves. Leaves or petals, she didn't know – she'd never seen such a tree, even in the Botanical Gardens at Leiden.

'It looks like paradise down there,' she said to Leonard.

'But not Port Moresby, I'm told,' he said, taking her hand. 'I hope you won't be disappointed.'

By the time they landed, clouds had come in over the mountains, the sky had lost its blue and hung low and heavy. When they'd crossed the tarmac to the hangar that served as a terminal, Rika was streaming with moisture. All around her people jostled, selling watermelon and carved masks, touting for business, calling out in singing voices. While Leonard lit his pipe and watched for the trunk with his film equipment, she waded into the crowd, pushing past the Australians who'd been on the plane and were now standing in groups, mopping their foreheads and calling across to the porters. She went on, into the colour and the smells, into this strange world where even air and trees had changed their nature. She lifted her camera to a tall woman with tattoo lines radiating across her face, a cigarette tucked into the bush of her hair. Rika smiled. The woman did not. She held Rika's gaze until she'd returned the Leica to her basket. The woman nodded, a ghost of a smile, and turned into the crowd.

*

The host, coming to greet them on the veranda, was Alex Penrose, a plump man whose glasses slid down his nose in the heat. He was the professor of anthropology.

'Welcome,' he said, his arms out wide. 'Come in. Come in. Let me introduce you.'

Professors. Wives in those terrible slacks. The vice-chancellor. A politician from the new indigenous party, serious, with neat, cropped hair. A sea of hands shook Rika's. Names skimmed through her head and were gone.

The room was sparsely furnished. The chairs were pushed to one side, and standing back against a wall was a group of young men with springy hair – students, she supposed. They had beer bottles in their hands; they held them as the white men did, but their faces were hesitant. There seemed something transitional about them. She liked that. Maybe she was too. She smiled and a ripple passed between them as they watched her, all blonde fringe and pale legs. Her indigo shift was getting more attention than Alex Penrose's story of how he'd lured Leonard to this new university that was still being built in this dry valley.

He'd been visiting the Martyrs School across the mountains, over on the north coast, where the Japanese had landed during the war. 'Named for the Anglican nuns who left their retreat too late,' he told Leonard. 'Foolish creatures, they trusted their god to save them.' He paused for laughter, which duly came. 'Still, it's a good school – we've a lot of students from there. I'd been there all day and was about to leave, when a boy came up. Smaller than the others, lighter-boned. From the mountain, the headmaster said. I thought the boy wanted to ask more about coming to the university, but, no, my introductory talk doesn't usually get such a response.' He paused for effect. The vice-chancellor laughed. The men crowded around laughed. 'The boy said, "The mountain asks for you," and I said, "You mean the chiefs," and he said, "No, the mountain." It was one of those moments. I might as easily have said no – it's not as if they don't keep us busy here' – another pause, another laugh – 'but how can you turn down an invitation like that?'

'If you hadn't gone,' Rika said, 'we wouldn't be here.'

'I suppose you wouldn't,' Alex said.

'Or maybe you would,' the politician said. 'More than one road can lead to where we're going.'

'Yes?' Rika looked at him. Cautious. She couldn't tell if he was mocking her. She thought not.

'You people have strange ideas of causality. You like to see the link and prove it.'

'How else would we get here?'

'Maybe the boy was right and the ancestors were calling you.'

'To here?' Rika was doubtful.

The politician smiled. 'I meant to the mountain,' he said. 'But maybe here as well.'

More laughter, though not from Rika.

'As an anthropologist, I wouldn't dismiss the possibility,' Leonard said. He had turned to the politician. 'I've seen evidence of other causalities.' He took a long draw on his pipe, and the conversation, with Alex conducting, returned to the mountain.

'A powerful place,' he said. 'You feel it when you're there.'

He'd accepted the invitation and gone up with the boy. Before the climb, he hadn't thought much about the bark-cloth they made on the mountain, though the headmaster had shown him a small piece on his wall, a gift sent down from the chiefs. He had felt the fibrous texture of the fabric and looked at the strange irregularity of the pattern, but the cloth was ill-lit and crowded by the lists and schedules pinned around it. He had had to climb the steep ridges of the mountain, a two-day journey, to reach the villages high above the morning mists. There he saw the bark-cloth hanging from houses and gateways, adorning the people. He saw that the black lines were painted with a free hand, the patterns heightened with rust browns and reds, dabs of yellow, a vibrant vocabulary of the mountain. It was then that Alex thought of Leonard. He'd seen his film of the canoe-makers of Tuvalu, and knew his reputation to be among the best.

'And here he is!' he said, arms flung wide. It was an achievement, persuading Leonard to come from Oxford to this new university, and for the film he'd shoot on the mountain to be associated with his department. So the faces turned towards this tall, slightly stooped man with a bony face that made him look more than ten years older than his wife.

The circle of men closed around him and Rika was left to Susan Penrose, a small woman who'd had too many children and didn't like the heat.

'Let me introduce you to the women,' she said. 'I'm afraid we're rather old-fashioned up here. With the men working, we have to make our own amusements.'

More faces, more names to miss, Rika thought.

The wives coming forward with their hands outstretched were matronly. Rika's dress felt appallingly wrong and she gave the skirt a surreptitious tug. Then she saw the bark-cloth tacked to the wall. Not a good position, but there it was, a pattern of abstract, semi-triangular shapes hanging imperturbable beside the door to the kitchen, where she could see people slicing chicken, arranging dishes, washing glasses.

'Beautiful, isn't it?' Susan said. 'The women paint the cloth, and one of their chiefs sent me this one. Not to Alex. To me.' She laughed. 'What a different world if our chiefs were women.'

The wives thought this hilarious. Something inside Rika sank. Was this what awaited her? This and the raw house where the car had left them that morning? There were still building materials piled outside. From inside, there was nothing to see but sparse trees. All afternoon she'd sat staring out, as if the hills might hold some surprise, some hint of possibility. But there was nothing. All this way, and nothing.

Later, Rika would say that if it hadn't been for Martha, she'd have run home to her father there and then, all the way to the Netherlands, and begged him to turn back the clock. As it was, Martha was standing near the kitchen, under the bark-cloth, and when she saw Rika look up at it, she smiled. In their exchange, hope rallied. Beside Martha was Laedi, with a child on her hip. Both women looked young – the same as her, Rika thought, with hair that was long and skirts that were short. No slacks for them. Martha was smiling, making small movements with her hands that said *keep going, don't stop*, as Rika extricated herself from a woman in a tie-dyed skirt who ran art classes and another who was starting a choir. When eventually she reached them, Susan Penrose didn't have to make the introductions. They did it themselves, as if the wait had been too long and they had a lot to catch up on. The child on Laedi's hip cackled with pleasure at Rika. Rika hitched her onto her own hip, saying, 'Come, it's hot. Let's go outside.'

Leaving the wives to their offers of sewing bees and coffee mornings, she turned, and with Martha and Laedi behind her manoeuvred through the party out onto the veranda, where the air was cool.

A young Papuan in a green shirt was leaning against the railing, rolling a cigarette. He was a student, not much more than twenty, with large, slightly hooded eyes and shorts that hung as if too large for him. He'd positioned himself where he could hear the professors and the politician. Leaning there, looking back into the room, he'd noticed the ripple Rika made as she abandoned the wives.

'Hey, Jacob,' Martha greeted him, as Alex appeared beside them. Behind him came Leonard and his pipe. Rika was looking out into the dark valley, which at dusk had been washed in garish streaks, transforming the swamp into a golden lake.

'I thought I'd walk over in the morning and swim,' she said.

'Where?' Jacob asked, following her gaze.

'There,' Rika said, pointing into the dark. 'Earlier I saw a lake.'

'Lake!' Alex exclaimed. 'It's a swamp! The only things that swim there are mosquitoes.'

'Still, I'd like to go,' Rika said.

'We can't have white women walking around alone in the scrub,' Alex said.

'I'll take you,' Jacob said. His face was curiously impassive. Impossible to read.

'It's a long walk, Jacob.' The roar had gone out of Alex's voice. 'Much too far for her.'

'We can take the old track.'

'I'd like that,' Rika said.

'Rika, darling,' Leonard said. 'Tomorrow morning we must go to the bank, arrange a car. There are chores.'

'Then Friday,' Jacob said. 'We should go at dawn.'

It was April, 1968.

RIKA WAS UP, WAITING IN THE EARLY LIGHT OF MORNING, WHEN Jacob tapped at the door of the newest house at the edge of the compound. She'd plaited her hair against the heat and pushed the plaits up under the white cotton cap she'd bought in town the day before. She was wearing jeans, so recently indispensable, which were now impossibly heavy. Still, at that hour the air was cool, and the hills and trees, even the bare earth, were transformed by the low slant of the sun that fell around the house in golden streaks.

Jacob nodded in greeting, one hand raised, and Rika echoed the gesture as they set off along the packed gravel road between the houses in which university families were waking for the day. Radios, a child crying, a hose on a garden. After the last of the houses, the road ended abruptly, with earth banked up where the grader had turned around. Clumps of tough grass were already growing over the mound of scraped-aside soil, a small track was worn into it, and on the other side they were in scrub, on a path she could see was well used.

'Who uses this road?' Rika asked.

'There used to be a camp out here,' Jacob said.

'What happened?'

'It was moved.'

'Where to?'

'Not to anywhere. To nowhere.'

'And the people?'

Jacob turned and looked at her. Didn't she know anything? 'They had to go,' he said.

'Why?' Rika asked.

'The university was built,' he said, and from the hunch of his shoulders she realised that whoever had lived here had been forced out, made to move on.

'Show me,' she said.

He cut through the trees to a cleared patch of scrub. Jacob didn't know how many people had been displaced. She looked at the crushed wood, the sheets of rusted roofing, splintered crates that had once been furniture, a broken chair. An old man and a boy were scavenging on the other side. Jacob called out to them. The people had moved to a settlement near the airport, the man said. He hadn't lived here. He was looking to see what he could use. At the edge of the clearing, growing into the bush, were sweet-potato vines. Jacob pointed to them with his foot. 'Not ready,' he said, and then nothing more as she followed him back to the track that led to the swamp. The sun still cast its golden beams, and all around birds were calling, swoops of colour through the shadow of trees. In the distance, the mountains were purple against the sky.

At the swamp, Rika stood beside Jacob, looking into the marshy water where tree roots bent and curled. There was a sweet, slightly fetid smell. Birds were scrapping in the trees, some great, raucous squabble going on above her, and she laughed. How could she have thought this swamp a lake? How could she have seen it at all?

'The sky,' Jacob said. 'You saw the sky.' He too was laughing.

'You tease me?'

He shook his head. No, he wasn't teasing. 'The sky catches the water,' he said, 'and makes it what you saw.' But still she felt the edge of doubt.

She took the Leica from the bag of woven bush-string that she'd bought the day before. She and Leonard had been at a market beside the harbour early in the morning, when fresh-caught fish were hanging from lines under the trees. The water was shining, reflective. She'd have to learn her camera all over again to accommodate its brightness. Its *shimmer*. Here at the swamp the water was stained, shades of brown and dark green. She took out her exposure meter. Even here she'd have to stop right down.

'Not much to look at if you're not a swamp-dweller,' Jacob said, and yet through the lens she could see that this grey-green world was alive.

'What do you see?' she asked him.

'Mud,' he said. 'And you with your camera.'

She laughed. 'No,' she said. 'Really?' She leaned forward, focusing down low. Pattern and texture, that's what she saw, the roots of swamp trees, the tracery left in the mud by crabs. She focused in tight, handed the camera to Jacob. 'Look,' she said. 'It's like art.'

'Art,' he said, handing it back. 'Why is everyone so interested in art? My roommate writes plays.' There was exasperation in his words. A severity. Then he smiled, a wide, straight smile that lifted his eyes so they no longer seemed hooded. 'Shall we go up? Look at the sky,' he asked, pointing to the nearest of the hills.

Rika followed behind the green of his shirt, along the narrow path back to the tall, aromatic grass, past large boulders, the strange papery trees. More birds were chattering, more sudden swoops of colour. The hill grew steeper as they approached, and the path, which had been rising towards it, turned at its base, skirting its steepness. Jacob walked ahead, off the path, and began to climb. It wasn't as if the earth had tilted, which is what Leonard said of the hills in Wales when they went to visit his parents. This was more like a child's drawing of a hill, as if an upside-down U had been given substance and dropped there by some mighty hand. Up close, it was a green wall, a kind of embankment. The ground was dry, stony. Her shoes slipped. She used rocks and branches to help her up. When she went down on her knees, Jacob put out a hand, grasped her by the wrist and hauled her up.

With every step the sun became larger, hotter as it swelled in the sky, and the stiff leaves of the trees gave no protection.

'*Zon*,' she said when they reached the top and had regained their breath. 'Our word for sun.'

'*Iji*,' he said, and she repeated it as he coached her inflection.

'*Iji*,' she said. 'Your sun. I like that. It has light in it.'

He nodded, looking ahead into the mountains. Rika wanted to ask what it was he saw when he looked across to those steep ridges folding away into the distance, pink and purple in the morning sun. The mountain where she and Leonard were going was way beyond, on the other side, unimaginably distant. All she saw was a barrier, impenetrable, featureless. She wanted Jacob to tell her how life was lived there, how houses were built, rivers crossed. How things grew. Instead she asked him where his home was.

'Home?' he said. 'My village?'

'Yes. Your village.'

'Over.' He pointed to the east.

'Near the mountain?'

'Your mountain? No. Not near there.' A slight emphasis on *your*, and she felt a blush add to the heat in her face. 'Further east, in the fjords,' he said.

'Fjords. Like Norway?'

'So they say.' He turned from the mountains to face the way they'd come, back towards the valley and the harbour. His shirt was a beacon against an unruffled sky, his face closed, impassive again. She looked with him across the sweep of valley. After the mountains it seemed strangely familiar: the distant speck of the university building site with its cranes and the neat rows of its housing. Through a saddle between the hills she could see the harbour and the outline of a tanker anchored off the port. Small dark shapes of canoes were skimming across the sheen of water like water beetles. She took the Leica from her string bag and leaned back to take a panoramic shot that'd capture the pattern of hills continuing beyond the frame, an impression of unbounded space, and, nestled somewhere in the middle distance, the toy town of the university.

'Is it real?' Jacob asked.

She turned to him, her face a query.

'Your husband comes from Oxford,' he said. 'He should know. Do they teach us here what they teach them there?'

Other than a year of photography in Amsterdam, Rika hadn't studied since school. She thought of the students on their bicycles in Leiden. 'I think it's real,' she said. 'Why wouldn't it be?'

'In town they call it the *bois'* university.'

'Boys? Like children?'

'No. *Bois*. Labourers.'

'Oh.'

'What does your husband say?'

'He doesn't say anything.'

'He comes all this way. From *Oxford*.' A note of what? Sarcasm? Disbelief? 'And he says nothing?'

'He says Alex Penrose knows more about Melanesia than any living man,' and before she could wish the words back, she saw anger flare. Anger and humiliation, that's what it was. 'Any *university* man, I think he meant. Any *anthropologist*,' she added, but Jacob was already bounding down the hill, skidding in the gravelly soil, kicking up dust. He came to a stop halfway down, by a large boulder where a few of the sparse, papery trees were bunched together. Shade.

Rika didn't know – how could she? It was her second morning in Papua – that from Jacob's perspective it was a serious question. Why wouldn't this be a lesser university, a lesser place, as his high school had been lesser? And before that, the primary school, with woven sago walls and windows open to the rain, and the teacher who lined up the children, caning the ones who called out the wrong answer. And now this, hidden away in a dry valley a university the like of which he'd never seen, seven miles from town. This university with no buildings. It was his second year, and still his classes were held in cramped rooms at the college where they trained the clerks. Clerks. Not much better than *bois*. Or in huts with roofs that leaked when the rain came. Nothing about this university bore any resemblance to the stories he'd been told by his clan-brother Aaron, one of the few who'd been chosen for study in Australia – and that was a concession to the United Nations. So Aaron said. A delegation had come, a visiting mission, and had seen how few students matriculated. The UN had insisted: send out some of those who are ready, fast-track a university for the rest.

The University of Queensland, where Aaron was sent, had colonnades and sweeping steps, clock towers and a library with floor after floor of books to the ceiling.

*

Alone on top of the hill, Rika felt like a flag, up so high, with a view in every direction. Not a flag to mark the spot, not an English flag. A flag waving into the future. All this way, and here she was, looking across at mountains that were nothing like her idea of the mountain that had beckoned. It was a perilous feeling. She sighed. The heat must be addling her brain and she could see that she'd offended Jacob. She put the camera in her string bag and began the climb down towards him. She stepped carefully; it was harder going down as she could see where she'd fall.

Jacob was still at the boulder, halfway down. He was watching her, though he'd angled his head as if he wasn't. When she slipped down on her arse, grateful for the jeans, she grasped the rough grass to stop the slide. Fine lines of blood appeared on her palm and Jacob came fast up the hill, offering his hand. A small smile, an apology, and his face became clear again. That's what she liked about him – the way he smiled, when he did. He knew as little as she did. A different little, but still, it was little. This new world coming.

'My clan-brother was at university in Australia,' he said. They were leaning against the rock into the shade, resting. Her breath was coming fast. She wiped her face but it made no difference – the air was heating up, its wetness settling on her. She took off her hat and took out the Leica.

'Is he still there?' she asked, lifting the camera, focusing tight on his face. It was a good lens. It'd manage this light.

'No. He's in Europe. Doing an MA.' A note of pride.

'What subject?'

'History. Colonial trade. Copra. Rubber. The trade in art. Plumes.'

She thought of her father at the museum in Leiden. 'Has he been to my country? The Netherlands?'

'Maybe. To Germany. You can ask him yourself. He's coming home.'

'To your fjords?'

'No. To here. He has a job at the university. In the history department.'

'What's his name?'

'Aaron.'

'Like the bible.'

'His father was a catechist. We all had mission names.'

'Jacob and Aaron. They were brothers?' She tried to remember the story. Her father hadn't believed. The stories he taught her came from the museum, not the bible.

'No. That was Esau.' Jacob laughed. 'The hairy one. Jacob was the smooth one.' He put out his arm. It was as smooth as a girl's. 'He had twelve sons.' He raised a thumb as if the achievement was his. 'Twelve tribes.'

'And Aaron?'

'He came later. With his rod.'

'I remember. It turned into a snake.'

She lifted the camera, adjusted the exposure. Click. Click, click, click. A fluke, she said when she developed the film, cropped in further and pinned his image on the line strung above the sink in the library's makeshift darkroom. Jacob's face, soft as putty.

'Time to go,' he said. 'It'll be hot soon.'

'And this isn't?'

She put her hat back on, pulled it low, tucked her plaits under.

They slipped and skidded their way down the rest of the hill back to the path, through the scrub, past the desolate wreck of a camp, retracing their steps until the houses came into view, the graded road, cars driving children to school. When they reached the bald house on the building site, Leonard was up and coffee was brewing.

IT WAS THE HOUSE RIKA DIDN'T LIKE. WHEN LEONARD WENT TO THE university, silence drew in around her. The house on the canal had moved and groaned with the water. This house was dry, untried. True, there were times when the house in Leiden had tormented her with its sounds, its memories. The cry of her mother at night when the cancer grew and her father was powerless to stop it. His night-weeping after the funeral. And the nights when she had wept and the house creaked in sympathy, grieving for her dead mother, and for herself, and then for the ache in her heart and the mornings she woke up nauseous, flushed green bile away with the water. The clanking of pipes as it made its way down to the basement, to wherever it went, drains and sewers under the canals. She didn't want to think about that, or the man in the orchid house. He'd come upon her when she was learning to use the Leica, a gift from her aunt in the dreadful weeks after her mother's death. The orchids calmed her, she found, as did the concentration it took to capture their texture. The man had come one day, then another, until he was there often. He told her of his high island in a blue ocean. He took her to a café, ordered her mint tea. She didn't want to think about the sudden rush of feeling that had come upon her unawares, or its consequence: the shame on her father's face, his sorrow, or the term away from school. Little wonder she had married Leonard, with his stories of a new moon, a new sun to hang in the sky. The promise of a life elsewhere.

After she'd accepted Leonard, her father kissed her on the forehead. 'Now I'll know you're safe,' he'd said, and she'd seen his relief, able at last to grieve alone, without worrying about a daughter he could find no way to console, and who had turned instead to a stranger – a man he'd never met. How could a father comprehend that? It was to Leonard, his young colleague from Oxford, that Piet turned for an answer. He saw that Rika spoke easily to him, and when Leonard first came to stay that she'd shown him the photograph of her mother on the mantelpiece. 'She gave me my first camera, a Kodak,' she told him. Leonard looked at the photo of a woman with a pale face, oval like Rika's, and her hair in a roll. 'I took it,' Rika said, her eyes brimming with tears. 'See, there's sun on the water beside her. She framed it.'

It was a symptom of her grief, Leonard told Piet later, speaking as an anthropologist might, that she had turned to the man in the orchid house. It was a symptom of her sensibility, and the enormity of the loss, not a betrayal of it. With the curtains of the house on the canal closed against the sun, it was an attempt at salvation: a grasping at life.

When Leonard had shown her the map of where they were going, she'd seen a bird-shaped island leaping from the blue of the Coral Sea and imagined a world to match the names she read: the Trobriand Islands, the Arafura Sea, the Louisiade Archipelago. Her father took her through the museum's gallery of canoe prows and ornaments, beautiful things airless behind glass, and into a research room where he'd opened a long, flat box. Carefully folding back the tissue paper, he lifted out a spray of brilliant orange plumes. It took a few moments for Rika to see that these delicate feathers were attached to a shrunken bird: a hardened tube of a body stripped of wings and feet. That's how the birds were prepared for trade, her father told her, and when they were first brought to Europe like this, without wings or feet, it was thought that they lived in the sky, forever flying towards the sun. *Birds of God: avis paradiseus.* Just the look of the plumes, vivid colours from a closed box, made Rika sad. So beautiful and so dead, wrapped in their tissue and closed in a drawer.

Back at the house on the canal, she looked at the photographs of the mountain bark-cloth Leonard had given her as part of his invitation to marry and cross the world with him. Even stilled to a monochrome image, there was movement in them. The cloth sent in a parcel from Papua, leaves falling, a moon rising, zinged with existence.

Pinned to the wall of Leonard's study in Oxford, it had more life than the shadows moving outside the window. Yes, it was the bark-cloth that was the invitation. That, and the map.

And the photographs of faces taken before the war by an Australian anthropologist Leonard was researching. Like the cloth, and like the story of the old woman with her string bag, these gave life to the prospect of being there, so far away. The question, in the form of a private thought that she carried with her, as much a part of her as her camera, was to know how the eyes of the people in the photographs saw. What did that young bride see, photographed in the year her mother was born? She looked at her festoons of shells, at her painted face and decorated head; she could sense the solemnity of the girl and the husband who stood close beside her. She could see the shyness between them, but nothing told her what it was they saw, looking back at the camera and the white man holding it. The old woman making pots from spirals of clay, what was she thinking as she looked not at the camera, but at the clay in her hands? The child leaning against her, staring at the lens with curiosity, would grow into a world which her mother could no longer avoid. And the old man with the ravaged face and matted hair? For whom that grim expression? These were questions she'd put to Leonard and her father as they passed the photos between them in the upstairs study of the house on the canal.

They were questions that vanished from her mind when a girl scarcely older than sixteen arrived on the veranda and announced herself as Mela, Rika's *haus gel*. It was the Monday after the welcome party. Leonard had gone to the university, and she was alone in the house. '*Haus gel*,' the girl said again. What did she mean? Where had she come from? The questions showed on Rika's face and were mirrored back to her by the sweet-faced girl in a clean dress.

'Agnes,' she said. 'My small mother. She send me. You tell her.'

Agnes. Yes, Rika remembered. A tall woman, stately, with hair growing high from her head, a flowered apron. She'd been at the party carrying trays of food. Rika had said she didn't think she needed help in the house, it was too new, and Agnes had said again that she had a niece, the daughter of her sister, a good girl, she would work hard. She'd let the statement stand for agreement, a way of speaking Rika didn't yet understand and which left her unprepared for this encounter at the door. Her attempt to explain that the idea of a *house girl* was against her expectations and upbringing was met with a steady, disbelieving gaze. Her offer for the girl to visit whenever she liked was brushed aside as the empty gesture it was. A demonstration of bare cupboards in a bare house that needed no cleaning sent the girl for reinforcements, leaving Rika with a faint and guilty hope that she'd given up and gone home.

Half an hour later Mela was back with Dolly, Martha's house girl, who had come to her by the same route, with a note from Agnes. 'This is Mela,' the note read. 'Your house girl. My sister's child.' Dolly had her two small boys with her, and they all trooped into the house and stood there looking stern and determined.

'Where's Martha?' Rika asked.

'She take the car,' Dolly said. 'She not there.'

Martha had gone to a lecture over at the university, where she was enrolled as a student. So Rika made the only move she could and took Mela, Dolly and the two boys to Laedi's house.

Laedi and her husband, Don, a tutor in the anthropology department, lived further into the compound, where the houses had been occupied since before the last rains. Hibiscus hedges flowered, pawpaw trees leaned with fruit, vines trailed over veranda rails and water-sprinklers sprayed coarse grass. Mats were being shaken from doors and mops squeezed over steps. Dolly called across to some young women sitting in the shade watching white children in a rubber paddling pool, giving them the news that Mela had come to work for the new *missis*.

'How many people have you got working for you?' Rika asked Laedi when she saw the women in her house, the confusion of

27

buckets and mops, the tea being brewed, and the large jugs of lemon squash.

Laedi didn't know. She didn't count. 'Tamba always,' she said. 'She lives here. The rest come and go. They live in town and come here during the day when Don's at work. They're my mother's people. Her language. *Wantoks*, we call them. Our friends. It's a complicated sort of arrangement.

'Don't think of them as servants. They don't. Think of it as part of the exchange that goes on every day in this country. They clean your house. You give them money and status. Though, I tell you, when the wind starts and the house fills up with dust, you'll be grateful.'

In the party atmosphere of the house, Rika saw that she was defeated, and turned her mind to the more interesting question of Laedi being 'half and half'. That's how she put it to herself, looking at Laedi's skin, a dark honey colour, and the strands of hair that had escaped the bright yellow cloth wound around her head. 'So you're half and half?' she said.

Laedi, who'd never heard the question put like that, even from the girls at school in Brisbane, looked at Rika. Milk skin. Milk ignorant. 'Mixed race is what they say round here. But half-caste – *hapkas* – is how I was born, and when I'm in town, that's what I am. A mongrel.'

Rika looked at Tamba. All the same ingredients. Tamba was darker and the curls of her hair were tighter, but her nose had the same hook to it. And the child, Bili? She was a smooth, nut-brown.

'So how did you get to be mixed and half?' Rika asked. 'Who was your father?'

'He was Australian. He stayed on after the war.'

Rika still thought of the war as mostly European. The Netherlands had starved in an occupation that left her mother malnourished and her father deaf in one ear. It was from Laedi that she learned about the soldiers fighting in the mountains she'd seen with Jacob. She tried to imagine what loneliness could have kept Laedi's father here after the war was over. 'Didn't he have a family?' she asked.

'A mother, that's all. She worked in a pub way out past Adelaide.'

Rika was unsure where Adelaide was. Somewhere south, in Australia. 'I went there once,' Laedi said. 'Don was at a conference and I hired a car, drove out there. A long, flat road with snakes on it. When I got there, it was just a pub at a crossroads. A couple of houses. An old man was nodding over his beer. I asked him if he remembered her. *Carol?* Yes, he remembered. That was all. I couldn't get another word out of him.' She gave a sigh that might have been a laugh.

'And your father didn't go back?'

'No. He stayed on,' Laedi said. 'The Highlands were opening up, coffee was being planted, there were jobs for men like him.'

'Coffee? In these mountains? They look too steep.'

'Not *these* mountains.' How could she be so ignorant? 'Haven't you looked at a map?'

'The Arafura Sea,' Rika said. 'I like the names you have here.'

'Well, most of them aren't ours!'

Leonard showed Rika the map again, pointing to the thick body of the bird, where, for years, the settlers on the coast thought the mountains were as impenetrable as here in the tail, too steep to use. He pointed to the old colonial division between New Guinea to the north and Papua to the south, cutting straight through the Highlands, which were thought to be empty. The colonial governments paid them no attention, until the gold miners went up the rivers and found wide valleys up there, fertile and full of people. That wasn't long before the war, Leonard said, and why someone like Laedi's father would have stayed on. 'Did he work on a plantation?' he asked.

'He managed one,' Rika said, and returned to the more interesting story of Laedi's mother, a girl from across the valley, who had hidden when white men first came to her village. The older women said they had penises just like their own men, only white, so the girls had better look out. They weren't sky travellers or returning ancestors. Their shit smelled bad.

'I thought Laedi went to school in Brisbane,' Leonard said.

'She did.'

'And she told you this story?' She knew that he meant this *fanciful* story.

'Yes. Her and the other women. Her *wantoks*. You should hear them laugh. There's one called Tamba, who lives with her.'

Leonard took her hand, kissed it. 'You've found a friend,' he said. 'I'm so glad.'

It was evening, and they were sitting inside with the fan whirring overhead and the flyscreen closed against the mosquitoes. Leonard poured her a glass of wine – Australian, and not very good – which he'd found in the supermarket in town. With the map spread on the table, he showed her the rivers the gold miners had gone up, and the ridges the explorers had crossed, the lakes beside which the first planes had landed. He pointed to the towns, to the large centres of populations, and the coffee. And all the while Rika was thinking about Laedi's mother with a name such as she'd never heard, Simba-ikan, who went to live with Laedi's father in a house with a tin roof that made a noise such as she'd never imagined when the rain thumped down on it.

'Did her father marry her mother?' Leonard asked.

'He paid five pigs.'

'That would be customary. Did he register the marriage?'

'I should think so,' Rika said.

'Didn't Laedi tell you?'

'She said it was unusual.' The women had laughed when she asked. No, Laedi had said, it wasn't usual for a white man to marry a girl from the village. But something had cracked open in him when Laedi was born, and he'd signed the register with the patrol officer, the kiap; he'd raise his daughter like a lady.

'Ah,' said Leonard, lighting his pipe. 'Lady. That's where it comes from.'

'Not Lady, not an English lady,' Rika said. 'An Australian *Laedi*. Long vowels.'

'What did she want to know about you?' Leonard asked.

'She wanted to know about Jacob and going to the swamp. She wanted to know what Jacob wanted.'

'What did you tell her?'

'I told her he wanted to know if the university was real.'

Laedi had pursed her lips. 'Was that all?' she'd said.

FOR MARTHA, THERE WAS NOTHING EXOTIC ABOUT NEW GUINEA.
Rather the reverse. For her, the bird-shaped island north of the
large flat continent where she was born evoked jungles, stretchers,
an uncle fighting the Japanese during the war. Mud. Mosquitoes.
Tent hospitals. The only reason she was here at all was because she'd
married Pete. She'd met him at a dance at the end of her first year at
Sydney University. It was a hot night just after the exams. A band was
playing, and Pete came through the crowd and asked her to dance.
He had long hair and John Lennon glasses. She had a fringe that
covered her eyes. They danced all night, bought hot dogs at dawn,
went back to his house and made love for a week. She was doing
English which, he pointed out, was a great deal easier to move than
anthropology. He was a postgraduate, and what with the job as a
tutor at the new university, and the prospect of his own research,
he could be in New Guinea for years. So they married, and even then
she had to wait for months before she could join him. The Australian
authorities didn't give out permits lightly. Occasional stories made it
into the newspapers of entry denied – to a Russian journalist, or
a member of the African National Congress, or a researcher from
an Australian university who'd come to the attention of the security
service. There was no way a girl like Martha would get an entry permit
for no better reason than that she wanted to keep sleeping with her
boyfriend. So they married, and he went on ahead, in time for the
start of the term. She was barely twenty, lost a year of study during
the long wait for the permit, and when she got to Port Moresby
she wasn't at all sure she'd made the right decision. She was in love
with Pete still, and while the sex remained good, it had a lot to
make up for. The endless heat. The mosquitoes. The dreariness of
the hills.

It took telling Rika this story to make Martha see that it wasn't just a list of events, and that it mightn't be so dull, being here, in this place she'd been close to considering a penance. The story of growing up over the shipyards where her father worked suddenly seemed a story worth telling. She described her mother taking in ironing, and the library at the top of the hill, with its books from Europe – a place no one in her family had been, except her grandfather, who was shipped there during the First World War and returned with shrapnel in his knee. If that story could take on colour, so could the town where they were, with its harbour and dry valley, which she came to see anew through the eye of Rika and her camera.

Wherever they went the camera was with them, and in those first weeks they went everywhere – to markets and street stalls, to beaches and villages. They drove out of town, along the edge of the harbour, or followed the road inland, along the river, or up onto the plateau behind. Wherever they went, they talked, even as Rika circled them, accustoming her eye to the brightness of the light.

Martha talked most volubly, and as she told her story, elaborating each detail, she asked questions that had Rika open up as she hadn't for a long time, not since her mother died. There'd been no one to talk to but her father, then Leonard, and she couldn't speak to them, not as she did to Martha and Laedi. She hadn't spoken to the girls at school. They'd had too many questions about the term she missed when she was sent to Amsterdam and they couldn't visit her.

Laedi's classmates had called her 'Coffee' – for growing up on a coffee plantation with skin that was 'coffee-coloured', and having to come to Brisbane to discover how to drink it. 'Coffee's drinking coffee,' they'd taunt. 'Want some coffee, Coffee?' She escaped to the cinema when she could, and even when she shouldn't. But Don, who was a student at the university, liked the colour of her skin. He made her feel a whole woman, not a schoolgirl. His parents called her Carol after the name on her birth certificate and passed her off to their neighbours as 'Mediterranean'. He took her with him on fieldwork in the Trobriand Islands, off the toe of Papua, and they talked each morning as they woke to the light of the sky through a woven door. When she fell pregnant, he married her in the Port Moresby registry office, with only her mother as witness. But when Bili was born and they moved to the university, somehow Don was different with her. Not that she talked to Rika and Martha about that, though she felt the tension ease in her as she lay under the trees at the top of the town beach and smiled into the camera as Martha asked her why she didn't find Jacob attractive.

The film Rika used was black and white, and she developed it in a darkroom at the back of the library's temporary offices. Leonard had made the arrangement, and went with her to a meeting set up by Alex Penrose with Gina, the manuscript librarian, a tall woman with an intelligent face. Her dark hair, showing the first signs of grey, was escaping its clips. Rika had seen her in the supermarket and outside her house in the university compound, where she was growing a hedge of red hibiscus. Her office, a small windowless room, was piled with archive boxes and folders. There was barely room for Leonard and Rika to sit down.

'Donations,' she explained. 'They come in by the week from the old-timers, missionaries, patrol officers, magistrates. A few from you lot,' she said, looking at Leonard.

'Good material?' he asked.

'Most is surprisingly good. Good enough to have the historians in here, working wherever we can fit them.' She gestured beyond the door to other rooms as congested as hers. 'But the photos – what a mess they're in!' She opened a folder on her desk. Inside was a jumble of small photographs, with the negatives pushed into envelopes that were showing the wear of time. 'The Anglican mission,' she said. 'A fabulous collection, going back to the 1900s. The north coast of Papua. Records from the war, including the journal of a priest who was mending a deck chair when the Japanese battleships appeared off the coast!'

Leonard laughed.

'The mission kept its papers in good order,' Gina said, 'but not when it came to photographs.' She handed one of the envelopes of negatives to Leonard. 'Can any of these be salvaged?' she asked. 'Looks like the cockroaches have been in there.'

Leonard held them up to the light. 'Some,' he said. 'But it'd be a tricky job. Looks as if they were developed in a lab.'

'Yes,' Gina said. 'They were sent down to Australia.'

'Rika could do something with them. Couldn't you, darling?' he said, turning to her.

So Rika began to work for Gina – half a day here, half a day there – fitting herself onto the table where the historians worked. In the darkroom, makeshift but adequate, she worked from the old negatives and developed her own film. She hadn't liked Leonard offering her up like that, but she became fond of Gina, and the library with its bustle and noise that didn't concern her. And she liked the silence of the darkroom, as she always had. It was where things settled, internal things; or if they didn't settle, they moved and morphed so that the edges that jabbed at her one time were different the next.

Every time she was there, she felt the present growing in her. She put it down to Martha with her clear gaze and unguarded talk. And to Laedi with her stories of moving between the cinemas of Brisbane and the village across from the plantation, where she slept by the fire with her skin-sisters and woke in the morning to sweet potato cooked in the ash. Neither of them was split as Rika was split; they hadn't had to leave one place so far away to find another. Or was it another part of herself she needed to find? But in the darkroom, developing her film, she felt a subdued sense of excitement, remembering their drives around the harbour, their afternoons on the beach. The talk. The talk surprised her. Not theirs but hers, after so many years of keeping fast to herself. She told them about the Botanical Gardens, which she passed on the way home from school, and how she went there to escape the girls and the gloom of the house on the canal, with its drawn curtains.

Until Leonard began to visit, her mother's books had lain untouched where she'd left them. When Martha looked surprised at this, Rika saw it in a way she hadn't before. In the unexpected release of that moment, she told them about the man from the Antilles who'd found her in the orchid house. She told them about the rush of feeling that came upon her, but nothing of its consequence. Was she a fool to admit to that? Would they see beyond what she'd revealed? She hoped not. If she kept it to herself, maybe it would vanish eventually as if it had never happened.

Outside the darkroom Rika rarely thought like this. Each day swept her along. Martha said Gina was having an affair with Alex Penrose. It was the talk of the anthropology department.

'Imagine sleeping with him,' Martha said. 'She'd have to be desperate.'

'She doesn't look desperate,' Rika said. 'I like her.'

'It'd be like sleeping with a jelly. A bristly jelly.'

Rika and Laedi laughed. They were driving out of town again for the day, taking Rifle, who'd bestowed himself on Rika as her gardener, to the rubber plantations, where he had *bisnis* to do with his *wantoks* in the labour barracks. He was another distant relative of Laedi's, and he'd arrived at Rika's door with a band of men carrying shovels. Before Rika and Leonard knew it, they too were living surrounded by mounds planted with corn and pumpkin, stretching all the way to the road. Not even the side of the house was spared. When Rika had presented Rifle with packets of seeds – capsicums, aubergine – thinking she might as well have some vegetables of her own, he'd looked mournful and begun a long story about bad soil, and Rika hadn't had the heart to insist.

Now he was in the front seat of the car beside Laedi, urging her on, chin forward, clicking his tongue in disapproval as Martha and Rika laughed in the back. He said something to Tamba sitting beside them, whose expression was equally dark. Bili, on Rika's knee, joined in the joke.

They'd left town early, driving past the last of the trade stores and roadside markets, inland along the river until the road narrowed and began to climb, twisting up through bends so steep that Martha and Rika stopped laughing. Ferns and vines hung over the cliffs that rose above them on one side and dropped away on the other. Above was rainforest; behind a hazy ocean. At the top the land flattened out, as if catching its breath before rising again to the mountains. Rifle urged Laedi on, past hamlets and villages, until they left the dappled light of the forest for the strange silence of the plantations. It was as if the birds had taken fright at the rows of rubber trees marching over their land. Rifle had the window down, calling out to men who were walking with buckets hanging from their shoulders.

At the barracks they let him out with the bag of cigarettes and bottles of rum he'd bought from the sale of his cabbages. An old man came over to greet Laedi, pushing his face into the car to marvel at Bili, the little *hapkas* child. He grinned at her, his old hand gentle on her cheek, his few teeth stained red from chewing betel. 'You go this way,' he told Tamba in their Highland language. She got out to follow his gestures that seemed to point upwards into the sky, directing her to the best place on the river. 'All the same as a Highland river,' he said. 'Very good.'

Back in the forest, birds chattered and flew and the air was perfumed and sweet. It was less humid. Tamba sat in the front watching the sun, her head out of the window as Laedi turned the car from this track to that until they came to a stop beneath whispery casuarinas. They walked down to the river, spread out a rug and lay under the trees. They had books, a picnic. Rika took her camera into the trees to experiment with the dapple of light. She stood on a rock in the river and focused down on the tumble of the water.

When the sun passed the high point of noon and Bili and Tamba had fallen asleep on the rug, Martha, Laedi and Rika followed the river along a steep path, down through the boulders to a wide swimming hole. On the side where they stood were flat rocks. In the centre water tumbled from above, and on the far side was a projecting rock face:

green fronds, green water, a deeper shade, trapping the light in its depths.

Laedi took off her shirt and looked down at her stomach.

'I'm pregnant,' she said.

Rika's heart gave a thump. 'How much?' she asked.

'Twelve weeks. A bit more.'

'Were you sick?' Rika asked. 'Those first weeks?'

'A little. Not very.'

'Are you pleased?' Martha asked.

Laedi didn't answer right away. She let herself into the deep green water. 'Don wants a son this time,' she said. Beneath the water her body appeared a greeny brown. Her head in the shining air was brightly lit.

Rika hung the Leica from a branch and swam out after her. She felt tremulous, her limbs heavy.

'Can you smell something?' she called. She'd swum to the far side, near the rock face, past the water falling from the rocks above. There was a faint perfume, reminiscent of cloves.

'Orchids,' Laedi called back. 'See?'

'Where?' Rika followed the direction of Laedi's hand to the rock face. Green leaves, ferny things, vines. Rika swam up close, into the shade of the projecting rock, treading water and squinting up until she found the ochre-brown blooms, no larger than a child's fingernail, sprays of tiny flowers tucked into the green. Tears coursed down her face, and she swam into the water tumbling from the rocks above to hide them. The thought came to her that there might be no escape, even in a place as far away as this.

When her heart returned to a steady beat, she swam slowly back to the flat rocks, climbed out and lay face down beside Laedi and Martha. The thought retreated, back inside, underneath. In its place an emptying-out that left her weary.

Laedi reached out a hand and rested it on her shoulder. 'The orchids turn yellow in the sun,' she said. Her voice was gentle. 'Didn't you see them when you went out with Jacob?'

'I don't think so.'

'They'd have been there. In the grass. On the melaleucas at the swamp. Port Moresby Gold, they're called.'

'Port Moresby Gold!' Martha gave a short laugh. What kind of contradiction was that?

'It's not so bad here,' Rika said. 'I'm beginning to like it.'

THEIR HUSBANDS DIDN'T GET ON SO WELL. LEONARD AND PETE WERE fine, both of them easygoing. The problem wasn't with them. It was Don. He and Pete were friends of a sort; they had to be as the two most junior members of the department. They disagreed easily, had a beer afterwards, and yet it was always Pete who ended up with extra tutorials while Don got himself another field trip. Visiting botanists, geographers, it didn't matter – Don would find a reason to go with them, something he could write up, and every time Alex Penrose would let him go. 'Good for the department,' he'd say. That semester Don was on a committee organising a conference on the history of Melanesia. Timetables! Tutorials! How could he attend to them? He was busy writing letters to anthropologists in Berlin and historians in New York. The success of the entire event depended on him! As usual Pete took up the slack.

As a visitor to the department and a speaker at the conference, Leonard commanded a certain respect, and Don made sure he gave it. But it came with an edge; over the weeks he queried more and more the efficacy, even the legitimacy, of ethnographic film. Wasn't there something retrograde about *capturing* tribal cultures on film and showing them stilled in time, as if they existed outside the dynamic of change? Of *decolonisation*? Times were changing, didn't he know, and the questions were changing with them. Then, in a manoeuvre that was typical of Don, having raised the doubt, he neatly came up with a solution to a problem Leonard hadn't thought existed. He should accompany Leonard to the mountain and observe the filming as part of his own research into the impact of modernity on a tribal culture. It was the last thing Leonard wanted. Alex was already going with him, and that was enough. He didn't want the quiet eye of the filming disturbed. And he feared that if Don came to the mountain, Rika wouldn't.

Rika didn't like Don. She didn't like the way he rolled his eyes when Leonard used words that he considered affected. When Leonard called their wives *ladies*, he said, 'Well, you got that right. Laedi was meant to be a lady, and look at her now.' Laedi had blushed and looked down. Rika especially didn't like the way Laedi became quiet and subdued in his presence.

No, she wouldn't go to the mountain if Don was to be there.

Gina was at Alex's dinner the night the matter was decided. She was sitting a few places away from him, and nothing about her suggested an affair. She seemed more interested in the conversation between Leonard, who was seated beside her, and the visiting historian seated opposite, next to Rika. They were talking about F. E. Williams, the nuggetty Australian who'd been the government anthropologist for Papua between the wars, and the photographer of the bride adorned with shells. Leonard was giving a paper at the conference on his work with the low-land neighbours of the mountain people, which was as close to the mountain as anthropology had come by 1968. The historian was interested in him for his influence with the governor of the time, the brake he exerted on planters who wanted more labour, and missionaries who wanted to ban more tribal custom. Several times in the course of their conversation Leonard used the word *sensible*.

'*Sensible*,' Don said. 'Whose idea of sensible are we talking about?'

Leonard said something soothing, deflecting.

'Do you think polygamy is *sensible*?' Don persisted, and Alex gaffawed. 'No? Well, a headhunter might if he needed to produce sons fast.'

'In that case,' Leonard said, 'one would talk, surely, about the integrity of the culture. Consider it on those terms.'

Rika looked straight at Don. 'Williams' photographs,' she said. 'Have you seen them?'

'Some,' he said. 'They're ethnographically insignificant, most of them.'

'Some of them are marvellous.'

'He was a functionary,' Don said. 'He had none of Malinowski's flair.' For fieldwork, Don had chosen the very islands and exact village where the great Malinowski had worked.

'Williams' portraits are of *character*,' Rika said. 'They're of people he *knows*. You see it in the way they look at the camera. Malinowski may have been a better anthropologist, I don't know, but he's not a better photographer.'

Don's eyes narrowed.

'He named the people he photographed,' she said. 'How many anthropologists do that? Do you?'

'Rika.' Leonard put out a restraining hand.

'Have you noticed how he framed his shots, the way he went in close? Malinowski kept his focus in the middle distance – most anthropologists do – as if you can explain everything by putting in more of the surrounds. How do you say, *context*?'

The smirk had gone from Don's face.

'Well done, Rika,' Gina said, lifting her glass. 'Well done!'

Don, conceding nothing, shifted to the safer ground of Williams' work during the war, when he was liaising between the villages and the army with its great need for labour.

'He was trying to get the soldiers to understand the local people? Yes?' Rika took up the challenge. 'He spoke on their behalf?'

'Quite right,' the historian said.

'He was getting them to fight his war.' Don's voice was steely.

'It was more complex than that,' Leonard said. 'Given your interest in social change, I'd have thought you'd find him helpful. He faced the dilemma more acutely than any of us ever will.'

'He was manipulating the terms of change.'

'Isn't that what you say we all do?' Leonard said. 'We anthropologists?'

'That's what I'm working on.'

'I read your thesis,' Leonard said. 'It was impressive. There are ideas there that need considerable testing.'

'Where better to test them than on the mountain?' Pounce. Poor Leonard. He was accustomed to deflecting, but useless when it came to a direct assault. Laedi looked down at the table. Rika's attention turned to her, leaving Leonard to argue on in his measured way. If he was to film the bark-cloth as a living part of the mountain culture, and not as an object, he knew from experience that the fewer strangers there were, the less disturbance there would be. Don answered as if an intellectual puzzle had been posed. Would another 'stranger' mean 'disturbance'? What were these terms? How did a living culture understand them? Respond to them?

The dinner came to an early end.

'What happened to Williams?' Laedi asked Leonard at the door. She was wearing a red satin dress patterned with golden dragons. It was tight across her bust.

'He died in 1943,' Leonard said. 'He was in an army plane that came down. Not far from the mountain.'

'Terrible flying weather,' the historian said. 'It took a month to get confirmation of his death from the Americans.'

'His widow didn't get a pension,' Leonard said, 'because that one month put him short of the twenty years' service required.'

'That's what comes of flying with the military,' Don said.

'It's shameful,' Leonard said.

At the office the next day, Leonard suggested to Alex that it might be better if Don didn't come with them to the mountain. But Alex was vulnerable to Don's argument that this was an opportunity unparalleled in anthropological literature: one anthropologist watching another in disciplined research. The effect of a 16 mm camera, as a metonymy for modernity, on tribal art and culture. A seminal paper from a new university.

'He's headstrong, I agree,' Alex said. 'But he's doing some good work. Pushing the debate.'

'It'll make it hard for Rika,' Leonard said. 'With three of us men up there.'

'Always best to go ahead of the women,' Alex said. 'Make sure there's a house that'll suit. Latrines and so on. You'll need to prepare. Especially as she'll be the first white woman to go up there.'

'The first?' Leonard looked surprised. 'I suppose she is.'

'It's a hard walk. The only whites who've been up there are kiaps and missionaries, and then only on patrol.'

'In which case, wouldn't it be better to keep our numbers down?'

'Don't worry,' Alex said. 'It won't be for long. I'll have Don back here in time for second semester.'

OUR GROUND

OVER AT THE DORMITORIES, JACOB SHARED A ROOM with Milton. Two narrow beds, heads to the window, two desks, two lamps, two rails for their clothes. Not that their clothes amounted to much. Their stipends were a constant reminder that they were students in a poor country. A form of charity, Jacob said. Milton didn't mind. He put his T-shirts on the rail, his one shirt, and enjoyed them hanging there like characters in a novel. He lay on his bed reading James Baldwin. *Another Country*.

Jacob didn't hang anything on his rail. He felt foolish and resistant. He was studying law. He was going to make something of himself. Know their law, know their ways – that was his thinking. 'Lazy boy,' he said to Milton. 'Where's reading novels going to get you?' But Milton wasn't lying there lazing. *Another Country* was a set text. He was doing English and he was writing. He was on his third play. 'Drama,' he told Jacob. 'It's our tradition too.' His first hadn't really been a play at all, more a kind of poem. He'd acted it out to students in the canteen. Even he agreed there wasn't much use in that if he was going to change the minds of Australians in their offices and his compatriots in their villages.

The second play had attracted a crowd of labourers and a trickle of staff. The drama group had started, and they put up notices in town, on trees, on shop windows in Boroko, where the road from the university met the road that went to the airport in one direction and the town in the other. But no one from Boroko came to the play. It was a white suburb in those days. From the university, Martha and Pete were in the audience, Laedi too, and it had been hard to believe that the skinny fellow they knew as Milton, all edgy energy, never still, was under the cloak of the *samuna* man who spoke with such gravitas of the land that had come to him from his father and forefathers and which had disappeared creek by creek, hill by hill, under the oil palm trees. The *samuna* man, clown and actor, carrier of ritual knowledge, stood bowed before them, lamenting that he must prepare for death watching his sons labour on the plantation that had swallowed the ground of their birthright. He had walked off with the slow dignity of an old man, disappearing behind the screen at the back of the hall, and Milton reappeared in his own shape. Jangling Milton, all arms and legs, and wide hair.

The third was a real play – three acts, a cast of characters and a title: *Our Ground*. It was in rehearsal when Rika and Leonard arrived. It was the son's story, the labourer on the plantation. The first act was one of wretched humiliation as the white planter strides over the men, and the old man father is sent away, too feeble to work. In the second act, the planter comes to the village, tries to snare the hero's sister, sets traps for her and brings a bottle of rum to divert the men. They trick him in turn, and talk of revenge and revolution. Are they not men? Melanesian men? The sons of warriors as well as of *samuna* men? In the third act, they rise up – how could they not – and Milton, who played the lead, defeats the planter, rescues the girl and reclaims his people's ground. Not a subtle plot, but what was lost in subtlety was regained in the quality of the words Milton wrote, the string band and the high energy of the chorus.

The drama group was presenting *Our Ground* on the last evening of the conference, when the university would be full of visitors. That'd stir things up. Jacob didn't think much would come of it; still, he offered some advice. 'If you want to get an audience, you should ask that Dutch woman to photograph a rehearsal. Put it in the paper.'

'The one you took to the swamp?' Milton was on his feet and laughing. 'Your girlfriend, eh?' Some students had pinned a white centrefold on the wall over his bed. Jacob had ripped it off, punched out a louvre, and had to report to the warden. This time he slammed out of the door. Gone.

'Hey, brother,' Milton called after him. 'You ask her.'

Rika did take the photos. 'Publicity shots,' Milton called them. Jacob didn't ask her. Milton did, though not directly. He asked Martha to ask her. They were in the same English tutorial, or were meant to be. Since reading *Another Country*, Martha had avoided tutorials and made do with lectures. The flaw in Pete's theory about English being mobile was that it didn't take account of the curriculum. If Martha had stayed at Sydney University she'd have read her way from Chaucer to the Victorians. Not only that, but all the students would have looked like her, and many of them would have been women. Well. Here, almost all the students were men, and black at that. And the courses on offer at the university that was still being built had titles such as New Writing from Emergent Nations, or the Literature of Oral Traditions. That semester, Modern World Literature 2, the class she was in with Milton, began with *Another Country*. At first Martha kept quiet, shrank herself down to the smallest possible size, and it wasn't as if the rest of them didn't have enough to say about the anger of black men. Their tutor tried to draw her out by asking her what she thought of Rufus Scott's relationship with Leona. She took it to be a question about Leona. How could she answer a question about a white woman who took whatever a black man gave in a class like that? Black. White. She didn't even want to say the words. Better to think that underneath everyone's the same. Anyone would despise Leona. Martha's face was scalding and Aro, their round-bellied Samoan tutor, took pity on her. The white girl might be craven at the level of what she does, he said, but consider what she says. Isn't she a voice of truth about Rufus? In that classroom it didn't help. Martha was barely able to breathe. It was all sex, that book. Rufus was all body. 'Flesh, bone, muscle, fluid, orifices, hair and skin', as Baldwin put it. So was Milton. So was the class. So, come to think of it, was she. She missed the next class, and didn't go back until they were on to *A House for Mr Biswas*.

It was after a class on Naipaul that Milton caught up with her to ask if she'd ask Rika to bring her camera to a rehearsal. Martha saw that he was nervous – of looking foolish, she supposed, if Rika said no. She liked his nervousness. It made hers less onerous, and something about his shyness made him less flesh, more person, more like her. Her step lightened. 'Okay,' she said, and he grinned, doing a little jig as they walked, admitting that it was Jacob who'd had the idea.

'So you reckon she will?'

'Yeah. I'm sure she will.'

At the rehearsal of the third act, Milton, in torn trousers and with his chest bared, was pacing around like a nervous mother. A string band was playing: a guitar, several ukuleles, a drum and bamboo base, as well as village instruments made from halved coconut shells and tin cans. The chorus line of plantation workers was practising its steps – hands, feet, laughter. For Martha, as much as for Rika, it was stepping into a world she'd not known how to join.

In the doorway, the threatened sister – a student from Mela's village on the harbour – was reading a book. Over at the side, Laedi was talking to Wana, a student she knew from the Trobriand Islands. Wana was small-boned, a girl still, with soft brown skin and wide, high cheekbones. She was hiding her black curls under a beanie, and stuffing cushions under an apron to turn herself into the planter's cook.

The director was Aro, the tutor from the Modern World Literature class. He'd worked in theatre in Auckland. 'Okay,' he said. 'Let's start. Remember, this is a rehearsal for Rika. Have you all met her?' A round of applause. 'Yes? Good.' His hands were up, quietening everyone. 'Are you listening? Yes? Good. The thing is, having remembered Rika, you're to forget about her, and forget the camera. Okay? Don't look at her. Don't look at the camera. She'll find you. Okay? Then let's start.' He clapped his hands and jumped off the rickety stage.

The white planter, whom Milton had created without a redeeming quality, was being played by Sam, a friend of Pete's from the history department, and though he'd never acted before, he entered into his role with good humour and a modicum of success. His flame-red hair was slicked back and darkened, his face painted with scowling lines and a mean black moustache. Somehow he managed to narrow his eyes to malignant specks, and there he was, bookish Sam striding around with a shotgun! Rika used three rolls of film that evening, and among them was an image of Milton standing with the gun over the prostrate figure of Sam. She moved in close and crouched, accentuating the threat, catching the sweat on Milton's back and the shine of Sam's painted moustache. Aro sent it into the *South Pacific Post*, who refused to run the photo as publicity, and then, in a twist of its own peculiar logic, published it on page three as an outraged news item. A warning, the editorial said, that the university was indeed a centre of subversion and a threat to order. Action should be taken before it became a 'Mau Mau factory'. The vice-chancellor made a statement about the integrity of drama and freedom of speech. The Australian administrator's office put out its own statement 'regretting' the involvement of university staff in the play. Sam and Aro wrote a good letter; they gathered signatures and waited for it to appear in the *Post*, which, of course, it didn't.

Who cared? At the next rehearsal, Aro said it proved the power of theatre, and the warrior chorus danced in victory.

In the library's darkroom Rika developed the film from the rehearsal, and when she finished, Gina came in to see the prints as they dried on the line. She looked at them carefully and said, 'Why don't you photograph the performance? For the library.' And then she asked, 'Is there a script? Or is it improvised?'

'I think there's a script. I'll ask Milton,' Rika said.

When she did, Milton stiffened his back. What kind of a question was that? He was a writer, and yes, there was a script. When they made changes in rehearsal, he added them in; Aro, the director, said he should, it's what writers did. The script was a mess, in the sense of being untidy. Did that matter?

'We'll ask Gina,' Rika said.

So they drove to Boroko, where the library's temporary offices were above the Toyota dealership. On the way, Milton told Rika about his *samuna* grandfather, and the plantation, and his father's land that was going to oil palm, and nothing growing underneath. Rika had never heard of palm oil. Oil, from palm? For soap? When they got out of the car, there on the street in Boroko Milton lifted his arms and turned himself into a squat, brooding oil palm with an aura of silence spreading out around him.

'Even a tree,' she told Laedi and Martha at the beach that afternoon. 'He can even make himself look like a tree!'

In Gina's cramped office, he was himself again, a student sitting across the desk from a librarian, scrunched next to Rika, their knees up against the desk. Books and papers were piled up against the walls, and the desk was a sea of folders. They sat, watching for clues, as Gina looked at the script of *Our Ground*, turning the pages, frowning, turning back again before she went on. When she finished, she put the script on the desk, turned it to face Milton.

'Is this what you're working from?' she asked him.

'Yes.' He sounded dubious. Was that the right answer?

'Perfect,' Gina said. 'How would you feel if it came into the library with Rika's photos? After the performance.'

'Fine,' Milton said, without a hint of the eagerness that had had him grinning in the car.

'Though first,' Gina said, 'we should get it typed out and give you a clean copy. You'll need it. You never know, it might get published.'

Published! Yeah! In the darkroom Milton hopped from foot

to foot. Maybe this talk of being a writer wasn't just *hambak* and *gaiman* – humbug and lies. Maybe someone like him could publish a book. James Baldwin had. Milton thought of Rufus Scott as if he was Baldwin, as if he'd written the novel, which he knew he couldn't have, as he'd thrown himself off the George Washington Bridge. Dead. Still, to Milton, Baldwin and Rufus Scott were one. In class, Aro said that maybe Rufus was one of Baldwin's selves, and jumping from the bridge was the fate he imagined for himself, had he not escaped to France. That made sense. But did it mean that white characters were other selves? Did Baldwin have a white self? Did he *want* a white self?

Rika hadn't read the novel, she was pouring chemicals into dishes. She switched on the red lamp, it turned her a weird colour. She wasn't listening. She was concentrating, running film through the enlarger. Her face was set, as if she'd lost all sense of herself. A vessel – that's how Milton's grandfather had been, the old *samuna* man, knowledge acted through him as he became *samuna* spirit.

Milton watched Rika work, and when the image shimmered up through the paper, he was back where he was, in the darkroom. He watched as she manipulated the lens of the enlarger. Photography was like writing. A small move here, a little more, a little less, a slide this way or that, and the image changed. Or if not the image, then its meaning, its emphasis. You didn't just look through the lens and press, any more than you tell a story, full stop. She handed him the wet sheets and he pegged them onto the line. First there were the ones he wanted from the play. One of him leading the chorus, another in which he barely recognised himself from the ferocity of his eye. He liked the way he could become someone else, anyone really, if he put his mind to it. And he liked it in the darkroom, with Rika working and him thinking. So he stayed on while she made some prints for Mela. They were of a visit to Hanuabada, Mela's village on the edge of the harbour. White people didn't go there. Mela with a row of children, their mothers grinning and beckoning. These were duty photos, he supposed – what the village wanted. The shots of Laedi were more interesting. He saw fascination in them, Rika's or the camera's, he didn't know – all those sharp, close images of her face, her skin, her belly. He wasn't sure what to make of this frank gaze. And then a series of images that might be poems: a roof dipping towards water, the play of reflected light.

'Those roof lines,' he said as they drove back to the university. 'They put a song in my head.'

'Sing it,' she said.

'*San I les, olgeta les*,' he sang.

'*Kilaut go kam.*

'*Na tevil bilong solwara pairap long kappa.*'

'What does it mean?'

'Idle day.

'Shadow of clouds.

'Salt water spirits sleep in the roof.'

'Teach me,' Rika said. And he did. Her first pidgin song.

'*Tok Pisin,*' he said. 'That's what we call it. A language. Pidgin's what the planters call it.'

'No good, that,' she said, and they sang all the way back along the road.

'*San I les, olgeta les.*

'*Kilaut go kam.*

'*Na tevil bilong solwara pairap long kappa.*'

Rika was happy – *hamamas*. She was learning a new language. New faces, new names. She felt herself part of something. It was a feeling she hadn't known for a long time, since before her mother died, before the house on the canal darkened with grief. Before Leonard rescued her from sorrow and shame. While the prospect of being alone in the house without him wasn't what she'd expected, she found she wasn't daunted. When they'd first arrived, the weeks had stretched ahead, empty as a plate, but looking back, they'd moved fast already and everything had changed. Even the house. She'd bought striped cotton cloth at the trade store to cover the table. The gallery of photos pinned on the wall kept growing. The house took a shape that was hers, and

Rifle even planted pawpaw trees along the side of the house. She'd never felt the house in Oxford was hers. Well, it wasn't: Leonard had lived there for years. She'd moved in with his books, his paintings, his furniture, and though he offered to change anything she wanted, she couldn't see how else the house could be. She'd made curtains for the bedroom, that was all. Creamy cotton, a discordant note, but she liked to wake in the morning and watch the light shine through the cloth. The old curtains with their heavy backing had kept the room dark, and if Leonard rose early to work, she could sleep on till noon without knowing the morning had gone.

In this new house on the edge of the valley, it was Rika who woke first, rising with the sun. She went out into the cool air and golden light. She looked across to the hills and to the mountains rising up. Though it was June already, not long before Leonard was to leave for the mountain, her heart was light and full.

THE CONFERENCE BEGAN WITH A RECEPTION AT THE VICE-chancellor's house, and among the guests who'd travelled from cities as distant as Auckland and Manchester was Simbaikan, Laedi's mother.

Rika had been in the hot, crowded hangar when Simbaikan's Fokker stopped with a roar, and she'd thumped down the steps calling 'Laedi, Laedi,' striding across the tarmac in a brown check shirt and sturdy walking shoes. She took Bili in her arms, sniffing her as if breathing the scent of generations. She put her nose to Tamba, and then drew a long, deep breath at her daughter's shoulder. 'Laedi, Laedi,' she said again, showing all her teeth, the hook of her nose pushed forward by the wideness of her grin. She took in Rika with a look that could raise a mountain, and put her nose to the hand Rika offered. 'Good spirit woman,' she said, sniffing again. Tamba lifted the sack of taro that came off the plane with her. Rika took the suitcase and Laedi a bundle wrapped in banana leaves. Simbaikan regarded them with a monarch's eye. 'Very good,' she said with a regal nod, 'gutpela tru', and the crowd parted in front of her as she forged ahead towards the doors, her granddaughter held aloft in her arms.

At the reception she stood like a pillar looking into the packed room, watching the guests with their smiling teeth, the thick swirl of cigarette smoke, waiters cruising the room with drinks. When Rika saw her, she left Leonard with the visiting professors and jostled her way towards her on the wide veranda that looked out towards the building site of the university, and across the scrub to the wild country behind. The cast of *Our Ground* was there, all dressed up, looking good and feeling good. Milton was wearing a tie, grinning, just for being there, with all those white bastard professors. Not many students had been invited, but the play was on the conference programme as the closing-night event, so Aro had sent in the cast list – chorus, stagehands and all.

Rika, Laedi and Martha were leaning against the veranda rail, talking to Wana, the girl from the Trobriand Islands who played the big fat planter's cook. Rika recognised her from rehearsals, where her sense of her had come through the lens of the Leica, and here she was, transformed, in a dress nipped in at the waist. Without the cushions under her apron, she had a perfect hourglass figure. That would have added to Alex Penrose's alarm when, at the end of his lecture on Malinowski's *Sexual Lives of Savages*, she'd asked if he believed this account of Trobriand girls, or had the great anthropologist been duped, spun a tale of sexual excess the men thought he'd enjoy?

'Was he duped?' Rika asked her. 'Malinowski?'

'Partly,' Wana said. 'Anthropologists are.'

'Why are you studying it then?'

'I'm not. Moved to history. It's cleaner.'

Simbaikan tugged at Rika's arm. She was standing there, close to Laedi, with her back to the view, scowling as if she was watching a bad film.

'All I see,' she said, 'is Highland men outside minding the cars. Are we Highlanders good only for building and digging and cleaning? Look inside – all Papua man and island man. Same these students.' She pointed her nose at the cast of *Our Ground* and gave one of her celebrated snorts. 'Where are the Highland students?'

'Are there any?' Rika asked Wana.

'Some,' she said.

'Why not many?' Simbaikan's chin was jutting out.

'Because education came late to the Highlands,' Laedi said. 'You know that.'

Simbaikan sniffed. 'I don't see none here.'

'Not all the students were invited. Too many,' Laedi said.

Wana took a step towards Simbaikan. A smile, and a hand on her arm. 'Highland students are clever,' she said. 'They don't waste time at parties. They study for the time to come.'

'You are from where?' Simbaikan said.

'From the Trobriands.'

'Huh,' Simbaikan scowled. *'Ol nambis lain.'* A coastal girl.

'Yes,' Wana said, arranging her face in a mock-sad smile.

'Why are you here? Not studying, the same as Highland students?'

'I come to see Laedi. To speak hello to her mother.'

Simbaikan looked doubtful. 'You speak true?'

'Some true,' Wana said, and Simbaikan sniffed again. Not quite a snort. Rika wanted to laugh. There was something comic about Simbaikan's ferocity. Her face had settled into an expression that wasn't a smile exactly, but was no longer a scowl. 'You a friend of Laedi?' she asked Wana.

'Good friend,' Wana said.

Simbaikan lifted her hand, sniffed the back of it, turned it and pressed her nose to the inside of her elbow. Another sniff, then a wide grin. 'Saltwater woman. *Strongtru.*' Relief.

Laedi put her hand on Simbaikan's arm. 'Okay?'

'Now I have a beer,' Simbaikan said.

A waiter had come out to the veranda with a tray. Bottles of beer were sweating in the warm air. Milton took two, balanced them on the veranda rail. He leaned over to see where they'd fall, moved one to the floor. Trucks on the road into town blew up a trail of dust that drifted slowly upwards. The vice-chancellor's house was on the edge of the valley, higher up, across the road from the housing compound. The sun was setting, a gold rim of light behind the mountains to the west.

The vice-chancellor was making his way through the crowd with Michael Somare, the new leader of the new party in the House of Assembly. Every eye was on him, the man of the future, formally dressed in a tailored *sulu* that wrapped around him like a kilt. He was nodding to long-socked bureaucrats from the administrator's office. A benign smile. The vice-chancellor stopped for an introduction, Somare shook a visiting hand, touched a local arm. On his other side was Derek, an Australian from the politics department who was already acting as an advisor. They spoke to a professor from Harvard, another from Melbourne. Leonard was introduced. Somare already knew Alex Penrose. Gina was next to him, his hand on her back as if to encourage her forward – Martha and Rika raised a querying eye – and Somare gave a slight nod of his head. He tapped Alex on the shoulder, said something to Leonard. More laughter, more smiles, and on they went, Somare flanked on one side by the vice-chancellor, and on the other by Derek.

Rika watched. It was like a novel, she thought, arriving in a new place. It took a while to learn the characters, to know who to watch. Somare. Had he been the politician at the first party? She didn't think so, it had been a blur that night; she knew nothing. Now Wana was standing next to her giving a commentary. The House of Assembly had just had its second election, she said. 'We've got our own members at last. The UN pushed and Australia gave way, same as with the university. And still the Australians talk of slow progress.' Rika could hear exasperation in Wana's voice. 'They're supposed to act on the bills passed by the House, but the minister is good at putting in amendments.'

Rika didn't know there was a minister.

'He's in Canberra,' Wana said. 'He's ancient, looks like a relic from another world.'

'And he can tell us what to do up here?'

'He's the *minister*.' Wana laughed at the surprise on Rika's face. 'Don't worry, it won't last long. Somare will get self-government. Five years, I reckon, not much more.'

So that's why the vice-chancellor had Somare in tow.

'He'll take us to independence,' she said, 'but that'll take longer.'

After that, Wana didn't know. Something else would be needed. She was running ahead into the future, Rika barely abreast of her. Leonard said Australia wouldn't let Papua and New Guinea go, not for a long time yet – for them it was a bulwark against Asia to their north, a mountain range necessary to their sense of security – and here was Wana saying, soon we will be independent.

*

The rest of the cast of *Our Ground* didn't seem interested in the procession of Somare and the vice-chancellor. They were fooling around with Milton, until a Papuan in a loose white shirt was picked out for introduction. Then they turned as one to watch. The Papuan was standing in a group that included Jacob and Sam and staff from the history department. Jacob and Sam were both wearing ties. The Papuan who was shaking Somare's hand had no tie, just that loose, elegant shirt.

'He's beautiful,' Rika said. 'Who is he?'

'That's Aaron Nabuka,' Wana said. 'Jacob's clan-brother. He arrived last week.'

'He's brought back some good music.' Milton did a little jig with his feet.

'He is who?' Simbaikan asked.

'He's been to university in Australia,' Laedi said. 'Been to Europe. The place Rika comes from. He's clever. Come back to teach.'

'He won't live long,' Simbaikan said.

'You talk humbug,' Laedi said.

'He's strong yet,' Milton said. 'Good dancer.'

'He'll be prime minister one day,' Wana said.

'Not him,' Simbaikan said.

'If not prime minister, then vice-chancellor.'

'Or a poet.' Milton grinned.

'What does he want for himself?' Rika asked.

'That's not a question he'll get to ask,' Wana said.

'And the other one?' Simbaikan asked, her chin jutting towards Jacob. 'Same skin.'

'His brother,' Laedi said. 'Clan-brother. From the fjords.'

'Him trouble,' Simbaikan said, and they laughed; yes, Jacob was trouble. Somare was leaning forward, still talking to Aaron. A long stop, this. When the vice-chancellor moved on, Derek lightly punched Sam on the arm, and the crowd opened and reshaped itself like an eddy in a pool, as Somare was steered towards the next introduction. Back to the visiting professors.

Through the roar of faces Rika saw that Jacob was making his way towards her and the cast. He was wearing dark glasses, a gift from Aaron.

'Did you see my brother?' he asked her. She was curiously light-headed, though she'd only drunk one glass of wine. Another of punch.

'Take off them glasses,' Simbaikan said to Jacob. 'I don't see your face.'

Jacob took them off and Milton put them on, and, swaying there against the evening sky, he became a black American jazz player, saxophone and all.

Rika watched Aaron disappear from view as people crushed around him. She watched Sam work his way through the crowd until he came to a stop at Wana's side. His red hair was bouncing up from his head. When she saw Wana smile at him and slip her hand into his, her mind was pulled back to the lens she'd watched them through at rehearsals. In that world, Sam the planter with his slicked-back hair had shouted at her in the guise of his fat, waddling cook. Rika had caught the moment he sent her flying across the stage with a backhander to the face. A powerful shot. Gina liked it. And now, here they were, hands together, smiling at each other.

Martha leaned in towards Rika, who was standing next to her, and let her head rest on her friend's shoulder. 'Are you happy too?' she asked.

'Yes,' Rika said. 'Very.'

On the last afternoon of the conference, Aaron spoke to a crowded hall. The sun beat against the windows, and still people pushed in, standing at the sides and at the back, filling every space, spilling out through the doors. Labourers came from the building site to watch through the windows. Somare was there, sitting towards the front, with Derek beside him. Politicians from his party filled the row, talking affably and calling out to people coming in through the door. The Australian administrator was there, every visiting professor. Martha and Laedi were sitting halfway back, straining to see the front, where Jacob and Milton were leaning against the wall near Rika and her cameras. She was on a job for Gina, photographing the speakers. She turned the Leica towards Somare and the politicians, then took a wide shot of the full hall. She took a notebook from the back pocket of her shorts, looked at the camera, wrote something, then switched to the Rolleiflex – a gift from Leonard to mark their engagement – when the vice-chancellor came to the podium to introduce Aaron.

'Our first Papuan member of the academic staff,' he said, listing his achievements and degrees. 'Welcoming him to the university is a moment of pride for us all.' Outside, over the applause, labourers who'd come off the work sites to see him could be heard whistling and stamping their feet.

Aaron walked to the podium. He shook the vice-chancellor's hand. The applause was loud, and Aaron raised his hand as he greeted the crowd outside. It was good to be back, he said, thanking Somare for attending and the other members of the party that'd formed during the years of his absence. Pangu, it was called, for the union of Papua and New Guinea, and it stood for an early move to self-government.

It had chosen the bird of paradise as its symbol, and in the few days since he'd returned, Aaron had seen its logo on student notebooks, on classroom and canteen walls. What better symbol for an independent Papua New Guinea, he asked, than the rich spray of plumes that are worn in headdresses, traded between tribes, the hallmark of an island that is itself shaped like a bird? But symbols, he said, can represent warnings as well as ideals.

'The plumes of our birds have a history that holds a mirror to this country and reflects onto it not our character, but the character of the colonists and traders, the collectors, the naturalists, the bounty hunters – and it is their view of us, mirrored on to us, that is given as our own.

'When Magellan carried birds of paradise, stripped of feet and wings, to the king of Spain, the misconceptions that accompanied them had a life as fanciful as the plumes themselves.' Aaron was reading from the pages in his hand. 'Accounts of the *passaros de sol* and the *avis paradiseus*, living in the air until they died on the wing, became a metaphor taken into the poetry of Europe, and we went with them – people as strange as the birds.'

Through the lens of the Rolleiflex Rika focused in on Aaron's face, framed by his hands, palms open to the audience. She knew she'd get some good shots and, watching for the moment – the camera moment – her mind drifted from his words back to Leonard, who'd be leaving for the mountain in the morning, leaving her here with life unfolding.

'Consider these facts,' Aaron was saying. He turned towards her, to the side of the hall, to the camera. Or maybe it was Jacob behind her, he was looking to.

'By the end of the nineteenth century,' he said, 'the discarded plumes of the naturalists were not enough to supply the milliners and satisfy the desires of European women for hats.

'By 1913 the plumes of the greater bird of paradise, *paradisaea apoda linnaeus*, were fetching just short of twenty-five American dollars each, and that year alone over sixteen thousand plumes were taken from German New Guinea.

'The hunters brought disease to the villages.

'The threat to the species brought the attention of conserva-
tionists, who, in their eagerness to protect the birds, told a story of
tribal debasement that had less to do with the disrupted realities
of tribal life than with European political agendas.

'From birds circling the sun, marvellous creatures, we became
wretched victims, acted upon, no will of our own, captive to Europe
and Australia.

'How, then, do we tell *our* history?' he asked.

At the end of the afternoon, people were jostling to shake Aaron's
hand, calling out as Somare walked with him from the hall, one hand
on his shoulder. Rika got a shot of him lighting a cigarette, the strain
visible on his face.

'Impressive,' Leonard said, emerging from the crowd, looking for
Rika. He was smiling. The day was ending well. The conference was
ending well. Congratulations were in the air, and outside the hall in
the shade of the building, the temperature was surprisingly pleasant.
All around, people were shaking hands, mopping their faces, exchang-
ing addresses. Rika, still at work with the Leica, heard only the shrill
of cicadas. A strange and unexpected sadness had come upon her,
and she couldn't shake from her mind the disturbing after-image
of a small, shrunken bird's body laid out on a table in the museum
in Leiden.

WHILE AARON SPOKE THAT AFTERNOON IN EARLY JUNE 1968, NO ONE in his audience knew that in Los Angeles, when the clock ticked over from midnight, Robert Kennedy had been shot dead on the floor of a hotel kitchen. Those who missed the radio news from Australia that evening saw its impact on the faces of colleagues when they returned to the hot, packed hall for the performance of *Our Ground*.

Poor Milton. A gun fires in California and in Papua a play gains an unwanted edge.

The atmosphere was still festive, and there were plenty in the audience for whom the assassination was not news, or not news of any significance. For others, and not only visitors from the United States, there was a chill that couldn't be thawed by the heat. From the top of her ladder, Rika caught the roar of approval from the labourers and kitchen staff as the gun was held to Sam's head. She caught the alarm on the few whites from town who'd made it their business to come, to see for themselves. She got Simbaikan's scowl as she raised her fist to Milton. *Raskol man!* She also caught Jacob, his eyes narrowed, as he watched the audience, not the play, and the moment when Sam's face, framed by Milton's legs, betrayed a consternation that had not been there in rehearsal. But it was when she didn't have the Leica at her eye that she saw Aaron watching her. How long, she didn't know. When he saw her see him, he smiled, and she felt something smile deep inside her. In that moment, no longer than a heartbeat, she saw that Jacob had intercepted the exchange.

The next morning Rika drove Leonard to the airport. Rifle was with them, bustling about, taking charge of Leonard's luggage: the camera trunk, his tripod, oil cloth and bedding, lamps, a small generator to charge the camera, and film to last several months. He whistled up a troop of carriers and led them to the counter where everything was to be weighed. Leonard too. There was a great deal of shouting and gesticulating, and everywhere were lines of people, piles of boxes, out-of-shape sacks. It was morning, hot already, with small planes taking off over the mountains before the cloud set in.

When, at last, everything was loaded onto their plane, Leonard held Rika close. She knew that their last night together had not been as he'd hoped. She hadn't meant to, but she'd turned from him. She didn't know why; she was tired and something inside her resisted. A surge of tears stung his eyes. He blinked them back, kissed her carefully, once on each cheek, then softly, briefly, on the lips. 'Goodbye,' he said. 'Enjoy yourself,' and something in his voice triggered tears in her as she watched him cross the hot tarmac with Don and Alex. He turned to wave, then climbed aboard. On the other side of the runway, the hills were vivid green in the morning sun.

She stood beside Rifle, waving as the plane took off like a buzzing insect, rising into the sky as it flew towards the mountains and vanished into the haze of distance.

Just walking beside Simbaikan changed the view. At the market she strode along with Bili on her shoulders, squinting suspiciously at the garish colours of reef fish. She didn't like the water, and scowled at it, letting out long, hissing breaths as if the ocean itself was of doubtful value. Laedi had told Simbaikan that in the time of history, the Highland ancestors had lived on the coast. All this had been theirs until the sea people came in their canoes with their different languages, different songs, and chased them away, up into their high, wide valleys. It enraged Simbaikan that now, here on the coast, her people were considered credulous and backward just because when she was a girl there were villages across the valley that hadn't seen white-skinned men. And if this country was now to be one, and the Australians were to go, as everyone told her would happen, then what would become of her people, made strong from growing on strong ground, but not with time to grow strong on the new ways? At the market she hollered at every Highlander, asking what they did, sitting under the trees smoking. She'd tell them to go find work, get strong, think of the government that comes, gathering a retinue that accompanied her back to the car, carrying her load of sweet potato, *kaukau* that could never measure up to Highland varieties.

'She's a grandmother patriot,' Rika said.

'She's like a yam,' Laedi said. 'Part of her root stayed in the ground.'

And, like a yam, she took root in the garden of Laedi's university house. Rifle found a kerosene drum from somewhere, which he lined with river rocks, and at the swift transition from day to night Simbaikan lit a fire and sat beside it prodding the dark, roasting vegetables in the embers. Rifle took her presence as a tactical advantage and brought his *wantoks*, with their betel nut and lime gourds, to the side of the house. Milton came with students from the drama group, drawn by the smell of the fire after the soft food of the canteen. Wana was often there, and when she was, Sam came from his house with a frying pan and a bag of sausages, and a kind of absurd theatre took place as he and Simbaikan negotiated the cooking and the fire. Martha went most nights, after Pete returned to the extra marking that had landed on him in Don's absence. Rika drove straight there on her library days, going into the house, where Simbaikan was brewing up leaves from the market for the new baby to grow strong. Rika stayed there, talking to Laedi as if they hadn't seen each other for weeks, and when night fell and Simbaikan lit her fire, she'd take up a seat beside Simbaikan, leaving the veranda to Laedi, who liked to sit within sound of the house, a midway zone she made her own.

There were no guests in Laedi's garden, and no hosts. There were no invitations, no program. Time slipped its accustomed mooring; people came, or didn't come. Sometimes six turned up, sometimes twenty. Things happened, or didn't, direction came without direction. There was Simbaikan, hawk-faced by the fire, and fruit bats in the pawpaw trees, the whine of mosquitoes. There was the friendship growing between Rika and Laedi and Martha. And above, a night sky charged with forces, which set Rika thinking about what it might mean to have an 'unlocked heart'. It was a phrase she'd learned from the surrealists, and André Breton's *amour fou* with the place where she was. 'Oceania. It has always had the supreme ability to unlock our hearts.'

She'd been in the library, working at her table, when Gina opened an archive box that had arrived from Melbourne. It was from the widow of a prominent dealer in 'primitive and tribal arts' who'd worked in Paris in the 1920s, and then in New York, before returning to Australia. 'We didn't lead a life that would accommodate children,' his widow wrote in her accompanying letter. 'You'd be doing me a kindness if you could make good use of these papers.'

Inside was the record of the Oceanic section of her dealer husband's business. There were neat ledgers of every item traded over forty years or more, folders of letters and exhibition notices, catalogues and articles. The folders that caught Gina and Rika's attention that day were of photographs, professionally taken, black and white, and large, not the wretched stamp-like prints Rika was sorting, and all of them labelled and dated.

'Look at this,' Gina said, putting a folder on the table. She was wearing library gloves as she unwrapped the tissue and slowly turned the images of tall, intricate carvings: an ancestor figure with arms that morphed into a diving seabird; a man whose nose joined up with his penis. 'There are times when I love this job,' she said. 'When the past takes you in its grasp and shows you its power.'

The past or the place? Rika didn't know, though everything felt too immediate, too alive to belong to *before*. The blinds were drawn against the heat, and even if they weren't, all she'd have seen from the window was the street in front of the Toyota dealer. Yet she knew that these *things* – she didn't have a name for them, these beautiful *objects* – were still being made up rivers, on islands, on mountains. Ask Wana. Ask Milton. Ask anyone.

In another folder were photographs of *maro* bark-cloth from Dutch New Guinea. Rika put on her library gloves and stood for a long time looking at the dancing beings painted on a flat surface. She thought of the mountain bark-cloth, with the same flat surface, the same exuberance. But those were of mountains and leaves, the fruits of the forest. The *maro* bark-cloth was of fish and birds, creatures that were neither man nor bird, strange poetic imaginings floating in the large space of the cloth.

'Miró painted like that,' Rika said. 'He must have seen these. Do you think he *took* them?'

'He was inspired by them,' Gina said. She meant it as a joke, a half-joke, but Rika didn't laugh. She was reading the accompanying notes that these were among the bark-cloth the surrealists had seen in Paris in the 1920s at the start of their love affair with Oceania. Rika read from André Breton of the 'irresistible need to possess, hardly equalled in any other domain', and from Paul Eluard praising the 'disintegration of categories . . . colours and forms, laughter and tears'.

She translated for Gina, who, being Australian, didn't have French, a monolingual fact that continued to astound her. 'The bird takes root in the woman, the man in the nest.'

The surrealists, she read, would travel anywhere to find Oceanic art. Travel where? She flipped a few pages. To Rotterdam! Breton meant they'd travel as far from Paris as Rotterdam!

'Easier than coming here,' Gina said. 'None of them got anywhere near.'

'None?'

'A dealer, that's all. If it was a love affair, it was with an *idea*.'

'With art,' Rika said. 'That can be a love affair, yes?'

'Oh, yes,' Gina said. 'The greatest of love affairs.' She paused for a moment, looked at Rika, smiled. 'But not necessarily the best.'

Outside their door, a phone was ringing in another room, typewriters clacked, and beyond the blinds over the window the sun rose in the sky. The room was still, a world unto itself, *somewhere else*, until Laedi and Martha came clattering up the stairs. They had Wana with them.

'Do you want to swim?' Laedi asked, and it wasn't until Bili was tugging at Rika's hair that she was back in the present. It was well into the afternoon and she was hungry.

'We can stop at the bakery,' Martha said.

'First look at these,' Rika said, holding out the photographs as if they were treasures lifted from the sea.

Wana, her hair tied up in a strip of bright cloth, put on a pair of library gloves, turned over the images, read the dates. Whistled.

'We must tell Aaron,' Rika said.

'I already have,' Gina said.

Rika cleared more space at the table. She was used to Sam being there, and Aaron, like him, was teaching on the Melanesian history course. He, too, would need to read documents and letters in Gina's care. Until the library on campus was finished, there was nowhere else for them to work. With few published histories – most that there were belonged to an earlier age, not much use for students who'd go from their tutorial rooms to create a new nation – it meant writing lectures, many of them from scratch.

When Gina apologised for the cramped conditions, Aaron said he wouldn't mind the squash, or the smallness of the room, or people coming and going outside the door. It was better than the chilly reading rooms of libraries and museums in Europe, where he'd felt invisible; even when he insisted, no, he didn't come from India, or Africa, but *New Guinea*, still people thought he meant West Africa, or some part of India, or Indonesia, a spice island maybe. Somewhere comprehensible. It took the paradox of the surrealists' love of a land they could imagine as not real to get anyone interested in a place that, to him, of course, was intensely real. Talk of the surrealists' *amour fou*, more lasting than the love of any woman, and people reached for the atlas!

In the tearoom overlooking the cars in the yard at the back of the building, Sam laughed and Gina made more coffee, but Rika was thinking that if no one had any idea of a real place, after a while it'd vanish into some strange memory zone. When that happened to her, not places but events, it was a kind of relief. Gone. She liked the feeling, and there were times when she encouraged it. But what if it was everything, the entire world you came from. It took a stretch for Rika to imagine that – Europe was *mapped*. No one didn't know Europe.

'When you were in Europe,' she asked Aaron one day when he was there alone, working beside her at the table. 'Did you go to the Netherlands?'

'Yes,' he said, looking up. A slight smile.

'To Leiden?'

He nodded. 'Your home town.'

'You knew?'

The smile widened. 'Jacob told me. But I'd have known from the way you asked.'

'My father's a curator at the Museum of Ethnology.'

Aaron knew that too. His smile was rather like Jacob's, without the edgy watchfulness. 'Some of the earliest plumes taken from Dutch New Guinea are there,' he said.

Was this a point of pride, or of shame? Rika didn't know. 'Did you see my father?'

'No. A woman showed me the plumes.' When he saw the disappointment in her face, a hint of embarrassment, he said, 'You must miss him.'

'Yes, I suppose I do.' She didn't like to think of him too much, alone in the house on the canal, with her mother gone, and now her.

'It's hard being away from your own ground,' Aaron said.

'It didn't feel like ground when I was there.'

'No,' he said. 'All that water,' and she caught the smile of his eyes.

'So much, it sometimes goes under the houses.' She laughed. Cautious.

'Like the villages here. Have you seen them, built out over the harbour?' He gestured to the window, oriented himself and turned to point towards the harbour.

'Yes,' Rika said. 'I've been there, to Hanuabada.'

'How?' he asked, surprised.

'Mela took me.'

'Mela?'

Rika gave a little shrug, embarrassed to admit to a *haus gel*.

'It's okay,' he said. 'When I get a house, I'll have someone to clean too.'

'Where are you now?'

'In the men's dormitory. I'm a tutor there.'

'Oh,' she said. 'Two jobs.'

'I don't get paid for that one. It doesn't take much work.' That smile again. 'Stopping them rioting, that's all.'

Rioting? She couldn't imagine Milton rioting. Jacob maybe, but not Milton.

Aaron was laughing, and she was blushing. 'No, not rioting!' he said. 'Being unruly. Noisy. Sneaking girls in.'

She liked the way he spoke, his odd humour. 'Where did you stay when you were in Leiden?'

'In a room near the station.'

'No riots there.' Her own small joke, and he smiled.

'No. No riots. No one to sneak in.'

'Were you lonely?'

There was no smile this time, just a small nod. 'I suppose I was,' he said.

She could imagine how it would have been: nothing nasty, no sneer, no jeer, just the bland certainty that tolerance requires no gesture.

The door opened and Sam came in. 'You two chatting again?' he said, putting his folders from Gina on the table.

Aaron returned to the primitive and tribal arts dealer. He was concentrating. *Working.* She wasn't. She looked at the little prints from the Anglican Mission that only the day before she'd found interesting, and her eye, her mind, wouldn't stay there. They returned to Aaron. Something about his nose, the flare of his nostrils, and the way the eyes were set reminded her of Jacob. Yes, she could see they were clan-brothers, there was something similar about them. And yet, also distinct. Quite distinct, as if the features that were prominent in one receded in the other. The jut of the forehead in Jacob, the power of his shoulders, didn't draw attention in Aaron, though when she looked at him they were there, just as clear. And the nose, so striking in Aaron, seemed quite different in Jacob, though both had the same high arch.

'Did you see these?' Aaron startled her. He was holding out a colour photograph of a fine plumed headdress. Yes, she'd seen it. It had passed in front of her that afternoon with Gina; another folder, another elaborate spray of feathers, that's all she saw, nothing more. Her plaits were pinned up against the heat again, and she'd cut her fringe short so it stuck out from her forehead like a tiny awning, and still she could feel the sweat at the back of her neck, her brow. She brought her attention to the headdress. She saw the fineness of the black, dancing plumes. Attached to them were tufts of soft white feathers. 'Are they sewn on, these white ones?' she asked. It was hard to make out.

'Yes,' he said. 'It's big work. Underneath feathers from a cockatoo.'

'And the black feathers?'

'Black cassowary.'

'Not bird of paradise?'

'Not those. These.' He passed her another photograph, the red of the *ragianna*, the red plumes she'd seen attached to those shrivelled bodies. The colour of henna.

'And here.' Another photo, another angle on the black cassowary headdress. 'A very good one. Old. Collected 1908.'

Sam came round the table to look. 'Would it have come through the traders?' he asked.

'If it's in Europe, yes,' Aaron said. He looked at the back. 'Unless it was part of a collection. There's no note to say it is. Just the village in Papua. Owen Stanley Range.'

'How do they do it?' Rika asked, looking at the white feathers.

'They're tied on,' Aaron said. 'It's delicate work, sometimes they use a flying-fox bone as a needle.'

'So much work,' Rika said.

He smiled. 'There's nothing like it,' he said. 'A lazy afternoon, in the shade, talking as you work.'

'How long since you've been home?'

'Too long. Not since before I started my MA.'

'Are you going back?'

'At the end of the semester break, in July. There's a feast and I've got permission to go.'

Sam looked up. 'The old man's letting you go already?'

'How long?'

'Only for a week.'

'For a *feast*?' Rika asked. A whole week, for a feast?

'Not just any feast,' Aaron said, with that half laugh of his. 'A ritual feast.'

'You are getting the treatment,' Sam said, amiably enough. Aaron was on a local salary, half what he was getting; he didn't begrudge the perks.

Rika returned to the photograph Aaron had handed her. At the back of the headdress, low down, was a kind of cape – enough to cover the neck – of white and black cockatoo feathers, alternating, overlapping, cut into regular and precise patterns. Above them, the seeming disorder of the black plumes with their carefully sewn white.

'At night they dance,' Aaron said. 'All you can see are the white feathers moving.'

'They dance at night?'

'When the moon is full. On the mountain, your husband will see it.'

'Leonard,' she said. 'Yes.'

Rika liked having Aaron at her table, and Sam. She arranged her days so that the two she spent at the library would coincide with theirs. She liked the way they sat back in their chairs and talked. She liked the contrast of their hair, one red, one black, both springy, growing long. She liked the way they joked and then became serious again. She liked the lunches they ate in the tearoom, fresh bread and tomatoes from a stall on the street. More coffee. There was a spring in her step as she came up the stairs in the morning. She stood at the window, looking down on the drab street, at white mothers shopping with small children, at local women with their string bags, *bilums*, set out for sale on woven pandanus mats, at groups of men smoking in the shadow of the awning over the bank. Her mind felt wide and capacious. Aaron had shown her the *Surrealist Map of the World*, and she saw how it pleased him that the surrealists had redrawn the map in 1929, doing what the European powers had done only ten years before with the Treaty of Versailles, carving up the world, remaking boundaries to suit the victors of war. Only the surrealists' was not a map of conquest. Theirs was a map to celebrate the creative. 'The poetic sublime,' Breton called it. 'Glittering visions of something other than that which we can know.'

Bang in the centre of the *Surrealist Map of the World* was the great Pacific Ocean. Off to the left, Russia was huge (they approved of the Revolution); Africa and China were small but well visible. To the right

73

Mexico was large and so was Labrador, but between them the United
States had very nearly been erased. Gone! At the left-hand edge of
the map, England was a dot off the east coast of a large Ireland. Rika
liked that. Australia had shrunk to the size of Tasmania (which didn't
feature at all) under New Guinea and its islands, which were so large
the equator has to bulge upwards to accommodate them.

Rika traced the *Surrealist Map of the World* and made an enlarge-
ment of it on a large sheet of art paper. With ink and a fine pen, she
decorated the map with tiny *maro* figures, and pinned it to the wall of
the room where they worked.

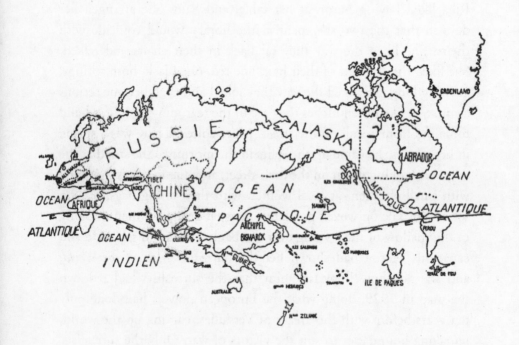

LIFE, BEING AS IT IS, CONTINUED IN WAYS THAT WERE RESOLUTELY realist. Personal slights and rivalries arrived in Laedi's garden as surely as the ukuleles and the gossip. The stars still shone in the sky, but down on the ground of the garden Milton didn't forgive the editor of the student newspaper for abandoning a review of his play in order to write about the Kennedy assassination.

'We shouldn't be ruled by what happens to them,' he grumbled, to which Eremiah, the editor, answered along the lines that it was his point exactly. 'Shooting a planter, that's easy. What to do next is the question.' He told Milton to read what came out of the United Nations. 'What will you know if you lie about and read novels? They're seducing you. Making you angry. You kill the planter. They hang you. Go to the archives. Read the court reports.'

That the play was reviewed by a visiting Australian journalist who said all Milton could have wanted, didn't reduce the slight. The journalist from the Melbourne *Age* included the play in his article on the new university. 'A new voice, a challenge to Australian colonialism. A people rising up in their own language.' Two weeks later the arts editor invited himself up to investigate this new direction in Black Writing, but even that didn't shift Milton's mood. 'May his penis refuse to piss,' he said when he saw Eremiah strut across the road towards Simbaikan's fire. Simbaikan's view was that Milton had fallen into sickness from the bad thoughts of his play. They'd weakened him and left him wide open to any marauding spirit that passed.

The marauder Simbaikan had in mind was the niece of an Australian official in the colonial administration, who was in Moresby 'killing time' before starting at Melbourne University. Her name was Tessa, and her fingers were loaded with rings. She'd been at the play and had turned up uninvited at the cast party afterwards. Never mind the assassination, she was in party mood. Maybe Milton was particularly vulnerable that night with the off-balance atmosphere at the play, or maybe it would have happened anyway. Tessa went straight up to him, looked him in the eye, flicked back her hair, and that, as they say, was that. Another *amour fou*. He might as well have been drugged. Or sorcered by the rings on her fingers and the chain around her ankle with its little silver bells that chimed as she walked. She arrived in the garden on the night they heard that the arts editor of the *Age* was coming up. There was talk of taking the play to Melbourne. A good opportunity, Aro said. Tessa sat herself on a crate and crossed her legs. The silver bells tinkled. 'You'll like Melbourne,' she beamed at Milton. 'Cheer up,' she said, rearranging her legs.

In the presence of this long-haired Australian girl, Milton fell into silence. He didn't join the talk of touring plays to the remote villages, though it had begun as his idea. Otherwise, he'd said back in the days before he was dazzled, everything happens in Moresby, which just proves the fears out in the villages that independence will mean the rule of town sharps and *raskols*. If roots are to be grown for the future, they have to start in the villages.

'*Useless*,' Eremiah said. 'They're white-man plays, not village plays.' Plays, novels, this whole idea of creating a nation through art, nothing would come of it. He had no time for James Baldwin. Self-indulgent. Drinking and fucking and killing off characters who should know better. '*Art* doesn't change anything.'

He was a tall man with a long face and hair that grew straight up from his head, giving him a look of permanent outrage. He was one of the older students, in his late twenties, who'd been kept waiting for the university. He'd done a stint as a clerk in the colonial government's administration, and had seen how entrenched the old attitudes were. From the island of Bougainville, his skin was true black, not the red skin of the mainland. 'Black like a saucepan's arse,' Milton growled. He could jeer, but Eremiah was proud of his skin. Black skin, black power. There was nothing compromising about Eremiah. Not like Milton, leaning in towards Tessa.

'Write a play about the *haus boi* lynched for looking at *missis*,' Eremiah said. 'That'll wake you up.' Milton ignored him. 'Write a play about Martin Luther King.'

'Mister Preacher Man,' Milton said, his eyes still on Tessa. Her long hair, her throat, those legs. 'Mister Newspaper Man.'

Simbaikan scowled. 'He looks at her too much. He looks at her and sees all wrong.' She poked at the fire. *Hapkas* babies, she said, need strong mothers, not a harlot, a *pamuk meri*. 'Empty girl. No ground in her.'

She rolled a sweet potato out of the fire, scraped off the ash, cut it, gave a chunk to Rika. She liked this girl, Laedi's friend. She didn't know why she had the white skin of the new people, for she was like her long-dead husband, sanctified in memory, with an inside the same as the old people, the dark-skinned people. Her husband had been a good man with a good smell, and it made no sense to her that his skin was white. It had burned in the sun and peeled like the bark of a tree. Same with this girl, who was too white, she complained to Laedi, her spirit must have gone astray. She patted Rika's arm and handed her another chunk of sweet potato.

She looked across to Eremiah, who was still arguing with Milton. Aaron's hands were reaching out, to one, then the other. She liked him, a good man from the coast, but Eremiah gestured over him and a big noise started, with everyone shouting. The card game stopped, and Rifle was standing up. Simbaikan scowled.

Eremiah's fist was in the air. 'They shot Martin Luther King,' he shouted. 'They shot Robert Kennedy. Wake up!' This soft talk of plays and love and dancing together, black skin and white, was a diversion. 'The road to independence will be a hard road,' he yelled. 'We must be ready to fight.'

Tessa's voice came chirruping in. 'Don't you worry,' she said. 'Things are changing in Australia. Independence will come soon enough.'

Eremiah's tall, thin head shot up another few inches. 'We're not waiting for a gift from you,' he said. 'If we want independence we'll have to demand it. *Take* it.'

It was too much for Simbaikan.

'*Raus!*' she shouted. She was on her feet. 'No good, this independence talk, your head is too hot. You sit down and learn the white-man law. You go! You go and study!' She stomped over to Rifle and told him not to listen, shouted at the Highland labourers with their scruffy beards and gappy teeth to clean out their ears. She'd rather white men as kiaps and teachers and doctors and pilots than a black *munka* with his tall hair and angry vanity. She poked at the fire and wouldn't be placated until Eremiah left and the last of the comments shouted over his shoulder had disappeared into the dark. His supporters thumped away with him, and Rifle returned to his card game.

A ukulele started up, then another, a jews' harp, a counter current, ironic, playful, like a voice from another world, another layer of existence rising up as if from the earth, and there was movement again, people dancing. Sam and Wana swayed softly against each other. Tessa took Milton by the hand and let the moon do the rest. When the drums started, Laedi and Tamba tapped out the rhythm on the veranda. Rika moved, weaving through the dancers, letting the music enter her, swaying with the trees that moved against the sky. When she came to Aaron, who was making his way towards her, she asked him who was right, Eremiah or Milton.

'Both,' he said. 'Both hot-headed.'

'Who would you trust to tell your history?'

Aaron laughed. 'Neither.'

'Then you should do it,' she said. When he smiled, a slight shrug, she turned it into a question. 'Surely,' she said, 'it should be you?'

Still he didn't answer, there being no answer, not easily, not that night. Instead he told her that when he was a child, he'd had an uncle who'd been a bird-catcher, a man who could think like a bird. There in the garden with the ukulele playing, he held out his hand, moving his fingers as if drawing a bird towards him, and Rika felt something move deep inside. He swayed, and she swayed, not dancing exactly, not together, but close, until she continued towards the veranda, where Martha was sitting with Laedi, watching.

'Look at her,' Martha said.

'She'll get over it,' Laedi said. 'She'll have to.'

*

In the garden, Rika and Aaron might sway, but they never quite danced. When Martha asked her why not, she shrugged and said she wouldn't dance, not with Leonard on the mountain. Martha danced with Jacob so she knew the stab of disloyalty, with Pete only a few houses away marking essays. She also knew that the person Jacob wanted to dance with was not her, but Rika, and that too she experienced as a stab. Still, it was the end of term, the winds would soon start, and everything would change. So Martha danced, and Rika stayed with Simbaikan by the fire, or talked to Milton and Jacob, or to Eremiah and Aaron, who'd arrive together discussing politics. She wasn't interested in the politics of independence. She wasn't *unin*terested, she just accepted that history would sweep them along and required no help from her. When the arguments started, her mind would drift into that expansive space that opened to the night sky, until Aaron came with her to the steps of the veranda. She dabbed herself with citronella and leaned into the smoke from his cigarette.

For a while they'd sit there quietly, until they turned to each other, their words floating up towards the house, or out into the night air, so that anyone who passed could catch a fragment of their stories weaving together, and Rika's first hesitant attempts to learn his language. She learned to call her string bag *jávo*. She learned that the word for breath also meant emotion. To breathe was to feel. 'Oh yes,' she said, breathing the soft garden air and looking up at the stars. She learned the word for story, *kiki*, listening as Aaron spoke of the fjords, the home he hadn't seen for two years.

'Will you tell me about your bird-catcher uncle?' she asked one night in the last week of term.

'You don't think it strange?'

She smiled, and shook her head.

He looked at her, a long pause as if he was testing her, or maybe himself, before he told her that the best birds weren't in his village, on the edge of the water. They were found up higher, in the forest behind his mother's village. They looked across to the fire, where Jacob was standing, on the edge of the dance and the talk, watching them. He'd been there when, as small boys, they went with their uncle into the forest, to the trees where paradise birds collected at dawn and dusk. He didn't want to climb up; even then Jacob didn't believe. It was Aaron who went after his uncle and sat on a branch near him as he made the sound of the red-plumed *raggiana*. *H-hu-how-how-how-how-how-how-how-how-HOW-WHAIWIH*. There on the steps, Aaron's voice transformed itself into the call of a bird. Jacob looked across, recognising the sound. Rika saw the flash of his eyes before the lids came down, and he walked off in the direction of the road that led into town.

'He knew the habits of birds,' Aaron was saying. 'He shared their spirit. And now he's gone, and I don't know who has that knowledge. The knowledge of generations. It may be that it's gone. Too many of us went out to school.'

His hand was open, outstretched. Rika's hand lifted, fluttering for a moment like a shy bird, but it didn't land. She brought it back to her side, held it in her lap. Aaron closed his gently, as if a bird had landed there.

Without warning, or reason, Rika wanted to cry.

THE HEARTS OF WHITE-SKINNED MEN

THE FIRST RIKA HEARD OF TROUBLE ON THE mountain was when Gina knocked on the darkroom door. 'Let me know when I can come in,' she called. She wanted a private place to talk. No listening ears. She'd had a letter from Alex Penrose. She made no pretence – yes, they were lovers. Rika had known that for weeks. These things happen. Children, families – sometimes not everything fits.

'How does Leonard seem?' she asked when Rika let her in and had pulled out a stool from under the bench. The only light was from a pale-red bulb.

'Fine,' she said. A plane had been up with supplies and returned with letters.

'Has he written about Don?'

'Not much.' She made a show of concentrating, running film through the enlarger.

'Rika, listen. Alex is worried. Don's interrupting the filming.'

'Yes,' Rika said, still looking through the enlarger. 'Leonard said.' She was finishing the last of the shots from the South African ambassador's talk to the university politics club. She was looking down on Eremiah standing on a chair calling for a protest.

'So will you go up?' Gina asked.

'There's all this work here.'

'It can wait. The job can wait.'

There was something ominous about Gina's tone. Rika turned to her, stopped the pretence of work. 'Why are you asking?' she said.

'Alex thinks it'd help if you went up.'

'Not while Don's there.'

'Alex and Don will be back soon.'

'What's it really about?' Rika said. 'I don't understand. Leonard says Don's playing music. Using up the batteries. It doesn't sound much.'

'It stirs up the young men, upsets the chiefs.'

Rika's heart slowed to a very small beat. She didn't want to think of Leonard up on the mountain, needing her.

'Look,' Gina said. 'Don's ambitious. He wants to be out early with his book on culture and change.'

'So?'

'He's using the mountain as one of his case studies, as you know.'

'I thought the point about the mountain was that it hadn't changed.'

'Everywhere changes. That's Don's point. He wants to take an example of a place that's thought not to have changed, and show that it has.'

'What's playing music got to do with it?' Rika said, irritated. 'It's not much of a change if it's only there because of him.'

'The music's symbolic,' Gina said. 'It starts something off, uncovers the tensions. That's what he's after. Alex says the young men flock to him, he has them smoking cigarettes, listening to music, talking of independence. The chiefs hate it.'

'Poor Leonard.' Rika sighed. 'He thinks anthropologists should be neutral.'

'Yes, I know. Influence government behind the scenes. Alex

used to think that. Don doesn't. He says that if Leonard has his way, independence would be another twenty years.'

'That's unfair,' Rika said. Poor Leonard. Poor, kind Leonard.

'Apparently there was a row.'

'I didn't know that.' Leonard's letters said that Don was obstructive, and that he was behind schedule with the filming, but nothing about a row.

'What's happening with the film? Did Leonard say?'

'He's not doing as much as he'd like, that's all I know. And that the chiefs want the film made. They think it's good for the mountain. They want it told as their ancestors would tell it.' Rika sighed. 'There must be something else going on. Something *personal*.'

'It is personal. That's why he needs you.'

'He made his other films without me,' Rika said. 'He might do better up there on his own.' Her words sounded hollow, even to her. If he was asking for her, she should go. He'd brought her here, all this way, Leonard and the mountain, and now, suddenly, she didn't want to go. Not now, on her own.

'What's going on with Aaron?' Gina asked.

'Nothing,' Rika said.

Gina's face was a question mark.

'*Nothing's* going on.' A flash of anger.

'I'm not judging you. Heaven only knows, I'd be the last person to do that.'

'Then why are you asking?' Rising tears.

'Rika, Rika.' Gina got up and put her arms around her.

Rika bristled. 'Is it so bad to *like* someone?'

When Gina left, Rika sat on the stool, her shoulders slumped forward, and wished she could cry. Instead, a dry, shut feeling.

That evening Rika didn't go to Laedi's. Exams were over, students were returning to their villages. The winds had started, blowing a fine-powdered dust under doors and sending sudden gusts of leaves across the road. With Simbaikan about to depart and Don about to return, Rifle had sold the drum from her fire. Those who were left stayed inside, and that evening they noticed a car parked in the road outside. Martha thought it was the neighbour from the bursar's office who yelled at them to keep the noise down. Sam had seen him cruising around the housing compound at night as if on a patrol. But it wasn't him. No one recognised the driver who sat in the dark, smoking a cigarette, and when Sam walked over to ask him what he wanted, he wound up the window and drove away.

When Rika hadn't turned up at eight, eight-thirty, nine, Wana and Martha walked over to her house and found her sitting in the middle of the floor. She was looking at her wall of photographs. Jacob on the hill was there. The pattern of swamp. Mela at her village. Close-ups of Laedi, her hair, her bare feet. Simbaikan at the market with Bili on her shoulder. Sam and Wana at a market; Milton with his ukulele; Rifle and a sack of vegetables. A close-up of Aaron in the library, his face turned to the light of the window. A gallery of her new life.

Pinned to the side were the morning's shots from Eremiah's protest at the South African ambassador's visit, the first demonstration in Port Moresby. There was a shot of the ambassador scurrying up the steps of the plane that'd take him back to Canberra, his alarm visible as he turned to look at the students with their placards. *Go Home Racialist!* Another of Eremiah, his hair on end, looking more than ever like a carving on the top of a house pole, his fist in the air. There were the shots she'd taken from the bonnet of the car as the police ran towards her, and of Jacob yelling at her to get down, seconds before Aaron reached up and pulled her into his arms. Beside them was the picture cut from the *South Pacific Post* of Rika flanked by Aaron and Jacob, each with an arm pinned behind them by the police. Her face was turned to Aaron. A very public moment.

And now in the silence of her house she sat on the floor. In front of her, in its tarnished silver frame, was the small photograph of her mother that she'd brought from Leiden.

Wana picked it up. 'Your mother?' she asked, looking at the young woman with her hair in a roll.

Rika nodded. Tears were close.

Wana's mother was a nursing sister. She took canoes between villages to deliver babies at night when there was no one to drive the hospital dinghy. 'She's a *vegu*, a grasshopper creature,' Wana said. 'Like you. Long, sensitive feelers.'

Rika smiled wanly. 'Thanks for coming.' Her hair was in two fat, untidy plaits.

'What's happened?' Martha asked.

She told them about Gina, and Alex's letter. Martha wasn't surprised, Pete had also had one from him.

'I should go up,' Rika said, and the tears spilled over.

Martha put out her arms and this time Rika let herself be comforted.

'Why does nothing ever stay the same?' she said, when she sat back on her heels, the tears spent. 'Something seems to be one way, quite certain, then it turns into another.' She took the photo of her mother from Wana and held it in her lap. 'She was there, with me, just as she was, and then she was ill and nothing could bring her back. Not to how she was. At the end she turned away when I came in. Can you imagine that? Your own mother couldn't look at you.'

'She was protecting you,' Wana said. 'Grasshopper girl.'

'And now it's happening again.'

'No one's dying,' Martha said.

'Everything's shifting, and I can't get back.'

She got up and went to the desk, searching around in one of the drawers. Then she went into the bathroom and closed the door.

Wana and Martha looked at each other. 'Something's got her,' Martha said.

'Got both of them. Look.'

Aaron, treading carefully, was coming up the steps onto the veranda.

'Where is she?' he asked.

'In the bathroom.' There was no sound. No running water. No flushing toilet.

Martha put on a kettle, a reflex learned as a girl. Any sign of crisis, make a pot of tea.

'Don't say anything.' Rika was in the doorway. She was holding the plaits in one hand like limp animals, and in the other she had a pair of scissors. She'd cut unevenly, up on one side. Her hair was thick and it sprang out, giving her face an entirely different look, as if she'd leaped forward five years, from a girl into the skin of a woman.

Aaron took the plaits, held them in his hands.

'Are you okay?'

She nodded. 'You?'

He nodded. She knew that it was true, and also not. Same as her.

They sat on the floor, in the middle of the room, facing each other. Aaron picked up the photograph on the mat between them. 'Your mother?' he said. 'She's lovely.'

'She died.'

'I know.' His voice was quiet as they sat there, beneath the fan, looking at each other. Wana and Martha, like chaperoning ghosts, were at the table behind them with the pot of tea, in which they were showing no interest. 'What happened?' Aaron asked.

'Cancer,' Rika said. 'We had a year in England. My father was working at a museum in Oxford and I was at school. Didn't I tell you?'

'Only that. Nothing more.'

'She caught a chill on the ferry going home and it became pneumonia. They said she'd recover, but by the time she did, they'd found the cancer.' She put her hand to her chest, the top of her left breast. Over her heart. 'Here.'

The wind had stopped. Outside, another car drove slowly past. Wana stood up and went to the door.

'And you?' Rika asked. Aaron, too, had lost his mother young. He'd still been at the primary school and had heard the drums from the canoe.

'The crying carried over the water,' he said. 'She'd been well when we left soon after dawn, and by noon she'd collapsed by a stream she'd known all her life.'

'Was it a snake?'

'No, her skin was intact.'

'There was no doctor?'

'There's an aid post at the airstrip, near the school. No one went when it was sorcery.'

'Was it?'

'I know enough to say it wasn't, but somewhere inside I think it was.'

'Why wouldn't it be possible?' Rika asked. 'Under the surface the currents are strong.'

'There was a root of ginger on the rocks by her canoe,' he said.

'And Jacob?' Rika asked. 'Was he there?'

'He was with me in the canoe when we came back from school. I saw that there was magic. Even then he didn't believe it.'

Another pause. Rika watched the blue curl of his cigarette smoke. 'Do you think of her often?' she asked.

'Sometimes,' he said.

'I try not to, but it's like a skin. A part of me.'

'A double skin. That's what we call a tattoo.'

She smiled. Everything about her felt doubted; he surely could read her skin.

He reached across and took her hand, lifted it to his face. A soft kiss. One soft kiss.

'When will you be back?' she asked.

'At the end of next week.'

'And Jacob?'

'He'll stay longer.'

'Is it okay? Between you two?' She knew that it wasn't.

'It has to be,' he said. 'We're the only two who are educated for the future. We have to agree.'

'You go tomorrow?'

He nodded.

'So soon.'

'You'll be here when I return?'

Her eyes didn't waver. A smile. A slight nod of the head.

One morning while Aaron was away, Rika ran up the stairs from the newsagent with an Australian tabloid newspaper. She put it on Gina's desk with a flourish and opened it to the bikini girl. 'I've just seen a Highlander chased out for looking at this,' she said, jabbing her finger at the grainy picture. 'I told the man at the counter that it wasn't illegal to look at a newspaper, and he called me a coon lover, said he knew all about me, *filthy coon lover*, I should go back where I came from.' She was flushed and breathless. 'Coon. I've never heard that word.'

'It's like nigger,' Gina said. 'They use it in Australia.'

'We should report him.'

'He's an old-timer. He'll be gone soon.'

'That's no reason. We must report him.'

'Who to?' Gina asked.

'The police.'

Gina shook her head. 'They won't take you seriously. Especially since the demonstation. You were in the paper, remember. They'll be on his side and on your back for ever. It's not worth it. Things are changing, and they will more.'

Rika sat down. Her hands were shaking, a tremble running though her.

'They got rid of the White Woman's Protection Ordinance,' Gina said.

Rika hadn't heard of it.

'I'll look it out for you. It was to protect white women from black men. You know, looking at them in the shower, that sort of thing. Black peril, they called it.'

'Did they look at them in the shower?'

'Probably not. There were stories and some incidents. Occasionally they were nasty, but most of it was fantasy and paranoia. Some people blamed it on white women wandering round the house, or out on the veranda, in a towel. It was a huge issue before the war.'

'When did it end?'

'1958.'

'Only ten years ago.'

Laedi said there was something hardwired into the hearts of white-skinned men that refused the claim, any claim, however slight, that a man who is black may make on a woman who is white. All that year there were letters in the *South Pacific Post*; they'd come in an ugly run, then stop, only to start again, provoked by changes that were a daily challenge to that hardwiring. Papuan men were returning from study in Australia, and some of them arrived home with fair young wives. *Hapkas* babies were pushed in prams by mothers with flowing hair and no shame. It was not an uncommon sight to see white girls drinking with black students in bars and beer gardens. Tessa wasn't the only one enjoying a holiday from Melbourne. In the paper were cartoons of black devil figures having their way with voluptuous white maidens. Talk of 'hotbeds of sin' and 'coffee-coloured babies'.

Out at the university, those who saw themselves as moving with the tide of history, not victim to it, grimaced at what they took to be the last shudder of a retrograde world. White staff members joined students in beer gardens and saloon bars to make the point that a change in law meant a change in practice, and when the *South Pacific Post* warned its readers to 'Beware the Congo', they laughed. In their minds, with independence coming so late to Papua New Guinea, they would learn from the mistakes of Africa. There'd be no carnage here; on the contrary. Instead of reading the *South Pacific Post*, people in town should read the student newspaper. Read Eremiah on the true equality of man, which will come only when each looks at the other as if he looks at himself, no matter what his tribe, or his race.

*

Two days after Alex Penrose returned from the mountain, he was standing in the door of the room where Rika worked. 'How do you like the bark-cloth?' he asked. His paunch had vanished and his face was thin. There was a sore on his ankle.

'It's beautiful,' Rika said. Against a background of muted yellows and reds, delicate black shapes crossed the cloth as if a form of calligraphy.

'The women chiefs sent it especially, as a gift to Leonard's wife,' Alex said.

'Yes,' she said. There was an accompanying letter from Leonard. 'He told me what the markings mean, the pattern of the vine that used to be tattooed onto the women's faces when they became artists.'

'Not quite,' Alex said. 'More to do with initiation into clan mythology.'

'Into the ways of the bark-cloth, no?'

'When you go up there,' he said, 'you'll be able to ask them yourself.'

She said nothing.

'Have you thought when you're going?'

'No,' she said, looking him straight in the eye. 'There's a lot of work to be done here.'

'Your husband could do with a visit,' Alex said. 'It's been hard for him with Don.'

She wished she'd had the wit to say it was a pity then, that Alex had taken Don up in the first place. The unfairness of it, that she was made to feel guilty about a situation entirely of Alex Penrose's making.

Don came back with several bark-cloths. They, too, were beautiful, but they weren't given to him as a gift to his wife. He complained that he'd had to buy his, as if, somehow, it was Leonard's doing. With an air of incivility, he went to the library on Aaron's return from the fjords, sat at the table where he and Rika were working, leaned back in the chair and looked from one to the other. He quizzed Aaron on the lectures he was writing, as if to suggest that whatever he was doing there was an excuse, a paltry cover. Looking straight at Rika, he told Aaron and Sam, who was also working at the table that morning, how little a camera could do, what an outmoded form it was when it came to anthropology and the representation of culture.

That evening he went out of his way to drive past Rika's house, and saw Aaron on the veranda.

'What do they think they're doing?' he said to Laedi when he returned home. 'It's brazen.'

'Sam and Wana were there,' she answered. 'And Martha.'

'Don't quibble.'

His bad mood went on and on.

Aaron and Rika were exposed in a glare of light harsher than the sun over their heads. On the morning Aaron returned from the fjord coast, leaving Jacob there for the last week of the vacation, he'd gone straight to the library. It was on the way, between the airport and the dormitory where he lived. Typewriters stopped and every person in the office looked up from their desks. Rika had barely had time to ask how it'd been, going home after so long away, before one person after another found reason to visit the table where they sat, though they talked of nothing more compromising than the character of an Anglican priest whose photographs showed him more interested in orchids than souls.

Gina kept her door closed.

The next day, when Rika was at the beach with Laedi and Martha, Aaron joined them there, as he had many times before on his way back from town. And she, as she had before, went to meet him as he came through the trees. But the light seemed brighter, their every move magnified as they walked down to the water and swam out towards the reef. Martha was with them, not that it made any difference. Sea birds cruised overhead, as they always did, and outside the reef canoes slid past on their way home to Mela's village. An ordinary afternoon, the water calm with a shimmer of haze over the reef, but on that day even the children stopped to watch, and their mothers stood in groups, turning their heads and whispering.

At the university there were rumours that Rika and Aaron had been seen coming out of a hotel room, or buying airline tickets. Ridiculous rumours. It didn't matter that none were true, or that Aaron and Rika were never alone, for those who judged them saw what they feared, and wanted, to see.

Alex Penrose confronted Aaron in his office. He walked in, closed the door and told Aaron that Leonard was greatly respected in Oxford and Canberra. All this talk might reflect badly on Aaron's career. One day he'd be needed to head up the department, or the university; he should consider these things.

'I know,' Aaron replied, opening the door. His professor had already said the same thing.

'BE CAREFUL,' LAEDI SAID. IT WAS ONE OF THE FEW TIMES SHE'D BEEN to Rika's house since Don's return. Term had started, Aaron hadn't been back to the beach; Rika had barely seen him except at the library. And still there was whispering talk. Laedi's eyes were puffy and she was wearing a drab pregnancy smock.

'Are you saying I shouldn't see him?'

'I'm saying you should be careful.'

'Do we have to be careful of nothing? There's nothing to be careful of. *Nothing*.'

They were in the kitchen. Rika, in an apron, was cooking fish curry. Aaron was coming to dinner, and so were Sam and Wana, Pete and Martha, Aro. She was making a statement, refusing to be cowed. She'd grown up on stories of the war and people who'd hidden Jews in their attics. Several times her father had kept people overnight at the museum. If he could do that, she could do this. 'It's a *meal*, that's all.' Her chin was out.

'Don't think I disapprove,' Laedi said. 'It's not that. I don't want you hurt because you don't understand how vicious this place can be.'

'I've seen the letters in the papers. And Gina's told me about the White Women's Protection Ordinance. Wana says it's a white-man fantasy that white women are irresistible to Papuans.'

'That's her being naïve. Or hopeful. White people are powerful. It gets into our fantasies. Why do you think I married Don?'

'This isn't a fantasy,' Rika said. 'And it's got nothing to do with the colour of our skins.'

'Now you're being naïve. Or stupid.'

'Do you think of me as white?'

'Of course I do.'

94

'I think of you as Laedi, not white, not black.'

'There you are. You think of me as mixed race. *Half-caste.*'

'No, I don't. I think of you as you.'

'And that's who I am. Always wrong. Black when I should be white.' A deep flush spread across her face. 'White where I should be black.'

'What's Don done? What's he done to you? Laedi?'

There was a long pause. Laedi looked at Rika, and her eyes filled with tears. 'He says I'm a white cunt.' Her voice was quiet. 'He yells it at me, so Tamba hears. And Bili.' Barely audible. 'He hates me for it. Says that all the things that should be white about me are black, and the one thing that should be black is white.' Tears were dripping onto her horrible, servile smock.

'You should leave him,' Rika said. Her voice flashed with anger and shock.

'How can I? I'm pregnant and I haven't any money.'

That evening the mood was sombre. Aaron talked about his return to the village, his old uncles weeping, and the feast and dancing. He and Jacob had both dressed in plumes. They'd come to an agreement – *a pact*, Aaron called it – that neither would use the new ways against the old. Rika wanted to ask more, but whenever her eyes met his, they couldn't stay there. A car was parked outside on the road. When Pete went out to investigate, it drove off before he could see the driver's face. Then it was back again, the same car, and this time Sam and Aaron went out. 'Watch out, you black fucker,' the driver called as the car slid away again. 'Coward,' Sam shouted as it turned the corner, out of sight. Half an hour later a different car drove slowly past, turned and stopped where the driver had a clear view to the window. Rika wanted to pin a sheet across the louvres that were open for the air, but Wana said, 'No, it'll look like we've got something to hide.'

Washing up with Martha afterwards, Rika was incandescent with fury. The unfairness of it, the impossibility. The prejudice. That was one thing. Worse was the self-consciousness that had her feeling she couldn't look at him, not as she used to. Not with everyone thinking what they thought, when there was nothing to think. *Nothing*. And anyway, all she wanted was to be with him. Not *be with him*, just be there, *be here*, knowing him.

'Oh, oh, oh,' she cried. 'What is it with everyone?'

It was Aaron who decided they shouldn't see each other 'for a while'. They should be cautious, let the rumours drop away. He went to the library to tell her, let her know his sorrow, his regret, and found that she'd gone to Mela's village for the day. The table was neat, there was no sign of her. A lecturer from Geography was working alone at one end, looking at maps from the war. Aaron sat at his usual place, reading documents from the United Nations; but his concentration was bad and his eye kept returning to Rika's empty chair.

'She's not there, mate,' the lecturer said.

Aaron went into Gina's office. 'Will you tell her I won't visit for a while?' he said. He was putting her at risk, he said. Leonard was alone on the mountain, Jacob had returned, and teaching had started. He'd come to the library on days she wasn't there. Could Gina tell her that? Just until things calmed down.

'Prudent?' Rika said to Gina. 'What do you mean, *prudent*?'

Two days went by, then a third and fourth. For Rika, each might have been a month. Energy drained from her. At the beach, she didn't swim. She lay under the tree and stared into the branches. She turned towards the road as if Aaron might suddenly appear, as he had back in the days when the only person to object was Bili. She looked out to the rippling line of the reef, out to where she'd swum with him, his body curved in the water as he took her hand and showed her how to dive down, into the silence beneath. *Irivi*. The word for water in his language. It was as blue out there, the canoes still slid by, men still fished with their nets off the rocks, but Rika, who once saw everything, saw only that Aaron was not there.

At night the sly car continued to keep watch on a house where there was nothing to see. Another was parked outside Aaron's dormitory.

A day passed. And then, late one evening, Rika was on Martha's veranda.

'Are you alone?' she asked, tapping quietly at the flyscreen. Pete was over at Sam's playing music with Milton and some students from the drama group.

Martha was at the table writing an essay, the first of the new semester. *Heart of Darkness* – another book that was hard to talk about. No one in the class liked the way the Africans came across as backward and credulous, but Martha was the one who made the mistake of assuming theirs to be the darkness Conrad, or Marlow, meant. They had a different lecturer that semester, a brilliant man, everyone said, but to her he was alarming. He'd been in Africa and wasn't interested in teaching Australian girls. Was it the darkness of Africa Marlow found? he asked in response to her blunder. Or was it the darkness of colonialism, the darkness that the whites bring with them, that Kurtz has cast around him? Whose hearts are dark?

'I think I've done a terrible thing,' Rika said. She was sitting across the table, leaning on one elbow, her head in her hand.

'It's not terrible. Don't let them make you think it's terrible.'

'It's not what they think. It's what I think.'

She looked worn. Tired. There was a pimple on her chin and Martha wasn't yet used to her hair. She'd had it tidied up in town, but it remained lopsided.

'Oh, Martha,' she said. 'What shall I do?' Tears pooled in her eyes.

It wasn't Aaron she spoke of that evening, it was Leonard. She spoke of his goodness, his steadfastness, his generosity. She spoke of the house where he grew up on the side of a Welsh valley, and his elderly parents, and the household of dogs and no television. It was hard to imagine a child running free there, she said, and yet he had, in what he called 'the most blessed of childhoods'. 'It didn't make him strong,' she said. 'That's the strangeness of it.' She was quiet for a while. Pensive. 'At night I wake to someone crying, but I don't know if it's him on the mountain, calling for me, or if it's me, or a dream. Or an animal outside.' She looked at Martha as if she was about to announce her own death. 'I must go to the mountain,' she said. 'Make him understand. Tell him. I must be the first to tell him.' Before rumours and letters could reach him. 'Will you ask Aaron to come and see me? Please?'

'Of course.'

Early the next morning, Martha drove past the building site, where the new library was taking shape, to the offices which, with the dormitories, were all that were in use. She parked in the dust and already the sun was hot as she walked across to find Aaron. There were no telephones in their houses – every message had to be delivered in person. His office door was open, his desk was neat, but he was not there. Martha was writing him a note when Sam, whose office was opposite, arrived. 'Rika wants to see Aaron,' she said.

'I'll tell him,' Sam said. 'He's at a tutorial.'

'Today, if possible,' Martha said.

Sam looked at the timetable. 'His last class finishes at four-thirty. He should be with her by five.'

'Thanks.'

'It's getting difficult,' he said. 'Don was asking me yesterday. Very aggressive about it. Nothing's happening, I said, and he swore at me.'

'Is Aaron okay?'

'He's been in a dark mood all week. Not saying much, and I can't get him out for a drink.'

*

99

At the library Rika was standing at the window alone in the room. She turned as Martha came in. 'Of course,' she said, sounding oddly like Leonard. *Of course*, what she'd meant to say last night was that it was time for her to join him, that'd been the agreement, and after the injury from Don, though its true nature remained obscure, she couldn't inflict another. She must go to Leonard, go back and be his wife, he was a good man. Please, she said as if she was talking to someone other than Martha, would she not misunderstand her. It was time for her to go, that is what she had meant.

'Do you still want to see Aaron?'

'Oh, yes.' She looked down onto the stalls across the street. 'Yes,' she said again, very softly. 'Yes.'

When she turned back to Martha, her eyes were bright with tears. 'What should I do?' she said, and Martha knew from the way she looked that she was cast as herself again.

Maybe, Rika said, it'd be better if she went somewhere with Aaron, and not to Leonard at all. Not yet. Maybe she and Aaron should go to Townsville or Cairns. Or Darwin. Singapore. It didn't matter. Anywhere where there were no eyes watching; it was impossible here, everything was impossible with everyone watching, and too much talking, and everywhere people who knew who they were. Yes, that is what they should do. Go away until it was over, until these feelings had gone, these . . . She raised her hands at the absence of words to say what it was that must go, be expelled, overcome.

Gina was in the doorway. 'Go home,' she said. 'Try and get some rest.'

'I can't.'

'Martha will stay with you.'

'I've got lectures this afternoon,' Martha said.

'Aaron's coming at five,' Rika said.

'Then you must make a decision,' Gina said.

'I can't,' Rika said again, and tears spilled over.

Gina came into the room and closed the door. Her face showed every one of her forty-five years. 'Sit down,' she said. 'Listen.' In these situations, she said, we women are too often acted upon.

'You talk about Leonard and his film. About Aaron and his future.' Gina's question to Rika was about *her* future. 'What do you want for yourself?' she asked. 'For your own future.'

Rika shook her head. She didn't know.

'You don't have to decide for Leonard's film,' Gina said. 'That's his job. And Aaron's future is his future. The film will still be a film, and Aaron will still be whatever it is he's meant to be. And you. You have a life that in the long run will amount to more than being with either of them. What do you want by the time you're my age? You could be a photographer.'

Rika sniffed, gave a small laugh, a long moan.

'I'll back you whatever you decide,' Gina said. 'Other people will too.'

She'd back her if she decided to go with Aaron. If he asked, Rika said, which he hadn't. For the rest, Gina said, they'd have to ride it out. *Don't be frightened off.* Change was coming, and it was coming faster than this town realised.

'Independence,' she said. 'Think about it. Its widest meaning. For you, for me, for all of us.' A bracing concept, independence.

'Now go home,' Gina said. She kissed Rika on the cheek. *Courage*, she said. She took Martha's hand, a slight squeeze as if to say they were in this together, all of them, and that she, too, must measure up.

Back at the house, with nothing to do but wait, Rika couldn't rest; she couldn't even sit. She felt singed, as if her nerves had moved closer to the surface, a form of sickness, maybe, or of sorcery.

'We'll clean the cupboards,' she said, startling Mela into a rush of activity: furniture-moving, cupboard-emptying, bucket-filling. Lizards dozing on the walls and ceilings watched in disbelief.

The afternoon wore on. Rifle watched from the shade with the men who came and went, joining him for a smoke as they picked their way between the houses. There seemed more of this traffic than usual; Rika could see them nodding their heads and looking towards the house. Towards her. Mela came out with a bucket and Rifle called across to her, a stream of language that had her tutting and shaking her head.

'What?' she asked Mela. 'What's happened?'

'Sorry,' Mela said. '*Sore tumas.*' There'd been a row. A big row in the canteen between Jacob and Aaron. One of the *bois* from the kitchen was outside under the tree. He'd seen it all.

'Tell me,' Rika said, going out to Rifle. 'What happened?'

The story emerged in a torrent of words. Jacob had brought back *kago bilong tumbana* – traditional artefacts – from the fjords. 'He sell them for money,' Rifle said. He'd sold them for money to a no-good Chinaman, who had come to town last week on a *balus*, an aeroplane. 'Tomorrow he go.' Aaron was angry. *Kross tru.* He'd shouted at Jacob in the canteen. Many bad words.

Rika was confused. Aaron hadn't said anything to her about ancestral objects. What were they exactly? Lime pots, Rifle said. Necklaces. Plumes. She still didn't understand. When had Aaron found out about this?

The sun slipped down the sky. Four o'clock became five. Still no Aaron.

At five-thirty, Sam arrived with a message.

'Apologise,' Rika said. 'Why should he apologise?'

'He has to go to town. It's important and he's sorry. He didn't expect it. He'll come as soon as he can.'

'Why's he gone to town?'

'I don't know. I mean, I don't quite understand. Something to do with things Jacob brought back with him from the fjords. Carved lime pots and head-rests. Bird of paradise plumes.'

'*Kastom kago,*' Mela said.

'Wana knows,' Sam said.

Wana had seen it all. She'd been in the canteen eating lunch when Aaron came in. It was hot, as usual, and the food was mush. The milk was going off; it'd been left out since breakfast. The mood was desultory, with people talking idly or reading for their afternoon tutorials. The moment Aaron came through the door the atmosphere changed. It was clear from the way he walked that he was angry. He went straight to Jacob, who was sitting at the same table as Eremiah, reading the newspaper. Aaron had a man with him, a relative from the fjords who worked at the hospital, an older man with cropped hair. 'Is it true?' Aaron demanded, standing in front of Jacob. Was it true he'd sold the *koána*, the emblems of the elders? Jacob accused in turn: what would Aaron know about what the elders wanted? He'd been out of the country for years, and now he was sorcered by a white woman. He spat out a vile word: *cunt-struck*. The older man lifted his hands in warning. The word Aaron used against Jacob was the word for *lesser* – lesser man, lesser brother, lesser rank; the impetuous, treacherous one who brings trouble and dishonour to his people. The word Aaron used came laden with contempt, and he used it in front of students eating their lunch and kitchen hands, who understood the full impact of the insult.

Jacob had broken their pact, their agreement. After Aaron left the fjords, Jacob had talked big, and on the promise of bringing back wealth, he'd persuaded the old men, the elders, to give over some of the treasures that had come down to them from their fathers. He'd carried them back to Port Moresby and made the enquiries that took him to the hotel room of Mr Lim, a man who understood how to convert one kind of wealth into another. That morning the kinsman who worked at the hospital had walked out to the university to warn Aaron that Mr Lim had the *koána* and was about to leave, flying out the next day to Kuala Lumpur.

In the canteen, Jacob was on his feet. 'Arrogant man,' he accused Aaron. Who was he to decide? It wasn't a pact they'd made; on the contrary it was a giving-over by Aaron, a surrender of old privileges, a sharing of responsibility. How else were they to get the money to begin the business of bringing wealth to the fjords? To Jacob it was of minor significance that among the items he'd removed were treasures said to have come with the first ancestors from their place of origin deep in the ranges. Handed down through the generations, they would rightfully come to Aaron when Noah, his eldest uncle, died

and returned to the spirits. They would not come to him as personal
wealth, or even as symbols of the power of lineage and history. The
point, which Wana struggled to get across, was that their power was
not separate from the lime pots and plumes and head-rests that Jacob
had taken to Mr Lim. They were not symbols, or representations.
They *were* the power.

Jacob said no lime pot lasted that long. New ones were always
being made. One lime pot or another, no difference. But Mr Lim
understood. It cost Aaron all he could borrow from Sam to buy back
the lime pot and stick that his uncle had rattled, as his father had
before him, and before that their father, Aaron's grandfather, when he
called the clans to attention.

'Why didn't he tell me?' Rika asked. 'I had no idea. None.'

'He only knew this morning,' Wana said.

'He didn't tell me about the treasures, that they'd be his. Didn't he
think I'd be interested? Didn't he trust me?'

'No one explains these things to white friends,' Wana said. 'We
live a different life here at the university. It's too hard explaining, and
no one other than us understands anyway.'

'You could try,' Sam said. 'I'd like to know.'

Wana disregarded him. *Later*, she seemed to say with a shake
of her head. It was tiring, this role of go-between. She had a pile of
books, and essays to write.

'There are some other things you should know,' Sam said.

'Like what?' Rika snapped. She felt adrift, closed out, alone.

'Like Tessa's uncle is sending her back to Melbourne already,'
Wana said.

'So soon?'

'She goes tomorrow.'

'Sooner or later the family would put a stop to it.'

'It's not just that,' Wana said. 'There are rumours in town.'

'Rumours. There're always rumours.'

A woman from New Zealand was threatened in her hotel by a
group of white men who'd seen her in the bar with some Papuans.
They said she was leading them on. 'Do it again and we'll show you
what it is to be a whore.'

'Rika. Listen,' Sam said. 'It's important. Reports have been handed in to the administrator's office. Derek from Politics knows. He hears these things. Last week he warned Aaron. There are groups forming, and it's all about Papuan men with white women. They're expecting incidents.'

'Like what?'

'We don't know,' Wana said. 'Even Derek doesn't know. But the cars at night – you've seen them. They've been on the campus during the day, outside the offices, white drivers sitting there watching.'

'They can drive around as much as they like,' Rika said. 'There's nothing to see. *Nothing.*'

'It's what they *think*,' Sam said, 'not what they see.'

'You two go to films together. Nobody complains about that,' Rika said. 'I haven't been anywhere with Aaron, unless it's all of us.'

'This is different,' Wana said.

'Why?' Rika's chin was pushed forward, her mouth set.

'Because you're a woman,' Wana said. 'They've never minded white men with a woman like me.'

'And because you're married,' Sam said. Then, looking at her, he said, 'Sorry, Rika. But it is obviously a factor.' He took her hand. She pulled it away.

'And because you look good together,' Wana said. 'Very good. It makes people jealous.'

Darkness came and the hands of the clock continued to turn. Rifle and Mela refused to go home. 'No, you go,' Rika said. They looked at her, united. '*Nogat*,' they said. 'For Aaron, we stay.'

Mela cooked pumpkin and rice, and Rifle came into the house, sat at the table. Mela, who not so long ago had refused to take tea out to a Highland man, refilled his cup, spooned in sugar and counted out the biscuits. Rika counted the hours. Martha came to sit with her. Seven o'clock. Eight. Still Aaron didn't come. Rifle walked over to Laedi. There was no news from Tamba. Laedi and Don were sitting in chairs, he could see them through the window.

Outside, the wind was blowing in the trees. Inside Rika's house, the radio relayed a serial from Australia after the nine o'clock news. Rika switched it off. Mela put out a mat beside the door for Rifle, and pulled a mattress for herself into the room with Rika. 'Thank you,' Rika said. 'The two of you good. *Gut tru.*'

All was quiet. No car drove past, no one seemed to be watching. Eventually the man from the bursar's office turned off his lights. The moon shone on the leaves of the trees. Rifle was like a shadow, circling the house. He wouldn't sleep, he told Martha when Pete arrived to walk her back to their house.

Rika lay on the bed she had shared with Leonard and listened for footsteps. She heard fruit bats in the pawpaws, Rifle going out and chasing them away. She heard him tie up the fruit. Against her will and intention, she fell asleep into a dark nothingness that had barely begun before she was pulled out of it by the jolt of headlights in the window and a thud of cold, sinking fear.

Rifle was out on the veranda when Laedi got out of the car. Pete and Martha were coming across from their house; Laedi had stopped to wake them as she passed.

'What?' Rika said. 'What's happened?'

'Aaron's been attacked,' Laedi said.

'Attacked,' Rika echoed. She had a vision of wolves. Lions.

'Some men got him. He was on his way over to you.'

'How bad?' she asked. She was still. Calm.

'Bad,' Laedi said.

Aaron had rescued the elders' treasures and returned to his room in the dormitory. He was on the way to Rika, cutting across to avoid the road. A group of men was waiting not far from the turn-off. He didn't hear them, and he didn't see them until they jumped, dark, hooded figures pulling him into the scrub. They had a bat of some sort, and their fists in hard leather gloves. He went down, felt a boot in his ribs. 'Stay away from our women. Use your own black cunt.' Another boot landed on his shoulder. 'Stand up, you prick.' They hauled him up, another fist landed on his face. He felt something move. They dropped him. Another boot, and he lost count, until the boots crunched away through the dry grass and a car's motor started up.

For a while Aaron lay there, drifting with the movement of wind, smelling the dust, listening for the rustlings of creatures. He was alive and the earth smelled sweet, grass stems a memory of the dry grass along the ridges above the fjords, where he'd wept as a child after his mother died. He knew he wasn't far from the road, but still he lay in the grass and let his mind move to the stories he'd grown up to: of Papuan warriors, the men who raised themselves up from defeat and led their people to new victories, new villages, new conquests, new lives. He remembered the morning in Leiden when he was woken by a bird outside his window. The day was pale and cold and the bird insistent. Though he didn't know the bird's name, he knew it'd come to tell him that in the fjords his father had died. All that day he walked, and all that day he heard the bird. When he closed his eyes, down there in the grass, it wasn't his father's face he saw, but Rika's on the day he told her this story.

Lying in the savannah grass, bleeding into the dry dust of the earth, a thought came to him as if it were a voice as clear as the bird that had woken him that day. *You will rise*, the voice said, and he knew that far from beating Rika out of him, these men had beaten her in, into him, and into the new future of his land. His head throbbed, there was blood in his eyes, his nose. His ribs sparked with pain each time he moved. His legs hurt. Everything hurt, even his teeth. But for the rest it was clear, there was no longer doubt and confusion. No more hiding. He hauled himself on hands and knees to the road, and when he heard the slow grind of a truck he moved to the verge, lay in the gravel, lifted his head into the arc of its headlights. The truck stopped, there was an exclamation and feet dropped lightly to the ground, the welcome sound of *Tok Pisin*. He laid his head on the road, surrendered to the dust and to the strong hands that lifted him, steadying him on the platform of the truck, which jolted on broken suspension and delivered him to the door of the hospital.

He was there, Laedi said, sedated against leaving, refusing a transfer to a white ward.

Again Rika asked, 'How bad is he?'

'Concussion. A split lip, a deep cut over one eye, stitches, a broken nose. His face is a mess, Rika. You must be prepared.'

'That face,' she said. That flesh, that beautiful man. 'Who did it?'

'We don't know. They jumped him before he could see. White. Hooded. The words they said were foul.'

Rika was trembling as if she were cold. Mela squeezed lime into hot water. 'How did you hear?'

'He sent someone to find me,' Laedi said. 'Me or Martha.'

'Why not me?'

'He's protecting you.'

'What about Don?'

'Too much rum with his lime.' Laedi gave a small, sad smile. 'Much too much. He's snoring. Drunk. *Spak*,' she said, as if to herself.

*

Aaron had multiple contusions and haematomas. Those were the words the doctor used when he met them at the entrance to the ward. A rib was cracked, he warned Rika, and a shoulder dislocated. He led them down the long line of beds. It was the early hours, yet the ward was alert, only the illest of patients asleep. Despite screens hastily brought from somewhere, Aaron's bed was visible to everyone – orderlies, patients, the families that slept around their beds – and already a small crowd had gathered to look at this man whose name was known across the town. His face was swollen, his lip was as large as a liver. His eyes were small slits, barely distinguishable. His words were slurred.

Rika knelt on the stained concrete floor beside the bed, laid her head beside him and, weeping without a sound, let her hand move across his battered body until she found a place where it could rest without hurting him. He moved a grazed and bloodied hand and rested it on her head.

It was a tableau that would remain with Laedi and Martha like the cover of a book, a bit tattered and worn, but nevertheless a moment when nothing ceased to be nothing.

THE MOUNTAIN

WALKING ONTO THE MOUNTAIN, IT SEEMED TO RIKA that she could have been on a sea voyage, rowing a small boat through a large ocean of waves. Yet an ocean would have left her exposed, open to the sky, while this journey took her deep under the green surface. From above, nothing of her progress would be visible, only the turbulence of the forest canopy rising and falling like unsteady currents. She'd watched the vast movement of forest from the small plane that took her over the high spine of the island. It had landed twice at narrow grass mission strips perched on precarious spurs, viridian green in the dark ocean of forest. At each a crowd had met the plane, old men gathering to shake the pilot's hand as crates were unloaded and the mailbag handed to the clerk from the mission. Women crowded together, their string bags heavy with sleeping babies. It surprised Rika that so many people emerged from the forest emptiness.

On the northern side of the mountains, the land flattened onto a plain cut by rivers and crossed by roads, pocked with houses and villages, tin roofs of plantations and government stores, the square grid of Popondetta. The plane circled the old military airfield and landed on the one strip that was maintained. While the plane was reloaded for the run that would put her down on the mountain, Rika walked along the edge of the strip. Tall grass grew through rusted, burned-out tank remains. There was no sign of the town, ten miles away. A man with a scrawny dog gave her a stick of sugarcane and walked on across the airstrip. A group of women with string bags for sale sat in the shade of the shed, where boxes of cargo were being weighed for the plane, which rocked as they were pushed into its tail. She looked across to the mountain, jutting forward from the range, a crown of cloud concealing its peaks.

Leonard was up there somewhere, waiting, not knowing that she was coming. She hadn't sent a letter ahead. 'Don't write,' she'd said to Alex Penrose. 'I want to tell him myself. Face to face.' He'd nodded, and all he'd said was to take shoes that were strong and accustomed to her feet.

'You sure you're okay?' the pilot asked when he let her off at the strip and saw there was no one to meet her.

When she'd written the envelopes that took her letters to Leonard, delivered by this same plane, the name of the village had conjured up a settled place, with the sort of things settled places have, and now she could see that even a post office was a fanciful notion. There was a bush school from which children came running, and an aid post, a small building with the only tin roof she'd seen as they landed. The medical orderly from the coast was on the strip to greet the pilot and take the mail bag.

'I'll take care of her,' he said.

'Good man, Tobias, mate,' the pilot said, giving him a week's supply of newspapers.

'My paper service,' Tobias said, and the men slapped each other on the arm.

'So long, then,' the pilot said. He looked up at the sky, checked the clouds, and then, as if an afterthought, turned back to Rika. 'He's a good bloke, Tobias.'

When the plane took off, Rika and the medical orderly were left standing with boxes of supplies at their feet. The schoolchildren were watching them, a few teenage boys hanging back. Rika felt as if she'd let herself get stranded just over the edge of the known world.

'Your husband is at the villages up on the mountain,' Tobias said. 'We can send a message up to him.'

'I'd rather surprise him,' Rika said.

'There are no surprises in this place. He'll know you're here long before you get there.'

The teenage boys were coming shyly towards them on soft bare feet and in tattered shorts. They were slender, with fine features and solemn eyes. 'These are the boys down from the mountain to meet the plane,' he said, sorting the boxes marked for Leonard. 'This is the wife of Leonard,' he said and the boys shook their heads. 'Too good, too good!' the tallest of them said as Tobias rattled off their names. Obi. Albert. Jefferson. 'He waits for you every week.'

'How far away is he?' Rika asked.

'Long way.' The tall boy pointed towards the high peak of the volcano. '*Huvaemo*.'

'Plenty far,' said another.

'They're right,' Tobias said. 'It is a long way. Six hours, for you maybe seven. They can do it in four. You must stay here tonight. They'll take you up in the morning.'

'Oh,' she said. This was not what she'd anticipated.

'Okay, boys, you can stay? Stay in the schoolhouse, yes?' Tobias was loading them with boxes marked for Leonard.

'With Hunter,' the tallest boy, Obi, said.

'You take him back with you tomorrow,' Tobias said.

'He don't want to come,' Obi said.

'No good he stay here.'

When Tobias had sorted the supplies for the school and the aid post, he took Rika along the path to the village, past a large church up on stilts like the houses, with painted crosses along the side and JESUS in large, shiny blue letters.

'That's new?' she asked.

'A few years now.'

After the newness of the church, the houses that straggled on either side of a wide, bare path looked dilapidated. Women carrying firewood on their heads lowered their brows and didn't let Rika catch their eyes. Her camera was in her string bag, untouched. Men in small groups nodded as Tobias greeted them, or melted away, leaving only the dogs to watch them pass.

At the aid post a young boy-man was sitting on the ground outside the door. His bare knees were drawn up, his head hung down. When he looked up, Rika could see the shadow of a first moustache on his upper lip.

'You okay, Hunter, man?' Tobias asked. 'You want to come in?'

The boy sprang to his feet and was gone, running across the cleared ground where women were waiting for Tobias with their babies.

'He's in trouble, that boy,' Tobias said. 'He should go back up the mountain with you tomorrow.'

'What's wrong?'

Tobias waved his hand vaguely. 'A girl he thought he'd marry.'

'Isn't he too young?' Rika asked.

That night, the rain thudded down. Rika, Tobias and Lucas, the schoolteacher, ate sweet potato and a tin of fish in the house next to the aid post. The lamp flickered in the wind that gusted under the door. The room was plain, with a rough table and hard benches, where they sat as Tobias poured from a bottle of the beer that had come on the plane. There were several books pushed to one end of the table, yellowing newspapers, a box of batteries and a radio. On a shelf were more books: a medical dictionary, *Cry, the Beloved Country.* Tacked to the wall was a photo of Tobias receiving a certificate from a white man in a tight tie.

When Rika asked what it was with this village, its strange atmosphere, the men fell quiet from their talk of hoped-for postings, their next trip to Popondetta, their dreams of Port Moresby. She could sense their longing for escape. It wasn't just that this village was small, isolated in the mountains. It was an uncomfortable place, pinched between the large population of Orokaivans down where the land flattened out, and the mountain people above. When the Orokaivans had come up on a raid, Tobias told her this was the first village they hit. Since the colonial government had put a stop to war-raids, the village had tried to appease the marauders by joining their churches and marrying into their clans, but the advantage never came their way; instead their border had shrunk, bit by bit, with land rightfully theirs now gardened by others. Meanwhile, up above, their mountain relatives, unscathed, maintained their borders and their art.

The rain stopped, and in the quiet that fell their voices were suddenly loud. Tobias opened the door. Across at the church, Rika could see men moving in the light of a hurricane lamp, occasional flashes from a torch. She could hear voices raised in rapid talk. From the way Tobias and Lucas listened, she judged that they didn't like what they heard.

Lucas went to the door and called out, then left. 'I'll be back,' he said.

'He's gone to see if the boys from the mountain are in the school-house,' Tobias said. 'He doesn't want them getting into trouble with the men here. That's why we want to send Hunter back.'

'Why doesn't he want to go?' Rika asked.

'He's been shamed by a girl up there,' Tobias said.

'How?' Rika asked.

Tobias got up from the table, went to the gas refrigerator wheezing by the door and took out another bottle of beer. 'There's a new mission here,' he said, in place of an answer. 'In competition with the Anglicans. The pastor is from the coast. He tells the village that their custom ways are no good, that they must obey the new laws and believe the word of the pastors.' He sighed, rolled a cigarette. 'That way they'll be rewarded with easy *kago*.'

'Do they believe it?'

'Some do. It fits our custom to think that fortune comes from the ancestors and our behaviour. Ideas like that can get twisted. They see what's happening down on the flat, they go down to the town and see trade stores, they see *kago* come for us on the plane, and they have nothing and don't understand why. They're easy prey for a mission that preaches rules and rewards.'

The rumble of voices from the church was low and mournful. Beyond, the dark forest, and Leonard.

'There's bad feeling. That's why your husband has gone up. Custom is strong up on the mountain. The Anglicans still go up there, but the villages don't take much from them. They like the stories and disregard the rest. When the priests go up, which isn't often, they're more concerned with how they treat their pigs than converting them. It's a powerful place. I hold clinics up there sometimes.'

'How hard is the walk?'

'Hard enough to put me off. I'm sending some medicines up with the boys. There's a woman called Janape – you'll meet her. She's a natural nurse. She came down for school here when she was in her teens, and spent most of her time at the aid post. The best assistant I've had!' There was warmth in his laugh. 'I trained her so there'd be someone on the mountain with basic skills. Lucas says she should have gone on to high school.'

'Why didn't she?'

'She didn't want to.'

'Because of the church?'

'No. What I'm saying is that they're different up there. They don't like being away from the mountain.'

Rika slept that night in a narrow bed in the empty aid post. No one from the mountain would sleep in there for fear of the spirits that could enter, unimpeded, through the windows that regulations required. The blankets were damp and musty, the pillow was hard. The weight of what she was doing lay heavily with her. In Moresby, the prospect of being here, on the mountain, had been abstract. Now Leonard was close, and she had to face what lay ahead – and behind.

Outside, the moon was a thin slice of light in the sky. The church seemed to have emptied out. She could hear nothing but the scratching of bush-rats in the walls.

At dawn the small troupe of guides led Rika through the village. Hunter wasn't with them. The village was already awake; she could hear the murmur of women's voices in the houses and smell the morning fires. There were men in the church as they passed.

'Those men sleep in the church?' she asked.

'Maybe,' Obi said, giving a shrug, a smile. 'Sometimes.' His face was as smooth as a girl's. He was sixteen maybe, no more. He took her rucksack and then held out his hand for the basket that had come with her from Leiden. When she resisted, another boy mimicked her walk with a large exaggerated basket bowing her down. She laughed, put her camera in her string bag, and gave the basket to the mimic. 'His name is Albert,' Obi said.

Beyond the village, the path narrowed through gardens cut into the forest. They walked in single file, climbing on up to a hamlet where women called out as they passed, through more gardens until they were in forest. The great trees rose so high that they walked among the buttress roots. Far above was a pale sheen of sky, a distant source of light, while underneath it was dark, brown and olive, barely green at all, and strangely quiet but for the sound of her boots.

For each ridge they climbed, they plunged down the other side to the roar of water, a tumbling stream in a swathe of sunlight. Her guides waited as she cooled herself in the water, wetting her head, her shirt, before climbing on, up and up, the great peak of *Huvaemo* appearing to be first on this side of her, then on that. With each rise the path became steeper, and when she couldn't reach a handhold of root or vine, Obi took her hand and pulled her up, his broad, bare feet treading gently while she swayed and slipped. As the sun lifted into the sky, it became hot and moist underneath, with a pungent smell of growth and decay. Images came to her, dark shapes on a flat canvas. And Leonard's legs, the thin tendons working, his feet splaying out as he walked. She thought of him, uncomplaining, never asking *how far, how far*, as she did, his Welsh heart beating down exhaustion, making himself feel nothing. She knew he didn't feel nothing, but, still, the stoic capacity that had drawn her to him unsettled her. He'd made this journey for anthropology and art. She was making it for love. He'd made it as an act of faith for the bark-cloth and his film. She had no desire to take out her camera. The bark-cloth faded from her mind. Instead, an image of a bird of paradise coming into the hand of a small boy perched in a tree. Aaron was a heartbeat inside her, not so much thought as being, present in each step as she climbed on.

When the sun was high above the forest, they came again into gardens, and the world returned to a vivid green, loud with the sound of birds, and full of breath. Banana and pawpaw trees leaned with fruit, long beans hung from their vines, but though the gardens were well tended there was no one working in them. At a circle of houses built on posts around a clearing of swept earth, doors were closed and open platforms bare. An old woman came from a house on the far side and spoke to Obi. Everyone had gone with Leonard to the big village to prepare for the dancing. She gave them a pineapple, but when Rika wanted to lie on her platform and rest, the old woman gestured them on.

'Keep going,' she said in language. 'Take the *tauba* lady before it rains.'

Rika lifted her head and there, coming over the peak of the mountain, was a billow of cloud. Albert, a mimic with Milton's capacity to transform himself, became bedraggled in warning of the rain that would fall.

Her legs trembled as if no longer under her command, yet somehow she walked on behind the boys with their boxes of *kago*, down another steep path with a hand for help as her balance lurched, then up, until they came at last to a long ridge and she could hear voices coming from the narrow valley below. The guides hollered and when an answering yodel reached them, Albert picked up his pace, whooping down to the river. Only Obi waited, slowing his pace to Rika's.

At the river women and children were washing, water beading their hair as they shook themselves, calling out to her and waving. Rika waded waist-deep into the pool where they were and fell back in the water, her heart like a caged animal pacing inside her ribs. Hands came to her, stroking her arm, touching her head, a reception of angels. A young woman stretched towards her, a shampoo bottle in her hand, but even as she came forward through the water, she was called back, a name rising up – Josephine – and she was absorbed into a group of girls calling out their names, too many to remember. Rika sank back into the river. Above her the land rose in a rocky scarp where even the trees seemed to have difficulty clinging. When she lifted her head from the water to the sound of more people singing out their names, at that moment she wanted only to sink back under the cool water, let go her hold on the rocks at the edge of the pool and allow the current to pull her down the mountain, all the way to the sea, where she could rest, quiet and contented, until the tides carried her gently along the coast, eastwards to Aaron's village.

A man was standing on a rock at the edge of the river. He was wearing a shirt she recognised as Leonard's, shouting to her over the roar of the current. An older woman with eyes like dark jewels took her hand and steadied her through the running current to the rock where he stood.

'Boja is my name,' he said in formal English. He was a stocky man with a broad nose and round, prominent eyes. 'The chiefs are waiting. You must come. The women bring you.' And then he was gone, up a waterfall that seemed also to be a path.

On the last steep ascent, she was overtaken by small children light on their feet, and women with string bags heavy with vegetables. She could hear the *kundu* drums in the village on the ridge as people gestured ahead, encouraging her forward.

'Leonard?' she asked, a single word, a name, all she could say over the beat of her heart.

At the top, the land flattened onto a spur that widened like a stage, the forest dropping away on either side, peaks forming an amphitheatre across the steep valleys. Ahead, a hedge marked the start of the village. Two pigs, one behind the other, were trying to find their way through. The gateway was closed by crossed saplings, and from them hung a large bark-cloth of mountains painted in browns and rusty reds. Something about the irregularity of the peaks made Rika draw in her breath.

Small girls in soft, feathery headdresses came through the gate from the village and took her hand. They were wearing cloth painted in the same colours, wrapped around them as skirts.

'Leonard?' she asked and a young woman from the river pointed beyond the gate. 'We wait yet,' she said. The last gap in the clouds had closed, a grey veil descending.

In clothes wet from the river, shivering at the prospect of what lay ahead, Rika let her mind drift back to Aaron and the few days she'd tended him, the nights she'd slept beside him, their first moves towards each other made in small, careful moments; a soft hand, a lip, the sweet taste, salt and blood, skin on skin, the insignificance of all difference. And here she was, cold from the river, with the clouds rolling over, and Leonard waiting.

The drumming stopped. A voice called out, an invocation perhaps, and then the singing began again, the women's voices rising above the beat of the *kundu* drums. The gateway was opened, the bark-cloth pulled back, the saplings removed. Rika was to enter. In the large grass circle of the dance ground, dancers moved in welcoming pairs, advancing and retreating in a rhythm she couldn't quite take into her body, the pause and repetition rhythmic, yet at odds with her own experience of rhythm. The headdresses of the men bounced like the tails of the birds whose plumes they wore, and all around the painted cloth worn by the dancers moved as if it was itself made up of movement. Through the double lines of dancers she saw Leonard with the Arriflex on his shoulder shooting straight towards her, breaking his long-held practice of filming only that which was ethnographically authentic, and never contaminating the view through the lens.

The dancers ignored the first spots of rain as they led the slow advance back and forth across the grass. Boja ran towards Leonard with an umbrella for the camera. Rika's clothes hung clammy against her. She was cold, her feet numb in wet boots. And still the dancers danced and chanted their high rhythm, until a crash of thunder and slashing rain sent them running for cover. The chiefs hung their feathers under the eaves of a large covered platform. The camera was closed and Boja hurried towards a house with it. Leonard came fast towards Rika across the boggy grass, his hair flattened on his head.

'You've come at last,' he said, taking off his glasses. His voice was rich with pleasure.

For the rest of the afternoon, rain pounded and poured. Rika changed her sodden clothes for a dry shirt and trousers rolled down against the mosquitoes. She rubbed her hair in the small towel Leonard had brought, and wrapped herself in a blanket. Mist was blowing in under the eaves; bark-cloth hung limp from the wall of the covered platform, which stretched between the enclosed sleeping rooms. Along one open side was a half wall of plaited pandanus; the side facing towards the dance ground and the village was open to air and cloud. Leonard was sitting in the centre on a woven mat. He was thinner, hollowed out, wearing an anorak and sucking at his pipe.

The strangeness of seeing him after all that had happened had the unexpected effect of reversing the distance Rika had become used to. Here was Leonard, immediate and present. Port Moresby had retreated beyond the cloud, its dusty streets barely imaginable. She knew she should speak at once and not let this familiarity spill over and silence her, but even as she came to sit beside him already he was talking of Don, the bruising details of that conflict obliterating everything she needed to say as effectively as the rain had removed all sight of the village.

'I know how little anthropologists get right.' Leonard's voice was aggrieved. 'Better than Don, I know. All I claim is that it's a valid task, a way of safeguarding something, preserving it against the onslaught of change. Don can't accept that. To him it doesn't matter that a film can observe small cultural details. He won't accept that my work isn't political. It's quite different. It's a move towards understanding something human and complex.'

'Like a dance,' Rika offered, 'that goes from one generation to the next. The feet change and the steps continue.'

'Yes,' Leonard said, taking her hands in his. 'You always have the right image. How excellent that you've come. I knew you would. You're so good, giving up the library. When we get back to Oxford, we must find another job that you'll enjoy.'

She stood up, walked to the top of the steps from the platform, her heart thumping. The rain was easing, smoke was coming from the cookhouse door and she could see people inside. How could she tell him now?

'I wish you'd warned me, though,' Leonard was saying. 'I'd have come down to meet the plane.'

'I wanted to surprise you.'

'And no surprise could be better.'

Boja came in, tutting at the rain, a black palm leaf held over his head as an umbrella. '*Kago*,' he said. 'We open the *kago*.'

Rika was grateful for his presence as he opened the boxes carried up by Obi and the boys, retrieving tins of fish, packets of sugar, tea, rice, nails, laundry soap. Newspapers.

'Good man,' Leonard said. 'I'm telling Rika about the trouble with Don.'

'Full of humbug,' Boja said, tearing a strip from along the edge of a newspaper, rolling tobacco from the packet he'd extracted from the depth of a box. '*Tauba* humbug.' He handed the tobacco to Leonard, who filled another pipe.

'If Don couldn't accept what I was doing,' he said, 'he should have kept away from the filming.'

'But wasn't the camera what he wanted? I thought that was the *point*.'

'If I had a penny for each time Don told me the camera isn't an innocent eye!' Leonard took a long draw on the pipe. 'He took me for a fool. I know the arguments. But the fact remains, a camera can be disinterested. It depends how it's used.'

'Did you say that?' There was an edge to Rika's voice. A kick of irritation. Did Leonard really believe the camera was disinterested? She knew there was no scene, no situation, no moment, no detail that couldn't be reinterpreted. Hadn't he taught her that himself? 'Did you *say* that it was disinterested?'

'I said it was a record, not an argument that I was making.'

'And what did he say when you said that?'

'He shouted at me. *Crap!* That's the language he used, and the small boys would hear and go running back to the houses shouting, "Crap! Crap!" Boja would shout at them. Wouldn't you, Boja?'

'No good,' Boja said. 'The small boys, they go crazy, calling out.' He shook his head and drew on the tobacco. Leonard watched him, bleak and pale behind his glasses. Rika steadied her breath, stretched her arms above her head. Boja looked at her, looked at Leonard, and, having learned the English salve of tea, rose to his feet and said he'd ask the women to cook the water. Rika watched him hurry away under his black palm leaf, climb the steps to the small cookhouse, where smoke from the roof was vying with the rain. She'd rather be there, where the women were, learning names for the faces she'd seen at the river.

When two young women came from the cookhouse with a kettle, she climbed down the steps onto the grass. Her bare, bruised feet sank gratefully into the wet ground. Cold, but soothing. Mist hung in the valley and moisture dripped from every roof and tree. Two men were crossing the open space of the dance ground with a python looped between them on a pole. The rain was letting up.

'Josephine?' The name swum up from a watery memory; the girl with the kettle was the girl with shampoo at the river. She was young and pretty, with pert breasts high on her chest. She smiled and seemed to blush.

Behind her, another woman was carrying several tin mugs. She was less young, maybe the same age as Rika. Her face was restful, and there was something about her that struck Rika as remarkable, but before she could see what it was, Boja was tugging at her arm. 'The chiefs are coming,' he said, gesturing towards the house, where Leonard was calling to her from the steps. Two old men were picking their way through the sodden grass, and coming to join them from another path was a woman chief with a headdress of white feathers.

By the time Rika turned back to the woman, Boja had taken the cups from her and she was returning to the cookhouse. There was a slight sway to this woman's hips, her back was held straight and tall. The walk of a model, Rika thought, and an image from the 1920s superimposed itself, from the camera of Edward Steichen perhaps. No. The picture was wrong, not because of her limp skirt, but because she walked without self-consciousness. The greatest photographers were pressed to find that in a model.

'My sister Janape,' Boja said as the woman climbed the steps into the smoky interior of the cookhouse. So she was the woman Tobias had talked of.

'I have medicines for her,' she said. 'From Tobias.'

'Tomorrow,' Boja said. 'Now chiefs come.'

As Josephine approached the house, Leonard went abruptly inside. Had he not seen her? The girl hesitated as if uncertain, and handed the kettle to a boy who was sitting in the doorway.

'Why doesn't Josephine go in?' Rika asked.

'She no good girl,' Boja said. 'She go to cookhouse.'

Instead of asking how a girl so young could be no good, Rika asked Boja if Janape could come and drink tea?'

'Tomorrow,' Boja said. 'Maybe tomorrow.'

As light drained from the sky, the old chief climbed the steps to the platform. He stood to attention, heels together like an ancient soldier. Round his neck a pig-tusk necklace hung like a mayor's chain. Behind him was another clan chief, his teeth worn down to their stumps, and the woman chief in her soft feather headdress. She came to Rika, took her arm, put her nose to it, breathed her in. The woman from the river, with the eyes like jewels.

'Nogi,' Leonard said. 'The paramount chief of women.'

A soft murmur of words. Those dark eyes.

'She welcome you,' Boja said.

The three chiefs, the *duvahe*, sat on woven mats facing Leonard and Rika. Their backs were straight, their legs crossed. Boja spooned milk powder, sugar and coffee into round tin mugs, then poured water from the kettle, and carefully passed them to the chiefs. They warmed their hands, looking into the steam. Leonard had the Nagra tape recorder running, but no camera.

The platform was filling up with people, crowding in. More were gathering in the fading light outside. Boja was standing by to translate.

'Listen,' the first of the chiefs said. The old man. 'Hear me! I am Nanaji, chief of all chiefs of the mountain people. My house is beyond the dance ground, in the village where the path to the far river starts. I have six sons.' He named them all, beginning with Boja, who accepted the mention as his due. The chief pointed to his other sons among the men who'd squeezed onto the platform. 'My gardens grow many yams, and my pigs are plenty.' He listed the virtues of the gardens and hunting grounds of the clan. 'Hear me and listen.'

'This is the formal welcome,' Leonard whispered. 'If it hadn't rained, it'd have been outside, after they'd danced you in.' He gestured to the edge of the dance ground, to a tall, narrow pulpit of saplings, a dark outline in the misty light. 'Everyone would have been there to hear.'

'Leonard, man of yours,' Nanaji went on, addressing himself to Rika, with Boja and Leonard both supplying the meaning, 'he holds the knowledge we give him well. We are pleased to see this man, this man with white skin, come into our land. He takes news of our art to the place that belongs to him. This is good. This is good for *Huvaemo*.'

Leonard made a small bow, and spoke a few words in the mountain language. *Huëmae*, thank you.

The old man then spoke of the mountain, breaking into a chant – a long account of the life he was born to before the kiaps came, and the strange shock of the war between the *tauba* Australians and the Japanese. The clan chiefs nodded, and added their stories of when they were boys and went down to the town. The old chief sang of the dangers that came with the army men, disturbing an initiation, taking the boys to war before they were tattooed, catching them like birds in a trap.

'Why are they telling us this?' Rika whispered to Leonard. 'Is this a warning?'

'It's a history. Listen.'

The chiefs sang on, a rhythmic telling of disruptions to the mountain that came with the new ways of government and plantations, the bad spirit of money. Boja refilled their tin cups from the kettle and the coffee jar, while Leonard began a long explanation to Rika about the tribe's system of causality and the ways in which disruptions are understood as supernatural, upsetting the mountain, which became distressed, bringing sickness and trouble to the clans.

Listening to Leonard, and watching the solemn row of chiefs watch her, Rika felt bloated. Their stories were burying the story of love in her. In the limelight of a small campus, her betraying heart had been a beacon. Here on the ridge top, with nothing shining on it, it had become invisible. Looking into the faces of the old men, she felt the impossible distance between that world and this. She wanted to stop Leonard from talking. She'd never know anything if she blocked up unknowing with too much knowing. She wanted to sit, quiet beside the woman chief Nogi, *absorb* her.

There was an uneasy sensation low in Rika's back. It surprised her, sitting there, to look down and see that her legs still existed, neatly folded on the mat. Nogi smiled across to her, made a gesture with her hands and stretched her legs out in front of her. Rika followed her example, and, yes, it was better. A nod from Nogi. A smile in exchange. She wanted the evening to end, she wanted to lie down, retrieve Aaron, be with him in her mind. But the old chief Nanaji still had the welcome song to sing with Nogi. The song welcoming her, the first *tauba* woman to come to the mountain, wife to the man Leonard who came in service of the mountain. Boja was at the door calling for Obi to translate. He was Boja's brother's son and the chief's grandson.

'He do grade five,' Boja said. 'Nanaji say this boy must stay on the mountain, learn the custom stories. The teacher want Obi to go to school. *Duvahe* say plenty young men go to Popondetta to work on the plantations. They make small money. Learn bad ways. No good.' Boja sighed, then added, 'Nanaji, he old man.'

'He's right about the plantations,' Leonard said. 'But maybe it'd be good for Obi to go to school and learn the ways of government. Independence will come one day. Maybe sooner than we expect.'

The chief looked mournful as Boja translated. He didn't like the idea of independence. He hadn't liked the Australian kiaps, the few times they'd come, but the prospect of an Orokaivan government was worse, and closer. Nanaji didn't smile until Obi came in and sat by the door. He gave the boy a soft greeting. The single cowrie shell tied round his neck shone as Boja pumped the lamp.

'It's a fine line,' Leonard was saying, his voice low, 'between the old ways and the new. In every circumstance it's hard to know what's best, when to hurry or slow down the process. It almost always cuts both ways. What does Aaron think?'

'Aaron?' Rika's heart gave a thump. 'Aaron Nabuka? Why do you ask?'

'Alex thinks highly of him,' Leonard said. 'Says he's one of the best, and I gather you've become friendly.'

Could her heart leap through her skin and land at their feet, there on the ground between them? Leonard squeezed her hand, returned his attention to the *duvahe*, who were singing the rhythmic words of the welcome song, while another old man beat the *kundu*. Song filled the space of the roof, billowed out into the dark.

Obi stood to translate. 'This song, it is a song of welcome to *Huvaemo*. This place, our mountain, it is the place of our ancestors, the place of our art. You are welcome. Walk. Walk in and see.'

'One, one, you walk,' Boja said.

'All walk,' Obi said. 'Walk one by one, walk all together. Walk in and listen. This song of *Huvaemo*. This song our art. This place our mountain, this place our art.'

'Thank you,' Leonard said. '*Huëmae*.'

The old chief rose to his feet and took Leonard's hand. 'You have come, you have listened. Leonard's wife, *tauba* lady, you are welcome,' he said.

Leonard went to a box that had come on the plane and took out a blanket for the other old man *duvahe*. Another for Nogi. She sniffed at it, handed it to a woman behind her. Nanaji gestured to Obi.

'There aren't enough for all the young ones,' Leonard said.

The chief's face clouded. He said something that wasn't translated. Outside there was a hushed quiet.

Leonard gave the boy a blanket.

'I couldn't go against Nanaji,' Leonard said when he and Rika were alone in the windowless cave of a room where they were to sleep. 'We're guests on their land. That's what Don could never grasp.' And he started again, a catalogue of the arrogant ways in which Don behaved. 'Apart from anything else,' he said, 'it's discourteous.'

Despite her dislike of Don, it seemed absurd to Rika that on this mountain, in the midst of bark-cloth it had taken such endurance to reach, Leonard's bitterness should be so great. 'Could it have been something else that you were arguing about?' she asked. 'Something personal underneath, maybe, that has more to do with our world than theirs?'

He was undressing, folding his clothes. There was a faint smell of him in the bed that made the room less alien. Rika lay on the plaited sleeping mat, waiting beneath the mosquito net for her husband. Her heart kept its rapid, guilty beat. She turned away as Leonard climbed under the net to join her.

'You're tired,' he said as he arranged a blanket over her. He was still talking about Don when she fell asleep, his hand resting on her back.

AT DAWN THE NEXT MORNING, THE SKY WAS GOLD TOWARDS THE rising sun. Women were hanging paintings on lines of bush-rope strung along the far side of the dance ground, ready for Leonard's camera. The bark fabric of some was heavy, slightly spongy, painted in reds and blacks. Others were delicate as if the bark had been spun into lace. Creamy buffs, ochre yellows, rusty reds. It took two women to position a large cloth so that the rope could hold its weight and its edge didn't rest on the wet grass. A landscape of mountains. Smaller cloths were painted in the pattern of the curled vine, like the one sent to Rika in Moresby. On others, a tumble of leaves, cassowary eggs, the design of the bush snail, the teeth of river fish. Some were wild and free, a perfect play of line tumbling across the cloth in celebration or joy, conjuring something, Rika didn't know what, the mountain perhaps, a deep seat of emotion, the balance that can be found in the disorder of forest.

More women, their backs as straight as house poles, were arriving with bundles of folded cloth. They shook them out and added them to the lines of bush-rope. The mist in the valley had gone, the peaks rising into a clean sky.

'What is that?' Rika asked Boja, looking at a painting quite different from the others. 'Is it the sun?'

'*Nogat*,' Boja said. 'It is the spider who lives in the ground.'

The background was painted black, and the legs that stretched out from a small centre were made from strips of pale cloth, sewn over the black. Spider legs? To Rika they looked like the rays of the sun.

'They sew them on with a bone from a flying fox as a needle,' Leonard explained. 'It's an old technique they use for the most important cloth. It's a cape to wear at a ceremony.'

'Who painted it?'

'The paramount chief make it,' Boja said.

'Nanaji?'

'Lady chief,' Boja said. Waving his arms and talking fast to the women, he called out across the dance ground. Turning with him to look, Rika saw Nogi coming towards her. She was wearing the same headdress of soft white feathers, and looped across her chest were beads and necklaces. Fresh, pungent herbs were tucked into her armband. Her eyes took in Rika, uncompromising and direct.

'She say you are welcome,' Boja said.

'Please tell her I think it is very beautiful.'

'Ancestor story,' Boja said, translating as Nogi spoke. It was the mark of the female ground spider, who taught the first woman on the mountain how to weave a string bag.

Listening to the story of the spider weaving her web, and the ancestor woman feeling its strength that could carry a baby, everything in Rika went towards that cloth, and she wanted it. Spider-leg sunrays. She wanted to show Aaron, she wanted it as proof. Of what, she didn't know. That the mountain existed? That she was there? Even as she was thinking this, Nogi took off one of her necklaces and placed it over Rika's head with a quiet run of words.

'She say you are welcome, here on the mountain,' Boja translated. 'She and the other women chief will take you into the forest. Show you the trees.'

As he spoke, and Nogi watched, Rika felt as if she were transparent and this woman could see her greed, her covetousness. And still Nogi smiled.

Back at the house, Leonard prepared his notebook and Boja gathered up the cameras. They were to record the cloth that day, filming it in the sunlight with the artists who'd come from distant villages.

'Janape will stay with you,' Leonard said. 'Boja's sister. You'll like her, she's smart. She should do more school. I've offered to help, but she says no. She's not married, which is unusual at her age.'

'She doesn't look so old,' Rika said. Janape was coming across the dance ground towards them with a small girl in a headdress of white cockatoo feathers.

'She's old not to be married here.'

'Why isn't she?'

'Hard question for me to ask. Boja shrugs when I ask him. It'd take a woman anthropologist to find out. One should come up here. The women have a lot of authority.'

The young girl in the white feather headdress came up onto the platform with Janape. She was about twelve years old, maybe less. Looking into eyes that were small jewels, Rika asked what her name was, and the girl took her arm. Another deep breath.

'Lilla,' Janape answered for her. 'Small girl of daughter of Nogi chief. Nogi is her granny.'

'Your granny too?' Those eyes. Those dark eyes full of light.

'All the same. My mother, sister of Lilla's mother.'

'The same family,' Leonard said. 'You can see the likeness.'

'It's the eyes,' Rika said.

'Beautiful, aren't they?' He turned, smiled to Janape. 'You will look after Rika here?'

'All the same,' she replied with a pretty laugh. 'First we do the medicine. Later I take her to the gardens.'

'Very good,' Leonard said, pulling his hat low over his brow. 'Excellent.' He touched Rika's cheek. 'Shout out if you need me.'

Rika watched him cross the dance ground, the *amorire*. When he turned to wave, she could see his pleasure at having her there. Fear pressed up in her. She could smell it. How was she to tell him, when he looked at her like that? Perhaps, after all, a letter would have been better.

In the quiet of the house Janape opened the box from Tobias. She took the notes he'd written, counted the jars and bottles, and arranged them on the floor. Pills. Liquid medicines. Powders. Bandages. Sugar water for children with diarrhoea. Iron tablets for pregnant mothers. Rika, watching, could imagine her in a laboratory, that intelligence turned to test tubes and experiments. She was sitting on the mat, and beside her Lilla was making shapes on the floor with her finger, turning to Rika in query, asking this large white spirit with strange hair and no language if she understood the alphabet she drew for her.

'They are roadways of the paintings,' Janape said. 'See? The snail, the vine, cassowary egg, skin of snake.'

Outside, Leonard continued on with his notes, drawing sketches of each painting, naming each recurring design as instructed by Boja and Obi. How slow he seemed. Had he always been like this, pinning everything down?

'A good man,' Janape said, and for a moment Rika thought her irritation, her treachery had been revealed, as visible as Lilla's alphabet. But there was no rebuke; Janape's smile was wide and clear, her eyes kind. 'Come,' she said, choosing from Tobias's jars and putting them in her string bag.

Janape and Lilla led Rika past a line of houses, down a small slope to a cluster of dwellings built on stilts at the edge of the forest. Flowering plants grew close to the path. Two boys were climbing a pandanus palm for nuts, throwing them down to the ground.

'I'll wait here with Lilla,' Rika said when they reached a house with people calling to Janape from the platform. She could see a woman lying on a mat. Better she waited here, out in the air, under the tree with large red flowers. But Janape beckoned to her. 'It is good that you come,' she said.

The sick woman was struggling to raise herself onto her elbow; her breast was swollen, drum-hard and hot. Janape took her whimpering baby, spoke quietly to the woman and pressed her hand against the breast. She tried the baby on the other side. A little sticky fluid came out.

'Good,' Janape said. She took a jar from her bag and gave the woman four pills.

'Will she live?' Rika asked as they left. What would happen if she didn't? Up here, so far from anywhere?

'We come back tonight. More pills. They are good. Two days. Four. She will be well.'

At the next house, built almost in the forest, Rika didn't go up to see the man whose cough she heard through the plaited walls of his sleeping room. She walked back up the path to a small bank that looked down into a gully. White trumpet flowers were hanging from a branch beside her. She thought of her mother, face turned to the wall. And of Aaron in his bed in the ward, the police coming to take his statement. A ruddy-faced Australian with a spiral notebook, the whole ward watching, the crowd at the door, and not a word said as she sat beside him. 'An investigation,' the *South Pacific Post* reported, implying it was a *raskol* gang that had beaten him, when the whole town knew the truth. 'The wife of Dr Leonard Powell, the ethnographic filmmaker, was present to offer comfort.'

When Janape rejoined her, they sat still, without speaking, the sun shining through the leaves of the tree. Rika could feel her strength, and let it comfort her. Memory loosened its grip; in its place, a welling sadness.

'We go now,' Janape was standing up. 'Sister friend.' Lilla took her hand and pointed across to the peak of *Huvaemo*, still clear against the sky. The air was fresh, birds flew in the trees and the grass of the path was soft.

Coming into the village, a woman with a worn face called Janape onto her platform. Rika listened to their voices, one soothing, the other forceful. Without language, she listened as she might to music, and something in the timbre of the frayed, angry voice struck her as a warning. When Janape called to Rika, she climbed the ladder steps warily. The woman was sitting with her legs straight in front of her, her back ramrod straight. She was painting black pathways on barkcloth folded on her knee, a mass of angry shapes whirling across the fabric. She beckoned and patted the matting next to her, where Rika was to sit. She took a betel nut from a small bag and offered it to Janape. Curious children appeared at the edge of the platform and were shooed away. 'Go now!' she told them, including Lilla. 'Women talk.' She looked straight at Rika, fixing her with sharp, determined words that seemed, though Rika couldn't be sure, to be making Janape uneasy. Janape was stripping the skin off the betel nut and didn't look up when she translated.

'She is the mother of Josephine boyfriend,' she said. 'Big trouble for boy. He is in the village at the airstrip.'

'Hunter?' Rika asked.

'All the same. She wants him come home. That village at the airstrip is making him sick. She ask you to bring him.'

'How?'

'Maybe Leonard will bring him.'

'How?'

More words came from the woman, spoken slowly, directed at Rika's eyes.

'What is she saying?'

Janape shrugged. 'Mother of Hunter crazy a little maybe.' Was she being evasive? She stood up for them to leave. The woman went back to her painting – roadmaps of fury.

Underneath the house two pigs were resting. As Rika climbed down the ladder they blundered off towards the bush. She felt clumsy herself, following Janape and Lilla through the village, not recognising paths, not knowing where they led, not knowing what was said.

Under another house, a boy was sitting hunched as if he were cold. 'Diki,' Janape called quietly, and the boy hobbled towards her. She took the soiled bandage from his leg and frowned at the putrid sore. It was not healing. It was long and narrow, running the length of the boy's shin, with raised, puckered sides and a deep ugly crater.

'This one no good,' she said. 'It go down and down.' She filled the crater with white powder and counted out more pills

'Will that fix it?'

'Maybe. Maybe no.'

'Should he go to Tobias?' Rika asked. 'Can someone help him get there?' The boy was limping as if the pressure of his weight was painful. 'He could stay there and go to school.'

'He go to school before,' Janape said.

'Why isn't he still there?'

'It not a good place. He want to come back to the mountain.'

The boy said something to Janape, a low murmur, and looked towards Rika, his eyes pooling with tears.

'That place give him the sore,' Janape said. 'No good for him, going there.'

'What do you make of it?' Rika asked Leonard when they took the lamp to their dark bedroom.

'Williams has a very good book on Orokaivan magic and sickness,' he said.

'This isn't Orokaiva.'

'Many of the same broad principles apply. He categorises sickness in four ways, and most of them have a supernatural component. The most dangerous are caused by malign spirits and sorcerers, though their origins—'

'I don't want to know what Williams said.' She was struggling to keep her voice even. 'I want to know what you think.'

'About what?'

'About if it's possible that the boy has been, how do you say, *sorcered?*'

'Darling, it's almost certainly yaws.'

'Then he should go to Tobias.'

'Of course he should, but he won't if he thinks it's magic sickness from down there.'

'So what do we do?'

'I'll talk to Boja.'

'Wouldn't it be better to send a message to Tobias and see if he can come up?'

'We must be careful not to interfere.'

'Leonard, if we don't, and it's yaws, he'll die.'

She lay on her back, watching as Leonard checked his notebooks, put them in a pile on the floor with his glasses on top. She watched him undress, straightening his shorts, hanging his shirt on a nail, careful as if it were an evening suit he'd hired. She saw the fold of flesh at the base of his buttock, purplish balls hanging low in their sack.

'There's that other boy too,' she said. 'Hunter.'

'What about him?' Leonard's voice was sharp.

'His mother wants you to bring him back here.'

'Best to leave that for the chiefs to deal with,' Leonard said.

'Why?' she asked.

Leonard didn't reply.

The lamp cast shadows, making him look gaunt and slightly sinister. When he lifted the mosquito net and came into bed, he turned to her and she accepted the arm he offered. But when he put out the lamp and in the darkness moved his mouth to hers, his hand to her breast, she lay very still, drawing herself into the smallest beat of a heart.

'What is it?' he asked.

'I can't,' she said. 'I'm sorry.' She could feel tears sliding down the side of her face.

Why didn't she tell Leonard then? Why didn't she take the opportunity that presented itself? This was the question that would plague her when she thought of that night afterwards. Laedi would say it was because she didn't want to hurt him, not after what Don had done. And then there was the filming. The great dance of the clans was coming up, when the moon was full: the dance to the mountain that he'd waited and watched for. But that night she'd not thought of Don or the dancing, or even the film. That night she was angry, and registered only the shock she had not expected, that his skin had become unwelcome to her, contrary to her heart, almost repugnant, and it was this that tipped her into a place of no words.

'Don't cry,' Leonard said. 'I know what it's like when you're first in a village. Everything is raw, and there are none of the things we're used to.' He kissed her forehead. 'Go to sleep now. There's plenty of time for us. Years and years.'

RIKA WENT TO THE MOUNTAIN EXPECTING TO CATCH ONE PLANE IN and the next plane out. But instead of staying two weeks, she stayed for four, held first by the dancing and then by the rain. In those weeks, time was divided. It seemed both to slow and to speed. Without a watch, she couldn't tell what hour it was. She might think it noon and find it was ten. The sky was no help; mountains, clouds, the canopy of trees confused the angle she might expect of the sun. As time slowed to the ticking of her heart, a week could pass without her knowing the day. Tuesday had no meaning, Friday was an idea that belonged somewhere else. Her mind was similarly divided. The part occupied by Aaron remained a pulse-beat of longing. The days without him could stretch the distance of a life, but elsewhere in her mind the mental settings she had brought to the mountain slipped the relentless catch of the clock.

During the time that accompanied the moon's movement towards full, when the dancing for the mountain would begin, days that were not counted but passed one by one, she went into the forest with the women when the morning sun was low and the grass of the dance ground patterned with shadow. Nogi led the way with a chief who wore unpainted bark-cloth and red parrot feathers in her hair. Unlike Nogi, who was adorned with many necklaces, Kimame wore one strand plaited with a single cowrie shell. In the pierced septum of her nose was a short piece of polished bamboo. Her realm was the mountain. She knew when it was disturbed, and how to placate it. She knew its pathways and boundaries, its rituals and language. She knew where gardens liked to be cut, where rivers could not be swum. 'Kimame is a strong woman,' Janape told her. She'd been to the edge of the volcano's crater, where the heat turns skin white.

As they walked, Lilla showed Rika the bush-snails from her alphabet, flat and green. Kimame taught her to recognise the curled vine that was a clan insignia, and the pattern on the fat caterpillar that lived in the black palm. Each day, with Janape at her side, Rika learned a little more. She could greet a chief, *duvahe*, and call out as she approached a house. She could name a baby or a child, a pig or cooking fire, a string bag or yam. She could repeat the names of certain birds, though she'd get them wrong often enough, when she saw them fly from one tree to another, her errors sending the women rippling into laughter. They took her hand in theirs, and taught her a new word: friend of ours. Though her language was sparse and the words she knew were paltry, she could hear the tone in their voices, and she knew that they could hear the response in her voice, the humour, she hoped, and her respect. But did they also hear through the woven walls of Leonard's house the sharpness in her voice when she talked to him? How much did they know, did Janape know, of those unruly, ugly feelings of hers? What did they hear in the language she and Leonard spoke?

She showed her camera to Kimame, turned to Janape, gestured to the forest. 'Can I take it?' she asked.

'It's okay,' Janape said.

Her thought was not to photograph the women but to capture the dark and pungent place where they climbed, the ground that was their ground. Instead of standing back, she came in close until her images were almost abstract. She took a patch of moss, a section of buttress root, the sharp hook of a curled vine, a snail, the mark left on the path by the slide of feet on wet earth. Sometimes she swung the camera up towards a flash of white, a bird rising like a wish, a blade of sunlight reflected from a broad leaf, but she did not take the shot, returning instead to wet rock, dark earth, leaf mould, the patterned tangle of undergrowth.

She was shy of raising the Leica to the faces of the *duvahe*. She had no interest in documenting them, in making a record. She had no impulse to catalogue or categorise. She made no notes, kept no journal, wrote nothing down. Only her camera was put to use: knees and feet, a backbone, an elbow, the back of a head, a band of fabric, a woven armband tucked with musky herbs. Texture and resistance. The paint stick meeting the cloth. Mallet on bark.

In a glade where a small river tumbled from the mountain to form a perfect pool, Kimame took several heavy wooden mallets from a small hut so that the young women could beat the strip of inner bark she'd laid over a hardened log. Rika took a place beside Janape as the thwock of the mallets echoed through the trees. It was hard work, transforming bark into cloth, and as Janape sang beside her, Rika thought of Aaron and the men who'd ambushed him. She'd asked him if she should go back to Europe, so that he would be safe. He'd turned his head towards her, taken her hand. 'If you are afraid for yourself, then you must go. If it's for me, better you stay.' He'd lifted her hand to his lips. 'White men think they can beat things out of people. We believe we beat things in.'

Spirit. The women had taught her the word for spirit when they'd shown her how a tree was cut for cloth, and she'd felt their exasperation when she couldn't grasp how spirit moved from tree to cloth, from cloth to painting. When she'd asked Leonard, alone in their room that night, his answer was filled with distinctions and discriminations that had nothing to do with the experience of beating the cloth, or walking the mountain, feeling its pulse through the soles of her feet. He turned to his notebook. Some trees have spirit, he reported, but others do not. He read the list he'd made. The mountain has spirit. Rivers have spirit. Bush spirits can make gardens grow, or can send in the pigs. Pigs don't have spirit.

In the glade where the women beat the bark, and no man could enter, Rika's thought moved, changing shape as she contemplated the possibility that spirit wasn't something that existed in this thing, this person, this tree, this cloth. Maybe it was more like negative space in photography, the connective tissue that joins the things that are seen, bringing them together through angle and light. Emboldened, she stood up and walked to the water. It was fresh from the mountain, a shallow pool lined with smooth pebbles, but when she took off her boots, tucked up her skirt to step into the water, Kimame's hand went up in warning. More language, more words she did not understand.

'Not this river. Not this water,' Janape said. The spirit of this water was to go into the cloth.

Walking back to the village, Nogi stopped at the top of a ridge and fixed Rika with a shrewd look. They were on a rocky outcrop looking across to the peak of *Huvaemo*.

'In the big war, many soldiers died and no one to bury them. Their spirits walked about, lost and angry. It upset the mountain,' Janape said, translating Nogi's tale of the last eruption of the volcano in 1951, when the mountain breathed scalding, angry air that burned everything that lived, incinerated villages, buried gardens under ash. Before the eruption, there had been signs that the mountain was angry. Cassowaries and bandicoots came into the village, wild boars came close to the houses. There were great storms with lightning in the sky, and though the rain fell, the rivers ran dry, the water pulled back up into the mountain. When the water returned it was hot.

'She wants you to know,' Janape said, 'some things happen are no good. No good for the mountain. It's a very big job being chief. Plenty work to do.'

'Is there something wrong now?' Rika asked. There was nothing rising from the peak, not a wisp of smoke, or even of cloud.

'The snakes, maybe a little,' Janape said. 'They move around.'

'Is it us being here?' Rika asked.

'You are welcome,' Janape translated. 'You white lady, you are welcome. You and Leonard are good spirits, both. When no good *tauba* come to the mountain it makes trouble. The mountain does not like.'

'The kiaps?' Rika asked.

'They okay,' Janape said.

'Is Nogi afraid for independence? Maybe bad strangers come then? Into Papua New Guinea.' Rika imagined the threat of plantations coming across the plain right to the base of the mountain, driving the Orokaivans up to these villages for water and gardens, and the rivers overflowing, silted up below, the sky rumbling with thunder.

'Maybe,' Janape said. 'Maybe no.'

'What can I do?' Rika asked.

'Understand,' Janape said. 'Nogi, she want you to understand. Leonard is a good man, but other *tauba* caused much trouble. Nogi say you must know. Keep trouble away.'

'Don.' It was Don. 'What did he do? Was it the music? The camera?'

The chiefs watched her, Janape too, and Rika knew she had not got it, whatever it was that had offended them.

'Janape?' Her voice was asking. 'Janape, friend of mine? What happened? What did Don do?'

Janape looked away. 'We go now,' she said, and Rika felt it as a rebuke. As the women walked quietly down the spur to the river, she felt the disappointment that had registered on Nogi's face. The sky was clear, there was no sign of clouds, *Huvaemo* glowed in the afternoon light. But among the women, the mood had changed. The knowledge of being closed out even as she was welcomed in bred an edgy anxiety she could not quite place as coming from them or from herself.

For the first time, Rika felt that she should not be there. Not her, and not Leonard either.

WHEN THE TIME WAS RIGHT AND NANAJI GAVE THE SIGNAL, THE GATES opened and the clans from the high villages burst into the *amorire*, singing their arrival. Feet stamped the ground, *kundu* drums kept the rhythm, each with its own voice, plumes mimicked the birds of the sun. Young men set the pace with a high step and perfect timing. Behind them came the women singing the cloth that moved against their skin. Nogi, in her soft white headdress and with the ground-spider cloth with its sunray legs hanging from her back, led the women. Beside her was Kimame in her plain bark-cloth and red parrot feathers.

Janape took her place in the dance, small Lilla dancing beside her. At the end of the line, Josephine's hair sprung out, dark and glossy. The woman whose breast had been swollen came out of the dance to take Rika's hand. Even Hunter's mother took a turn, her voice rising into the piercing staccato of the women's voices above the drums, before she returned, glowering, to the long trench of earth oven where pig was cooking for the feast when the dancing ended.

Leonard stood well back to film. Boja had had three small platforms built for him around the dance ground so that he could capture the wide circling of the dance. While he stood back, those too old to dance, or too young, came in close – almost touching the dancers – moving in and out as the double lines looped and circled. Rika moved with them. She squatted low and filled her lens with the dancing cloth, as if by taking the small space of the paintings, she could draw into the image the spirit that was evident in every step of the dance, and that she was struggling to comprehend. She filmed cloth, and she filmed feet stamping the ground, calling up the ancestors. She raised the camera to Janape's face, and Lilla's, to other women and girls she was learning to call friend.

She took Lilla's place and joined Janape in the dance, with its strange pauses she never quite anticipated. She circled the *amorire* with her, in the midst of the cloth and the plumes and the *kundus*. Dancing beside Janape, held by the sureness of her step, Rika understood that the quality she had not been able to name in her *sister-friend*, but had seen in her from the first, came from contentment. Janape lived in place. And Rika felt sorrow in the split of her own life that had brought her so far from the place where she started, and the premonition that she would live all her life out of place.

When darkness fell, the dancing continued into the night. The moon shone, catching the white feathers sewn into the plumes, exactly as Aaron had said. The peak of *Huvaemo* was outlined against the sky. Rika changed out of the cloth Janape had dressed her in; the dance had gone beyond her ability to accompany it – whatever was happening out there on the *amorire* belonged to the mountain, not to a pale visitor.

As the dance continued, its numbers dwindling towards dawn, when only the strongest would remain, she dozed, and woke, and watched, and brooded, her thoughts returning to Aaron, always to Aaron. To those first sweet days, her skin and his, the opening, the closing that took them under, beneath the surface, into the heart of each other. Longing rose in her, and a fretful fear that she may never find her way back to him. She put her mood down to bad nights, the unyielding beat of the *kundus*, the thinness of the air and the tension of days passing with nothing said to Leonard.

When she watched him film, his cumbersome equipment, his cards and notebooks seemed a barrier. She despised the platforms he'd had built. As she watched him labouring, first in the sun, then in the light of the moon, Boja at his side with the Nagra and a clapper, the camera separated him from the dancers. Even when he came down and moved among them, even when he turned the Arriflex to follow someone out of the edge of the frame, still she registered it as an imposition. An imposition and a limitation. When she took her own camera, the small, neat Leica, into the midst of the dancers, it was in contemplation of all he left out of the frame. Maybe the notion of frame needed to go in this landscape of spirit, if anything was to be known of feet moving over forest tracks, feet dancing, a hand raised with the paint-stick. Foot and earth, plume and brow, cloth and skin – these were the gestures she tried to catch.

At dawn, when the dancing was finished, she sat with Janape, watching the sun rise, gold over the outline of peaks. Janape had danced the full night. Her legs trembling from the work of it, her feet bruised. It was only the second time she'd found the strength to stay with it to the end. She was sucking a piece of sugarcane, preparing for sleep, when Nogi came towards them across the *amorire*, which had been beaten into mud by the feet of the dancers. She was still wearing the ground-spider cape, which hung from her back like the rays of the sun. She spoke to Janape. Not many could dance from dusk to dawn for the mountain. When Nogi was young, she had done it, and now it was her granddaughter, as it should be. Then she took Rika's hand, and gestured for her to lift the camera. *Lift the camera. Look at my face. At all our faces. Now that you have seen us dance.*

In the golden light of that morning, Rika brought the lens in on Nogi's eyes. She shot off a roll of film, capturing the clear gaze of a woman who had no reason to pose, no concept of vanity. And as she did, the thought came to her that she had an exhibition. It was a thought that excited her, and also made her ashamed.

When the dancing had finished and the clans had returned to their villages, Rika was at the river with Janape, sitting on the stones, enjoying the warmth of the sun. Above them, parrots were darting back and forth, squabbling for seeds. In the river Josephine was squeezing the last of the shampoo onto her hair. Women on their way back from their gardens were washing sweet potato and taro in the shallows. A baby was asleep in a large string bag hanging from a tree on the shady bank.

Rika lay in the water and let her mind return to swimming with Aaron at the town beach, out past the children, floating as he dived beneath her, his body liquid in the water, and bursting up through the surface into the air, saying, *come down with me*. Diving down, her hand in his. And then she was back in another river, far back when her mother was alive, a holiday somewhere, when she swam in the shallows of a smooth, gentle river, opening her eyes to the silky movement of weeds, surfacing to sunlight and her mother on the bank in her apple-green dress.

Though the current was turbulent in the mountain river and she could hold her head under for only a moment, she felt something in herself that was both grief and resolve. The time had come: she must face Leonard, her own failure of courage, and find her way back down the mountain to Aaron. She'd sent a letter to Popondetta with a man taking peanuts to the market. Otherwise there was no way to tell him that she loved him no less, that it was not Leonard but the mountain that had snared her. She dipped her head under again, and coming up into the air she was comforted by the presence of Janape. Was friendship the word? She didn't know what the word would mean to Janape, with its implication of choice. Friend joined to sister. She didn't understand enough to know if there were friendships within the clan that were different from the way they understood the web of connections that held each person as part of the whole. Could an outsider be a friend? Or was it a word that belonged in the *hapkas* world of exile?

Rika heard voices hollering from across the river, at the top of the ridge. Janape stood up.

'From the airstrip they come,' she said.

The women washing vegetables stopped to listen as the shouts bounced across the valley to the village and answering calls ricocheted back. They joined the yodelling, but from all the talk, the raised excited voices, the dropping-back into a busy silence as the vegetables were returned to string bags for the climb to the village, Janape said only, 'A policeman brings home the boy.'

A group of women was already hurrying towards the village. Josephine ran to join them as a band of young men came down the waterfall path. In the open space beside the river, Albert crouched with his hands in front of his face and looked at Rika as if through a camera. Obi spoke briefly to Nogi. Across the water, a tall Orokaivan policeman emerged from the trees. He was carrying a rifle, and with him was Hunter, his head hung low, looking at the ground.

Rika made a move towards the path. The clouds had come over, obscuring the sun. Janape put out her hand to restrain her. 'Wait,' she said.

When the riverbanks were quiet again, and the voices had disappeared into the bush, Nogi came up close to Rika, taking her arm in a hard grasp. She looked straight into her eyes. 'Josephine,' she said. 'Will Don come for her?'

Alone with Nogi and Janape at the edge of the river, Rika understood what she had been slow to grasp, and Leonard had not told her.

'No,' she said. 'He will not come.'

Hunter, betrothed to Josephine and shamed by Don, had fled to the village by the airstrip. Just that week, after the big rain, he had been caught under the pastor's house. He had pushed a stick up between the bamboo slats of the floor to wake the pastor's daughter, in the hope that the girl would creep out and join him. Instead he roused the father. The village woke to the thwack of the pastor's belt and Hunter's cries as he fled into the bush. When he slunk back to the village at the end of the day, the pastor was calling down the wrath of heaven, declaring him a sinner, cuckolded by a white stranger, the centre of a scandal, hanging around where he had no land and no rights. Compensation and righteousness were on the pastor's mind, the more so as he had attempted to save the boy and bring him to Jesus.

Tobias rescued Hunter that night and kept him in his house with the policeman, who'd arrived in the village on his way up the mountain to find the *tauba* who was making a film. Tobias, taking advantage of the policeman's presence, persuaded him to escort Hunter to the high village. It was an arrangement the pastor accepted, knowing that the presence of the policeman would strengthen his demand for recompense, and shame the boy.

Climbing up from the river with Janape, Rika stumbled under the weight of her ignorance.

'You did not tell me,' she said.

'You did not see.'

When they reached the village they found Leonard, and a large crowd gathered in the *amorire*. Men were shouting back and forth, and Hunter was crouched on the ground with his knees drawn up. Clouds were rolling in over the peaks. 'Uncle of Hunter,' Janape said, as a man walked over to the boy, yanked him to his feet and thrashed him with a long switch of vine. Hunter shrieked and leaped until he was knocked to the ground and lay there taking the blows with his arms around his head.

'Should we stop it?' Rika asked Leonard.

'We can't,' he said. They wore the shame of Don's skin colour.

When the boy was whimpering, his hands over his head, no longer moving under the lash, the chief Nanaji walked across and put up his hand. Hunter's uncle stepped back. Nanaji helped the boy to his feet and took him to the chiefs' house.

'Should we see if he needs medicine?' Rika asked Janape, as people trailed away to their houses.

'He must walk with his shame,' she said. 'In two days we can go to him.'

Josephine had vanished from sight.

'Why didn't you tell me?' Rika asked Leonard when they were alone on their platform.

'You're a friend of Laedi's,' he said.

'So?'

'I didn't want to put you in the position of knowing something you couldn't tell her.'

Fury rose in Rika as the policeman came across the *amorire* calling out to them, and climbed the steps to the platform. Behind him Albert swaggered with his stomach stuck out and an imaginary rifle the size of a bazooka on his shoulder.

'Come in,' Leonard said, putting out his hand. 'Leonard's my name.'

'Sergeant Thomas,' he said, shooing away the boys.

'It's okay,' Leonard said. 'They can stay.' But the sergeant persisted and the boys trailed reluctantly away.

'You here to look at paintings *bilong sampela*?' the policeman asked.

'That's right,' Leonard said.

Sergeant Thomas looked at the bark-cloth nailed to the walls and pulled at them, demonstrating to Leonard that the fabric was out of shape and the designs were crooked. He shook his head. '*Nogut tru*,' he said, sorry that Leonard had come all the way up here – bad road, steep mountains, bringing *missis* with him, a big trip too much.

'You come to my village,' he said. 'My people make very good cloth.' He squared off his hands to demonstrate the regularity of his people's cloth. 'All the same, square sides, and the pattern very good, all the same, this way, this way, all the same.' Plenty of kiaps had bought it, and the missions too, and a *tauba* had come to see about sending it to a shop in Moresby. 'With independence coming up,' Sergeant Thomas said, 'plenty tourists will come. Come to my place, we will give good rates, very good deal.' Leonard could make a film for the tourists so that everyone would know where to buy good cloth, he said. 'No good buying cloth like this. It goes crazy in the corner.' His eyes were glittery and unblinking.

'That's very kind,' Leonard said, 'but I am filming for the university, and the university likes this art. They are thinking about it in a different way.' He started a speech about the record he was making of bark-cloth in a place where there hadn't yet been other influences.

Sergeant Thomas was unimpressed. As far as he was concerned it was no good keeping the villages the same as yesterday. Independence was coming and progress with it. Only old men wanted the villages to stay the same. Old men and bush *kanakas*, he said, gesturing towards the village. It took several cups of sweetened coffee and a stick of tobacco before he accepted Leonard's answer. He shook his hand, called him a friend, and agreed to take a batch of film down to Tobias, where it could be kept cool in the gas refrigerator at the aid post.

'You change your thinking,' he said as he left the veranda, 'you find me at Popondetta police station. Sergeant Thomas.'

The next day the rain came crashing down the mountain with an angry, slanting force that sent sago-leaf thatch flying from roofs, chickens squawking into the eaves, pigs blundering about, trying to find shelter. All night it thundered down, dripping through roofs, gusting into rivers and streams, pooling on the ground beneath the houses. Leonard and Rika moved their sleeping mats from one side of the dark room to another, avoiding the drips and the wet that slid through the plaited wall.

Did Don have any idea of the consequences of what he'd done? This was the question Rika wanted answered.

Leonard didn't know. At first, he said, Don had obeyed the sensibilities of the village; Josephine hadn't come to him at night until the village was still, and she'd left again before dawn. Leonard never liked it. For a start, he said, the girl was too young. But Alex seemed to think the village knew what was happening, and that as long as Don recompensed the father, they accepted it. It wasn't the first time he'd encountered this in the field.

'*In the field?*' Rika shouted. 'The *field* is their *lives.*'

She shouted again when Leonard said that Alex had told Don to be careful not to humiliate the family, and to be sure to leave the girl's father a gift. But there came a time when Don wanted more than a short visit. In full view of everyone he took Josephine's hand, gave her gifts, and during his last week in the village he'd persuaded her to sleep through the night with him. When she emerged from the house in the full light of day, it was tantamount to a declaration.

'Alex should have made him leave,' Rika shouted over the thud of the rain.

'He wanted him to write his book.'

'Is that more important than *this*?' She was standing, with Leonard's anorak around her, gesturing out towards the village, barely visible through the rain. They were in cloud. *Swé*, it was called.

Nanaji came across from his house with a wide banana leaf held over his head. There had been a meeting of the *duvahe*. Nanaji and Leonard sat face to face on the mat, Boja hovering between them. Rika's secret burrowed deeper from view as the two men came up with a financial settlement for Josephine's father and another one for Hunter and Josephine to marry. There was also to be a pig for the preacher, and Leonard agreed that this, too, should be paid for by Don, though it was he who went to his trunk and counted out the notes.

Rika watched with furious eyes, unable to intervene as Leonard and Nanaji made decisions that would determine the shape of two young lives. She left them to it and ran through the rain to the cookhouse.

'Did anyone ask Josephine if she *wants* to marry Hunter?' Rika asked Janape. She was crouched by the fire, arranging the sticks over the embers, blowing the fire into life for the kettle.

'The chiefs decide,' Janape said.

'Did Josephine think Don would come?'

Janape shrugged. 'She hoped. Maybe.'

'Did you think he'd come?'

'No. I did not like Don.'

'He has a wife in Port Moresby,' Rika said. 'And a child. A girl.'

'What name this girl?'

'Bili,' Rika said.

'A good name,' Janape said.

'She's a strong child. There's another one coming.' Rika held her hands out from her stomach to indicate the state of Laedi's pregnancy.

Janape shook her head, clicked her tongue. 'No good,' she said, looking out into the rain. 'Don brings much trouble to the mountain.'

Rika was angry. She was angry with Leonard. She was angry at his patience when she could not let him touch her. She was angry with herself for the night she'd given in to him, and to herself, and for the dark pleasure of her double betrayal as Leonard sweated above her. She was angry at the kindness of the hand Leonard rested on her back when she turned from him on their hard sleeping mats. Most of all, she was angry that he had not told her about Don, that he'd left her clumsy and childlike before Nogi. And all the time she knew that her failure to speak, her lack of courage, far outstripped his.

EVENTUALLY THERE WAS NOTHING FOR IT – NO ESCAPE, NO REMEDY –
but to say the words. So when she was alone in the house with Leonard,
watching the rain, Rika took a deliberate breath.

'Leonard,' she said, putting her hand on his knee and then wishing
she hadn't. 'I think maybe I'm in love with Aaron.'

The ease drained from his face.

'I'm sorry,' she said.

'When?' he said. 'How long?'

'I don't know. It crept up. Over the last month before I came up,
I suppose.'

'Why didn't you tell me sooner?'

'I couldn't.'

Leonard was shivering, wrapped in a blanket. Outside, everything
had vanished into the thickness of rain. There were no mountains, no
forest, no gardens, no houses, no village. Occasionally figures moved
close enough to glimpse. Otherwise they were alone on a small ship,
two crew members, each grappling with a different sail.

'You're very young,' he said. 'I've always known that. Infatuations
happen. I remember what it was like.' He took her hand, swallowing
hard. 'I can wait for it to pass.'

'I don't think it's like that,' Rika said. 'I mean, at first I thought
maybe. But it's come to be more.'

'Don't do anything hasty.'

'I have. I already have.'

Even that Leonard said he could understand, accommodate, bear.

'I think I have to leave you, Leonard,' she said.

'No. You don't have to.'

'I need to.'

She heard the harsh tone of her voice and knew that it had shocked him as much as her words. She saw him understand that he'd missed the transformation signalled in her voice, and knew only that it had occurred. But she didn't see anger. He got up and wrapped another blanket around himself. He walked onto the open platform and looked into the void. The ghostly shapes of banana trees bowed in the rain like exhausted soldiers. Against a waste of sky, Leonard began to sob.

'I think I have a fever,' he said. He held a damp handkerchief to his face.

For two more days it rained. Leonard lay in bed, hot to the touch, shivering and sweating. His skin was a pale grey, his eyes without his glasses looked sunken and moist. Rika read Tobias's instructions for the remedial dose of quinine, Janape counted out the pills.

With Leonard trembling, unable to speak, remorse filled the hours. The rain fell and the river rose. Boja stood tutting at the door and called into the foggy rain for Janape to boil up water. Hunter's mother was in the cookhouse with her and she cackled when Rika went in.

Janape sat beside Leonard. She held his head as he drank and coaxed him to eat the yam she'd prepared. She sang quietly, as if to a child. Leonard smiled at her, fell back to his fever.

'For better or for worse,' he murmured when Rika went in with lime and ginger in hot water. 'Love and curse. I promised your father. Old Piet. Love and worse.' Tears and sweat covered his face.

Janape helped him up to drink the liquid she had prepared and turned the damp pillow. The clouds rained grief and fear, the duty of tears. Rika stood looking out into nothingness. Aaron was beyond the cloud, beyond the reach of her mind, and yet she wanted him with the full force of her being.

On the last day of the rain, as it began to ease, Leonard's fever abated. Boja came to sit with him. Janape and Rika sheltered in the low-roofed, smoky cookhouse as yams roasted in the ashes. Rika's legs were restless; whichever way she sat, they wanted to move. Her fingers tapped impatiently on the floor.

She wanted to tell Janape, explain why she would soon be leaving. She felt she owed it to her new sister-friend, and suspected that anyway Janape had heard enough to know. She wanted to ask her to look after him. But Leonard didn't want the village told; they wouldn't understand, he said, and could turn against her. And she didn't want him humiliated here as he was by the talk in Port Moresby. So her fingers tapped on the floor while Janape sang a low, quiet song with words she didn't translate. 'Just a song,' she said, when Rika asked.

The rain stopped as suddenly as it had begun. Where there had been an intolerable emptiness, the peaks of the mountain returned to view. Wisps of cloud hung in the valleys below, but above was a taut blue sky. Lines of bush-rope were strung between houses; blankets and bark-cloth were hung out to dry. Thatched roofs steamed in the midday sun. Roosters crowed again. Albert mimed old men walking through mud. Dark patches on the walls began to fade as they dried. Children came back to the platform and Leonard, coughing and pale, crept out to sit with them while Janape attended to their sores.

The punishing thought of pneumonia descended on Rika.

Boja went down to inspect the river. He said it would be three days yet before Rika could cross, maybe more. He and Leonard played a hand of cards.

'I won't leave till you're better,' she said to Leonard.

'You go,' he said. 'I've had malaria before. The worst is over, and Janape is here.'

'Should you come out for a break? To Popondetta.'

'I'll stay here. Maybe in a month. That'll give you some time, and perhaps you'll feel differently then.'

'Aren't you angry?'

'Rika, Rika. Would it make it easier if I were?'

*

Her last days in the village were strangely calm. Leonard was quiet, as if all emotion had been drained from him with the fever, as if his weariness was too great for expression. He sat in the sun and ate the yams Janape cooked for him. She boiled up a root she'd found by the river. The prospect of pneumonia receded. Women came with vegetables, and Obi and the boys went into the forest to catch lizard for him, a delicacy to make him strong.

The angry spirit that had inhabited Rika vanished as entirely as the rain. Affection rose in her again, for Leonard, for this good man weakened with sickness, who remained kind even in the face of betrayal. As the time approached for her to leave, she felt she could have stayed. Not to be with Leonard, but to experience more of this place where time changed its nature and spirit lived in the air.

'Maybe,' she suggested to Leonard, 'their idea of spirit is more like photosynthesis.'

He smiled and did not correct her. She looked at him through the Rolleiflex and saw a kind of veil around him, an aura perhaps, a trick of the light, the spirit of the mountain working on him. She knew that both of them had been moved in ways that would stay with them for the rest of their lives.

Rika sat on the steps to the platform, sombre, pulling on her boots, ready for the long walk down to the airstrip. Her eye was idly following four small pigs, poor pigs without spirit. The first blundered into a fence, the ones behind colliding and squealing, disoriented. It took several attempts for them to find the path. And then it dawned on her.

'Leonard,' she shouted. 'They're blind!'

Leonard, who was checking the film he'd packed for her to take back to Moresby, didn't look up.

'The pigs! Leonard!'

Still he didn't look up.

'They're blind, aren't they?'

She could see from his expression when he turned to her that it was true. 'When do they do it?'

'At birth.'

'How?'

'With lime. They rub it into their eyes.'

'Why?'

'To keep them out of the gardens.'

'It doesn't work.'

'I know. It's custom. They blind their pigs. Other tribes fence their gardens. It's tradition.'

'It's horrible.'

She went into the dark bedroom and wept. She wept noisily, taking in sharp breaths, not caring if she was heard. When she returned to the platform, Leonard hovering beside her, she stood looking at the painted cloth on the wall. 'Look at them. How can their art be so sure, so balanced, so *absolute*, when they *blind the pigs?*' She leaned against him and sobbed. Her eyes were red and her nose wet when Nogi appeared, carrying two folded cloths.

'A gift for you,' Janape translated, as Nogi handed her the cloth Rika had seen her painting with Janape's mother: a pattern of mountains, row upon row of them; black lines and a burned orange paint that glowed like the sun. 'They make it for you.'

'Thank you.' Rika bowed her head. What to give in return? Money was a crude offering. Even so, she contemplated putting a note in each hand – an incongruous gesture, like tipping a maid. She looked into their eyes and the thought faded.

'*Huëmae*,' she said. '*Duvahe*. Sister-friend.'

Then Nogi handed her the second cloth and the women who'd come to cluster around them fell very quiet.

'Nogi say, this cloth it is for you,' Janape translated. 'You have come to the mountain, the first *tauba* woman, the same as us. You have seen well, and we are proud.'

Rika knew, even as it came into her hand, that it was the ground-spider painting, the sunrays. She could feel tears rise and an impulse to say no, she was unworthy. But something in the way Nogi looked at her made it possible to accept, and when the tears spilled over, they were oddly calm, as if, just possibly, grief could be held in balance with the future.

'Thank you,' she said. '*Huëmae*.'

Their hands clasped, *tauba*-style, but the exchange was in the eyes. Nogi wasn't smiling exactly, but when Rika met her gaze she held it with kindness.

And so it was in some confusion of mind that Rika walked down to the river. When she stood on the rocks preparing to cross, Leonard leaned across for her Leica and took a shot of her and Janape, arms around each other beside the turbulent water. The sun was shining on their heads, the water was gleaming, and they were leaning in towards each other smiling. Then Rika took the camera back, turned it to Leonard and Janape, and there they were, Leonard pale and wretched, Janape shy beside him.

'Go back up now, you're still weak,' Rika said to Leonard. 'Let Boja help you.'

'I will,' he said. He put his hand to her cheek. 'I'll see you in a month or so.'

The river was high, covering the rocks where the women cleaned the vegetables. She waded across, one hand given to Janape, the other to Obi. Her every step was treacherous, while theirs were sure even as the current pushed at them and the stones moved under their feet. Albert crossed the river with Lilla on his shoulder.

On the far bank Rika waved as she watched Boja and Leonard disappear into the trees.

She climbed the next ridge behind Kimame and Nogi, the sound of farewell yodels bouncing over their heads from the village. *Kundus* called out to her, each with its own voice.

At the top she said goodbye to the women chiefs, who stood tall and straight. Nogi took off a necklace of shell and seed, put it over Rika's head to join the one she was given on arrival. *This place, this place* was all she could think. This place of extremes, this paradise that blinds its pigs.

She shook the hands of the women who'd climbed with her and were now leaving her to go on with Obi and the guides. Kimame would take them to the edge of clan-land. She took Lilla's arm, brought it to her face and breathed in.

Albert stood quietly with her old basket and did not mimic her large shiny tears as she went back along the line, shaking every hand, bowing to Nogi and the chiefs, until at last there was only Janape.

'Look after him,' Rika said.

'Remember us,' Janape replied.

HOHOLA

WHEN THE UNIVERSITY HOUSING OFFICER TOLD AARON that he was not eligible for married quarters, Rika said, 'Then let's move to Hohola.'

Leonard had come down from the mountain two months after Rika, head bowed, to work on a transcript of the film, with Obi's help. She had endured sideways glances and pursed lips. The eager questions were the worst, and then, after he'd gone, the feigned concern. A white woman living in Hohola? She liked the idea. And she liked Hohola, which had the advantage of being on a hill and closer to town. It was a well-established suburb, with gardens growing between the houses; the 'native clerks' it was built for had been joined by new players in the new order. On one side of them was a store manager from the big supermarket and his family; on the other, a journalist from Rabaul.

The house Aaron and Rika moved to was boxy, like all Hohola houses, and the rooms were small, without internal doors. The water that ran from the taps was cold, and there was a copper out the back for laundry. But when they walked into the empty house with its stained walls and concrete floors, they saw only that it was theirs.

Laedi and Martha tied up their hair, stood on ladders and in the space of a weekend the walls were painted white – a bit rough, but clean and bright. Wana went to the markets for woven panandus mats to cover the floor, and Rika hung her bark-cloths from the mountain over the empty doorways. At the side of the house was a large, bare slab of concrete. Aaron and Pete built a frame over it, Sam knocked up a trellis, and Rika planted vines, which grew to make a shaded veranda where people gathered, crowding around the table, or sleeping on the old bed against the wall. Aaron's kin came in from the fjords – no one was turned away. Rika sang as she cooked coconut rice and banana bread, food for many.

Their bedroom, the only room where they hung a door, was at the front of the house. The bed was low, a mattress on a propped-up board. The sheets were covered by a pale green spread, and the bedside lamp was on a painted tea chest. Books were piled on the floor, open where they'd left them. Light shone through the louvres, filling the room with tenderness, lingering on the rumpled sheets and clothes that hung from a rail. Outside the window were pawpaw trees, and beyond that the bare open space where kids from along the street played during the day. The sound of their games – the thwack of a ball, the drag of tin cans across the ground – was a daily accompaniment to their lives.

Sam and Wana were the first to join them in Hohola. Their house was on the street below Aaron and Rika, near the trade stores. Its condition was worse, with broken louvres and a leak in the concrete sink. The paint rollers came out again, another weekend on ladders, with the radio playing and yams from the Trobriand Islands cooking on the fire outside. The exodus from the housing compound had begun, and when boom gates went up at the university and guards patrolled at night, Martha and Pete, and Laedi and Don also made the move to Hohola. It was their way of saying they weren't temporary visitors safe in a white compound, where floodlights had been installed and tough wire put over the windows. Nervous Australians had begun their resentful exodus south, their absence barely noticed as new suburbs went up and cranes continued their slow move across Moresby's skyline. New staff arrived at the university from Africa and from India. In Hohola Martha read Chinua Achebe and Rika learned to grind the spices that appeared in the Chinese trade stores at the bottom of the hill.

They were good years, those Hohola years. True, there were mean dogs and rowdy boys and men coming home drunk, and unlike the university compound it all happened on the streets, or in the front yards. But so did the dancing and the flirting and the fires and the string bands. Hohola was a life of noise and smells and music, and everyone talking, always talking. Stories of love affairs and school teachers and credulous missionaries were told, tricks and rivalries and feuds were reported on. Everyone knew what had been said in the administrator's car, for his Papuan driver lived down the road from Sam and Wana. Porters from the Legislative Assembly lived in Hohola, and so did waiters from the hotels where deals were done. Good ears and soft feet, all of them. Visitors from Australia said they learned more about the place from one evening on Rika and Aaron's veranda than they did at the government meeting or university seminar they'd come for. As one year moved to the next, and the vines grew over the veranda, their house became a sure centre in the midst of the comings and goings that made up the life of Port Moresby during those changing years. And at the centre of the house were Aaron and Rika, shining with happiness.

Something powerful radiated from them, and no one could miss it. In town there was a muted respect. Aaron's response to the assault – *they beat her into me*, and beyond that a well-judged silence – had the strange effect of making him safe from further attack. When they walked through town hand in hand, not so much as a gob of spit came their way, which was more than could be said of other couples who linked brown arm in white. This despite the gleam between them, the spark that was palpable in the way they walked, the way they greeted each other, the way they spoke. They breathed the same air, read the same books, woke to the same patch of sky. When Rika danced to a string band, or to a ukulele on the bare earth in front of their house, where children played during the day, it was clear to everyone that Aaron had released something in her. When the music slowed and the rhythm dropped and he wrapped his arms around her with the full power of his attention, ignoring the holler and hoot of every kid in the street, no one could doubt that this was a true union of heart, the gold coin itself. For five years they were happy, with barely a cloud to ruffle their sky.

Martha and Laedi were also content in Hohola. Not the clear-sky happiness that shone from Rika and Aaron. Both were in marriages that were more like the two faces of a coin, easily turning them in different directions, than the solid metal between. Pete and Martha found reason to be apart without actually separating. He had his fieldwork and she began an MA, reading the writings of colonial travellers who had come to New Guinea, some in search of the 'cannibal queen' who'd make them a literary fortune, others to escape the grey skies of England, drawn to a dream of the South Pacific. Pete's research took him up rivers and out to the islands. Martha's took her to London, to Melbourne: to libraries that housed the books she was after. But when they came back together, it was always to Hohola. Dusty, noisy, happy Hohola with meals under Rika's vines and visitors from Fiji and Samoa, Sydney and Honolulu. Yes, for Martha they were good years, those Hohola years.

Laedi, too, was surprised to find for herself a sense of peace in Hohola, despite her increasingly unhappy marriage. She gave birth to Daisy, a serene baby who seemed to bestow her peacefulness on her sister and mother, and Don left for a new job at Melbourne University. By the time Laedi and the girls joined him there, he'd met the woman who was to be his next wife, a research student from Trinidad. The night before Laedi and the girls left for Melbourne, a string band played out the front of Aaron and Rika's house. People spilled down the street – half of Hohola must have been there. Daisy, who was not yet two, slept through it all; Bili, at four, danced as if these were her last hours on earth. She danced with Rika, and tears fell down both their faces.

'No need for sad,' Simbaikan said, though the lines of her face were grim. 'This is her ground. She'll come back.'

'And Don?' Rika asked. 'Will he come too?'

Simbaikan raised her arms as if to say it was of no account whether he did or he didn't. She'd never liked his smell, but he'd made two strong babies, had he not?

Rika laughed and was comforted. Yes, Laedi would return, Laedi and the girls, and somehow at that moment she knew it would not be long.

It wasn't. A year and a half and they were back. They moved in with Martha and Pete until the house next door came free, and by the time their boxes arrived from Melbourne, Rifle had built a shed for the chickens he gave Bili as a gift to welcome her home, to Hohola.

BETWEEN MARTHA'S KITCHEN AND LAEDI'S WAS A PATCH OF BARE ground. After a few months of tramping back and forth, eating in one house or the other, carrying plates and dishes, and never enough chairs, Laedi had the idea of a platform. Highlanders who'd set up camp on the hill behind them built it, the design emerging from many hands and many beers. When it was finished people came from streets away to look. It was a raised platform, just that, built between the houses, with a roof of iron sheets and sago palm, and large enough to accommodate a long table, also knocked up by Highland carpenters, from offcuts Pete bought at the sawmill. Two sides of the platform had low plaited walls, but otherwise it was open to the air. Breezes came down the hill, and from it they could see who was walking up the road. During the day, washing hung along the open walls, and Simbaikan was there often enough to guard against intruders and theft. At night the Coleman lamp hung from the rafters and they talked in its shadows, all of them gathered in, neighbours and visitors, everyone together, breathing the pyrethrum of mosquito coils.

Laedi's return, Rika said, had them back on their rightful pathways.

In the European summer of 1971, Rika's *Mountain* exhibition opened in Amsterdam. The treacherous thought that had come to her when Nogi made her own relationship with the camera and met the lens without posing, without vanity, proved prescient. Here was a new face, a new set of eyes looking.

The exhibition was noticed, and so was Rika. There was an interview with her in the cultural pages of *de Volkskrant* and a photo of her at the opening wearing a white crocheted dress. Her hair was loose, grown long again, cut straight at the shoulder. In the interview she said that during her one year of art school in Amsterdam, she'd learned that the task of art was to make the familiar strange. On the mountain, she'd understood that her task was to reverse that maxim. She wanted to let something that is familiar, common to us all, show through the strangeness. She gave each woman her name, and that is how their images were titled, though to her chagrin not a name made it into the reviews. 'The Strange Made Intimate' was the header over one, 'Savage Beauty' over another.

Martha was in Amsterdam when the exhibition opened. She came across from London, where she was researching her travellers, for the small civil ceremony at which Rika and Aaron were married. Again Rika wore her white crocheted dress. Aaron, in a suit and tie, gave her father the trochus shell amulet he'd brought as a gift for the occasion. At the restaurant afterwards, old Piet spoke with the grace of a Melanesian. Rika shone with the happiness she'd brought from Hohola.

But Martha wasn't there when Rika took Aaron to her mother's grave, and walked with him past the school she'd attended, into the Botanical Gardens whose gates she had passed on her way home each day. Near the end of their visit she took him into the orchid house, where he read the labels, learning the Latin names for the Port Moresby Gold, *Dendrobium discolor*, and the pale, spidery sprays he recognised from the rocky cliffs of the fjords: *D. cyrtosepalum*.

'Our worlds are not so far apart,' he said when they were lying on the grass outside, in the afternoon sun. 'How peaceful it is.'

Rika, lifted on one elbow, looked at him lying there with his eyes closed. She traced the scar over his eyebrow with a soft finger. 'Aaron,' she said, and he opened his eyes, looked at her, smiled. '*Kómbo-ko.*' My love, my lover.

'What is it?'

'There was a man. When I was a girl. That summer after my mother died.' The words came fast as she told him about the man who came across her in the orchid house, and how they'd talked, and he'd come again the next week, then the next. He was older, a graduate student, a long way from his home, and when it was time for him to return to his island he'd kissed her, there in the orchid house, and she'd let the tide carry her, and made no resistance. 'Just that one time,' she said. 'Can you forgive me?' And Aaron saw the shame and dismay that could still raise tears, and did again that day. But she said nothing of the hospital room in Amsterdam, the term missed from school. Or the sorrow that dropped her into a silence that lasted for weeks, months, and had come upon her again in the gardens with Aaron. All that was hidden deep in her, beyond the reach of words. Aaron held her close and with her face concealed in his neck, he told her she shouldn't be ashamed. He'd grown up in a culture that did not shame the young for their promiscuity, and, though she bridled at the word, she leaned into him and let the buried remain buried.

Rika saw Martha again a month later in London, when Aaron was invited to speak at University College. The paper he gave on the colonial division of the Pacific at the Treaty of Versailles, the first from a historian whose lands had been traduced, brought him a respect that complemented Rika's success. They were invited to seminars and galleries, and Aaron saw that Europe need not be closed to him. When he disappeared into the libraries where he no longer felt invisible, Rika lured Martha out from the same reading rooms, and they walked the summer streets and squares. Flowers were in bloom, trees were a tender green that astonished Martha. It was on one of their walks, in Regent's Park, along the edge of the lake, that Rika told Martha about the afternoon on the grass with Aaron at the Botanical Gardens in Leiden.

'I didn't tell him I was pregnant,' she said, looking at Martha with such regret that Martha put her arm round Rika's shoulder. 'I wanted to tell him, and I didn't. I couldn't. It was enough of a betrayal as it was, that I'd felt so much. Nothing like it again until him. You know. You know how it is. That overwhelming feeling, that giving over, that *opening* that can't be for anyone else.' Yes, Martha had known that feeling – it was part of the problem with Pete, now that it had faded. 'At school,' Rika said, 'they made a lot of his age. There was talk of the police, but I was seventeen and nothing was forced. I wanted it. I didn't know what it was that I wanted, but I wanted it.' She turned to look at Martha. 'I welcomed him. That was the betrayal.'

'You can't betray someone in advance,' Martha said. 'What about Leonard? Was that a betrayal?'

'Oh, *Leonard*,' she said. 'That was different.'

'Are you going to have a ceremony in the fjords?' Martha asked. They were leaning on the rails above the lake, watching the ducks in their little wooden houses. The sun was warm, the light easy on the eye. So different, so very different from Hohola. Martha found it hard to put it all together, the mind map of where they lived.

'There's not really a ceremony to have,' Rika said, still looking at the ducks. 'He can't pay bride price, can he?' She laughed. 'He gave my father the trochus shell.' She was quiet for a while before she turned to Martha.

'Aaron says a child is more important than a ceremony,' she said. 'They're beginning to ask in the village. I'm still an outsider there. It'll be different when I am pregnant.'

'You can't have a baby for the village.'

'Why not? It'll change everything.'

'You'll still be white, if that's the problem.'

'I won't be clan, but the child will,' she said, off on a riff about a new generation for a new world, where schools would be places of opportunity and marriages for love alone. 'See why I can't live here?' she said, and Martha laughed.

When Rika took the job at the university's new arts centre, she insisted on a local salary. Didn't an 'unlocked heart' mean unlocking prejudice and unequal advantage? She had a studio to teach from, a well-equipped darkroom, and Aaron. She was on her right pathway. What more could she want?

In the years since she'd been on the mountain, Rika had had a lot to say about pathways. It was a term she'd learned from Nogi. She took down the bark-cloths from the doorways of her house and pinned them on her studio wall at the arts centre. 'Look,' she said to her students, running her fingers along the black lines of Nogi's mountains. 'On the mountain only the senior artists can draw the pathways. It takes many years of learning, and until the young artists have learned enough, all they can paint is the colour between the pathways.' She asked her students to consider what the colours would be like without black pathways. They'd have no form, no structure. 'That's why we're using black and white film. That's where photography starts. It's in the darkroom that we learn the pathways of the shot, the structure of the image. We take that into our seeing the next time we look through the lens.'

At the university, she felt herself part of the changes that were all around her. Her work flowed into the work of others, just as her life flowed between the houses in Hohola. She and Sam started *Village Shots*, taking their students into the villages and into the town, hers with cameras, his with notebooks and recorders for the essays they'd write. Milton said they looked like a bunch of tourists, with their cameras and shade-cloths and hats on their heads. He was back on a break from Melbourne, where things with Tessa weren't going well. But he'd had a play put on, and a job at a new theatre in an old warehouse. He was in Rika's class the day she pinned on the wall a photograph of one of Martha's travellers, a stout woman from Dublin who had lived for many years in a house above the harbour. She was photographed there, before the war, in a forty-foot room with shutters filtering the light. Standing to attention near the stairs was a Papuan servant with a bare chest and a high bush of hair, lit from the light of the window.

'What do we make of this photo?' she asked the *Village Shots* students.

'How do we answer them?' Sam asked. 'Can we?'

'Why don't you go there, and restage the photo?' Milton said. 'Make that your answer.'

The house was much as it had been thirty years before, with the same view over the harbour, a shaded garden and servants. A senior official in the Australian administration was living there, and his wife welcomed them with lemonade and ginger cake. In the forty-foot room, the students worked out where the photographer had stood, and rearranged the furniture. They chose the student with the highest hair to stand where the servant had stood, replicating the old photo, the shutters folded away as they had been. But in their composition, the figure in the light from the window wore a Black Power T-shirt and held a camera – which he turned to the wicker chair where the colonial writer had sat. In her place sat Rika, a white woman with a camera. The students directed the shots as if for the stage. In one, Rika had her camera raised, so that she and the student with the high hair vied for ascendancy. In another, her camera was gone, and she stood in the position of the long-ago servant. A student from Hanuabada, the village on the harbour, positioned himself to take in the view of the mountains across the harbour.

Back at the studio, students lounged on the floor smoking while others moved the prints around, arguing over whether it was Politics or Art that was on display. When images from the docks were up, was it the danger of the rigs or their silhouette against the harbour that was to be emphasised? When a deal was being done in a flash bar in a new hotel, was it the glimpse of money changing hands that gave the photo its power or the shapes made in the space between the heads that drew together? And all the while, Rika was bouncing on her toes, sparring with Sam. He wanted historical context, where she spoke of light and form. He spoke of documentary, where she saw the potential of performance.

When the *Village Shots* exhibition went up at the end of 1972, people came from all over town to see the displays, which spread from the studio at the arts centre to the exhibition space at the spacious new library. Straggling lines of schoolchildren trooped through with their teachers. Laedi brought a bus from the mission, where she taught, and the women from her literacy class stepped out of the bus in bright dresses from the screen-print workshop, their notebooks tucked into their string bags. Every day was festive. Hawkers set up outside the library with watermelon to sell. Old women settled down on their mats with their betel nut and cigarettes arranged singly for sale in front of them. People came from settlements and outlying villages, and so did visiting dignitaries and government advisors. Gina said she'd never done so much meeting and greeting, and Aaron, called on to show the dignitaries through, had never had so many lunches in the vice-chancellor's rooms.

Up on the wall was the image of the student in the forty-foot room. Around it were shots of house girls in bright dresses, a man carrying laundry through the kitchen and the servants' quarters, a small outhouse away from the view.

Some students had stood at the gates of a hotel photographing the faces in the cars that drew up. It was curiously interesting. Others had been at street stalls and markets, their shots displayed alongside the rumours Sam's students had collected: that Papua would become a state of Australia; that the Highlanders would make war on the coast, and everyone would lose their land; even that the Vatican was on its way to claim the palm oil.

A young man took a calmer route and photographed nothing but roof lines and house poles, slatted floors above water; he accompanied the clean, sharp images with 'If this roof could speak', a long poem of a house whose ancestor saw Captain Moresby sail into the harbour. That was Rika's favourite, and Aaron's.

Another series of shots taken over several weeks of the same old man as he adjusted to the camera and began to look back, then question, and finally repudiate it, found its way into the *Sydney Morning Herald*, and the series into a special issue of *Oceania*.

At the opening of the *Village Shots* exhibition, a historian visiting from New York gave a rousing speech. 'This great experiment! This extraordinary moment! A privilege to visit, to be part of this quickening!'

In response, Rika spoke of pathways. She was looking particularly beautiful that night, in a dress made from a cotton print designed by students at the arts centre. Aaron lifted her hand to his lips and said the camera made visible the task of the future, and the capacities of the students who were preparing for it.

Their pathways were strong, a string band newly back from a tour of Australia was playing, and the future stretched ahead with everything in place.

The one threat to this happy view was Derek. He had left the politics department to run Michael Somare's office, and he wanted Aaron there, working for the chief minister and the government that was coming. This was a greater task than to serve the university and its students. That was his view, and he'd put it to Aaron more than once. When it came to a particular request, a talk here, a weekend meeting there, Aaron would do as Derek asked, but he would not leave the university. He had the soul of a scholar. Martha saw him in the new, custom-built library most days, at his favourite desk by the windows with books piled around him as he worked. His lectures on Malinowski and Margaret Mead were becoming renowned, attended by staff from other faculties and patrol officers who were in town for a briefing. Yes, the life of the university suited Aaron.

Derek was at the opening of *Village Shots* with a bureaucrat from Treasury and an advisor from Canberra. They stood in the middle of the room and it was clear to everyone that they were more interested in Aaron than anything up on the wall.

'You're not getting him,' Rika said, warding him off with a smile.

'The time will come,' Derek said, also with a smile. The new prime minister in Canberra, Labor for the first time since 1949, wanted independence soon, and he wanted it fast. '"Australia is no longer willing to be the ruler of a colony",' Derek quoted. 'Remember?'

Rika needed no reminding of the cheers on their veranda when Gough Whitlam had been voted in as prime minister. Or of the doubts that followed and the questions that were now being asked. 'Divest' – what, exactly, did that mean? 'Gearing up' for independence was one thing, but who would control the 'terminal arrangements'? Not Derek.

Rika shook her head. 'Didn't you once teach that the future is formed of the past? That it needs to be understood? I've heard you myself, I've hear you say Aaron's lecture on the Treaty of Versailles is essential for anyone wanting to work with the government.' Her face was flushed. 'There are plenty of others to work for the government. Who else has Aaron's mind?'

'It's his mind that we need,' Derek replied.

Rika looked at him with a stubborn eye. Didn't he understand that it was a matter of pathways? Besides, she didn't think Aaron was strong enough. Physically strong enough. She hadn't forgotten Simbaikan's prophecy of an early death. Laedi said most of Simbaikan's predictions were wrong, and anyway she changed them to suit the way she was travelling. 'She was right about you coming back,' Rika told Laedi, whose reply was that any fool could have known that.

'He works hard enough as it is,' Rika said to Derek.

In the celebratory atmosphere of the opening, Derek backed off, biding his time. But as she danced that night, Rika could feel a crack in the happiness that had come with Hohola.

One Sunday afternoon the following July, some young men came crashing up the hill through the houses, scaring the chickens and setting off the dogs.

'The Highlanders want to kill us all,' one of them shouted to Rika. It was Doug from Mary's house opposite, the youngest of her boys to start on the wharves. He was back from the rugby league match.

'What's happening?' She went out into the yard and called across to Mary.

'They riot,' she said. 'Hear them.' From somewhere distant they could hear a dull roar of voices. Glass breaking.

'Where are they?'

'At Four Mile,' Mary said.

'Did New Guinea lose again?'

'Papua won,' Doug was flushed with excitement. 'Papua kill them.' There was a cheering roar from his brothers, who came running out of the house carrying knives.

Mary shouted at them to stop, to give over the knives, but the boys were already whooping down the hill. That in itself was an indication that this was no squall, that a storm was blowing their way.

At the bend above the trade stores, Rika could see over to the road into town. The Chinese store-owners were nailing boards across the doors; the women who sold betel and lime were packing up and hurrying away. The trucks that congregated there had gone. In the distance she could hear the crack of metal on metal, the wail of sirens. Standing there was eerie, as if she was on some kind of dividing line. Behind her the shadows were beginning their slow creep down the hill and from that direction the air was fragrant with the late-afternoon scent of eucalyptus. In front of her, out in the valley, she could smell danger rising like the dust drifting up from the road.

It was here that Martha found her, just as three boys, all soft edges and spindly legs, came scrambling up the hill towards them.

'Aaron says to go to Laedi!' It was Aaron's nephew Wilkie, his wiry plaits bobbing. He was breathing in wild gasps. 'Everyone's fighting. New Guinea want to kill Papua, everyone dead.'

'Calm down.' Rika caught him by the shoulder, holding him steady, and the others slowed, hopping from foot to foot.

'A big fight,' Wilkie said, pulling himself free. 'We'll chase them out.'

Rika kept her hand on his shoulder. 'Did Aaron say to go back?' she asked. The boy shot her a sideways look. 'He didn't, eh?' Her grip tightened. Wilkie hung his head and the other boys shuffled and looked at the ground. Fifty years earlier they'd have been on their way to warriors already, but the old initiations had ended and they were just kids in town for school.

They told Martha and Rika that they'd been on the stand with Aaron and Pete in a large crowd of coastal Papuans. At the end of the match they were cheering. 'Clapping and dancing,' Wilkie said. They didn't see what happened, only that people were spilling out of the stands to fight and it took a long time to get away. Girls were crying, and Aaron and Pete kept stopping to help them. Outside in the street were cars with smashed windows. 'A big noise,' Wilkie said. When the police arrived with batons and tear gas, the crowd ran on towards Boroko, breaking the windows of trade stores, stopping cars, smashing windscreens. Highlanders who were chewing betel at the back of the Boroko Hotel joined the fight and blocked the road.

'A white person's wedding got frightened,' Wilkie said. 'Ladies in white dresses were all running about.' The boys had recovered themselves and were laughing, imitating the white ladies and the hats on their heads.

'So how did you get back?' Rika asked.

They'd waited a long time, talking to some men Wilkie didn't know. 'A white man came talking to Aaron,' he said. 'Government man, maybe.'

'Derek?'

'Maybe.'

'You know Derek. Somare's man. White man.'

'Maybe.'

'So? What happened.'

'Nothing.' The car had gone away, back to town with a policeman. The boys had left at last, in Pete's car with Aaron. They got through the roadblocks, that's all they'd say, and then Pete stopped at the turn off and Aaron sent them up the hill to Rika.

'Where have Pete and Aaron gone?' Martha asked.

'They drive towards the university.'

'How was Aaron?' The real question, from Rika.

'He was cross, like this,' Wilkie said. He pulled down his mouth and for a moment looked exactly like Aaron when the weight of what was coming bore down on him. 'Smoking plenty of cigarettes.'

Rika frowned. She'd taken to wearing her hair tied back. It gave her a severe, uncompromising look. *Grim* was Pete's word, and he was right; there'd been a change in her.

On the stands at the stadium, Laedi and the girls had watched the match with the Highlanders from the camp on the hill behind their house. Neighbours wouldn't have put up with their shacks and their gardens, their tramping to and fro, if it weren't for Laedi, and because of Laedi not so much as a lemon was taken from a tree, or an egg from a chicken coop. They got water and an electricity cable from her, and were fiercely loyal, but that afternoon at the stadium they surged off into the fight, leaving her alone with two small children in a turmoil of shouting people.

Laedi got the girls out by a side gate, where she ran into a priest from the mission. He was surrounded by sobbing teenage girls with torn clothes, their hair messed up in tufts. They'd been taunting the losers when they found themselves surrounded by angry Highland men. The priest had waded in to rescue them, and having hauled them out had no idea what to do with them. At the sight of Laedi, he crossed himself and handed them over. All around people were vomiting from the tear gas, men were being loaded into police vans; an old lady was sitting in the middle of the road, tears pouring down her face. Laedi got most of the girls onto a PMV, one of the last to take passengers, pulled the old lady to safety and bundled the rest into her car. By the time they reached Hohola they were no longer crying, though in the space of a few miles their ordeal had escalated: they would be 'dead finish' if it hadn't been for the priest and the spirit of Jesus. For the rest of the evening the story grew: the savagery of the Highlanders, the bravery of the priest, the power of holy Jesus.

Bili was scowling. A Highland girl with her chin in a stance worthy of her grandmother, she went up the back to guard her chickens.

In Laedi's kitchen, Rika was slumped on a chair. Sweat was pooling under her breasts, but all she felt was cold. A creeping edge of fear was upon her again. Fear for Aaron, fear for herself, and for the child who hadn't yet come. His clan-sisters might think the inability to summon up a child was hers, but she knew it was his. She'd consulted a Chinese herbalist in town; she took her temperature each morning, and knew she was ovulating.

'Do you think this is it?' she asked Laedi. 'That this time Derek will persuade him?'

'It was always going to happen,' Laedi said.

'It'll kill him.'

'No, it won't. You talk *gaiman*. He's virtually working there anyway. How often do we see him before midnight? It might be better if he gives up the university and isn't stretched between two.'

Rika put her hands on her ears and moaned. Bili came in and started moaning with her. Some kids were arguing out on the street, playing 'independence'. 'Is it true we'll get to live anywhere we want?' Bili asked.

Laedi sighed. 'Of course it's not,' she said, and put the radio on. Aro's calm voice was reassuring. He'd moved from tutoring to work at the new radio station. 'Return to your houses,' his voice said. 'Do not be afraid. The town is coming under control.'

Wilkie and the boys took advantage of the radio and the neighbours coming and going to escape down the hill to the roadblock that
had gone up at the turn-off. Every car was stopped and each driver
was told that Hohola was now strictly Papuan. And then anyone who
lived there was let through! Including the coastal New Guineans,
who made up a good proportion of Hohola's inhabitants: families
from above the line drawn on the map from west to east – New
Guinea above and Papua below.

Which, Wana pointed out, showed just how stupid the distinction was. It wasn't New Guineans whom the Papuans wanted to keep
out, it was those tough-minded fighters from the Highlands, who
seemed to think that because they worked on construction sites across
town, they had some stake and ownership in the place. In any case,
Wana said scornfully, almost as many Highlanders are Papuan as New
Guinean, for the line drawn by the Europeans ran plumb through the
middle of the Highland populations.

She'd been at the university all afternoon, reading in the library;
she was a tutor now and she didn't have time to waste on football. It'd
been a quiet afternoon with most students at the match, and when
she heard shouting outside, she thought it was just exuberance. When
she realised the antagonisms of the match were being played out on
the campus, she went and found Aaron in the shade by the door,
smoking with Sam.

'The teams weren't even made up of Papuans and New Guineans,'
Wana said, when she and Sam arrived on the platform. 'Only five
New Guineans were on their team, *and* they had a Chinese captain.
And half the Papuans were white.'

'Which goes to prove Aaron's point,' Sam said.

'What point?' Rika's voice was sharp.

'The usual,' Wana said. 'That Papua's an artificial idea. That you
can trace all this back to the colonial carve-up. He's been getting the
students to understand the consequences of going to independence
divided.'

*

'Don't be fooled,' Aaron had said. 'You are students well able to understand the history of colonialism and the complexity of this moment.
Our relationship with Australia is changing, not ending, and we must
understand why and how. If nothing else, understand this: Australia
will always play this place of ours to its advantage, which right now
is to recast its relationship with Asia.' That's what Aaron wanted
understood. Indonesia had claimed Dutch New Guinea, and already
there were tensions along the border. The new Labor government
in Australia needed a decolonised Papua New Guinea, safe within
its influence, for exactly the same reason that their conservative
predecessors needed it as a colonial territory: as a buffer between
their large white continent and Asia. 'Don't be diverted by the wrong
fight. Australia isn't interested in Papua versus New Guinea, and if
any of you think it'll take on Papua's separatist cause, you're fooled
already.'

'Where is he now?' Rika asked, though she knew the answer.

'With Somare and Derek,' Wana said. 'They want him in the
office. Seriously this time.'

'No,' Rika said.

'Yes,' Wana said. 'Rika. This time it's yes. This time he'll *want* to.
We all do, we can't not be part of what's coming.'

Over the radio Aro's calm voice repeated that there was no cause
for alarm, the police were on the streets, stay inside, order would soon
be restored.

Wana understood what Aaron was up against. A western education
had pulled them both out of tribe and place; they understood what
it meant to be able to make individual choices about their lives. Yet
there was an ancient seam inlaid in them like the drumbeat of a heart.
Wana knew that had Aaron been able to live by temperament alone,
he could have chosen a life not unlike the one Leonard had retreated
to in his Oxford college. In that life he might have taken Rika back
to Europe and lived modestly as a scholar. But his was not that life,
and no choice could make it his. It wasn't just an accident of birth;

it wasn't just obligation, or the vanity of knowing they stood on the brink of history; and it wasn't simply a residue of tribal consciousness. It was a nasty little hook, an existential paradox that was like a curse laid on them: the knowledge that they had choice made choosing impossible.

This is what Rika would never understand. She thought choice meant being able to select a life for themselves, no matter how often Wana told her that wishing and wanting would get her nowhere when it came to Aaron's future. She might as well rail against the weather.

Milton understood the peril and consequence of falling in love across the lines of race and culture. 'She's doomed,' he said gloomily to Laedi. Their years in Melbourne had overlapped, and a bond of some sort had been forged between them there, each privy to the humiliations of the other in that foreign city. He'd arrived back earlier in the year, blistered with anger and shame. Tessa had tired of him, as anyone could have told him she would.

On the evening of the riots, he turned up on Laedi's platform after dark. He was living out at the river, and had hitched a ride into town on a truck. He'd looked at the broken glass, disappointed there wasn't more. He was after material. 'Policemen everywhere,' he complained when he showed up in Hohola.

When he saw Rika staring out along the street into the dark, as if that would bring Aaron back where he belonged, he said, 'He won't choose her. Not if it comes down to her or Somare. He won't even choose himself.'

But Rika's will was strong, and so was her fear. She pulled a crate to the edge of the platform and sat there looking down the street, brooding, waiting for Aaron.

When Martha took her a bowl of rice and vegetables, Rika moved across on the crate. 'Stay with me,' she said, toying with the food. They sat in silence for a while, listening to the sound of the radio coming from the house and people in the street calling out, asking where Aaron was.

'Two years ago, when we were in Leiden, I had my IUD out,' Rika suddenly said. 'Two years, and nothing. Do you think it's a punishment for not telling Aaron about the abortion? Do you think I've put a curse on myself?'

'Of course not,' Martha said. 'You were young, hardly to blame.'

'I was fighting them off as they wheeled me in. They gave me an injection. I let them kill it.'

'Rika, at that stage it'd only have been cells.'

Rika winced. 'Don't try to reassure me. It doesn't help.'

To Martha her voice was a blade, and it cut.

It was two in the morning when Aaron returned. A car came slowly up the street with Wilkie running behind. 'Government car again,' he said, swinging himself up onto the platform as Aaron got out, spoke to the driver and walked wearily across the yard, shaking hands with the men who'd gathered out on the street. When he came into the light, Martha noticed that his skin had a greyish tinge, and she saw Rika's face darken.

'You're right,' he said to Pete as if continuing a conversation already started. 'I have to leave the university.' He sat down, took a beer from Sam, rolled a cigarette and turned to Rika. He put a hand on her arm, a gentle gesture. 'I'm taking Somare's offer,' he said.

Her eyes met his, and held them. She said nothing, but her eyes spoke for her. *Are we to give up a child for this?*

'I have to,' he said. 'There is no other choice.'

'No,' she said, though the force had gone out of her voice.

In the distance they could hear the rumble of army trucks heading out of town. 'Roadblocks,' Aaron said. 'They're putting them up for tomorrow. To keep people from coming into town.'

'*Papua besena*,' Milton sang in a mournful voice. 'Papuan separatism, the forgotten *hapkas* child.'

He'd returned from Melbourne declaring himself *hapkas* – adrift between cultures, an existential misfit. 'It's our fate,' he told Rika. '*Hapkas*, both of us.' He was reading Camus and drinking too much.

Rika was glad to have him back.

AARON FACED AN EDGY, UNPREDICTABLE ENERGY IN THE HEAT OF THE next afternoon when he stepped forward to speak. He'd been on the road since morning, marching with students in support of unity. Angry Papuans joined the march at Koki market, where there'd been more rioting that morning. Rika and Martha drove past overturned stalls and tear-gas canisters and police vans. Unlike the marches of five years before, there was no place for whites, so they left the car at the mission and went on to the parliament building with Laedi. There they stood on a slight rise at the back of the crowd looking down to the harbour with its still, gleaming water. Highlanders came sloping along, keeping their distance in a show of strength that had the police hauling them away if they raised an arm to throw the small hard stones they carried in their string bags. Dockworkers came swinging up the hill, chanting as they ran with high prancing steps.

Outside the House of Assembly, Aaron was standing with Derek and Somare's people. Behind them was a row of stern-faced men with arms crossed and legs apart. A scuffle was breaking out at the edge of the crowd when Aaron stubbed out his cigarette and took the megaphone. Above him, the sky was wide and open.

'Many of us have carried the white man's *kago*,' he said, 'and we know its weight on our backs. Many of us here have seen our fathers stand in line for the white *masta*. Many of us have brothers or uncles who worked in the houses and hotels of white men, forbidden to wear shirts as they served. We know the humiliations of our people, we know our own humiliations, and they must never be forgotten.'

The crowd chanted their agreement. *Never. Never forget.* Aaron lifted his arms, the very image of a preacher. Rika watched in love and dismay. He was good at this; they'd not let him go now.

'But this is not all that we have seen. We have seen the dignity of our elders in the villages. They have powers the white man knows nothing of.' There was another roar from the crowd, and again Aaron raised his hand. 'We have seen the elders step into our meeting places when there's a dispute among the clans. We've heard them call us to listen. First we talk, all of us together, and then, when it's time, we let their wisdom tell us when to negotiate, when to compensate, when to fight.'

A sleek black car came edging up the hill, pushing forward, forcing its way through the crowd. Fists banged on the bonnet, someone shouted and Aaron glanced behind him.

'In the past,' he said, 'we have marched to these buildings to demand the right to make our own laws. That is what the people of all the tribes of Papua and all the tribes of New Guinea asked for. Only this: our dignity as men.' He said it again, repeating his words for the Highlanders, who were jutting their beards at him. 'Now we march to these same buildings to say we stand together for the coming of wise government.' Again the magisterial pause. Again the raised hand, again the chanted response. Eddies of dissent were rumbling at the edge of the crowd.

The car came to a stop, with a policeman at the driver's window. One of the back doors opened but no one got out. Rika's camera stayed focused on Aaron.

'*Bung wantaim! Ahebou!* Aaron slid between languages. 'Let us join together for this great task. Some of you here today will occupy these offices in the future. What men will you be then? Others will stand as teachers before classrooms of our children. What men will you be? With which eyes will you see, with which ears will you hear, how many languages will you speak? When we take our children to the hospital, do we ask, is this doctor Papuan? Is this doctor New Guinea man? We ask, can this doctor make our child well? Can this teacher teach our children the knowledge they need for the new world that's coming?'

The crowd had grown and the mood was turning.

'We must hear each other. We must hear all the people of Papua.'

Papua, came the response. 'And all the people of New Guinea.' *New Guinea*. 'We must hear what the people are saying, those who are afraid of this new day coming. Why are they angry? Why are they afraid? What injustices have they seen? We must ask these questions before we can know what can be negotiated, what must be compensated, what must be restored. Our elders know this when they step into the meeting place to speak to the clans.'

Martha caught a glint of sunglasses, and saw that someone had got out of the car and was leaning against it. With a jolt she realised it was Jacob, and that he was watching her and Rika, unwatched himself. He inclined his head towards them. So he was back from Malaysia.

Rika looked towards Martha. She'd spotted him too. The last time either had seen him was at a party, which Martha didn't want to recall. It had been at Hohola, with the string band playing. Pete was away somewhere; she and Jacob were dancing. The band was playing and they were dancing, closer and closer, until they fell into the cushions on the veranda bed. Hand, mouth, breast, breath. Then Rika was standing over them. 'Go home, Jacob,' she'd said. 'You're drunk.'

Below them, standing with the megaphone in his hand, Aaron was still talking.

'We know how to talk. Papuans can hear New Guineans, Highlanders can sit down and talk with coastal people. We do not need to fight. We need to listen with our many ears. We need to see with our many eyes. We need to come together. *Bung wantaim! Ahebou!* All of us together.'

By the time Somare appeared, the crowd was ready for him.

As Somare took the megaphone, Martha caught another flash from Jacob's sunglasses. Silver rims. He opened a small, shiny case, took out a cigarette and bent to light it. His law firm must be doing well. There were rumours that he had Malaysian money behind him. When Somare finished speaking, the crowd, primed by Aaron, rearranged itself to march with him in a gesture of peace to Hanuabada, the harbour village. The canoes that had been out over the reef for safety were returning there.

'Let us greet them in peace,' Somare said.

Rika and Martha watched Jacob tack through the crowd. He shook a hand here, stopped for a word there, offered a cigarette, slapped a shoulder. He was making his way towards Aaron. They shook hands, a quick exchange, then Jacob greeted the men around him and continued his way through the crowd, moving slowly towards Rika and Martha.

'Rika,' he said with a short bow, which in another age and place might have been accompanied by a click of heels. 'You've been in the fjords,' he said. '*Afa* Noah told me.' But whatever it was that *afa* Noah had said was left to hang in the air. Rika lifted her camera. Click, click. 'Is that so?' she said as she moved away. In the photo Jacob is standing beside Martha, looking into the sun. His hair is billowing out around his large black glasses. Her hand is raised against the glare.

'That man of hers is a pretender,' Jacob said, when Rika had gone. 'Did you ever hear anyone in a village talk like that? His elegant words are the white man's words.'

'Jacob!'

'He's doing the white man's work, as we always have.' His smile was at odds with his words. 'They made this mess and we're left tidying it up. We worry and grow old, we sit up at night devising laws. They don't. While we imitate them governing ourselves the way they tell us to govern ourselves, they take the money and grow fat in their chairs.'

'You haven't softened your line with age.'

'I know too much,' he said.

'Doesn't working in the law put you on their side?'

'It gives me a way of fighting.'

'Fighting for what?' Martha said. 'You don't seem interested in politics.'

'I'm not. I'm in for the real game.'

'Which is?'

'Who mines this country for its minerals. Who takes its wealth.'

'Isn't that a government task?'

'That's what the white men want us to believe.' He laughed so jovially that she wasn't tempted to say more. 'It's good to see you, Martha,' he said, and there was something in his tone that made her blush. 'You're looking well on Hohola life. Come and visit me sometime.'

OUT AT THE RIVER, MILTON WAS LIVING IN A SHACK LEFT OVER FROM the gold miners. They hadn't grown rich, and Milton didn't expect to. Money gave him bad thoughts. Melbourne had taught him that having it could do your character no good, and his sojourn on the back streets of Port Moresby when he first returned taught him that not having it wrecked you fast – body and mind. So he took himself off, out of town, and lived in the shack near the river. It had a dirt floor and flaps for windows that could be propped open with a pole. He built himself a table, a bookcase, a small sleeping platform. There was the river to wash in, a tank of sorts with enough rainwater to boil up a kettle; the fire was outside, an old grill set across stones he'd hauled up from the river.

Rifle had told Milton about the shack. He was planting a garden out by the river, in some complicated arrangement with the people whose land it was. He'd rigged up an irrigation system of bamboo pipes and he needed someone to keep it running. All Milton had to do was make sure that the section at the river was in place to bring the water to the vegetable channels overnight. In return Rifle kept him supplied with betel nut and beer. All in all a satisfactory arrangement, and Milton only came into town when he was bored of himself, or when he ran out of kerosene for his lamp, or exercise books for his writing. He'd arrive in Hohola, dishevelled and filthy. Laedi would send him into the shower and Bili would sit on an upturned bucket on the other side of the plastic curtain, waiting for him to come out. She wanted Laedi to marry him. She had plans, and would offer up eggs from her chickens, drawings from school, anything that she thought might tempt him. She even found him a typewriter, which Rifle put on the back of his truck and took to the river.

So Milton set himself up on his table and taught himself to type. For a few weeks, maybe a month, he looked better each time he came into town. All his anger poured onto the page as he banged away at the keys: anger against Tessa for when she'd turned her back as if he'd never been there. He'd made a *scene*, that's what Tessa called it. Okay, let it be a scene. *Thump, thump* went the typewriter. Anger at Tessa. Anger at the playwright who arrived back in Melbourne from New York boasting about having met Allen Ginsberg, swaggering around with a joint in one hand and Tessa in the other. The arrogant shit. It turned out he was a cousin of Tessa's sister's godmother, *whatever that was*. These white people who wander the world peddling their belief in the artist freed from the primitive demands of kin and clan, they're as highly regulated and interconnected as any Papuan. It turns out to matter as much to them who their families are, and who they have engaged in obligation and the play of status. It's just not as obvious, and they don't admit it. You'd need to be an anthropologist to make sense of it. He'd make the obvious joke, but no one much found it funny, though at first when Tessa dropped him, people still called out to him in bars; that was something. But when he drank too much and said what he felt, and let the anthropology joke not be a joke, there was a turning-away. Not a fight, as there would have been in Hohola; a fight and still a place to sleep. In Melbourne there was nothing overt, just a change in tone and eyes pitying him, and then even that was gone. Who would know, who would *care*, that he came from a line of *samuna* men?

No one wanted his plays anymore. His poetry was returned with a note. A new government was in power; hadn't the prime minister himself renounced Australia's colonial past? Times were changing. 'Wake up, man,' he was told. 'Write something else.' He'd thought it was the plantation manager he hated, but now he knew it was Tessa and her oh-so-smart white theatre friends.

Okay, if that's what they wanted, he'd write something else. He'd write about them, write about Tessa. Ha!

The problem was that Milton wasn't a good hater, and hating made him sick. The words that he thumped out by day came back at night and gave him bad dreams.

When Bili joined him in hating Melbourne, he wouldn't have it. When she said it was too flat with too many houses and too many white people, he made her stop. Laedi reminded Bili that her father was white and her mother half-white, which made her three-quarters white, so she'd better get used to it. Bili scowled and said the Highland quarter was a very large quarter, so large it made up to a whole. She wasn't bloodless like white people, she could bleed. And right there at the table she picked up a knife and nicked the soft pad of her index finger. A bead of dark blood swelled and dropped onto the table. 'See,' she said. Daisy, with her sweet nature, shed a tear for her sister, and for the white people of Melbourne. Milton picked up Bili by the shoulders until her face was level with his, and shook her. 'You ever drop Highland blood again, girl, and I'll beat you. You hear. You've got good blood. All of it's good blood. You be proud, girl. You be proud.'

It was advice he could give Bili, but couldn't use for himself. He frowned and moaned until eventually, on the platform in Hohola, he admitted that the anger he pounded on to the page was turning back on him. Useless. It was all useless. He was a no-good writer. The novel was a no-good white-man form. Who, here, cared about white girls? And those fuckers down in Melbourne would read it like the perves they were. 'All it'll do is prove what they think – that we can't keep our eyes off their girls.'

'Might make you some money,' Rika said, and Milton scowled. He drank a pot of strong black coffee and sloped off down the street like a vagabond.

Back at the shack, Tessa went into the fire.

It was quiet out at the river, half an hour from town, on a track that wound up over a small ridge and down the other side into a shallow valley. The shack was near a bend where the river pooled out before continuing on in a channel between the rocks. Laedi took the girls there at the weekends. Laedi didn't swim in the pool of tea-stained water, with its grainy beach. She lay on the rocks and read. Milton sat beside her with his ukulele, watching the girls. He and Laedi didn't speak much; there was a quiet between them, as if they were part of the quietness that fell over the dry hills and the sandy soil. At that time of year, after the winds and before the rain, it was hot and still. The air smelled dusty, the trees rustled their papery leaves, cicadas kept up their shrill, and at dusk snakes slid into the water. Milton saw them when he set up Rifle's water-catching system.

Rika and Aaron came most weekends too. It was dusk when they'd arrive. Rika was right – Aaron's hours had increased with the move to Somare's office. Up early, home late. And still he'd want to go out to the river on a Saturday night. He'd swim across and dive with the current. He'd wash the dust of Hohola from his nose, smell the hills and the wood smoke from Milton's fire. He'd pick up the ukulele, feel young again.

Milton was out there, tending his vegetables and contemplating his characters – he hadn't found a replacement for Tessa, at least not one that took – when the leader of the Opposition, a staunch man in his forties, dropped dead on the floor of the House of Assembly. The first Milton knew of it was the next day, when Rifle's truck loomed over the ridge and down the track. He was shaking his head with the drama of it, and in among his rambling account of the wailing around the town, and the talk of magic at the market, he said that even *waitpela* friends had gone crazy with the disaster. Rika, who everyone thought had calmed down, was shouting and crying, saying next it would be Aaron. Just the same. One day he'd '*dai pinis*' there on the floor. Rifle shook his head and told Milton it was so maybe. Hadn't Simbaikan said Aaron wouldn't live long. 'Was she right?' Milton asked. 'Maybe. Strong spirit, that woman, she knows *plenty*.' So Milton came into town on the truck, prowled around testing the air for character and plot, and turned up at the platform in time for pumpkin curry and rice. And an egg just for him, from Bili.

Rika was down the road at her house, in bed. It was true, she'd taken this death as a warning. Simbaikan continued to spook her, and when she reassured Rika of her own strength, which would keep her alive a long time yet, it made everything worse; the reassurance she wanted wasn't about her, it was about Aaron.

Standing by Rika's bed with a glass of fresh ginger and lime, Laedi said, 'Get up, Rika. Where's your courage?'

Laedi's view, given on her platform when Milton arrived, was that a fear spirit had got into Rika with her mother's death, that was all. Bad fears do that, they come in under the skin when you're weak, or open, or too young, as she was, just a girl in a cold country with no sisters.

Wana said Rika was the *vegu*, a grasshopper creature with long empathetic feelers, and that was the reason for her fear. But Milton said no, Rika *imagined* what other people thought or felt; she imagined what she wanted them to feel, or would have felt if she were them, but her thinking was always tied to herself, and when she got it wrong, her imagination turned her mind to fear, because in fact she wasn't a *vegu*. She put her feelers out into the world, touched other people and then let her own heart beat out the message that came vibrating back to her.

'Go down and see her,' Laedi said to Milton. 'She might listen to you.' For he was the *vegu*. He had the capacity to get inside other people, not her. It was what made him an actor. He could shed his own skin and inhabit another. Which may be why it was to Milton, more than to anyone else, that Aaron turned. He was the only person who could arrive at the office without disturbing its taut surface. Aaron would give the thumbs up if he could get away, and Milton would go outside and chew betel while he waited. Then they would sit in the shade, and Aaron would breathe in, taking strength from their talk.

Rika was sitting at the table with Wilkie, eating toast, when Milton came reluctantly down the path.

'Will you take Aaron out to the river this weekend?' she said, putting on more toast and passing him the jam. 'He needs to get out of Hohola.'

Wilkie rolled his eyes and put his hands to his head in a gesture to Milton that said Rika had become deranged by this death.

'If he wants,' Milton said, shrinking himself down to an ear.

'He's always better for being out there.'

'It's not me. It's the river.'

There was a pause, then Rika said, 'Eremiah's back.'

Milton snapped back into his own shape. 'When?'

'Last week sometime,' Rika said. 'Milton, listen. He's got *worse*. He says Aaron's sold out – though it doesn't stop him drinking our beer. You'll see tonight. He'll be here for sure. In *Hohola*.' Milton took the sneer in her voice to be Eremiah's, not hers. *Hohola, where the black actors and stooges live.* 'You'd better watch out, Milton,' she said. 'You really are a black actor.'

'A black writer,' Milton said with a grin, taking another slice of toast. He'd caught a whiff of possibility; Eremiah had returned and a character was taking shape.

In Chicago, where Eremiah had studied for an MA on Martin Luther King, he'd roomed with a student descended from slaves. Unable to compete with his roommate's tales of lynchings and slavery, his own childhood in the village world of Bougainville took on a renewed resonance: the spreading breadfruit trees, the canoes pulled up on the shore, the songs stretching back through the generations. All the more so because this world – vivid in Eremiah's memory, and still the ground of daily life for his relatives in Bougainville – was threatened by a mine that was digging out the rich seam of copper lying beneath the fertile soil. Entire villages had been evicted by helmeted riot police and by the time Eremiah was back in Moresby, the top of an ancestral mountain had been sliced off for the open-cut mine, which was making a profit so large even he didn't anticipate its size.

Out at the river, Milton was at his desk. Baldwin Rufus, with a history very similar to Eremiah's, was coming into furious existence.

Unlike most of them who returned home with foreign degrees, Eremiah didn't go to Treasury or a university job; or to a job of any sort. He reappeared on the campus, refusing offers with a dismissive wave of the hand. At Hohola, the string band played outside Aaron and Rika's house, and Aaron welcomed him back as a brother. Rika counted the beers he drank as he raged against the mine, and Somare for allowing it, and – even that first night – against Aaron for working for him. At the university, she watched as he gathered students around him – in the canteen, at the arts centre, in the forum. His talk was all of the mine, joining the voices demanding that Somare renegotiate the terms of the agreement. Can we trust our government to stand against the Australians and the mine? Can we trust them to protect our way of life if they're willing to sell the minerals under our land? Eremiah had read the legislation that had been through the House of Assembly.

'Is this the way we want to go to independence?' he asked. 'We're tribal. Think what that means.' He too had the gift of oratory, a voice touched with music, and each week his retinue of students grew louder and bolder. 'Yes, there are wars. But within a tribe there's also cohesion, law, authority, consensus. You want a Pacific republic? Make it worth its name! Devise a new form of black government that builds on the tribe! Why do Canberra's bidding? We're warriors! That's what we are, and that's what we should remain. Warriors!' He threw back his shoulders. Eremiah the warrior! Eremiah, who never had a book out of his hand. Eremiah, whose scrawny arms wouldn't know what to do with a club if you put it in front of him.

'Why don't you get a job?' Rika said one afternoon when he was at the arts centre stirring up trouble. 'All you do is *criticise*. How about joining in the work?'

'I'm not working for Somare. I won't do trade with the profiteers.'

'Nor does Aaron, so lay off him.'

She made him look at the images her *Village Shots* students had taken of Aaron leaning against a wall at Somare's office, phone in one hand, cigarette in the other. The shadow that fell across his face accentuated the burden, the weight on his spirit.

'Look,' Rika said. 'Have a good look at him. He's a *friend*. Think about it.'

But Eremiah didn't need to think. The answer was easy. Aaron should leave Somare, take off his white mask and become a warrior.

Under the sagging roof of the platform at Hohola, with neighbours crowded in and kids playing football in the light that spilled into the yard, Eremiah accused Aaron. 'Coconut man' with a dark skin, but white inside. A coconut advisor doing the white man's bidding. 'You ask us to hand over our resources to foreign companies and call it *development*! You turn us into wage labourers for a meagre royalty, and that small insult of a reward goes to Port Moresby! Have you been to Bougainville? Have you *seen* the mine? Have you heard the weeping? Why not a federation of tribes? Build out from the village meeting ground. Let Bougainville make its own decisions. An autonomous province, the first in a new Melanesian federation. *Why not?*' His hair was up on end, ablaze with indignation.

'Because,' Aaron said, 'we *have* to travel as a viable government, and with unity.' Not only because Australia demanded it; the reasons were obvious, and numerous. The world was imperfect, it had been shaped by colonialism, the mine would bring in much needed revenue, and at that hour of the night Aaron didn't want to discuss it. He was exhausted. 'For a start,' he said, 'if we don't have foreign investment, we won't have an economy.'

'My point exactly,' Eremiah was out of his seat. 'You're letting in the thieves and the plunderers. Making them legitimate. Ha! We think we've got this great thing called a state, *democracy*, and in exchange we welcome them in – help yourselves, sirs, our minerals are yours. Ha! You want our forests? Our fish? Our women? Help yourselves!'

'We are a *dem-oc-racy*.' Milton trilled on his ukulele. He didn't object to what Eremiah said – the Pacific republic, the plunderers and thieves – he agreed with a lot of it. It was Eremiah's manner he hated, his superiority. Milton would be off at dawn, back to the typewriter. Back to Rufus Baldwin, who, in that first draft, might as well have been named Eremiah.

'You think we're handing ourselves over on a platter?' Aaron's voice was defensive. 'We're *negotiating*.'

'*Compromising*.' Eremiah's slightly nasal voice added to the sneer.

'What do you want us to be? Some kind of pariah state?'

'You want us to leave ourselves without protection?' Wana weighed in. 'Without an alliance? Outside the United Nations? Who's going to stop the plunderers then? Who's going to stand with us against anyone with the power and the money to land here and take what they want? Have you thought of that?'

It was a bad night. The atmosphere was thick and heavy. The argument ground on and on. Eremiah was out of his seat, walking back and forth like a mad preacher, the sweat gleaming on his face. Insects were flying into the lamp and dropping onto the table. Aaron was lighting one cigarette after another. Rika said something to him, a short, whispered exchange, and pushed back her chair.

'We're leaving,' she said, and they walked down to the yard, out of range of the lamp.

'Hey, brother,' Eremiah called after Aaron's retreating back. 'You Melanesian man or what? Don't follow your woman. Stay and fight. Where's your pride?'

Pride. There was a lot of it around. Prides that could splinter in unexpected and inconvenient ways. Black Pride. Papuan Pride. Pride of ego. Pride of tribe.

The role given to Aaron was to be the voice that could soothe these clashing prides. Wana called it the task of the turtle dove. Forget the bird of paradise, she said. It might be okay for a flag, but it was too showy and temperamental for the realities Somare had to work with. Useless when it came to the task of quelling the disruptive prides. 'Look at him!' Eremiah said, opening another beer. 'He's cowed!'

'Shut up, Eremiah,' Laedi said. 'Have you forgotten what it is to be a friend?'

*

That night, in their bed in Hohola, Aaron lay on his back, silenced by the weight of all that was asked of him, of them, of this new country. Rika, beside him, wept for the distance that was opening between them.

JIWU'S CURSE

 RIKA WAS TWENTY-SEVEN THAT YEAR, SEVEN YEARS
older than her mother had been when she was born.
The starvation of war hadn't stopped her mother
becoming pregnant, yet here was she, well fed on
coconut and fish, and still no sign of a child. Worse, the absence she
referred to only in the most private of conversations had become present
in the talk that moved between the women up and down the street.
Laedi had been asked at the trade stores, was it true that white women
could stop the sperm of men? Rika wept when she heard of it. Wasn't
every great narrative of love consummated by the conception of a child?
A child such as she, who redeemed her parents' wartime suffering. A
child who would claim a role in Aaron's village, an exchange between her
and the women, his clan-sisters, who regarded her as essentially different, the bearer of new powers, maybe, but a focus for disaffection when
the new ways ground against the old. As the years passed, their suspicion
grew. Making a baby was not a simple matter if a woman didn't know
how to open her womb, how to draw the spirit of the child into her.

'Surely,' Rika had said after their last visit to the fjords, 'by the
time we next go, it will be different.' It'd been a punishing visit, made

at new year, just the two of them. Maybe that was the mistake – there was nothing to deflect from the flatness of her stomach and the small-ness of her breasts. Aaron said she was a natural concern to them – 'give them time to get used to you' – but for Rika time was exactly the issue.

'Come with us,' she said to Martha as the next visit loomed.

'Why not,' Pete said. 'It'll do us good. Get you out of the library.'

He'd been there before as part of his research on exchange and the gift. Martha had never been. She didn't go into the villages, not to stay, not often.

'Please come,' Rika said to Martha. 'You could be my second eyes. Aaron thinks I exaggerate and the women aren't turning against me. But he's always with the men, and I'm alone when things happen.'

Rika was hard to refuse when she wanted something, so they went, the four of them, and Martha accepted the role that was cast for her.

It was a clear morning when they crossed the ranges, with the peaks rising to a high dome of sky. Below them, the forest canopy swelled with such voluptuousness Martha wouldn't have been surprised to see cherubs or ancestor figures resting there. Pete laughed at her, and so did Aaron. The only beings they saw were the young boys, who crowded around the plane when it came down at a mission strip to deliver mail and supplies, and then ran along the grass, chasing it as it took off again, up over the vast expanse of forest. Rika pushed her hair back from her face and frowned.

At Popondetta, out on the flat, they landed on the old military strip and came to stop at a small shed beside a road. An oil-palm worker who came from the fjords climbed in behind a clerk from a store in town, who was some kind of complicated relative of Aaron's. Names were offered with much laughing and hand-shaking. They were on their way home, like Aaron, for the *vasái,* the ritual feast of the clans. It was the first since a cyclone had ripped along their coastline the year before, wrecking gardens and flattening houses – a bad omen with self-government coming up so soon, which was why Derek let Aaron go. There were enough troublesome omens along the coast and he could do some useful work while he was over there, smoothing the political path, so Derek signed off on a week. A whole week! By the time the pilot closed the door of the Cessna and swung himself up into his seat, there was a festive mood inside the small cabin. 'All aboard?' he said. 'Let's go.' And off they went, back down the runway, taking off over the oil-palm plantations, skimming the coastal forests until the fjords came into view, punching out from the mountains, their steep sides a vivid green against the rich blue of the Solomon Sea.

Coming into the government strip, which sloped up from the water, the plane circled out, low over the reef, and seemed almost to float back in, scattering sea birds, touching lightly on the grass and rolling to a stop near trees at the edge of a small creek. The kiap, a balding Australian with large knees, was waiting for them.

'Sorry, folks,' he said. 'There's some delay. I had to send the dinghy up to Spear Point. There's a kid who needs to come into the hospital. Nasty accident.'

'That's okay,' Aaron said, shaking his hand. 'Gives us time to talk.'

'There's the house, if the ladies want,' the kiap said, extending an awkward hand to Rika and Martha. One of those whose wife gave up years ago, Martha supposed. 'And George came up from the school,' he was saying to Aaron. 'Says you know him. Asks if you can come and talk to the kids. You know. Seeing you were once there yourself. Motivate them. Pep talk sort of thing.'

The sun was dipping towards the west when at last they walked down the steep path from the government station to the fjord, which opened to the small harbour that eighty years before had drawn in the *Merrie England*, the governor's ship, on its exploratory journey along the coast. A dinghy was waiting at the end of the jetty, and while the *kago* was being loaded, Aaron looked across to the dense, vibrant green of the opposite peninsula and the outline of the mountains beyond. A thin column of smoke was rising from a village somewhere among the trees, and canoes were rippling the still water. The way he stood there, the relaxing of his shoulders and the tilt of his chin, gave a glimpse of its power for him; the redemptive power of place and home.

'See,' Rika said. 'It changes him.'

Inside the fjord, the air was velvety and the water a clear, dark green. When the dinghy came out into open sea, the air chilled and the water turned an inky indigo. Rika sat forward like a figurehead, looking east along the purple bulk of mountains set against the darkening sky. Aaron, beside the boatman at the tiller, called out to canoes making their way home into the fjords. He pointed to new gardens cleared from the wreckage of the cyclone, and to the bare grass along the ridge tops. 'That's where the cyclone hit,' he shouted over to Pete. 'Each time the wind comes, it sweeps more soil from the top.' The word for ridge in his language meant barren, without fruit.

By the time the dinghy rounded the last point and they heard the drums, there was a reddish glow to the west and enough light to catch the plumes of the headdresses of the men who danced in welcome. Women with densely tattooed faces kept time with the drums. Small children with soft, pale feathers in their hair ran to Aaron and led him across the dance ground as his own feet tapped out the rhythm of the drums. An old man stepped forward to greet him. His face was deeply lined, the creases of his chest hung like an ancient garment, but his back was straight and his dry white hair swelled from his head like a stationmaster's cap. He was wearing a soft loincloth and he held a tall staff in one hand. This was *afa* Noah, the last of Aaron's father's brothers, and he stepped forward to greet Aaron with an expression of such tender pride that Pete turned and touched Martha's arm. Aaron leaned towards the old man and took in the aroma of patrimony. All around, women and children were calling out, clapping their hands. *Whaa! Whaa!* Behind the houses, at the edge of the village, chickens flew to the top of the trees to roost, squawking as if they too rejoiced at Aaron's return.

The dancers came to a stop outside Noah's house, and the old man climbed onto the steps, raised his hands to speak. 'He welcomes us,' Rika said. 'Aaron, the hope of their clan. Aaron, who will lead us into the future.' Martha could tell by her voice that she'd heard it before and didn't entirely like it.

'Tomorrow,' Noah said. 'Tomorrow he will speak. Tonight we dance.'

There was another roar of rejoicing, and the drums began again, feet beating the ground. Young women brought out pineapples, and from behind the house a young man appeared with a Coleman lamp, which he carefully hung from the rafters.

'That's new,' Aaron said.

'Jacob bring it,' came the reply. And then a rush of language, and Rika translating, consulting a young woman who had taken her hand, standing close beside her. *Sister mine.*

'Jacob's been here talking to *afa* Noah,' she said. 'A big talk. He gave him this lamp. He's up at the top village, his village, he went up there this morning. Boxes of *kago* for the *vasái*. Outdoing Aaron, as usual.'

Aaron's boxes were laid out on the grass in front of the guesthouse, where they were to sleep, across the grass from *afa* Noah. Built up off the ground, with newly plaited walls and wide eaves, the house was decked with herbs and hibiscus flowers. They would sleep well there, on woven pandanus mats with the windows propped open to the saltwater breeze.

The next morning they woke to the noise of birds. Outside the window the sky was a soft orange, and when Martha came out onto the grass in the centre of the village, she found herself in a golden world.

'It's always like this early,' Rika said, coming down the steps, yawning. At the cookhouse there was a fire already, and she went over to the women, took a knife, squatted down and joined them peeling sweet potato for breakfast.

'Can I help?' Martha asked, but no, she was a visitor, there was to be no work for her. A young girl, no more than sixteen, took her hand.

'I show you the village,' she said. 'I am the sister of Wilkie, the boy at school in Port Moresby.'

'A good boy,' Martha said. 'He works hard.'

'I work hard,' she said. 'Hard, hard. In Moresby I will work very hard. You'll see.'

Her name was Angel, and she looked like an angel, with a halo of glossy curls. She'd finished the last year of school at the government station, just enough to show her what lay beyond, but not enough to equip her for the hopes that had come upon her: a brazen angel dreaming of escape from the village she was walking Martha through.

'When the boat comes to take you,' she said, 'you can take me, yes?'

'What about your mother?'

Her lovely face fell like a clown's.

'Come,' Martha said. 'You show me the village, and later we will talk to Aaron.'

'Okay,' she said, picking up her pace again. 'Okay, good.'

The village was set out on a grassy slope running back from the water, a low dip between the forested ridge of the peninsula and a small rise before the final drop to the sea. Houses were arranged in family groups, with leisurely paths joining them to the dance ground and meeting place. Open platforms faced towards the breeze and people called out as Martha and Angel passed. Fires were being lit, men were stretching, women brushing the paths. Coconut palms swayed above, trees laden with fruit grew behind the houses, hibiscus bloomed, and at the edge of the fjord where the canoes pulled up, children were pushing off for the long paddle to school. Two women were already making their way across the fjord.

'Those women,' Martha asked. 'They go where?'

'For water,' Angel said.

'I thought there was a spring in the village. Rika told me.'

'In the dry season, it goes. Now we cross the fjord, climb up the other side.'

'Big work,' Martha said. There were no tin roofs here, no tanks. This village was as Gauguin might have painted it; for the women crossing the fjord for water, a tin roof and a tank would have made a better paradise.

'See,' Angel said. 'You take me to Moresby. I live with Wilkie and Aaron. It is good.'

'And Rika,' Martha said.

'And Rika,' Angel echoed with a merry, tinkling laugh that left Martha uneasy. Hard to know. Hard to interpret.

Martha was alert for signs of animosity, looking for anything that might indicate suspicion among the women. She was looking that first morning, and there'd been nothing else to suggest unease. On the contrary, there was much taking of hands and touching of faces. Small children wrapped themselves around Rika's legs. Young girls took her hand and cooed. Out of the crowd, faces Martha had encountered in photographs became people as Rika named them: Naomi with the mop of black curls and her next baby at her breast, Ruth with serious eyes, and strong Dulcie, mother of Angel and Wilkie, whose shoulders wouldn't be out of place in a Sydney gym. These were the women married to Aaron's father's brothers' sons. Cousins, *tambu* sisters to him, the mothers of his nephews, the boys he put through school. At the clearing beside the cookhouse, they made room for Martha beside them, patting the mats where they sat, welcoming and friendly. Rika, in her trade-store dress, was scraping coconut into a bowl. 'Good walk?' she asked, the picture of ease.

Martha squatted down on the mat next to Dulcie. Without language, her attempts to take up a task amid the food preparation were reduced to gestures that made the women laugh and hide their faces.

'No work for you, you're a visitor,' Rika explained. 'They mean you're untrained.' She grinned, still scraping her coconut. Some flecks of its white flesh fell on the ground and without warning a woman slapped her. Martha gasped as Rika's head jerked with the force of it. Angel stood up. Everyone else fell silent.

The woman was old, with hardly a tooth.

One eye was milky, the colour of an oyster, the other was beady and sharp. She let out a stream of words and walked off behind the houses, taking Dulcie with her.

Rika's face was tight, closed. 'It's what always happens,' she said when Martha went to her, put an arm around her. 'Aaron says it's how the old women are, scolding the young ones when they come into the family. It's their job as mothers of the clan.' *Aya* Aita was his mother's sister.

'If he says you're coming into the family, isn't that something to hang on to?'

'You reckon I'm family?' Rika said, letting her anger show. 'You saw how Aita looked at me.'

Yes, Martha had seen the veins knot in Aita's ancient face, and the angry finger jabbing first at Rika and then towards the young women. What was a white woman doing here, taking Aaron while there were girls in the village with the right relationship of clan and tribe? That's how it seemed to Rika when *aya* Aita strode away, out of sight beyond the hibiscus. And it's how it seemed to Martha, though later she wasn't so sure. Had that really been her reaction, or one put there by Rika? Why wouldn't Aaron be right?

Late that afternoon, old Aita took Rika's hand and rubbed her arm. She was wearing the dress Rika had brought for her. Bright red with orange flowers. 'Good,' she said, indicating the crispness of the material. 'Nice.'

SINCE THE MISSIONS, THE *VASÁI* HAD TAKEN THE PRECAUTION OF beginning with a church service. An each-way bet, Aaron called it. So the next day everyone – including Pete, who never went willingly into a church, even one with woven walls and an altar decorated with clamshells – sat through the heat of noon listening to the visiting pastor, a stout Tongan, praise at great length the will of God and his miracles. A number of babies were baptised, maybe a dozen, and almost as many old people were splashed with water to mark the gift of entry into paradise. There was singing and vigorous praying until, at last, in the name of God, the pastor blessed the coming *vasái*, which He, the Lord, had created, along with everything else, including the clans gathered in this church and the host clans awaiting them in their own church across the water at the top of an adjacent peninsula.

Aaron's village on the tip of the fjord was in *vasái* partnership with the clans from the village across the way, high on the next peninsula. Jacob was already up there. It was his clan village, Aaron's dead mother's village, whose clans who would be giving the feast for this *vasái*, and therefore making the signal to commence. Aaron's clans, in the village at the edge of the fjord, would accept the invitation, dancing in exchange for the gifts and the feast that awaited them. Pete, equipped with his notebook and field recorder, had told Martha the essentials. On one side, prestige was gained by the greatness of the feast, greater than the feast they'd received at the last *vasái* when the roles were reversed; on the other side, prestige lay with the perfection of the dance, the beauty of the feathers and drums. That was the role, this time, of Aaron's clans. It might seem a simple exchange, Pete said, but it wasn't. Rivalries were bound into the *vasái*, which presented an opportunity to shame the partner clans, thereby gaining an advantage, even as alliance was secured.

At the church, the pastor blessed the *vasái*, the exchange itself, which kept the fjord clans strong.

Out in the air of the dance ground after the church service had finished, two long hours of it, the dancers prepared themselves for the formal invitation from across the fjord. Any time now, Aaron said, the host village would summon them across the water for the start of the *vasái*. A conch would sound, they'd cross the water and the dancers would lead the way up the peninsula to the feast. Young men adjusted their heavy headdresses, old men with bulging calves beat the drums; young girls adorned each other's tattooed faces with fresh dabs of paint. The atmosphere was festive, a hum of expectation and talk. Martha and Pete were standing in the shade of the church when *aya* Aita padded up on dusty feet, with square-faced Dulcie and a school-aged boy trailing reluctantly behind. She had a question for the white-man visitor from the university, and the boy was there to turn the talk from saltwater language to English.

Aya Aita wanted to know whether being baptised, which she wasn't, would mean her passage to paradise could be extended to include her sister, Aaron's mother, who, being dead, she hadn't seen for many years, and also her dead husband. Pete said he didn't know, but Aita clearly didn't believe him. Would she do better to remain unbaptised, a woman of the old ways, and join her sister with the ancestors? She accepted that God had created the ancestors. But if he had, then wouldn't the new knowledge, like the knowledge of the ancestors, also have been given by God, and therefore divided into the ownership of separate clans? People were crowding around, joining the debate with noisy interjections. Pete tried to turn matters back to the *vasái*. But Aita wasn't to be deflected. Determination was glinting in her one good eye; another grandson was sent to find Aaron.

She wasn't asking Pete *about* paradise – the pastor was adept at that. She was asking who *owned* this white-man knowledge, who had the right to it. Pete, a white man from the university, a friend of Aaron, would surely know something as basic as that. The danger she seemed to be getting at was that, with Aaron and Jacob gone to town, no one knew who had the right to the new knowledge and the new ways, which clans it rightfully belonged to. As *aya*, mother of the ground, was it not her task to hold the rightful ways in place? If paradise was the way of the future, as the pastor said, then why, all around, were there signs of trouble?

She set her one good eye on Pete and slapped at the boy turning the talk. 'You tell us not what?' the boy whispered, ashamed to be asking such questions of this white-man visitor, friend of Aaron.

Afterwards, Pete said it wasn't an unusual suspicion, he'd heard it many times, and if you think about it, why wouldn't we white people keep our knowledge secret or give it out to the wrong clans, if it brings us such wealth? But Martha didn't think it was wealth Aita was asking about, but babies. Hadn't she turned towards where the women were sitting? Hadn't she put her hands to her eye, made the shape of a camera? Wasn't that what she meant when she said the pathways were confused between the old ways and the new? How could a woman who looked at the world through a camera know what was needed?

Pete laughed. 'You've been spending too much time with Rika,' he said. 'Don't read the worst into it.' And maybe he was right, for when Aaron arrived with a cheerful slap to Pete's shoulder, *aya* Aita's face changed. She lifted Aaron's hand to her face as they spoke, their voices a melody moving back and forth, with a chorus of onlookers breaking in.

'How did you settle that?' Pete asked when *aya* Aita had padded off.

'I told her that at her age, born *before*, she'll go to the ancestors either way.'

'Ah. The light hand of compromise,' Pete said, though to Martha it seemed hardly an answer.

'Come,' Aaron said to Pete, '*afa* Noah is asking where you are.'

Martha watched them cross the dance ground, a tail of small boys exactly getting their two different walks, before she retreated to the shade, where the women had spread mats and were swatting at mosquitoes and gossiping. Rika was chewing betel with them, spitting red, as they watched the dancers warming up, circling around, still waiting for the conch shell to call them across the water. Dulcie was opening green coconuts with the practised tap of a bush-knife. Sunny Naomi, the baby still at her breast, was leaning towards Rika, wanting to look through the lens of the Leica. 'There,' she said. 'There,' directing the camera to the small girls with feathers in their hair, ready to dance with their sisters. 'Everyone dressed for dancing.'

'Come and sit with me,' Angel said to Martha. 'Be my friend. Angel friend.' She was sitting at the edge of the tree's shade, where sun came through the leaves and danced on her face. Unlike the other young women, Angel had only one delicate line of tattoo marks high across her cheekbones.

'Why just that one row?' Martha asked.

'Because,' she said, 'I am half saltwater girl, half future.'

Naomi gave a snort and laughed. 'She is afraid,' she said, closing her eyes against the memory. 'It takes a strong woman, plenty pain, the face tattoo.' Her skin, a soft brown, gleamed beneath the lines that curved with the contours of her face. 'Fjord woman,' she said.

There was a light breeze coming from the water, and after a while Martha lay back on the mat. Up in the trees were rustling sounds; she couldn't distinguish what they were, though she knew that to Naomi, sitting next to her, each murmur would have a source, and each tree a history.

Could Rika ever be part of this place? Would her child be, if it lived in Hohola and not here? What life would the child choose? These weren't questions Martha could put to Rika. Even thinking them felt close to betrayal.

'Look,' Naomi said, standing up. 'Trouble, it comes.'

The carnival atmosphere had evaporated. Young men with painted faces and fresh herbs in their armbands had stopped dancing. Girls entering the dance for the first time retreated to their sisters. The signal to begin the *vasái* that had been expected at the close of the church service – Aaron had been sure of it in the morning – had not come. No conch had sounded in invitation.

Across the grass, in the shade of Noah's house, the elders of the chiefly clan leaned forwards.

'Pete will like this,' Rika said, looking across to him hovering on the edge of their deliberations with his notebook. 'They're figuring out how to placate the younger brother clans, without upsetting the *vasái*. I told Aaron that Jacob would try something. He'll be behind this delay, I'm sure of it.' She gestured inland, across the fjord to the adjacent peninsula, from which the host clans still hadn't signalled for the feast to begin. 'So much for alliance!' she said. 'It's all rivalry, and strategy. Look at them!'

Pete had drawn Martha a diagram before they left Moresby. Two pairs of reciprocal arrows pointed in two directions: one between the chiefly clans, who maintain alliances in the broader politics of the fjords; the other between chiefly clans and the younger brother clans with whom they share gardens and resources and the daily fare of village life. These clans might not be chiefly, may even be regarded as lesser, but they were powerful in their own realms, for they owned the knowledge that governed such essentials as the fertility of gardens and the availability of fish. And sorcery. The problem with them, as Martha could see from the stamping and the shouting, was that they were prone to be impulsive, rushing into conflict, if not constrained by the elders. From her vantage point under the mango tree, listening to Naomi's explanation as the mood darkened, it seemed to Martha that the aim of the *vasái* was as much to disturb Pete's neat arrows as to preserve their reciprocal neatness. Gift and enmity, Pete called his research.

Out on the dance ground, young men had hung up their head-dresses and were hollering. One line of dancers marched away, saying they'd not go when the invitation came, so great was the insult. Others, shouting in protest, walked over to the platform where the heads of the elders had drawn closer. Under their tree, the women were making soft whistling sounds. The children were quiet, their large eyes following the flurries of anger.

'What happens now?' Martha whispered to Naomi.

'The *kotúfu* will know,' she said. It was in their nature to be wise. They listened, they negotiated, they had the gift of talk. Their words were their wisdom, and their wisdom held the clans together. That's how she put it. The *kotúfu* made the path, the road, to success and riches.

Aaron was from a *kotúfu* clan.

'And Jacob?' Martha asked Naomi, 'Is he from a younger brother clan?'

It was Rika who replied, 'Yes, of course he is,' as if Martha should have known something so obvious. Angel turned up her pretty nose. She was a *kotúfu* girl, she said, reeling off the names that took her to Aaron and the elders deliberating on the platform, and before them all the way to the ancestor who built this village when his father's land was taken by the first kiap.

The young man who'd been sent across the fjord in a canoe came back with nothing. No message, no clue. Aaron climbed down from the platform to speak to the dancers, who were banging their drums with a menacing rhythm. 'We wait more,' Naomi said.

When eventually the conch sounded, daylight was vanishing and the chickens were flying up into the trees. Even Martha could fathom that if the old people and the children and the elders were to cross the fjord before the dancers, the drama of their arrival would be lost in the falling dark. Their splendour would go unseen. To accept an invitation so late in the day, and after such humiliation, would be to accept the insult – even if the dancers who'd stalked off could be persuaded to stalk back.

'And if we don't go at all?' Martha asked Naomi.

'*Nogat!*' That would be tantamount to war.

'Aaron will find the way,' Dulcie said.

'Not Aaron,' Rika said. 'He comes here for a rest. You know. You know how he gets easy here, gets well again.'

Earlier Martha had heard her telling Dulcie of the hours Aaron worked, how tired he got, *too tired*, and though Martha put a warning hand on her arm, she said it again, *too tired*, wanting Dulcie to understand that she meant too tired to lie with her and make a baby.

Dulcie turned her head away towards another sister-in-law. A glance passed between them, an intimation of the countercurrents running somewhere out of sight.

'Aaron isn't an elder,' Martha said to Naomi. 'Why must he find the way?'

'Aaron goes to Moresby and makes government,' Angel answered. 'Soon I will come,' and she was off again on how hard she'd work and how much she'd see. Dulcie hushed her with a slap. 'Listen, quiet.'

Noah was coming down the steps from his platform to speak. His pig-tusk necklace was in place, his wrinkled buttocks folding like fabric beneath his loincloth.

'He wants us to go,' Naomi said. 'The younger brothers, they say no.'

Noah returned to the platform and the heads of the elders moved forward. Outside, dancers continued to prance and shout, raising their fists and pulling the herbs from their armbands. Another pause, another deliberation. Then Aaron came down from the platform to speak. The crowd quietened; Aaron's voice rose above them. There were interjections and shufflings, but the anger diminished like a sigh as tension released, and though Martha couldn't understand the words, she saw their effect. He'd turned the mood. He'd found the solution.

A cheer went up and there was much shaking of hands.

'We go at dawn,' Naomi said. 'Good true.' Across the water food would be waiting, and it would go to waste. 'We arrive in the morning and they must cook again. To welcome us.' She laughed. 'You see,' she said. 'Aaron, he *knows*.'

In the dark, still hour before the sun rose, those who weren't to dance crossed the fjord in silence. On the other side, they stood grouped together, and even the smallest child made no sound until the first rays of the sun lit the tips of the trees. Then the dancers crossed on their canoes, plumed and adorned, chanting with the ferocity of warriors. They cut through the dark, glassy water with a wake of silver. The peninsula was a dark bulk; at its tip were palms silhouetted against a pale pink sky.

Ashore, the dancers led the way, leaping and drumming up the slope to where the finger of the peninsula joined the hand. There, at the top, looking out over the fjords on either side – waterfalls, a tumble of green – was the village where Aaron's mother had been born, and where Jacob's clans had their land. For the length of the climb there had been hazards; Naomi pointed them out as Rika and Martha brought up the rear – damp patches of soil, potent herbs sprinkled across the path, bent twigs in the grass at the edge of the path – and yet none of the dancers lost their concentration or footing, and the young women and girls who danced behind followed in unerring step. Aaron's clans went up that ridge like a travelling carnival. It was a triumph; a restoration of pride.

The hosts, shamed in their turn, could do nothing else but open the village and welcome the dancers in, past houses set out under the trees, clamshells marking the paths between them, and tall flowers, yellow and orange, around the perimeter of the dance ground.

The elders came forward in welcome, and behind them was Jacob.

'Smart move,' he said to Aaron.

'What did you expect?' Aaron replied.

ANGEL HEARD THE DINGHY BEFORE IT ROUNDED THE HEADLAND. It was two days later and they were idling in the village, replete from feasting. Rika followed the direction of her eyes as a small smudge came into view, its noise bringing people from their houses to stand under the shade trees along the water's edge. The dinghy crossed the fjord, swung round and cut its engine to drift neatly against the rocks. The clerk from the government station landed cleanly on the bank and handed Rika a telegram. It was addressed to Aaron.

'Kiap says you can stay at the station tonight,' he said in a loud voice, as if memorising the message. He was wearing shorts and long beige socks of the sort colonial bureaucrats in Moresby once wore. Chest out, feet planted square, he announced that there was a message from the government, very important, and Mister Aaron must go back to Moresby. 'The chief minister's office will radio at six,' he added, his voice modulated for Rika. 'A plane will come tomorrow morning early. You go to Popondetta, wait for the Moresby plane.'

'We have another three days,' Rika said.

'Tomorrow,' Angel was on her feet as if a sprint might be required. 'I can come tomorrow.'

Aaron had gone to the gardens with *afa* Noah and his father's brothers' sons to see the land they were clearing for him. They'd found old ancestor stones there and the blade of an axe fashioned by ancient hands. They were a message from the ancestors, an invitation to garden this land, they said – a doubtful story to Aaron's mind, a convenient discovery to reinforce his obligations to the village and counterbalance the gardens given to Jacob on the rival peninsula, where he was trying out vanilla crops. So Aaron was an hour's walk away, sniffing the wind of another politics, when he heard the dinghy's motor.

Pete, still in the host village up where the *vasái* had been, didn't hear the dinghy at all.

Rika opened the envelope. 'Return immediately. Arrangements made. Bougainville talks tomorrow 3 pm.' It was signed 'Derek'.

'Tomorrow,' she said. 'He has to go back tomorrow.'

That's when Martha saw dissent. Faces that had been open to Rika minutes before snapped closed. Naomi stared at the ground. A wail of complaint – or grief, perhaps – rose from *aya* Aita. Dulcie walked Angel towards the cookhouse, and it was clear from the way she handled her that she was angry. The women were talking so fast Rika couldn't catch what anyone was saying. It's what they did when they didn't want her to follow.

'I shouldn't have opened it,' Rika said. 'They think I wrote the words. Willed him away.'

For two days at the *vasái*, up in the high village, Martha had thought her doubts were misplaced. With the dancing and the feasting, the competing speeches and gifts, Rika had faded to the edge of proceedings. She and Martha talked more there than was possible in Aaron's village; Rika relaxed, let her fears subside. She went with Aaron into the forest at dawn to see the birds. Naomi took her to the spring deep in the forest, where the spirits of babies gather, and afterwards Martha lay with them in Naomi's brother's garden house, talking and sucking sugarcane. At the end of the *vasái*, Aaron took the camera from her so he could put her in the same frame as Ruth and Naomi, the kids piled in around them. *Aya* Aita posed beside her with a grimace that might have been a smile.

And now heads were turned, eyes hard, reminding Rika of who she was – an outsider; worse, because she had worked her way into Aaron and weakened his links with them. Why would she not be the cause of the telegram that had come to draw him away into a vanishing that with every season took him further from the daily reality of garden and reef and moon?

'My name is Dawson.' The clerk was standing next to Rika.

'Rika,' she said, putting out her hand. 'And Martha.' She, too, shook his hand. Then, looking towards the women, Rika asked, 'What are they saying?'

'The family, they are very sad.'

'They think it's my fault.'

He was apologetic. 'They're village people. No education. They think bad spirit has come. I tell them it is the government.'

Through the hibiscus clumps at the edge of the clearing beside the cookhouse, old Aita was rocking on her haunches. The women had retreated there, not working, or chewing betel in the shade, but moving around, talking in querulous voices. Naomi kept her face turned from Rika. Only hours before Rika had been with them, gossiping about the *vasái*, laughing at the flirtations that had rippled along the dance line, speculating on marriages and adulteries. Once again, she'd let herself touch that tender place of hope, and now this.

'You okay,' Dawson said to Rika. It was neither statement nor question. He was looking out to the reef. A few clouds were blowing in from the west.

'You fish?' she asked.

'I'm a land man.' He shook his head. 'This reef is dangerous.'

'Yes?' Rika said. 'Men go out on canoes every day. Small boys dive. Girls. Everyone. They seem okay.'

'They can die,' Dawson said. 'They come into the aid post. They tread on a stonefish. They catch a snake in the net.' He looked gloomy.

Martha had been out that morning with Jacob at first light, when the water was still and the wide sky opening like a steadying hand. He'd come down at dusk to sleep in Noah's house, ready for the plane that was due by mid-morning. With Pete staying up above with the *vasái* elders for another week of research, Martha had slept alone and woke to the first call of birds. She pushed open the window as Jacob emerged from Noah's house.

'Do you want to come?' he called as she came down the steps. He was walking across the grass towards the water. 'I'm taking a canoe out. A swim before I leave.'

'Sure,' she said.

The tide was high and the canoe slid out over the rocks.

Everything was still, no breeze to disturb the surface of the ocean. Shafts of golden sun lit rock that shone through the trees. For the rest, the land loomed dark and impenetrable, still in the shadow of sleep. Out on the horizon, a large island rose like another mythic land, freed from the clouds and mists that concealed it during the day. *Swoosh* went the paddle as Jacob dipped it first this side, then that, *swoosh* as they cut through the still water, along the edge of the peninsula to its tip, where three rocks jutted into the sea like giant stepping stones. 'That's Port Moresby,' he said, pointing to the first. The next was Sydney, and the furthest Australia. 'When Aaron and I were back from school, we swam out here and climbed up onto Australia and looked out.' He pointed straight ahead, north, towards the equator. 'Wrong direction, but that's where Australia was for us, and the world, stretching from one place of plenty to another. We were headed there.' He laughed. 'The little kids used to worry whether the ancestors would keep the canoe in a straight line and stop it from vanishing into some underneath place.'

'And you? Did you worry? Or Aaron?'

Again he laughed. 'We said we'd be on a boat, a ship like the ones that passed way out on the horizon. It never occurred to us that *they* could go down.'

This time it was Martha who laughed and, lulled by the soft morning air, she asked what his plans were for the vanilla they were planting up in his village. 'Are you going to have plantations up there?' She even told him, so lulled was she, so bewitched by the light, that there were rumblings of anxiety down here in Aaron's village. She said she'd picked it up from the women, they talked a lot of the trouble it caused with the men, this fear that on top they'd grow rich while down here on the edge of the fjord, they'd be left behind, subservient and shamed.

'Is that what they're saying?' The silky edge to his voice had gone. 'I've talked to Noah over and again,' he said. 'He doesn't believe me. He's stuck in the old ways and doesn't trust me unless I say exactly the same as Aaron. It's like a test. Every time.'

'Aaron doesn't want the balance of power tipped.'

'He's going to have to let them come into the modern world. Does he think he can keep them in some sort of ancestor museum?'

'Of course not. But if you bring lamps and radios and he doesn't, it stirs things up. They want a dinghy. He can't afford that.'

'That's why they should grow vanilla.' His voice was silken again. He looked at Martha and smiled. 'It's compact. It's high yield, they can grow it in the gardens. It grows well here.' And then, a note of sadness, everything amplified out there on the water, he said, more to himself than to her, 'Does Aaron think I *want* trouble down here?'

'I'm sorry,' Martha said. 'I spoke out of turn.'

'*Maski.*' Never mind. But he did mind. Martha saw it on his face; she saw it in the hunch of his shoulders, the darkening of his eyes.

They'd turned into the next fjord, no longer gliding towards the rising sun, instead facing the cliffs. They passed a small waterfall with a garden above it, gliding on until Jacob brought the canoe in under the cliff, where a high ledge jutted out above and vines hung down like a veil.

'Shall we swim?' he said, throwing a rope to a low branch of a tree. He let himself over the edge of the canoe, lithe, practised, the water barely making a splash. Martha plopped over after him.

Beneath the line of the water, the reef curved out in a series of ledges dropping deep below them. Jacob dived down, scattering small fish that darted out of his way and reassembled in their coloured squadrons to continue along the reef. On the surface, Martha held her breath, face in the water, watching as he swam along the edge of the reef, fluid as a sea creature. He picked up a brilliant blue starfish and rose up to let her touch its rough, rubbery arms. He grinned, pushed his hair away from his face, breathed deep and dived down again, returning the creature to its ledge. She knew that he knew how attractive she found him, and when he broke through the surface, she turned from him. She wouldn't give him the satisfaction of acknowledging it.

The golden light had gone. A canoe full of small children on their way to school paddled up; they were standing, ready to come in and swim with Jacob. 'School,' he said, in a voice that might have been Aaron's. 'You have much to learn. You go to school now,' and they paddled slowly away, into the sun, a silhouette of reluctance.

'We must go too,' Jacob said, heaving himself up into the canoe and leaning over to help Martha. He grasped her under the arm, and hauled her in. 'The dinghy's coming at eight.'

Martha sat at the front, looking resolutely forward, and by the time they rounded the tip of the finger and turned towards the village, the day had arrived, the land had regained its texture, smoke was rising from the cookhouse fires. A canoe, probably Naomi's, was crossing the fjord to collect water. Another canoe was rocking over the reef.

'Aaron,' Jacob said.

'How do you know?'

'Who else would be out swimming at this hour?' He screwed up his eyes, looking into the bright glare of water until he found them, two heads, all that showed of them, and slid the canoe alongside.

'You swim what?' he called. 'You tourist, eh?' And then to Rika, 'You watch him well. No good he drowns.' Martha saw his words register on her face. 'That'd finish you with the village.' He laughed, but there was nothing merry about it, and they pulled away, gliding on towards the village.

'Why did you say that to her?'

'She needs to watch out. There's talk of sorcery.'

'Don't put it in her head. She's nervy enough.' He was playing into her fear, *flirting* with it.

'What I don't understand,' Martha said as he brought the canoe into the rocks at the edge of the village, 'is what it is with you and Rika. I don't know if you love her or hate her. Nothing you do makes sense when it comes to her.'

'Ah, Martha,' he said, 'you read too many books.' With that he walked up the grass to Noah's house, and soon after she heard the engine of the dinghy coming from the station to collect him for the plane.

Now she and Rika were on that same stretch of grass, forlorn and alone with Dawson, the clerk, waiting for Aaron to come down from the gardens. The breeze had come up, ruffling the water. A small dark cloud was hanging above them, and though the sun was still out, it had turned the water a glittery mauve. It was hot and humid. Rika's face shone with sweat and distress. She looked wretched. Over at the cookhouse the women kept their backs turned. Only Naomi crossed the grass. 'Do not be afraid,' she said, and Rika's banked tears spilled over.

'It was not me,' she said. 'I do not want him to go. True. It is the government. Always the *gavman*.'

Naomi looked towards the women, hesitated, then gestured for her to accompany her to the cookhouse. They were boiling water for tea. Rika shook her head, refused.

'We go,' Dawson said, meaning over to the women, who had turned and were watching. 'For you, they make tea.'

Again Rika shook her head.

'I think we should,' Martha said. She could see from the way Naomi looked at Rika that it was an offer, a hand stretched back towards her. 'We should go,' Martha said again.

Rika swung round. 'Stay out of it,' she snapped.

A pulse in Martha's chest played an angry riff of fear.

The breeze was becoming a wind. Bright drops of rain fell from the small dark cloud. Birds vanished into the trees. They stood there, Naomi with them, for the minutes that passed, each as long as an hour, before Aaron and the men came running into the village. The boatman looked across the fjord to choppy water. 'Time we must go.'

The last sound from the village as the dinghy rounded the point was of women keening, calling Aaron's name. 'Son of ours. Brother. Come back. Return to us. Oh, misfortune.'

THE VERANDA OF THE KIAP'S HOUSE LOOKED OUT OVER THE FJORD to mountains that stretched, fold upon fold, to the south-east. It was sunset, six o'clock, and he was pouring gin and tonics. Martha and Rika were sitting in wicker chairs; they could have been colonial travellers from Martha's research.

'Cheers,' the kiap said, sinking himself into the chair beside Rika. He was dressed like Dawson, in long white socks and buff shorts. 'Used to be a good place, here, but even this is frowned on now.' He lifted his glass. 'The planter's drink.' His foot prodded at the half wall of woven pandanus. 'There won't be any of this left in twenty years.'

Rika made a noncommittal sound. Her lips were pursed, enough to register her mood. Aaron was in the office with Dawson on the radio telephone to Derek.

'How are you getting on in the village?' the kiap asked her.

'Okay,' she said. Her voice was flat, resistant.

'It's beautiful there.' Martha filled the gap.

'Yes, they're very picturesque, the villages. All those palm trees and the reef. We get young Australians wanting to dive here, and we try to keep them on the station. We've got a dormitory.' He waved his hand behind him. 'But they want to stay in the villages. It's usually a disaster.'

'Maybe because they're not invited,' Rika said.

'The villagers are on the make, looking for any chance. You should be careful, young lady, they'll be wanting a lot from you. They see us as cash cows.'

Martha blushed.

'I'm jaundiced,' the kiap said, getting up. 'Another?' Rika shook her head. 'Oh, they can be charming too, the Papuans.' A lot of gin

219

went into his glass, a splash of tonic. 'I've friends here I'll miss. But I've seen a lot of people hurt. Young people. Romantic people. They go to the villages and expect a paradise.' He paused. 'Has Aaron got gardens down there?'

'They're clearing one for him.' Rika said, and at that moment Aaron appeared with Dawson.

'G and T?' the kiap asked Aaron. 'A beer for you, Dawson, I suppose.' At least he gives him a drink, Martha thought, softening to him by just a degree, then rebuking herself; why should he be praised for a common civility?

When they were alone later that night, on the walkway to the rooms where they were to sleep, Rika said to Aaron that the sooner they got the likes of him out of the place, the better, and he replied that there weren't many of them left, the old-style kiaps, and they had their uses. Somare didn't want them back in another guise. 'At least if they're working for us, we know where they are.'

At dinner Aaron shut down any discussion about the demands, orchestrated by Eremiah, for Bougainville's provincial autonomy and the immediate resignation of its members in the House of Assembly unless the contract with the mine was renegotiated. When the kiap said they should let the place go – he'd been there, those black *munkas* were a stubborn lot – Aaron had come close to a rebuke.

'You're still working for the government, Dick,' he said. 'It doesn't help if our own people speak against unity.'

'It's only us here. We can talk it as it is.'

Aaron gestured to the open door, where *haus bois* came and went with trays, past a line of women sitting in the corridor.

'You know the last time your skin-brother Jacob was here, he had that Malaysian bloke with him?' the kiap said. 'Looking at the timber. That'll put money into the village.'

'There are regulations,' Aaron said, his tone even and neutral. 'It'll need thought.'

'No thought's going to be necessary if there are dollars,' the kiap said. Outside, the sky had darkened over the fjords and the forests. 'It'll be a job getting into the mountains, but Lim reckoned they won't need to if they log in from further down Collingwood Bay. The reef's a problem up here, coming in so close; they won't get barges in this far up unless they blast the reef, and that'd be a problem for the cray fishing.'

'Is Lim interested in cray?' Rika asked.

'He's got boats down at Milne Bay.'

Aaron was very silent. And then, in a mild voice, he asked the kiap if he knew the story of Jiwu.

'Who?'

'Jiwu.'

'Never heard of him.'

'Haven't you read Monckton's account of setting up the station here?'

'Can't say that I have,' said the kiap.

'Jiwu was a clan leader when Monckton arrived in the 1890s. But he hadn't been when the *Merrie England* went past on a reconnoitre a few years earlier. When the governor had staked out land for the station, he'd found the fjord clans fragmented and demoralised. They'd been scattered by raiding tribes from the west, and their villages destroyed. The people were suspicious and surly.'

'That'd be right,' the kiap said.

'The governor didn't meet this man, whom he called Giwi,' Aaron continued. He heard nothing of him. Jiwu's village was inland and he'd watched the raids from the ridge. When he saw the government boat, he realised several things. First, that the warfare with the raiders had to be settled before the white man arrived. Second, that the large canoes that could bring the sea-raiders round the coast in any weather were slow and clumsy when manoeuvring close to land. And third, that the enemy's war-spears were made of hardwood – heavy, capable of inflicting serious damage, but their range was short.

'So Jiwu devised a plan. He built a sham village low at the tip of a headland. And tucked in along the edge of the fjord, he hid the small canoes our people use for reef fishing. As you know, they can't go far out to sea, but inshore they are fast and manoeuvrable. He hid there with his warriors, and waited, their spears tipped with bush-poison.'

'Clever,' said the kiap.

'When the raiders came and saw the village, their leaders called out to the cowards who'd left their women undefended, and drove their canoes onto the sand. They charged the houses and found them empty, just shells and pretence. Shouting and angry, they pushed off into the water again. That's when the hidden canoes appeared, easily outrunning them. Jiwu's men kept the raiders away from the shore and threw their own poisoned spears from beyond the range of the raiders' reach.

'Only a few of the enemy made it back up the coast and they never came near here again. They were sometimes seen far out on the horizon but that's all. By the time Monckton arrived, the land here was secured.'

'Good story!' said the kiap, opening more beer, his expression jovial. 'The only one I know is that a man from one of these villages went up to the top of the mountain behind here just before the *Merrie England* came along the coast. On the way up he saw a snake that told him the ancestors were coming back in a new form, and when the people saw them they were to give them houses and be sure not to kill them. That's what set Monckton up. They thought he was an ancestor.'

Aaron didn't respond. It was a common story that could be heard from old-timers anywhere along the coast - which didn't make it true. He refused the offer of another drink, lit a cigarette and continued in the same level voice. 'When the *Merrie England* came back for the second time, putting Monckton and his supplies ashore, Jiwu was on the headland to greet him. Monckton recognised at once that he was a powerful warrior, and that something had changed. Standing with him were his seven sons. He was living here, right here where the station is. It was his mother's brothers' land. Jiwu invited Monckton to sleep in the house he'd built here, and showed him where to put his canvas bed. Just as he was falling asleep, Jiwu told him he was resting on the exact spot where he'd kept the dead body of the raiding chief.'

'Ah,' the kiap said. Then he rallied. 'Monckton got the land off the old bugger though, didn't he?'

'For a few trinkets, yes, and with a deceit Jiwu never forgave. The land the governor had chosen – and paid for – was further round the point. Monckton built right here, over Jiwu's house.'

'What did Jiwu do?' This was from Rika.

'Nothing this time. He knew he couldn't win head-on. So he watched and waited. Let Monckton think he was a friend. Got him to settle scores with the Doriri, their inland enemy.'

'A tactician,' Rika said. 'Like Somare.'

'And all the time he turned his mind with the ghost thought that when Monckton returned to his own place, he'd find it barren.'

'What happened to him?' the kiap asked.

'He left in disgrace when Murray became governor. Too many unexplained shootings. He went back to New Zealand and married.'

'And?' Rika asked.

'There was no child. He died soon after.'

'And the curse?' the kiap asked.

'It's still here, on this land that was taken from Jiwu,' Aaron said. 'If you believe these things.'

Which, of course, Rika did.

THE DECISIVE
MOMENT

 LEONARD ARRIVED WITH HIS FILM JUST AS THE RAIN began. It sent everyone running from building to building; dogs cowered under houses and trees bowed from the weight of the water that poured and slashed. Leaks sprang from the roof of Laedi's platform; his visit was accompanied by the drip of rain into buckets.

He had been at a conference in Melbourne – ethnographic film, very specialised – where *The Mountain* had been screened. Five years in the making, and for three of them it had looked as if there'd be no film. Yet now, here it was, and him, in their hemisphere. He flew up to Moresby; he couldn't not, though it was a hard return to make, and he kept it short.

The public showing of *The Mountain* was on his second evening in town. The university theatre was packed. There were people on the steps, standing at the back, crushed in the doorways. Over the years Leonard had grown into a figure of legend, the white man who'd lived on the mountain with a camera, who believed in the purity of observation, and had lost his wife to Aaron. That in itself would have been enough to fill the theatre, even if word hadn't flashed around that the film, which had been shown at a seminar that morning, was a knockout. The anticipation was high, even before Leonard arrived, and the higher it got, the worse Rika felt. In the week before he came she was sick to the gut at the prospect of watching it, and watching it in the eye of attention; so sick, in fact, that for a day or two she thought that this time she must be pregnant.

But it was fear that had her curled in her bed, where there was no Aaron to comfort her. He was off in the regions, a scout for Somare, soothing prides and calming aggressions. Since the visit to the fjords and the story of Jiwu's curse – *just a story*, Aaron said, but Rika knew that in this place nothing was just a story – the gap between them had widened, and they talked so little, Rika began to feel a stranger, to herself as much as to him. It was as if some essential part of her was draining away. Simbaikan boiled up roots of ginger and pieces of bark, leaves from the market, and coaxed her to drink. A child was close by, she said, and for a day or two Rika thought maybe the bitter brew had done its work. But, no. There was no salvation, and there was no avoiding Leonard's visit. In a resigned voice she said she supposed it was better that Aaron was away. 'I should do this alone,' she said, as if it were an ordeal.

As it turned out, it wasn't. On the first morning she went to the hotel where Leonard was staying, and even before the coffee came she knew that he had survived and she was forgiven. When Alex Penrose arrived to pick him up for the screening in the anthropology department, they were both relaxed, leaning back in their chairs. Leonard was telling a story about his parents' dogs catching a rabbit, which they brought into the house. 'An English sort of a story,' Alex told Pete, 'but at least they were smiling.'

In the car, driving to the university, Leonard looked out at the new suburbs and the crisscrossing roads that made the dry valley of his memory almost unrecognisable. Alex Penrose pointed to where the new centre of government would be, out there, off to the right, where cars and trucks were overtaking on a dual carriageway. He pointed to the buildings going up, and told Leonard of the others that were planned and who was paying for them: a national museum, a library, a new parliament house.

When they reached the university, Leonard looked at Rika and smiled. 'Why don't you come to the screening this morning?' he said. 'You might find it easier than watching it tonight.'

There was a pause and then, in a small voice, Rika said, 'You think? Okay. Yes.'

'Good I didn't wait till this evening,' she said when she went over to the library to see Martha. Although Leonard had warned her, another wave of nausea had coursed through her during the sequence – barely a minute long – of her arrival in the village, a rush of adrenalin hitting her knees and the back of her neck. On the screen she saw in her face all that Leonard had not seen. She contemplated how often he would have had to return to that short sequence in the solitary quiet of the editing room. She imagined him in the dark, rolling film back and forth, the flicker of light, and the consequences of her cowardice. Her cruelty. Five years. And there it was, a moment of her past replayed in a full seminar room. When Leonard asked if she would still come to the public screening, and to the party afterwards, she knew that she must. She also knew that when she walked into that theatre she might as well be branded with a scarlet letter.

'I capitulate,' the director of the arts centre said when he stood up to introduce *The Mountain*. 'Ethnographic film has been difficult for us. Remember Margaret Mead, wanting to "catch and preserve" us on film "for centuries"? A more effective way of putting the native on display!' He paused for the response. 'The imperial camera,' he said. 'Ethnographic film hasn't been a form we've looked to as we create our own arts of *piksa* film. But this one. Well, this one might change our minds. This one makes us proud.'

The famous image, regarded as a turning point in the history of ethnographic film, is of an adolescent boy with muscular calves – Albert – at the edge of the drama and the edge of the shot, mimicking not the dancers but Leonard, the filmmaker. Sometimes it is only the shadow play of the mimic that's seen. Sometimes Albert is dancing at the edge of the shot, the camera of his imagination heavy in his hands until the old chief walks across and takes the boy out of the frame. Young women slip across the edge of the dance ground, one holding a bottle of shampoo in her hand, and there is Albert again, his camera swivelled to take them in, and Boja waving his arm at all of them to get out of the way, and a troupe of smaller boys mimicking them both, another dance circulating at the edge of the dance.

At that first screening, there were gusts of laughter; *joy* on the faces lit by the film.

In a sequence that Rika thought he'd have cut, Don walks across the empty dance ground with his own tail of boys. A young man jives to music that's coming from the house, and off to the side one of the chiefs watches with a face full of sorrow. Boja and Obi frown at the pages of a ragged notebook, old women run for cover as the rain begins and the mountains vanish from view. A woman with a folded bark-cloth on her knee and a half coconut shell of black paint is in shot; behind her, a cloth of painted mountains hangs from a wall and a small girl leans against her, dressed in a pattern of spiralling bush-snails. The old chiefs talk on their platform where the dancers hang their headdresses, and Nanaji asks questions about the intentions of the camera, as Obi and Boja struggle to translate the words of the chiefs. All this without an explanatory voiceover, only subtitles and Obi's expressive eyes and his faltering translation.

In his closing thanks, Alex Penrose compared *The Mountain* to the shift that came to ethnographic film when Jean Rouch lost his tripod in Niger and discovered what could be done with the handheld camera. Twenty years later, Leonard had made a virtue of a different necessity. When unwelcome intrusions sabotaged his original intention to record the mountain culture with as little disturbance as possible in the presence of a camera, he had a choice. He could disregard the intrusions, leave them on the cutting-room floor, or he could let the experience change the film, and also him.

Five years tells the answer.

*

'The decisive moment,' he said at the next day's workshop with Rika's students. That is what the camera looks for. The decisive moment when something is present, illuminated as it comes into being, or as it vanishes. The look on a face. The moment of change, the dissonant note, the unexpected joke. You'll find it where you do not expect to find it. Where you do not *want* to find it.

Rika was standing at the side of the studio, leaning against the wall, her face half turned from the class, towards Leonard. Outside the windows, people were splashing past with plastic over their heads. Inside, everyone was attentive, none of the usual lounging around, no side comments, no flirting; instead a leaning forward, and stillness. *Village Shots* was up, and Leonard moved from one exhibit to the next, speaking with a conviction that had those whose work it was standing perceptibly taller.

'There, do you see? Those boys in the background. Do you notice their expression? What are they looking at? Not you, not the camera. We're in a settlement, yes? What are we seeing? Poverty, an old man with no teeth. Lack of opportunity. Another man with a discarded tyre. Yes. It's well composed. Are they resigned, these men? Making what they can from the scraps they pick up on the road. Yes? So, let's return to the boys. What age would you say? Seventeen? Are they resigned? Are they without hope? No. They're young, they're going to make a future. Look at their faces. What expression do you get there? If these boys became the subject, what would we be seeing? The beginnings of the gangs?'

Wana, who was sitting at the back with Martha, leaned forward. 'Do we only know that because we know the context? Because we know there are gangs? Because we know they begin in the settlements? If all we had was the photo, say we didn't know where it was from, would we be able to say the same?'

'Good question,' Leonard said. 'It goes to the heart of it. What can photography do? It can't write history. It isn't a biography. It's a moment, that's all.'

'Maybe the boys are watching a girl?' someone suggested.

'Now that's an idea. Do we agree? No? Because they would be

preening, showing off, if it was to a girl? Good point. Okay, we're back to the idea of them as alienated from the old man, their elders. Not interested in the camera.'

'Back to history,' Wana said. 'They show us that more than one thing is happening. They remind us.'

'And that,' Leonard concluded, 'is why you should never neglect the edge of the frame, or the edge of your vision. It's there that something is likely to reveal itself. The thing you overlook. See,' he said, pointing this time to a woman in the market with a child to her breast. A nice enough shot, but ordinary, commonplace. 'If you cropped this image.' His hands were over the print, shifting attention from the woman with the child to the woman behind them with a dollar note tucked into her armband. A small visual shift, a large shift of meaning. He moved on to a photo of a building-site foreman in a hard hat with his arm out in a gesture of authority; above him a young man, barely in focus, precarious and unprotected on a high steel beam. 'What have you seen? What have you not seen? What are you showing us? What are you neglecting? Go back. Test yourself. Where your eye turns away, look again.'

After the workshop, after the last of the students had shown him their folios, after Wana had left and Martha had returned to the library, Leonard went with Rika to her office. The rain had stopped – one of those interludes when the air was heavy with water and everything seemed to float. On the walkway to her office, students stood aside for them to pass, and there was respect in the gesture. 'They must admire you greatly,' Leonard said, though it was for him that they stood aside.

She opened the door to her office. It was a large room, but despite the windows along one side, it was gloomy with the cloud low outside. She opened the slats to let in a movement of air, hot, humid air, and Leonard's first impulse was to tell her to shut them again, shut out the damp – terrible for the photographs that were pinned on the walls and already curling inwards. Instead, his eye moved slowly across a portrait of her father that was familiar to him, roof lines in

Leiden, Nogi's face, images from the exhibition. And the shot he'd taken of Rika with Janape at the river on the morning she left. Until she looked at it that day with Leonard beside her, Rika had almost ceased to see that it was her and Janape; it'd become a study in light and shade, the two figures a solid structure against the dancing water. It was the last image Leonard recognised. After that, nothing. Rika's life without him. Aaron. So many of Aaron. At a table, with Somare; holding a megaphone at a rally; beside an old man, water glinting behind them. A short series in a village, near water, carved canoe prows, the woman who'd been at the seminar that morning, Wana, younger then, without glasses.

'The Trobriands,' Rika said. 'Three years ago.'

'I'd have liked to have gone there,' Leonard said. 'I have a colleague who's working on Malinowski's field photos.'

'Any good?'

'As ethnography, yes. As photographs, they're not in your class.'

'I never much liked them. The ones that I've seen.'

'My colleague defends them. We'll have to wait for his book.'

'Another book,' she said. 'This place will sink under the weight of them.'

He laughed. 'That bad?'

'Pretty much.'

On the working wall above the light table were shots of policemen and marketplaces, schoolchildren.

'More *Village Shots*?' he asked.

She nodded.

'Can I see what you're doing yourself?'

'From when?' She pointed to the flat boxes piled on a shelf beside the door.

'From now?'

'You sure?' she said. 'You wouldn't rather the Trobriands?'

'No,' he said. 'Unless you would.'

She opened her desk drawer, took out a slim folder, laid it on the desk and stood behind him as he picked up the prints one by one, looking carefully at the increasingly sculptural images: a hand, the back of a neck, the line of shadow on the muscles of a back, the movement of light and skin. Aaron, he assumed, but rarely his face, and then only the graze of a cheek, a curl of hair; coming in so close it was as if she wanted to get in under the skin. Unsettling images, hard to grasp.

'Are you thinking of another exhibition?' he asked, though he knew these were not for public view.

'No,' she replied. 'I can't go back to Europe, not now. There's no life there for me. I'm a Papuan now.' She smiled, and her eyes filled with tears. 'Only I'm not.'

'How did you reply?' Martha asked him. He was in the study room at the library where she was working with the letters and diaries of her travellers. He was standing at the window, looking out at rain that was sweeping across the valley again. 'I didn't,' he said. He was wary of false comfort; he'd had too much of it himself. He'd damped down the impulse to say, 'No, no, of course you can come back. I will be there.' Looking Martha straight in the face, he asked, 'What's happened? What hasn't she told me?'

He didn't speak easily, not of personal things, not of this, and as she watched him struggle to frame his words, a rush of memory came in on her: the shame of the cuckold. What a word, why recall it then, after the authority of that seminar; why that word and the image of Leonard five years before, back from the mountain, doggedly working with Obi to translate the soundtrack, and the house packed up already, and Leonard so restrained, so *English*; and everyone thinking that surely, beneath those sad eyes, those good manners, he must have been *murderous*.

'There's something wrong,' he said. 'I can't quite put my finger on it. There's a disjunction. The expansiveness of *Village Shots*, you know, her ease with the students. Then her own work. Have you seen the recent folio?'

'Some,' Martha said.

'What do you make of them?'

'I don't know.'

'They're brooding.'

She nodded. They were. Brooding and obsessive.

'There's something not right. I don't mean they aren't good. She's very good. That precision. It's as if they're coming in on something and I don't know what it is. I thought maybe you would, Martha.'

Martha hesitated. Would it be a breach of confidence to tell him? Would it be a betrayal?

'What is it?' Leonard asked again. 'What is it that's wrong?'

'She's not getting pregnant.'

He held her eyes long enough for her to see comprehension pass across his face, and maybe also pain before he turned to the window again, looking out into the rain. The valley was green, the round hills were green, plants that had been bowed by months of dust were pushing up new shoots. She doubted Leonard saw any of it. His gaze was turned inward.

'Has she been examined?' he said at last.

Martha shook her head. 'She's sure it's Aaron. And anyway, here, who —'

'She must go to Sydney,' he said, cutting in. Then he hesitated, as if this time there was something he wanted to say. But no, all he did was ask Martha to persuade her. 'She trusts you,' he said. 'Otherwise I wouldn't mention it. And if she needs money, can I rely on you to let me know?'

It was not until many years later that Martha asked him how, given the emotion of the time, he'd made a film that confounded all expectations. She was staying with him in North Oxford. The windows of his study opened onto a garden with a birdbath in the middle of an overgrown lawn. He hadn't remarried. He had women friends. There was a buxom don from Somerville who came in to return a book and stayed for a glass of wine. Martha couldn't judge the nature of their affection as they talked of concerts they'd been to, films they'd seen; there was something about Leonard that made personal questions seem improper, even from someone who'd known him as long as she had.

But later that night, after the Somerville don had gone, they returned to the mountain and Rika. It was then, swimming in the great ocean of the past, that the possibility of this other question arose. How did he do it? In a state of grief and shock, how did he make such a film? He didn't deflect the question. He simply said that it was hard. For a long time he couldn't play the rushes, he couldn't unpack the bark-cloth. It took Rika doing what she did, and the inconsequence of the two small films he made on his return from Papua, to force him up against himself, against his unacknowledged vulnerability, his 'intellectual timidity'.

'I suppose it's only when we're forced to, hard up against it, that we change,' he said.

After Leonard left this time, Rika said it was as if her memory became an involuntary impulse. Events from her past with him that had seemed commonplace took on a new colouring, and things she hadn't thought about for years came back to her as vivid tableaux: his visits to the house on the canal when, still a girl, she'd taken out her photographs and shown them to the tall Englishman. She could see herself putting the folio box on the table, and Leonard lifting out the black and white prints, asking: 'Who developed these?' and her father replying, 'She's been in the museum's darkroom since she was sixteen.' Now, eleven years later, the woman she'd become, the photographer she was becoming, understood what Leonard had done for her when he recognised the ease with which she could frame an image, her facility with light and shadow. And she understood that it had been in the mirror of his recognition that she'd come to understand it herself. Leonard had given her that, and it was worth more, far more, than even the Rolleiflex. And then she was back on the mountain, in another memory film, and there was Leonard, his arms out in welcome as she arrived in the village. Her harshness was vivid. Her silence and her cruelty.

She tried to close her mind against these intrusions and, heaven knows, with term ending and self-government so close, there was enough to keep her busy. But when she stopped, when she let her mind rest, Leonard would be there. She didn't want to return to him, or to that past, but she had the strange feeling that he was re-entering her. Not physically – she had no desire for him – but in some intrinsic way she felt that Leonard was returning to her. A nonsensical thought, when she considered it, but there it was, greeting her each time she swam out past the children at the town beach, or sat under the shade of the veranda and let her mind drift.

234

She'd had lunch with him the day before the plane took him back to Sydney and his flight to London. They'd sat on the shaded terrace of his hotel and he'd asked her if she'd had any contact with the mountains. She told him she hadn't. She thought of the people often enough, and of Janape saying goodbye to her on the path.

'Remember Janape?'

'I dream of her sometimes,' Leonard said. He leaned across the table and took Rika's hand. 'I feel I owe them. I know I owe them, and not only for the film. All of them. Janape, especially. After you left, she looked after me. She was very good. I owe her a lot.' He sighed. 'Exchange. How does it work in the fjords?'

Rika sat back in her chair. 'It's hard,' she said, 'with both of us on local salaries.'

A group of Australians came in and sat at the next table. They took files and pens from their briefcases and began a noisy discussion, as Rika told Leonard of the grand gesture she'd made when she took the job at the arts centre, refusing the expatriate salary that would have made everything easier. How could she have been so foolish? She told him about Jacob always with more to give, and the endlessness of clan demands: funerals to pay for, young men in town to be bailed out, kids going to school, babies and old people needing hospital. Leonard asked if he could help and she shook her head. There was Aaron's pride to consider. When Leonard asked if he need know, she looked at him, shocked. There was nothing she wouldn't tell Aaron, and even as the words came and her voice insisted on them, she knew it was not true.

She'd have liked to take Leonard to the airport right then, after lunch, when all had been said, and she'd heard about his life in Oxford, its quiet satisfactions, and knew that he no longer grieved at night. She'd have embraced him in the hot hangar and stayed to watch the plane take off. Maybe then these plaguing memories would have gone with him, back into the silence of the sky. But there was a farewell dinner to get through first. It was on Laedi's platform, with rain dripping through the roof. Wilkie spent the evening moving buckets around.

Rika would have preferred to be alone. She'd rather have lain on her bed with the door closed and the louvres open, and let her thoughts do as they would while she waited for Aaron. *Waiting for Aaron.* Had her life come to that? 'Don't make me choose,' he'd said. 'Don't make me choose between you and my people.' How could she make a claim against that? The *entire future* depended on him. On the work that they did, there in the office at all hours of the night. How could she say: *stop, we must go away, relax, become ourselves again, let the spirit of this baby find us. We're frightening it away.* How could she say that his sperm had become tired? No one could say that to a Melanesian man. Or: *if you can't choose me, then choose the child.*

These were the thoughts assaulting her as neighbours came up onto the platform to shake Leonard's hand and colleagues from the anthropology department splashed through the rain from their cars. Rifle came grinding up the hill in his ancient truck, all smiles and boasts, staying for the meal, a fair exchange for another load of the chicken shit soil he sold around the new suburbs. Leonard sat quiet at the end of the table, the smoke from his pipe lingering in the wet air. Alex Penrose was next to him, and between bouts of gossip from the street, they talked of appointments at distant universities. Under the thud of rain on the roof, it was a strangely muffled evening.

Aaron had come back from the regions that morning, and had gone straight to the office. He arrived home late, coming up the steps to the platform while Milton was telling a story he'd heard about a white manager on a plantation near Popondetta, who'd drunk himself to death and been found on the floor the next day. Rika was barely listening, waiting for the moment when Aaron would appear.

Leonard saw her look across and smile as he came up the steps, his face in the shadows, his rucksack over one shoulder. For a moment the tension went out of her and Leonard could see the girl he'd loved, the girl he loved still. When Aaron came into the light, Leonard stood up and put out his hand. The rain had stopped, and with only the drip from the eaves to distract them, the table fell silent. Alex Penrose also stood, making room for Aaron, giving him his seat. And there they were, Leonard and Aaron side by side. The muscles in Rika's neck were tense again as she passed a plate of food along the table to Aaron. It sat untouched in front of him, the smoke from his cigarettes adding to the heavy air. Leonard, pipe in hand, was asking him about Canberra and self-government. How well prepared were they? What level of support were they getting from Australia's Labor government? His questions were real, and though he'd heard the views of everyone at the table, he was interested in Aaron's answers, which were politely given, without elaboration. They were ready for self-government, he said, but not yet for independence.

'What we're asking for,' he said, 'is a larger gap between the two. Time, that's all.'

'And Whitlam?' Leonard asked.

'When Australia finally gets a Prime Minister who's anti-colonial, he's determined independence will come on his watch.' Aaron gave a laugh at the irony of it. Then a sigh. 'It's not our timing that's at issue. It's the next Australian election.'

'Is it vanity?' Leonard sounded perplexed.

'Partly,' Aaron said. 'It's also Indonesia. Now they've secured the west, the Australians are nervous. They think they'll have more traction if we're decolonised – and they can keep us safely in their sphere.'

'I see,' Leonard said. Of all the views he'd sought, no one else had told him that.

After Alex Penrose had driven Leonard to his hotel, leaving Laedi and Martha to clear the table of its empty bottles and overflowing ashtrays, Rika and Aaron walked back down the hill to their house and went straight to bed. Such words as passed between them were in the language of their bodies as they embraced each other with such intensity that Rika called out with the sharp surprise of it. *Oh Aaron, what will happen to us?* But he was asleep already, his breath coming in the slow rhythm she'd lain beside for five years. For her, that night, sleep was nowhere near. She left the warmth of their bed and switched on the light in the living room. Wilkie had left his schoolbooks open on the table. Aaron's rucksack was on the floor near the door. Home. Yes, this was her home. Then why was she so shaken by Leonard and his film? What she'd seen in it, and couldn't not see, was the return of a man and a past she thought she understood, in a form she didn't recognise. And with it came the question: had she misjudged him? It wasn't a matter of regret, or of changing her mind. Or if it was, it lay deep and low. It was a glimpse of a mind she'd once lived with in innocence. Had she lived with it also in ignorance? Doubt came exactly where doubt had not existed: in her own capacity to see. In the nature of her looking.

When you're certain of your approach, Leonard had told her students, question it. Trust your eye, and don't let your *idea* of what you see, or what you want to see, or what you think you should see, take the place of what you *do* see.

In the silence of that night, Rika took out her photographs from the mountain and looked again at the catalogue of her exhibition, and clippings of the reviews. What she saw revealed that the critical headings, offered as acclaim, now told her exactly what was wrong. 'The Strange Made Familiar.' Leonard had not made the mountain people familiar to a western audience, as she had done, or tried to do; he didn't bring the comfort of a familiar way of seeing into this other world, and turn them into friends like us. He didn't let his audience assume it knew what it was looking at. Nor did he let the mountain and its people be strange, a spectacle for the eye, something to gasp at and wonder.

He'd taken his viewers into Auden's 'land of unlikeness'.

NOVEMBER CAME AND THE RAIN KEPT FALLING. WHEN RIKA BLED AGAIN despite herbs from the Chinese apothecary, she took Martha's advice and booked in to see a gynaecologist in Sydney. Martha flew down with her, and Rika was grateful. 'Imagine doing this alone,' she said. They stayed with Martha's widowed mother, Gloria, in the house where Martha had grown up. The shipyards had been replaced by docks, a different noise coming up the cliff and into the kitchen, where Gloria fussed over Rika. She made her scrambled eggs and cottage pie, telling her to *eat up* as if a baby could be produced by another layer of fat beneath the skin. On the morning of Rika's appointment, she came down to the jetty to see her and Martha onto the ferry that would take them into the city. It was early summer, not yet hot. The harbour was at its sparkling best, a light breeze in the sails of the skiffs. The new Opera House was rising from the old tram depot. They walked up from the Quay, through the noise and the buildings and the traffic, to Macquarie Street. Rika grasped Martha's arm when they reached the gynaecologist's building and took the lift to his floor. In his waiting room with its leather sofas, framed degrees and piles of *Vogue*, they stood at the window looking out over the Botanic Gardens, until he opened the door and ushered Rika in to his consulting room.

He was a tall man with a boyish haircut, and on his desk was a brown seed pod the size of a small plump cushion.

'A fertility pod from Africa,' he said, and Rika put her hands on it.

It had been a long time, he agreed, for a healthy couple not to conceive. He looked at her temperature charts. She told him about her young self, who was so fertile that one ignorant event in an orchid house had filled her with a pregnancy nothing could save her from.

239

Not her father. Not the school. Not her own will. She spoke to the doctor as if he were a confessor. She told him everything, from her first period all the way through to Aaron and the pressure of his job, the exhaustion of his sperm and her fear that he would fall, without warning, dead on the floor.

'And that first pregnancy,' the doctor asked. 'How many weeks were you when you went into hospital?'

She couldn't mark that time in weeks, only that after the man had gone back to the rocky hills of his island, she vomited and couldn't eat breakfast. She'd stayed at home in bed, but the next day was no better. Nor the next. Her breasts hurt when she ran; she fell asleep at her desk. Her father, alarmed, sent her to the school nurse, who sent her to the doctor, who delivered the news. The school was pragmatic. She was given leave for the rest of the term and taken to a hospital in Amsterdam.

When she returned to school, she was wary, closed in on herself. She returned to her books, and to her camera, but not to the Botanic Gardens. Other girls in her class had boyfriends, but not her. She rarely went to parties. The feelings that had risen unbidden in the orchid house vanished as if they too had been scraped out of her. Only the smallest shadow remained of whatever it was that led her into a punishing nausea. In this way a year had passed before Leonard began to visit, and the dark feelings that she thought had vanished gave a small roll in the depths of her belly.

'And when you married him,' the gynaecologist asked, 'did you consider the question of pregnancy?'

'I don't think Leonard had babies in mind,' she said. 'I was barely twenty.'

She'd booked into a clinic not far from her old school and an IUD was fitted. It stayed in place during the marriage and on through the first year with Aaron, when everything was strange and intense and uncertain. Her periods came rolling along, one after another, with little pain and no trouble worth bothering a doctor with. She gave the whole process no thought, she told the doctor, until Aaron turned his mind to how he might make gifts to her father in preparation for a child.

The IUD was removed; a whiff of anaesthetic, and she was given it in a small plastic jar. A translucent sliver of skin was wrapped in its coils. What was it, she'd asked the nurse. A part of her? A baby trying to take? Something Aaron had left behind? It was nothing, the nurse said. Some tissue, that was all. Maybe a small infection. *Don't upset yourself.*

'As we can't test your husband,' the gynaecologist said, 'we'll begin by taking a better look at you.'

He took her into the small examination room. When they returned, Martha was brought into the doctor's office. She sat in the chair facing his desk, looking at the large, shiny fertility pod with a groove that made it look rather like child-sized buttocks. It was oddly reassuring. Everything about the room exuded confidence: the sun shining on the window, the doctor's notes on the desk, the leather-bound books and medical journals, the plastic models of ovaries and wombs. And, indeed, the doctor was hopeful. Apart from a cyst he'd found on Rika's left ovary, there was no other sign of abnormality. While he didn't think the cyst likely to be a cause of the *difficulty*, it merited further investigation, given her remoteness from specialist care. He could fit her in for surgery at the end of his Thursday list, in two days' time, and wrote the admission slip. Rika, her slender fingers back on the seed pod, smiled.

Two days later, Martha sat beside her as she surfaced, nauseous, from the anaesthetic. The ward was shaded; curtains separated her from the adjacent bed. The soft tread of nurses and the low moan of another patient were the only sounds. Rika opened her eyes and pushed the oxygen mask from her face. What? she asked. What had they found? Martha didn't know. When she asked a nurse, she was told the doctor would be along soon. Rika dropped back into a sleep of tears that seeped from her closed lids.

When at last the surgeon came to her bed, it was late in the afternoon. His voice was gentle and his manner kind, but what he had to tell her was not. He'd found evidence of a past pelvic inflammatory condition, almost certainly caused by the IUD. That, he said, would account for her infertility. The word no one had spoken.

'Was it the abortion?' she asked.

'No,' he said. 'It was the IUD that caused the infection.'

'How could I have something so bad and not know?' she asked.

'It's common for it to be asymptomatic.'

'But they recommended it. They *put it in me.*'

He was silent.

'What does it mean?' she asked.

'It means there's a residue of scar tissue. It's wrapped tight around your fallopian tubes. There's some on your ovaries.'

'Did you remove it?' The tears had stopped seeping. She was quite lucid.

'I did what I could. That's what took the time. Some of it went too deep to remove.'

'Will it be enough?' she asked. 'Have you removed enough?'

'I'm sorry, Rika,' he said. 'The scarring is extensive. There's only the smallest chance that you can conceive.'

'But a chance.'

'Small. Very small. I can't encourage you to hope.'

'I will hope,' she said. 'I can't not hope.'

'And I shall hope with you.' His voice was kind. 'But you must begin to prepare yourself for there being no child.'

'No,' she said. 'No.'

The tears began again, sliding down her face as if her entire being had become liquid. For a moment she was still. And then, with a juddering moan, she hauled herself up on one arm, jerking the drip in a cry of refusal, until the nurses came with a syringe. They laid her down and the moaning sounds lessened, her breathing quietening, until she was asleep.

ON THE EVENING OF PAPUA NEW GUINEA'S SELF-GOVERNMENT, THAT December of 1973, there was a reception that required dresses of a sort that were not readily purchased in Port Moresby. Rika and Martha had bought theirs in Sydney. The day before Rika had gone into hospital, they'd had lunch in a café near the park before wandering the shops. With the reception in mind, Martha bought a purple dress with a pattern of intersecting circles. Rika bought a red crepe dress with a keyhole at the breast. The young woman serving them had been to Papua with a schoolfriend whose father ran a plantation, and had some idea what it meant that self-government was coming. 'You're going to have to look good,' she said, bringing hangers with more dresses. Such was Rika's confidence that she told her she was going into hospital the next day. A small procedure, she said, touching her belly. 'All the more reason to look good when you come out,' the girl said, and Rika's thumb went up in agreement. When Gloria adjusted the hem for her that evening, Rika looked beautiful.

But when it was time to put on the red dress for the reception, Rika looked at it with revulsion. She hadn't taken it out of its bag until Aaron found it and asked what it was, and she confessed to spending money they could ill afford. It was a confession easily made as she was spared telling him of the abortion. 'That had nothing to do with it,' the doctor had said, and his words were like a wand. The relief was so great that to tell Aaron about the IUD and the scarring seemed almost a reprieve. Over that they could weep together. Words returned to them. Gone was the loneliness of sleeping beside each other in silence. With Rika's grief, gentleness returned, their private world of skin and fluid, and when they made love, it was no longer with the urgency of those last few months, which had brought orgasms that made her gasp. Now they rocked in each other's arms, and before they fell asleep as entangled as new lovers, he told her she was no less beautiful, no less able to love a child. They could adopt, it was not unusual in his culture. But when he coaxed her into that red crepe dress on the night of the reception, she felt a fraud, a parody of femininity, as vulgar as a transvestite. And as barren.

'Where did you get that word?' Laedi asked.

But that's how Rika felt. And that night it was how she looked. With the scar on her belly a purple welt, nothing Aaron said about adopting, letting one of his father's brother's sons give them a child – Naomi's next perhaps – could change the emptying-out that had befallen her. She knew, he didn't have to tell her, that when one sibling has no children, and another has too many, the children can move, still in the family with their many mothers. Fine, if that's your culture, but if she was to have a child, something of it must come from her. And she had no sibling.

So she took off the new dress and went to the reception in the old crocheted one she'd worn at the exhibition in Amsterdam and when she married Aaron. She clipped back her hair and wore no make-up. Even Laedi had a trace of lipstick for the occasion. Martha put on her dress and let Pete zip it up, with a long kiss to her neck that had him taking it off again. When they arrived at the reception, she felt as good as she had for some time. Until Rika saw her, and her face froze. They were at the entrance to the reception, near the door, with people all around. The evening air was soft, and so was Rika's voice. Soft, and fierce. 'How could you,' she said. 'How could you wear it?' Then she turned and walked past the tubs of orchids, in through the door. Rika might as well have stabbed her with a knife for the effect it had. *After all she'd done.* Pete, the only person who'd seen the exchange, said maybe it was all Martha had done that was the problem – she'd seen too much, come in too close. She was a reminder, he said, of things Rika wanted to forget.

In Sydney, for that week after the hospital before Rika was well enough to fly back, Martha had looked after her, as tender as a sister. Gloria made soup and Martha carried it upstairs; she went out for fruit, bought books and magazines that Rika wouldn't read. Gloria sat with her, day after day, and still Rika didn't talk. When she did speak, it was to tell Martha to leave her alone. In the kitchen Gloria asked questions Martha couldn't answer. And still she carried the tray up the stairs, saying nothing of the misery that had her pounding the streets at night. And after all that, after keeping her distance since their return, leaving Rika to talk to Laedi alone, now this stab about the dress. Was that fair?

'*Fair*,' Pete said. 'Fair has nothing to do with it.'

At the reception, the Australian administrator, now recast as high commissioner, gave an affectionate speech, and so did Somare as chief minister. Everyone smiled and clapped and raised their glasses.

'She'll get over it,' Pete said, handing Martha another glass, but champagne didn't dull the ache. As she listened to the talk of friendship between nations, she thought only of Rika turning away. She felt shamed by her dress, with its hem too high and it circles suddenly garish. Abiding friendship. Somare was replying to the high commissioner. Easy words. Everyone knew of the bitterness that came back from Canberra, and the extra work when budgets were cut and timetables for independence imposed.

Even Jacob, looking urbane in his suit with a dark ochre cummerbund, raised his hand in a salute to the coming nation. 'He's drunk,' Pete said, which, actually, he wasn't. But he turned as if he knew they were watching, and again raised his glass. Martha watched as he went to Rika, leaning to speak into her ear. She shook her head, as if to say no to whatever it was he'd asked, but the movement was gentle; she turned to him, let her hand rest briefly on his arm, and Martha remembered her musing, months before, that maybe Jacob, maybe Jacob was the solution, he was a brother, a skin-brother; maybe Jacob could give her the child. 'Don't be daft,' Laedi had said. 'It doesn't work that way, not when the first brother is alive,' and they'd laughed. Especially Martha. And there they were, Jacob and Rika, almost intimate. Rika smiled, shook her head again, and he moved on, across the room, speaking to Derek, to Aaron, to the high commissioner.

'Martha,' Jacob said later in the evening when he came upon her by the open windows. 'Enjoying yourself?'

'Not really. Are you?'

'Why not? On the road to independence and you're not celebrating?' He looked amused, and they stood together, watching the room from the cool of the night air.

'I saw your car in Hohola last week,' Martha said.

'Yes. I came to see Rika. After her operation. That's your way, isn't it? To bring flowers. Entertain her.'

Entertain. What did he mean, *entertain*?

'You and Pete,' he said. 'You seem happy these days.'

'Yes,' Martha said. 'Yes, I suppose we are.'

'A fine institution, marriage,' he said, bringing a blush to her cheeks. She thought he was jesting, maybe even flirting a little. He was leaning in towards her, conspiratorial, speaking softly.

'Do you think,' he said, 'that Angel will make me a good wife?'

'Angel.' Martha stepped back. 'From the fjords? She's *sixteen*. If that.'

'I intend to wait. I promised *afa* Noah.'

'Promised him what? Girls aren't for trade.'

'But it's a consideration, how it'll affect the village.'

What kind of a conversation was this?

'And in the meantime,' Jacob said, 'I'll send her down to Australia. To school.'

'Train her up, you mean.'

'I wouldn't put it like that.'

'Anyway,' Martha said, 'you don't know what she'll want in two years' time.'

'No?' They both knew what Angel would want.

'It'll be good for the village,' Jacob said. 'Noah agrees. It'll bring the clans together.' He smiled the smile she was susceptible to; still she couldn't see him and feel neutral. 'I'll teach her to love me,' he said, 'and I'll behave like a western husband.' He laughed. A very different laugh.

'Have you told Rika?'

'There's much to be arranged.'

'Don't do it too soon,' Martha said. 'Give her time.'

'I always give her time. You, surely, know that.' Those hooded eyes were open, eyebrows raised. 'Martha,' he said, lifting her hand to his lips. Then he moved off, into the reception, sleek as a panther, making his way back towards Rika.

MILTON HAD BEEN IN HOHOLA SINCE THE RAIN BEGAN. THE DIRT floor of the shack had turned to mud, and the road a slippery bog. Rifle had to carry out what was left of his vegetables by foot.

On the morning of self-government, Milton walked into town and joined the small crowd outside the building where the adminis-trator and Somare were signing the papers. He was there for history and for *art*, prowling about in the guise of Baldwin Rufus, looking for revolt, any small moment of resistance, troops for Baldwin Rufus's rebellion. Milton had no interest in troops for himself, or followers, or even rebellion. Well, he was ambivalent: he'd like to see some spark of something, not this giving over to the new version of themselves that had been handed down from Canberra. If independence was to come, it might as well come as *theirs*.

His novel was running amok, changing under his nose as he peered over the typewriter to see what he was banging out. Baldwin Rufus was no longer a crude version of Eremiah. Milton had grown to like him, or at any rate not despise him, and he saw that the interior life beginning to arrive on the page was an aspect of his own. He remembered back to Aro's classes. *Madame Bovary, c'est moi*. Not all of him, but a part.

Eremiah, or rather Baldwin Rufus, was no longer from Bougain-ville with a mining company to fight, but a boy from a village like Milton's, on the plain under the mountain, where the plantations were making their stealthy march. Milton knew nothing of mining companies and had never been to Bougainville; the fight was too serious to fake. But he knew the humiliations of his own people, the old men who watched their sons work on the labour line. When he heard the story about the plantation manager found dead beside the bottle, he rejoiced, improving on a man who (in Milton's version)

248

called himself 'king', not in memory of Martin Luther King, but in praise of his own reign. Dead on the floor! Perfect! What better stage for a rebellion, for the smouldering workers, who were young enough and educated enough to know the difference between a regent and a Baptist preacher. Let them take over the plantation. What better place to raise the bird of paradise flag. An autonomous republic! A republic of intellectuals! Why not? The first of the federated states of Melanesia! From Popondetta, Baldwin Rufus could march on Moresby, over the Kokoda Track, gathering recruits, arriving on the eve of self-government to find the town in turmoil, rising up against the new shape given to it by a new government in Australia. The offices would empty. The university would stand firm. The docks would come to a standstill. Logs would be placed over the airport runway.

So Milton was in Moresby looking for signs of revolt, and there weren't any. Hohola was quiet. Many of the women and children had gone back to their villages, or to camp out of town, safe from marauding Highlanders who, in fact, stayed in the settlements playing cards. There weren't even any drunks around. The pubs and hotels had been closed for three days and squads of police were patrolling the streets. The university was calm: no leaders practising their rhetoric there. No crowds gathering. No students reading aloud from Marx or Malcolm X. Oh well, he said to Laedi, if there wasn't material out there on the streets, imagination would have to serve in its place – which, for art, he supposed, was right. But he still had one ear cocked to the audience that had once cheered him in Melbourne. And that posed a problem. Would they believe a novel if it was too *fanciful*? The real place had to be somewhere on the page, or no one would believe and take notice. On the other hand, he couldn't have those Melbourne bastards thinking the place had lain down and taken it, whatever it was that Australia dished out. Bugger that. In fact, he said to Laedi, *bugger art*. Maybe you have to be in Africa, where there are coups and massacres.

Laedi told him to take a shower. Bili said there was no way she was going to live in Africa.

*

Another person in town that weekend was Tobias, the medical officer from the aid post on the mountain. He'd been transferred to the hospital in Popondetta soon after Leonard left, and had worked his way up to deputy director. He was in Moresby for a health department meeting and had stayed on for the proclamation. Like Milton, he thought it'd be an event, a historical moment, though in his case it wasn't for art that he wanted to be present. He wanted to be able to tell his grandchildren. So he was also among the small crowd that gathered while the administrator signed the papers and became high commissioner. It was a quiet event, not much of a moment, and walking back down the hill, he fell in with Milton. As boys they'd been at the Martyrs School together, and there was much to talk about as they walked though the empty town, and caught a PMV out to the suburb where Tobias was staying. His sister was living there, married to an orderly at Moresby General Hospital. It was somewhere along the road, riding in an unusually empty van, that Tobias asked Milton if he knew where Rika was. Still here, he'd heard, out at the university, married to Aaron – did he know of her?

'Sure I know Rika,' Milton said. 'Lives down the road from where I'm staying.' They slapped hands, there on the PMV. *Yeah!*

That was how Milton came to be the first to hear the story of Janape bringing Jericho, the *hapkas* mountain child, down to Popondetta to find Tobias, so that he could find Rika. 'A gift child,' they called him. It was time for him to be sent out to school and then to his father. 'Shit,' Milton said on the PMV, and then again that evening while Rika was at the reception. He pondered the news of this child coming now, when all hope of a child had gone, and whether, at this time of grief, Rika could accept him. 'Shit,' he said again, sitting in Tobias's sister's house, drinking too much beer. The blurry outline of a novel hovered somewhere, and with it the thought that the lives of friends were not the stuff of fiction. Or were they? A poem. Perhaps a poem. In the voice of the *hapkas* kid.

The next morning, Milton and Tobias set out for Hohola. Everything remained quiet, eerily so. The trade stores were closed; street-sellers had packed up and gone. There were no trucks. The PMV that picked them up was almost empty. It was as if the population had been cast under a spell.

At Hohola it was the same; trade stores were boarded up, and just one old woman was under the trees with betel to sell. Milton went across to her – they'd need replenishments with the task facing Tobias. He passed one to him with his lime pot as they climbed the hill to the house. Neither of them spoke as they walked, slowly, breathing in the quiet of the morning, a dog barking somewhere in the distance.

At the house they found Aaron and Rika drinking coffee on the veranda. Pete was there, and so were Laedi and the girls. But not Martha. Neighbours were shaking Aaron's hand as if self-government was his personal achievement, along with the order on the streets.

'How's the mood in Popondetta?' Aaron asked Tobias, moving along the bench to make room for him. 'It was hostile when I was last there, and we haven't had good reports.'

'Mixed and confused,' Tobias said. 'Frightened. They think people will come over from Moresby and take their land.'

'Not the Highlanders?'

'Highlanders or coastals, it doesn't matter. It's Moresby they hear about, and the pressure on land here. Some people think it'll be a free-for-all, a time of no more law. They're staking out which house will be theirs, threatening to kill anyone they have a grudge against. It's like here – a lot of people have gone to the villages.'

Meanwhile, up the hill, Martha was still smarting. Everything about the reception had had a lowering effect. Even Bili was in a state of despondence. She'd woken early, run up the hill to her chickens, finding them as she'd left them, and sat on the ground looking down at the roofs and gardens of Hohola. They looked exactly as they had the day before. 'What's the point,' she moaned, 'if independence comes and nothing changes?' Daisy was in Laedi's bed as usual and didn't get out until Wilkie came into the yard with a note from Rika. *I'm making banana bread. Come down.*

'I'm buggered if I'm going,' Martha said. 'Not after last night.'

'She's making amends,' Pete said.

'Don't be sour,' Laedi said. 'She didn't mean it.'

But Martha knew that she had meant it, and that morning she was not in a forgiving vein.

'Have you seen anyone from the mountain?' Rika asked Tobias, talking over the head of Bili, who had squeezed in between them. 'Janape? Have you seen her child?'

She knew of the child's existence from a geologist who'd been up there a month or so before. She'd sent in supplies with him, a small gesture of remembrance, and he'd come back with photos – awful, inept photos, but enough to see that Lilla had grown into a young woman, and that a small figure was leaning against Janape, surely her child. The geologist, who went through the villages quickly and on up the mountain to take his readings, could give her no details. When Rika had pointed to Janape in the photo he seemed unsure of who she was. A blur of women.

'Who's the father of Janape's child?' she asked Tobias.

Tobias looked uneasy. 'Maybe you should bring him here,' he said. 'Send him to school. He's five soon.'

'Five! Is that possible?' She was calculating on her fingers. 'Is that what Janape wants?'

'She came down to Popondetta. Brought him with her.'

'Was she ill?'

'No. She wanted to ask me.'

'Ask you what?'

'About the child going to school.'

'At the airstrip?'

'Janape says it's a bad place, that village. There's an evangelist in there now. He's not teaching the syllabus, and the inspectors don't get there like they used to. He says independence is coming up, he can teach what he likes. He doesn't have to teach the white man's way. Raise children for Jesus.'

'Janape never thought much about Jesus.'

'It's not only that.'

Tobias was looking to Milton as if for help, but he'd sunk down low, so low that the contortion of his face made Pete realise what Tobias was struggling to say. Don flashed into his mind. So that's what it was. A reckoning, long avoided, come at last.

'*Hapkas,*' he said. Just the one word.

'*Hapkas,*' Bili said with a wide grin. 'The same as us.'

'Yes,' Tobias said. 'He's a *hapkas* child. He looks it. He looks mixed race.' Tobias opened his hands in apology. 'He looks like Leonard.'

'You mean Don,' Pete said.

'No. Leonard.'

Rika stood up. 'Leonard?' She went very pale. 'It can't be. It's not possible.'

'It's what Janape says. She wants me to tell you.'

Rika sat down again. Put her head between her legs. There was a buzzing noise in her ears, and the voices above her grew distant and faint. She'd never thought Leonard would have a child. It wasn't a thought that in all those years she'd come near to thinking. There was something too pale about him. His penis was thin, and the stuff that flowed from it was pale and watery. Everything about Leonard was pale. She'd enjoyed herself with him, it wasn't that, but the enjoyment came from her; she made it, not him, and she enjoyed his pleasure in her as if something of her remained outside, watching. With Aaron she was helpless against the pleasure he gave and made for her. When her body swelled, awoken by Aaron, everything he left was a gift, and the giving of it so vibrant that her body could feel it hours later.

If fertility had a feeling, it was once her daily fare; if fertility came with rings of pleasure, then she should have been the most fertile of women.

The baby should be hers.

The baby should be theirs.

Above her, she heard that Janape had walked into Popondetta. Tobias had noticed her in the crowd of women outside the hospital. He

saw her in the morning and again in the middle of the day, his attention caught by the golden streaks in the child's hair, the straight,
prominent nose. Was that it? Or the urgency of the mother, and her
focus on Tobias rather than on the nurses and orderlies whose job
it was to move people into line. And he could see that this woman,
this child were not sick. He knew they were from the mountain, he
recognised the skin, and then, in the afternoon, he realised that the
woman was Janape, so changed was she from the girl he'd shown how
to dispense quinine and boil up sugar water for babies with diarrhoea.
He walked over to where she was waiting in the shade, and took both
of them into the hospital. The child had a large weeping sore on his
leg, others between his toes, in the crease of his buttocks. Otherwise
he was healthy. Janape too. A slight cough, nothing more. He took
them to his house and fed them. He had a little of their language.
Janape had taught the boy the English she knew. Obi had taught him
more. Tobias learned that the chiefs had started to teach the boy early.
Nanaji taking him to his house with the older boys, where he'd slept,
collecting his learning. Then Nogi had said to Janape, 'You take him
down to the flat land. You take him to learn the new ways. Find Rika.
When he grows more, she take him to his father.'

He was a solemn child. Tobias could see Leonard in him.
He touched the books on his table. It was a sign. He was called Jericho
to give him the power to blow walls down.

'How does the clan take it?' Pete asked.

'They say he's a gift child. Born with double spirit. An ancestor
gift.'

'Did Janape marry?'

'No. But it's okay. They're strong, the mountain people. The
women are powerful. The old chief Nogi accepts her. That's okay.
They like the child.'

'Compensation,' Pete asked. 'Is that what they want?'

'No,' Tobias said. 'That's not it.'

'Does Leonard know?'

'Of course not.' Rika flashed with anger. She was standing, bolt
upright, 'What do you *think*?'

'She can't have got pregnant long before Leonard left,' Tobias said, his voice apologetic. 'Neither of them would have known.'

'What do we do?' Rika sat down.

'We'll take him,' Laedi said. 'If that's what they want, we can take him. Raise him with the girls.'

'It's not the disgrace in our world it is in yours,' Aaron said.

'It's not the disgrace. It's what to do.'

'He can go to school here,' Aaron said.

'What do I tell Leonard?'

'Tell him we'll take the child while it's at school.'

'A boy. It's a boy. Him, not it.'

'Jericho,' Tobias said. 'His name is Jericho.'

'Jericho,' Bili echoed, her voice like a sigh.

'Leonard's in Oxford,' Pete said. 'He lives in a college. He can't take a child.'

'Even if he could,' Laedi said, 'a child of ours can't go to school in Oxford.'

'Why not? He's Leonard's child too.'

'He's had five years on the mountain,' Milton said. 'It's in him now.'

'We need him educated here,' Laedi said. 'Everyone who can make the future.'

'Why him more than any other child?' Rika said. 'He's never even seen Leonard. White genes don't make a difference. Why should Janape give him up? Is anyone thinking of her? *Imagine*. Just imagine how it will be for her.'

'She brought him to me,' Tobias said. 'To give to you.'

'To me? Or to Leonard?'

'To you. First to you.'

'Why me?'

'Janape said you'd know.'

'To me? She said to give him to me?'

'He can't have land if he stays,' Milton said. 'It's okay while he's a child. He can live and grow on his mother's clan-land. But not when he's grown. It happens all the time. Boys are taken out to find their fathers so they can have land. Otherwise there's nothing for him. No land, no wife, no man.'

'Stop,' Rika said. 'Just stop.' With the radio playing inside, one of Aro's serials floating out into a shocked silence, Rika narrowed her eyes. 'Stop shouting,' she said, though they weren't.

The thought of this baby astounded her. She tried to imagine Janape and Leonard, but it was too weak a picture. Did Janape loosen something in Leonard as Aaron had in her? But whatever it was in her that had been waiting for Aaron had been in her already, like an ache. If it was there in Leonard, she'd have felt it. It wasn't. It couldn't have been. He'd been sent away to school at seven, separated from his mother and stitched into a uniform. She remembered the stories he'd told, his voice even and conversational, as if what he reported was ordinary. The older boys taunting, his spectacles flushed down the lavatory. His mother driving off in the car while he stood on the step with matron, who smelled of carbolic and sick.

'Children don't belong to just one person,' Aaron was saying, as if she didn't understand something she understood perfectly well. 'In our world children are adopted, or taken up by other people in the family, in the clan. It's common. Not remarkable.'

'But not by white people,' she said.

'Rika,' he said. 'It can be ours. We can raise him, and then maybe another from the fjords.'

'Jericho,' she said, and her heart gave a curious leap. Was it possible? Could she turn a child who was Leonard's into a child of her own? 'A gift child', they called him. Could it be that redemption *was* possible? That she could return from the closed, dark place where she'd been these last weeks? That fear and shame need not rule all of her life?

'Are you sure it's what Janape wants?' she asked Tobias.

'Yes,' he said. 'It's what she wants.'

'Isn't she sad?' Rika looked at him, intent and insistent.

'Yes,' he said, meeting her gaze. 'She is sad. Sad *tru*.'

'She's sad and she still wants this?'

He nodded. She saw his eyes and somehow, just, she believed him, and while part of her wept for Janape, another part rose to the prospect of this child.

'Jericho,' Bili said. 'My Jericho.'

The gift child from the mountain.

BOOK TWO

2005–6

Birds of paradise
sing at brief intervals,
yet, as time would destine
this to be, vanish into the depths of massy
green, into the depths of some dark ocean.
Sometimes a lonely
bird whistles . . .

Russell Soaba,
Naked Thoughts: Poems and Illustrations, 1978

HAPKAS

FROM BILI'S APARTMENT HIGH ABOVE THE TOWN
beach there is a clear view out to sea. From her
balcony at the top of the building, if he risks vertigo
and leans right out, Jericho can see down, past towels
hanging over lower rails, to a sheer drop of rock. At
the foot of the cliff where the land begins its slope to the beach,
there's a tangle of vines and a high fence topped with razor wire.
It's the only place he's been in these first weeks of his return from
which there's no view of the ranges, not even a glimpse, or of the
clouds that shroud them. Looking out to sea, the high spine of Papua
is behind him – but he cannot escape the mountain, for when he
turns, there in the light of Bili's sitting room he can see the large
bark-cloth that hangs from her wall. The jagged peaks of mountain,
all reds and browns and blacks, pack the cloth with energy. Among
them, perfectly placed, is a large star, painted in burned yellow
behind the dots that give it light.

'What makes it so beautiful?' Bili asks, coming out from the
light and standing beside him. 'All these years I've had it, and it still
surprises me. I go for weeks without looking at it and then, suddenly,
it jumps out at me as if to say, *don't forget.*'

259

'Art does that,' Jericho says. 'It keeps us awake.'

'Like the old woman who climbs the mountain each morning, takes the sun from her string bag and hangs it in the sky. *The light by which we all see.* The mountain story. Do you remember?'

She looks at him, but he has turned, back to the dark ocean and the stars that glitter with the tears pooling in his eyes. Something has loosened in him, and right then, beside Bili, he does not want to cry. 'Look at you,' she says softly. 'Mountain boy.'

'Except that I'm not,' he says.

'No, you're not. You're English now.'

'Not that either.' He leans out. Far below, further round the beach, out of sight, are the low tin roofs that were once the international school and are now the NGO compound where Bili has her office.

'Remember Miss Bentley?' Bili says, following the line of his eyes along the cliff into the dark.

He nods, gives a small smile.

'Even prettier than Rika, Laedi said, with a queue of fathers on parent nights, and half of them didn't have a kid in her class!'

'True?' Jericho laughs and whatever it was that had risen in him – longing? fear? hope? – recedes, a tide washing out. Miss Bentley to the rescue. 'I still dream of her sometimes,' he says. 'I thought she was an angel.'

'She let me come into your class for reading, remember, and we sat like this.' Bili brings her head close, and they lean there on the balcony rail, side by side, looking out to the stars, remembering the afternoon heat of the classroom and Bili leaping to her feet each time he got a new word, calling, 'Miss Bentley! Look!' And icecream on the way home – 'Only if it was Martha' – and the strange, wet lap of the beach that alarmed him more than the books on his desk, so unnatural was this great flat expanse of water for which his language had no word. Then the slow forgetting as the colour crayons that drew marks across the paper erased the language of his mother, and the saltwater was no longer so strange on his skin, on his tongue.

'Mountain boy,' Bili says again and he breathes the scent of her, as fresh as the lemons that grew behind Laedi's house, remembering. He tells himself to enjoy the present of her presence, and he does, god alone knows, but everything about her comes swathed in memory, that long-ago classroom overlaid by Bili in London, the day he took her to the Courtauld, where he was studying, showed her the Gauguins, and she didn't know how to pronounce the name, she'd never seen a Gauguin before; why should she, she was studying law. Environmental law. Could any of his smart curator friends name any of the forest trees in faraway, out-of-sight Oceania? She shouted at him in the bus on the way back to his flat.

That flat. He'd loved that flat, his first alone – his cupboard, he called it – until he saw it through her eyes, her dismay at the dark stairs, the damp smell of carpet, the room that never seemed light even when the blind was up. In the morning, when they woke in his bed, he followed her gaze out to a low, grey sky, to the weathered brick of the house next door, the peeling paint of a window that looked across to his, and on its sill a geranium in a pot, a bright splash of red. It was lying there, just days before she left, that she'd said, 'Come back with me,' and, turning, had read the answer in his eyes. *Coward.*

The overlay of memory – the curse of memory – lives in him, *is* him, even as he feels her breath moist on his face. His hands know the shape of her shoulders, the curve of her waist, the swell of her hips, and it is this, only this, the now of her body, her warmth, her taste, her smell, that can banish the past, drawing him into a present emptied of everything but her.

That evening he does not return to Laedi's house where he's been sleeping since he arrived the week before. In Bili's wide bed, under the white veil of the mosquito net, he lies face to face with her and together their minds return to memory. Do you remember? they ask, and they do, all of it, right back to the first kiss the year Leonard brought Jericho back to the mountain when he was fourteen, she just sixteen, and the next, a year later, when Laedi brought Bili to Oxford to see Don, there between wives, a kiss at a fair in St Giles. So much remembering, and with each memory another kiss.

Before they fall asleep, still face to face, Bili rests her hand over his eyes. 'You're in Papua now, remember,' she says. 'If you look too long into a woman's eyes, she'll take your soul.'

Bili rises early. Jericho – who has been known to joke that he works in a gallery because he can do nights but not mornings – rises with her. His eyes open to the silver sheen of ocean outside the window, the cool of dawn, and he is awake, ready for the day. He drives with Bili to her office. She parks the car on a flat stretch that was once grass where as children they played netball, and together they walk up the steps to the Environment Legal Service. Within days he's ceased to wonder that this was once the teachers' room, as he opens the louvres, lets in the morning air and turns on the overhead fans. In other buildings that were once classrooms, other offices are opening for the day. People call out as they climb the steps, open doors, stand on walkways to catch the breeze from the water.

Bili has her own office within the office, a corner walled off from the large room that houses the service. Her desk is piled so high with papers that she's barely visible from the door that announces 'Director'. In the outer room three desks are arranged under the fans. Two are in use, one by the receptionist and assistant, another by a young lawyer, two years out of university. That is the full extent of her staff, though others come in to help, visiting lawyers who put in time *pro bono*. The third desk once had a salary to go with it, but funding is tight, and it is now piled with files waiting for attention. Bili clears them, adding to the piles already teetering on the floor. 'You might as well make yourself useful,' she says, dusting off the chair. Though Jericho has no knowledge of the law, she sets him to work.

On the walls, between shelves of books and filing cabinets, are aerial maps and satellite photographs of mining and logging sites. When Jericho first came to the office, driven there by Laedi soon after he arrived, she told him to look at the maps as he would a painting. Way to the west, a large expanse of forest runs under the soft belly of the bird-shaped island. Cut by rivers and lakes and areas of swamp, remote from towns, there are few roads out there: villages are scattered, gardens – visible from the air – nestle into the forest, a change in the canopy of trees that rise and fall, soft and billowing when viewed from above. Looking at the maps, Jericho understands why rainforests are called lungs. After the Amazon basin, New Guinea forms one of the great lungs of the earth. Scarring these forests, these breathing lungs, are bald, pocked patches the size of small municipalities. The logging camps are visible as pockets of activity, tin roofs set in straight grids along airstrips that are the only way in or out, unless you're a forest-dweller and know the paths that criss-cross the forest floor.

'Illegal clear felling,' Bili says, pointing to a large, bare area. 'We got compensation for the landowners. Not that it solves anything. It won't grow back the forests, or give the people back their gardens.'

Jericho looks at the aerial photos of white and empty earth, stripped of trees, gardens, everything.

'It's remote country,' Bili says. 'No one much has *Tok Pisin*, and it's hard to get in as the logging companies control the airstrips. They tear up your boarding pass if they don't want you there.'

'Has that happened to you?' Jericho feels a chill travel along his spine.

'Sure it has.' Her voice is cheerful, though he knows from Laedi that her work can put her in danger. There's worse than not being let on a plane, Laedi said. Bili's been threatened with a container. A container? Laedi had to spell it out for him. Being locked in a container and left in the heat to die. It happens, she said. People vanish, and if it's discovered, which often enough it's not, it's an accident, a terrible accident, nobody knew.

In front of the map, Bili brushes off his anxieties. She's telling him about the first time she went out there. 'We were taking statements from the landowners,' she says. 'We'd been working all morning, when an old woman insisted I came with her right then to see her land. It was a long walk – I could have done without it – and the woman was muttering in language and we only had a small boy who'd done some school to turn the talk. We came up a small rise to the edge of her land and the woman kept asking, "What do you see?" And all I could see, stretching into the distance, was silence and nothing.'

She stops and looks at Jericho, her face insistent. 'The sounds of the forest were gone – that was almost the worst, an awful empty silence, hard to describe. You don't notice till you step into silence how much sound there is in the forest. And then nothing. The earth had been bulldozed. The topsoil was gone, and there was nothing growing, some weeds and strangling vines. No birds, no rustling. Nothing. The creeks were silted up. That woman's land was dead. She looked me straight in the eye and I knew exactly what she was saying even without the small boy who was whispering, "You must help us." She poked me here.' With an insistent finger, Bili pokes herself on the ribcage just above her heart. "You," she said. "You must stop this."

'I think of that woman every time I go into court.'

The case Bili puts Jericho to work on concerns forests at the other end of Papua, north-east from Moresby, past the mountain, towards the tail of Papua. On the map tacked to the office wall, the forest is thick and pristine along the coast at Collingwood Bay, where Bili is pointing, interrupted only by swamp, areas of swidden agriculture, a curving river.

'Do you see where it is?' she asks.

'Well, there's the mountain.' Jericho moves his finger back along the ranges until he finds the mountain pushing forward onto the northern plain. Oil-palm plantations, marked on the map by a grid pattern of green dots, march like armies in all directions from the town of Popondetta.

'Forget the mountain for a moment,' Bili says, dragging his attention back to the forests along the coast. 'The fjords! See! They're there, at the top of Collingwood Bay.'

'Oh,' he says, and another file opens in his brain: more green, more water, more plumes, more dancing. Another rush of foreboding. Dark-green water. Aaron's body brought back on the canoe. 'Our lives. Why is it so complicated? So spread out. Everywhere. It's like a grenade going off.'

'Don't think of the past,' Bili says. 'There's work to be done.' She gives him a little shake, a smile, and he drags himself to the present, the map, the matter at hand.

'Are they logging the fjords?' he asks.

'No. It's too steep. But they want to log in Collingwood Bay. See, as soon as the fjords end, it flattens out. All that land is accessible from the beach, more or less flat to the mountains. Perfect for logging. Perfect for oil palm.'

'There's no logging on the map.'

'That's because we're fighting,' and she begins another long story for him to wrap his mind around.

He looks at the map, the swidden patches of agriculture. 'Gardens?' he asks.

'All along there.' She traces her finger in the strip between the coast and the curve of the river. 'Beyond that' – her finger moves towards the mountain – 'is hunting ground.'

'So if it's tribal land and the elders don't want it logged, then what's the problem?'

'False registration,' she says. 'If you want to make money logging, it's easy enough to find someone in town who'll make the claim. You pay them off and, if you're quick enough, the bulldozers get in before the villages know what's happening.'

'So how did you find out?'

'From a clerk in the forestry department. He comes from over there. He got suspicious, and some papers fell out of a cupboard.' Bili doesn't know how he came by them. She needs not to know. 'It happens often enough,' she says. 'It's the only way we find out.'

Because customary land is held by clan and tribe, it cannot be sold, she tells him. It is a provision of the constitution written back before independence. 'A beautiful document, everyone says, written to safeguard a way of life that depends on the collective ownership of land.' Bili gives a curt laugh. 'All that idealism Aaron and Rika were part of. They imagined a fine Melanesian future ruled by people like Aaron, but not a future ruled by money.'

Jericho wants to stop her, say Rika isn't idealistic any more, rather the reverse, but Bili is pointing at the files on her desk, requiring his attention. Should the landowners *want* their land logged, she is saying, they have to register it with the full consent of all clan-holders, which can take months, even years, if it's done according to the book. The registered land is then leased to the government, who leases it back to the logging company. 'A good system in theory,' she says, 'but in practice it's easily circumvented.'

In the Collingwood Bay case, a company was formed by business-men who'd been over there and seen the quality of the trees, and where their ships could come in. They then found landowners living in town, and as everyone in town is looking for money, it wasn't hard to persuade them to make the claim that would sign over the land. With a few more payments, a conspirator in Forestry and another in the Titles Registry, the land was registered and leased to the state, which then leased it back to the company that set it all up in the first place. A tidy profit all round, and the people living in Colling-wood Bay, on land they thought of as theirs, inalienable and eternal, would have known nothing about it until the bulldozers and chain-saws arrived. *If* the clerk in Forestry hadn't found the documents as the result of a word here, a whisper there, a countercurrent running against the wages of corruption. He knew exactly how to read them, and who to go to. When he arrived in Bili's office, barges loaded with logging equipment had already left Alotau and were moving slowly up the coast.

'We got an injunction against them landing with only days to spare,' she says.

FOR THREE WEEKS, DAY AND NIGHT, JERICHO IS WITH BILI WHEREVER she goes. He meets her friends, rides in her car, works out in the gym with her. He accompanies her to a conference, immerses himself in the labyrinthine politics of biofuels and *development*, a misnomer if ever there was one, and when the conference ends, he watches her speak to the press. 'Oil palm,' an Australian journalist says. He is belliger-ent. 'Shouldn't you be encouraging biofuel? Reduce our reliance on oil.' Bili smiles. Oh, that smile. 'Let me remind you,' she says in a voice that sounds like somebody else, 'that the island of New Guinea comprises one of our planet's largest stretches of unbroken rainforest. We must weigh that advantage against the cost of deforestation.' She talks on: the net increase in carbon emissions, the impoverishment of communities, and her colleague from Conservation Melanesia talks of the loss of habitat, frog species, bird-winged butterflies, botanical plants. Afterwards they go for a drink in the hotel bar. Their beers sweat in their hands, fans whirl above them, cicadas shrill in the trees, the sun dips into the mountains and while everyone else looks tired, as if the fight has drained them – they've smiled that smile too often – still Jericho is exultant. Just by being there, with Bili, in this land of his birth, he is exultant.

For three weeks, this is his life, at Bili's side. Three weeks of pure happiness, all he's ever dreamed of. At the end of each day he goes home with her to the apartment that looks out over the water.

On this night they are on her terrace again, after a dinner of spaghetti that Jericho has cooked while Bili works at her laptop on the Collingwood Bay case in preparation for a mention in court the next morning. Jacob's firm is acting for the other side, and his strategy is to wear down the landowners, exhaust them into compliance. With each new visit to court, each next adjournment, each next offer of money, again the landowners turn their backs, spit on the ground. They want to fight, and if this is the way they have to fight, this new court way, then they'll fight this way.

'He's a bastard,' Bili says.

But Jericho is not thinking about the landowners, or even of Jacob, whom he's heard enough of already. On this night, the stars are glinting, whole galaxies of them, in a clear black sky. The breeze is soft. Bili is soft. Her hair is loose, freed from the knot that keeps it back, smooth and tight against her head. It bushes out, a dark halo with strands of gold, just as her mother's once had.

Bili smiles, takes his hand. 'It's good you're here,' she says. 'Really good.'

'This time,' he replies, his voice matching the gentleness of hers, 'will you come back with me? When I've been to the mountain, will you come?'

'Are you serious?' She withdraws her hand and folds her arms into herself as if she's been taken with a sudden chill.

'You say it yourself – our lives are caught in the same net. It's time, Bili. We should make a life together. It's not as if we've done that well apart.'

'Is that what you came here to say?'

'Yes.' He looks at her face. 'No. Not only. I came to make peace with this place. With the mountain. With the past. Settle things.'

'*This place*. Is that what it is to you? A place?' Small lines pucker the corners of her mouth. 'If you do *make your peace with it*, whatever that means, and *settle things*, then you can stay here.'

He gives a short laugh of surprise. 'It's dangerous here,' he says. 'For you, especially. The container. You could be killed.'

'So?'

'We could move between. We're both both, aren't we?'

'Tourists in two lands, is that what you want? Get real.' And then her voice softens, no longer sarcastic. 'You haven't lived here since you were eight.' She sounds tired. 'It's okay, fair enough. You don't know it; why should you be loyal? You've given up being Papuan.' He hears the anger flare. Or is it disappointment? 'Okay, you go. Go back to London. Forget all this. You be a white man.'

'I'm not a white man.' He holds out his arm, his strong brown arm, pushes it towards her. 'I'm half. You're more. You're more white. Three-quarters, in fact.'

Her skin is darker than his, years in the sun drawing her closer to the place; he's paled with its absence. 'I'm New Guinea all through,' she says. 'Don't you see? Look. What do you see in this face? Tell me.' She comes up close. Close enough to kiss.

'Papuan. English. They're just words. We're people.'

Her face withdraws. 'Ha!' she says. 'Strip away the art historian, roll back the tape, cancel the Courtauld, cancel your expensive education. Cancel everything, return to the child on the mountain, and what would you be now, with no father and no rights to land, nowhere to garden? You'd be in Popondetta, if you were lucky. Working in the hotel. *If* you were lucky. A kina an hour. *If* you weren't dead. Papuan. English. Huh.' She goes inside, sits at her laptop again.

'I'd be the same person,' he says, following her in.

'You would not. For a start you'd have been raised in a clan. Made by a clan.'

'You weren't raised in a clan. I had five years. You had nothing. And look at your father. How useless is he? Remember that time you came to Oxford and he was never on time to pick you up? He *forgot*, remember? *Leonard* had to ring him. He's not Melanesian, but he believes in commitment and connection.'

'You're getting personal.' Her shoulders are up. Mention of Don touches a bad nerve in her.

'It *is* personal.'

He stands there, forlorn, abandoned, alone. She's pulled her hair back into its knot. Her face is stern, her nose an angry beak. Her eyes are narrowed, looking only at the screen. He feels as if he's been talking all night, all his life, talking and talking, persuading, convincing, making one thing into another, always outside, no matter where he is. Here. There. Nowhere.

'Go,' she says. 'Go back to Laedi's. I've got court in the morning.'

'It's only a mention.'

'*Go!*' she shouts.

On heavy, leaden feet, Jericho walks out of the flat, closes the door, softly – at least he manages that – and walks down the stairs. He wants the taste of salt on his lips, but is afraid to walk the beach in the dark. He asks the security guard, who is smoking with the guard from the block next door, to get him a taxi. While he waits he looks up at the adjacent block, all harsh edges, blank walls; from that angle you don't see the glass balconies that disguise its ugliness. Jacob owns it, Bili says. He must be making a lot of money. The taxi comes slowly up the ramp, low on its suspension. Jericho sinks into its sagging seat and returns to Laedi, through another security gate, past another guard, into the house.

Laedi is still at her desk, with a glass of whisky and papers from her department. She's a minister in Somare's coalition. Her electorate is in the Highlands, for the town near the plantation where she was born. She's got a strong following outside, which gives her a certain power in cabinet, though as a woman she's limited to the department of community development.

'I didn't expect to see you,' she says, turning her face to Jericho. If you're thinking of marrying, he's heard it said, you should look carefully at the girl's mother. That'll tell you what she'll be like when she's old. Would he want to be married to Laedi in twenty years' time? The creases around the eyes, the slight drop of the cheeks are harsh in the lamplight. Her eyes are tired, but her smile is wide and beautiful. Yes, beautiful still. The curve of her nose, so like Bili's, is accentuated by the cast of the light, and sitting there, she is splendid.

'Is Bili working?' she asks. 'Does she have court tomorrow?'

'Yes,' Jericho says. 'A mention in the Collingwood Bay matter.'

'How's it going?'

'Okay, I think.' He doesn't want to talk. He wants to slink off to his room.

'They're a strong community. They used to be warriors,' Laedi is saying. 'They're not going to give up. We've done projects over there. They go well as long as the elders approve.' She's about to go on, but she looks at Jericho, then at the clock. It's late, after midnight. 'You're tired,' she says. 'There's iced tea in the kitchen. Do you want some? You could add a shot of brandy to mine. It helps me sleep.'

Jericho puts a double shot in his, but it doesn't help him sleep. He lies under the lonely mosquito net and curses himself. What a moment to ask. With court tomorrow. He should have waited. He should have chosen his moment. *Thought* about it. The recriminations he can marshal against himself are vast and without mercy.

He gets up, checks that the fan whirring above him is on the highest setting. It is. He checks that the louvres are open. They are, but there is no breeze to let in. He stands under the shower. He dries himself, is immediately sweaty again. He returns to his damp sheet, turns the pillow, and lets pity flood him. Live here with her? That wasn't a thought he'd let lodge in his mind. What would he do? Could he live in this small, dusty, dangerous town? This small, *boring* town? Everything that has charmed him for three blissful weeks seems ugly and oppressive now that he is lying awake, exiled to a hot room. The round hills, the markets, the trees that grow above the beach, even the view from Laedi's house across the harbour, mountains folding away to the distance. *Especially* the mountains. Everywhere, mountains.

If he were in London he could get up right now and get a drink at a bar, he could buy the early edition of the *Guardian*. It would be day there now, and he thinks of his colleagues at the gallery where he has worked for five years, building its success, leaving exhibitions in place so he can take the time for this return. This *thwarted, mistaken* return. He thinks of the café where he liked to lunch. He imagines himself in a bar after work, drinking with friends, leaning back in his chair, laughing, carefree, the great city breathing around him.

In the heat of a Port Moresby night, Jericho, at thirty-six, feels tears of self-pity roll into his pillow. He hears the whirr of a mosquito inside the net and doesn't care. Let it bite him. Let him die up here, let them return his body to the earth of this accursed place.

He forgets the nights he lay awake in his flat in Shoreditch, woken by dreams of tall trees shading the sky, a landscape of dark ridges, sudden clearings of brilliant green inhabited by beings with high heads, feathers dancing in the white, shining light of the moon. He forgets the longing, and the fear that he will be expelled, cast out, never to return to that memory place of earth smells and comfort dimly recalled.

He forgets Leonard sagging low in his chair, his pipes arranged in the large clay dish beside his chair, saying, 'Yes, maybe it's time to go back. Time to reclaim it, or let it rest.' He forgets his response – 'But I couldn't live there' – and Leonard's reply that he didn't know that: 'It's one of the things you need to find out.'

He forgets the softness in his own voice when he speaks of Bili, and he forgets Leonard saying, as if it were a fact as certain as the stars in the sky, that his love for her should be enough to take him back, across the world, even to a town like Port Moresby.

PENANCE COMES IN MANY FORMS.

There is the craven penance that takes Jericho to Bili's office each morning, suffers her haughty displeasure and humbly performs the tasks she sets. He collates testimonies from the Collingwood Bay landowners. He catches the bus out to the university to look up cases, find reports.

It is penance, and he endures it. He doesn't retreat. He doesn't use his return ticket, or escape to Sydney. He sticks it out, day after day, into the winds of July when the town swirls with dust. He endures the heat and the mosquitoes, the blank evenings and long, exiled nights. And Laedi's kindness, which he takes for pity, until imperceptibly it transforms into impatience as the days pass and his mood does not.

Her view is that he's mistaken his longing for a forgotten mother and pinned it onto Bili. 'When you came down from the mountain,' she says, 'it was Bili you wanted, more than Rika. She was your replacement mother. Your sister-mother. Don't you see?'

He doesn't.

'You were little, only five – too young to remember. Janape came with you. Do you remember that?'

He shakes his head. 'I've been told, but I don't remember.'

'Rika insisted. She said that if you were to come to us, you needed a bridge. She didn't want it to be more of a wrench than it had to be, so Janape came, but she didn't stay long. She didn't like being away from the mountain. At least that's what we thought at the time, but over the years I've wondered. She was wise, Janape, and she knew that staying would make it harder. She was going to have to leave you sometime. It'd been decided.'

'What was she like?'

'She walked so quietly we never heard her coming, but we always knew when she was there. There was a force about her.'

'That's what everyone says, but it doesn't give me a fix on her, it's too cloudy. Isn't there something specific? Something she did?'

Laedi thinks for a while. 'That last night, before she left, she lay with you. Rika could hear her talking to you, singing as you slept. She didn't sleep. Nor did Rika. In the morning you went to school and Rika put Janape on the plane, back to the mountain. After that you slept in Bili's bed. It all goes back to then. Don't you see?'

He doesn't. 'Sort of,' he says, but a hard, stuck place in him tells another answer. 'Not really.'

'She gave you the cowrie shell she wore,' Laedi says. 'You must remember that. We rethreaded it onto leather for you, you wore it every day.' *That* hard, stuck place. Yes, he remembers the cowrie shell, and he knows it came from Janape, and he knows the story of his refusal to believe Aaron when he said it came from the sea and had gone to the mountain before coming back to him. It was a mountain cowrie with its own mountain name that he can't remember. But he can remember the feel of it around his neck, the comfort of it, and the boy in the playground at the Dragon School in Oxford who laughed at it. A boy's laugh that has grown over the years to become a terrifying roar. It wasn't the boy who threw the shell away, pushing it down in the rubbish bin. It was Jericho. He buried it, out of sight. Gone for ever. Like Janape, who died of a fever after Leonard took him to England.

In Laedi's house above the harbour in Port Moresby, he lies under the fan and weeps for the mother he doesn't remember.

Laedi tries another tack. 'Why don't you spend this time reading,' she says, and he can hear the effort it takes her to keep impatience from her voice. 'Be constructive. Prepare for the mountain.' He has stopped going into Bili's office each day. Twice a week is enough. More than enough.

Laedi puts a pile of books on the table. They are bristling with yellow stickers. Compulsory reading. More endurance.

And so, from the safe distance of the page, Jericho crosses the ranges to the plain at the base of the mountain, *Huvaemo*, a word that remains deep in him after the rest have flown. He starts with the early anthropologists, as instructed, and finds their language arcane and their kinship charts frankly boring. In any case, until Don and Leonard went to the mountain, none had ventured up to the small tribe perched at the top of its inaccessible flank. Don's book is too full of him to be of use, and Leonard's film has merged into the memory place that has become what Jericho sees when he thinks back. Other anthropologists stayed on the easier terrain of the flat land inhabited by the populous Orokaivans. His people's traditional enemy. Jericho thought he had forgotten, but the memory rises off the page, enough for his shadow to shrink and pull in tight around him. There are those who say you can learn the nature of a man from his enemy, but nothing Jericho reads brings him any closer to the mountain.

He tries the historians. At least they have narratives to tell, like the Japanese troops landing on the north coast in July 1942. They'd have seen the mountain from their battleships, looming over them as they crossed the plain. He reads of the old priest at an Anglican mission who was mending a deckchair when the ships came into view off the beach. Who knows, he said, they may be our friends: *otao naso*. Jericho likes that. But the old man was wrong. Nuns were massacred, villages looted. Men were taken for labour and women hid in swamps and forests. The Japanese didn't go onto the mountain. For them it might as well not have existed, just another peak in a fearful range. It was the Australians who walked up there, interrupting an initiation, rounding up men and boys to work on the Kokoda Track. It was heavy, relentless work, carrying wounded soldiers in one direction, and heavy ammunition in the other.

His mood does not lift.

More books and papers appear on the table. He toils his way through government reports on village resettlements after the war, and the spread of plantations. He even reads the regulations for village latrines. They are oddly interesting.

'How are you going?' Laedi asks.

'Depressing,' he says. 'Even the fonts they use are depressing.'

He'd rather talk of personal history, but Laedi is like Bili, resolutely in the present. He sees how hard she works, hears enough of the fights and manoeuvres that go on in her department. There's rarely an evening when she isn't at her desk. There was one, early on, when they talked of that long-ago visit to Oxford when she'd brought Bili to see Don. They'd all had lunch together at a pub on the river. Rika and Don had argued. What was it about? Jericho asked Laedi. All he remembers is feeling alarm at the adult order starting to tip, but Bili was there, and so was Leonard, and he took them for a walk along the towpath. Laedi said she couldn't recall what the row was about, and when he asked her how the afternoon ended, her mouth puckered. 'Not well,' she said. He'd wanted to ask, *What was it that burst you apart?* but he was afraid he knew the answer, and that it was him.

All he ventured to ask was whether it was true that after Aaron died and Leonard came for him, Laedi thought he should stay here, be educated in the country. For the country. 'That was the thinking, then,' Laedi said, smiling. Leonard said she'd wanted to adopt him, raise him with Bili and Daisy. He looked at her, wondering what it'd have been like to have her as a mother. Would he now be in London, looking for Leonard?

He doesn't let himself form the thought of Bili as a sister.

After days of reading – toil that goes unnoticed by Bili – Jericho begins to lose his taste for penitence. When Bili sends him out to the university on a task that will barely take an hour, he stays for the morning and walks over to the Literature department to find Simeon, who teaches there. He met Simeon with Bili when he first arrived. He's a poet. Laedi has his books, small volumes, which Jericho read during the bliss weeks. When he goes back to them in penance, he finds a language he understands in the words of a man who'd left his village for the mission school, who'd studied at Stanford University, who feels at home in America. There are poems about shopping malls and poetry readings and rap dancers, as well as poems about canoes and masks and *raskol* kids in the settlements. There is a short story about going home to the village, his children bored within days and his relatives emptying every kina from his pocket. And yet, for Simeon there is something there in his *place*, some painful something that can be found nowhere else but in poetry and the songs of his ancestors, who sailed to the beach in the evening sun.

Simeon is at his desk tapping his feet, listening to music as he marks the essays that are piled on his desk and on the floor beside him. He takes off the headphones. 'Hey,' he says. 'How's it going?'

'Not well.'

'Bili?'

'She's kicked me out.'

'Why?'

'I asked her to come back to London with me.'

'Man,' Simeon says. 'Bad move.'

Jericho sees the full scope of the disaster looking back at him in the mirror of Simeon's steady eyes, and immediately feels better.

Two days later, Jericho goes to see him again. This time he disregards the file Bili has left for him with her scrawled instructions. He puts his head round her door and says he's going out to the university, lingering just long enough to see surprise break through the mask of her face. There is a slight swing – a very slight swing – in his step as he walks down the hill. He takes the PMV, walks across the campus to Simeon's building, and climbs the stairs to his top-floor office.

When he tells Simeon about the books Laedi has given him, he says, 'Read us. What are you reading that stuff for? Read our writers.'

He goes to his shelves, and another pile of books lands in front of Jericho.

'When did you say you were brought to Moresby? Before independence? Read what was being written then. It was a wild time.'

'Rika was here then. At the university. She knew Milton.'

'Who's Rika?'

'The woman who took me.'

'Adopted you?'

'Sort of.'

'She knew Milton?' Simeon is impressed. 'Well, read him,' he says. 'He's the best. It took him a while to get over what happened to him in Melbourne, but once he did, he was the best. Read him on being displaced, between one world and another. Just what you need.'

'At least he wasn't mixed race. *Half-caste.*'

'*Hapkas.* It's a great word. My kids use it all the time. They call themselves *hapkas.* I'm from the Sepik, their mother's from Milne Bay. It's a point of pride. Makes them interesting.'

'Not so interesting in my case.'

'Haven't you heard of hybridity?' Simeon says. 'Brother, you've got it bad for Bili, that's all. You should get out of her office – she won't come round while you're like this. She's proud.' He shakes his head and lets out his breath as if he's contemplating a rescue mission. 'Highland women, they're tough. Get out of town, go over to the mountain, find yourself a good woman there.'

'I can't go to the mountain. Not yet.'

'Why not?'

'I'm not ready.'

Simeon looks at him, eyebrows raised in question.

Jericho is caught off guard, and does not want to admit to the inertia that has descended on him. 'For a start,' he says, trying to keep the gloom from his voice, 'they don't know I'm here. I didn't let Leonard tell them. And now, well, all this with Bili. I don't know where to start.'

'Build a link through the people in town.'

'There probably aren't any. There're less than two thousand of them all up. So few, even you hadn't heard of them. Us.'

'Them,' Simeon says. 'No one's heard of everyone. There'll be some in the settlements for sure. You can find anyone in this town. I'll do it for you.'

He stands up, puts the books in a bag for Jericho. 'Come,' he says. 'Let's have a coffee.'

*

Jericho reads Milton's poems, and thinks he recognises himself in the line about the *hapkas* kid who stands on the edge of the saltwater and watches the ships, waiting for his father from the other side of the strange wide ocean. He turns to the imprint page and reads the date of publication. 1978. Yes, it fits, and the line too about the bird of paradise. Aaron, he supposes, vanishing into the depths of the sea.

'Was Milton writing about Aaron?' Jericho asks Laedi.

'Don't take him literally,' Laedi says. 'He's not reliable when it comes to how things are.'

'Or were,' Jericho says.

'That too. He's a *writer*.' Her voice isn't dismissive exactly, but clearly she doesn't think it worth taking Milton seriously for an account of any facts.

He tries the same question on Simeon, even though he was just a kid on a river when Milton was writing of the *massy green*, the lonely bird whistle.

'It's sure to be true,' he says in a cheerful voice while he goes on sorting the papers on his desk.

'True how?' Jericho wants his full attention, and doesn't get it.

'True in the way poetry's true,' Simeon says, which is no more help than Laedi's dismissal of it as not *fact-true*. 'Have you tried his first novel? Plenty of truth there.' He stands up to take it from his crowded shelves. He knows exactly where it is. *The Jericho Road.* When he puts it on the desk, Jericho starts. He hasn't heard of the Jericho Road, and Simeon has to tell him it was where the parable of the Good Samaritan happened.

'You'd better read it,' he says.

Jericho starts it that very day, carefully opening the badly printed edition with pages falling out. Simeon says he'll kill him, should he lose a single one. Laedi is in the islands visiting community training centres funded by her department, so Jericho reads as he eats alone in the kitchen. He reads on in bed, the lamp angled through the mosquito net, staying awake into the night to finish the story of

Baldwin Rufus, once a mission boy, who goes to Chicago to study Martin Luther King; Baldwin Rufus, the impractical revolutionary who, on his return, seizes the plantation, sets up his republic, where reading is the order of the day and his small band of conspirators march around with the one gun they have between them. When they march over the Kokoda Track, that dangerous road, they are ambushed only by their own irrelevance. There is no rebel army to meet them. No police to arrest them. No press. Nothing. Singing as they march up the last rise into an empty clearing, there's nothing to greet them but forest, and an audience of birds. Behind them lies a track they don't want to walk again. There's nothing for it but to walk on past the plantations until they find a truck to give them a lift down the scarp. In town, Baldwin Rufus goes to find his liberal white friends. The wife is alone in the house and she lets him fuck her as if that's a revolutionary gesture in itself, and something about it disgusts him even as it adds piquancy to his rage, more so when her husband returns and gives him a beer. He gets drunk, vomits and sleeps on the couch of the forgiving whites who call him an intellectual as if all is redeemed if he makes a theory of it.

So which part of that does Simeon think is true?

'Don't be literal-minded,' Simeon says the next day. 'Anyway, it was the seventies,' as if that was explanation enough. He's got more inter-esting news for Jericho. He was right, you can find anyone in Moresby. All he had to do was ask someone from the settlement behind the university, who asked someone else, and yes, he tells Jericho, there are people from the mountain in town. Not many, but a few, and they've been waiting for this news. They'll be round to find you, he says. You don't need to do anything.

Sure enough, within the week a small, chunky man with a thick beard and eyes that bulge like eggs appears at the guard post outside Laedi's house. He is a clerk in Fisheries, younger than Jericho, and utterly unsurprised to see him. The chiefs had said he would return this year. Lilla, the chief of the women, had had a dream.

'*Wantok*,' he says. 'Brother,' embracing him with a hand to his arm and a nose brought close. '*Rovane.*' The mountain word for welcome.

His name is Young Albert. He has the air of a man executing a commission.

'Albert is my father,' he says, and Albert swims into Jericho's mind, the young mimic appearing and disappearing at the edges of Leonard's film. For the rest, Jericho is uncertain as Young Albert lists more names – an arc of kinship – names he recognises from the chart Leonard has made for him, but they are without faces, without blood or history.

Jericho takes Young Albert into the house. He stands in the large room as if he is an auctioneer making an inventory. He shows no interest in the view from the window, though he takes in the curtains, along with the size of the table, the number of chairs, the drawers in Laedi's desk, the telephone, the television, the books on the shelves. He stands in front of the bark-cloth on the wall, the filigree of the hooked vine the chiefs had long ago sent down to Rika.

'Nogi,' Young Albert says.

He goes to the framed photographs on the sideboard and picks up one of Bili and Jericho as children perched on the branch of a tree that is overhanging smooth water. In the distance, out of focus, is a wall of green.

'This is from where?' Young Albert asks.

'From the fjord coast,' Jericho says.

'Aaron's place?'

'Yes.'

Jericho sits with him at the table, and Young Albert's noticing eyes turn to him as if he, too, is on the inventory. Jericho feels at once too large and too small, encased in the shame of remembering back to the visit he'd made to the mountain as a young teenager, his surly behaviour, his rejection of everything he saw. Does Young Albert remember? Jericho cannot distinguish which of the boys he'd been; it was as if he'd closed his eyes, closed his mind. And now, here he is, wanting to open them, but not knowing how. Faced with kin, he's as uncertain as the teenager he'd been.

They sit like this for a while, Young Albert looking, and Jericho feeling less like a host pouring lemon water into a glass than a specimen laid before a naturalist. It is demoralising. Then Young Albert leans across the table, shakes Jericho's hand, says it is good, *gut tru*, that he's returned. He will tell the chiefs, and he and Jericho can go back to the mountain and set up a business. There's too much corruption in Port Moresby, and his children's teachers don't turn up to school.

'They learn bad ways,' he says. '*Bisnis* is better. We make money for school fees, for medicines, for ourselves.' He beams. 'No corruption.'

He is one of the boys who was chosen by the chiefs to go to school on Leonard's fees, paid year after year so there'd be men who could earn money for the villages, advocate for them, take over the role of outside provider. Jericho knows the agreement that was made when Leonard went to the mountain after Aaron died, the time he talked to the chiefs about bringing him to England. And he knows Leonard offered the school fees in part so that the burden wouldn't fall only to him. Leonard didn't want inheritance to become an encumbrance. But how can it be anything else when Young Albert tells Jericho that most of them who went to school don't like life in the town, and anyway there aren't enough jobs? There are a few in Popondetta, but there is never enough money. And in case Jericho has not understood what Young Albert is saying, he repeats that he's been waiting all this time for him to return, so that he can go back to the mountain ground where his children should grow. '*Bisnis*,' he says again, beaming. 'Together, we start a *bisnis*.'

'What sort of business?' Jericho asks reluctantly.

'Ecotourism,' Young Albert says, taking from his bag a large brown envelope of papers. The envelope is grubby, bent around the edges. He's done a *bisnis* course. He pulls out diagrams and columns of figures, and photographs of guesthouses from an ecotourism office in town. He passes them across the table to Jericho.

'I have a business plan,' he says. 'You and me, us two, we shall be manager. The Mountain Resort.'

*

'Oh my God,' Jericho says to Simeon. 'They want me to manage a resort. It's like now I've returned, what am I good for? Never mind, how are you, how's it been for you all these years away from us?'

Simeon laughs. 'Be realistic,' he says. 'You're an investment. That's why they gave you out.'

'No, it wasn't. I was *given*, if that's what it was, because I had no land and no rights. That's what the chiefs decided and what I've always been told. I was some kind of original burden.'

'That too,' Simeon says. 'What kind of a life would it have been, a *hapkas* kid hanging around useless? This way you're a resource. Don't you get it?'

'You're cynical.'

Simeon laughs again. 'Realistic,' he says.

'Anyway,' Jericho says. 'What do I know about ecotourism? I can't live up there running some crackpot guesthouse situation.'

'You don't have to. All you have to do is set it up, bankroll it, and then leave them to it.'

'I haven't got any money. It's all I can do to pay my mortgage.'

Simeon laughs again. It's becoming irritating. 'That's white-man talk. You've got access to money. They haven't. I haven't. That's the difference.'

'Who's going to walk up there?' Laedi says. 'Ecotourism won't work. It rarely does unless there's an airstrip nearby and a good reef. Tourists like the coast. You'll have to come up with something else.'

'Like what?' Jericho asks. What is it that's wanted of him? By Laedi, by Young Albert, by Bili? By this ache of a place?

An edge of panic enters the hot, lonely tent of his mosquito net with him. Sleep is a distant prospect. Instead Jericho conducts a conversation in his head with Simeon. A tirade. Didn't you say that *hapkas* was good, a state of being to celebrate? When all along a *hapkas* kid on the mountain is a *worthless burden*. You said so yourself. Janus-faced. Like Bili. And don't tell me Melanesian masks are multiple, face upon face, different registers of truth. Don't talk of the surrealists. I've heard it all before.

Hapkas. It's a state of penance, and that night Jericho does not like it.

SEPTEMBER COMES, AND WITH IT THE CELEBRATION OF INDEPENDENCE. Thirty years since the Australian flag with its Union Jack in the corner was lowered, and the bird of paradise flag raised. Thirty years since the Prince of Wales stood in the mud and saluted. Thirty years since Aaron died.

The town is filling with people travelling in by truck, by canoe, by foot, to join the celebrations. Driving past the stadium with Bili late one afternoon, Jericho can hear the rehearsals: school children drilled into formation, choirs belting it out, the drumbeat of dancers. Bili has unbent, Laedi has insisted, not that it makes it any easier. To add to his misery, Jericho has her determined display of *sisterliness* to endure.

'It's worse,' he says to Simeon. 'At least when she's angry, there's hope.'

Passing the stadium with its sounds of the pageant being rehearsed, Bili and Jericho are on their way to the university, where there's an exhibition of photographs from independence at the library. They are meant to be meeting Simeon, but he's not there. They cross the dry campus, over grass worn down to its stubs, and climb the stairs to his office. His door is locked. The light is off. They walk back through the dust, circle the exhibition, and come to a stop in front of a photo-graph of Aaron standing in a group of men behind Somare as he signs the papers declaring self-government in 1973.

'That's when you came to us,' Bili says.

'He looks so young,' Jericho says.

'That's how we remember him,' Bili says. 'We only knew him young.'

'I don't mean that. I mean at the time, when we were kids, he was old, and huge.' Jericho lifts his arm way over his head. 'And now we're older than any of them were.'

'Grown-ups are always large,' Bili says.

'It makes me sad.'

'Why? It's how it is. No reason to be sad.'

'If he hadn't died,' Jericho says. 'If he'd lived, would he have grown fat and slumped?'

'Would he be corrupt?' Bili says. 'That's the question.'

'God, you're tough,' Jericho says. On the phone Leonard had said to remember that she has her vulnerabilities too, but in the mood he's in now, he can't see them.

'Realistic,' she says. That word again.

'All that hope. It must make you sad.'

She shrugs. If it does, she isn't saying.

'Losing Rika,' Jericho says. 'That made you sad. You hated it. You said so. In London, remember?' She had, in his bed in that cupboard of a flat. He remembers the sorrow in her voice when she described how empty it had been, going back to the house after seeing him and Rika off on the plane with Leonard. Then Martha and Pete went back to Australia. Everyone gone, and they were just a family in Hohola, the platform no longer used, the tin taken off the roof, the table dismantled for its planks. Gone. All of it gone.

'A long time ago,' she says, and at that moment, just as her mouth settles into a firm line, Simeon arrives, flustered and dusty.

'We're looking at Aaron,' Jericho says, pointing him out in the photo.

'It's making Jericho sad,' Bili says, and this time Simeon is on Bili's side.

'Sentimental,' he says. 'Idealism's always sentimental.'

'I've heard you say it was the best of times, back then before independence,' Jericho says.

'For writing. That's different.' He's as sore as a bear. His mobile has been snatched on the road coming in and he's only had it a month. 'What are we celebrating?' he says. 'Independence for what? For this?'

'Come back to Laedi's for a beer,' Bili says and all the way in the car she and Simeon bicker. Did independence come too soon? Whose interest was it in? Papua New Guinea's? Australia's? Is neo-colonialism any better? Than what? Than the grip of Asian loggers?

Jericho has no opinion. He can't grasp the idea of Papua New Guinea as one place. It's too big, with too many parts, too many tribes, too many tampering hands. Split, like his memories. The mountain and the fjords: different places, different memories. Different masks. No. Different *deaths*. He skitters back from this thought. In the back seat of Bili's car, he consoles himself by looking at her head. Her hair is tied back, but wisps of curl escape and fall into the collar of her pale blue shirt. He can see the clasp of the necklace he gave her.

All evening he is silent as the talk flies around him. He hardly listens, it's the usual discussion of alliances and deals and betrayals that split one governing coalition and form another. Somare is prime minister again – three years of stability, Laedi says, and she expects it to continue. She serves in his cabinet. When Bili criticises his environmental policies, Laedi sighs. 'It's better than it used to be,' she says, and the talk returns to Somare back at the start, and the hopes they had. Real hopes. Despite all that they saw, all that they knew, there was still reason for hope.

'Did they work as hard as Rika says?' Jericho asks. 'Hard enough to kill Aaron?'

'He drowned,' Bili said. 'It was an accident.'

'It could have been a heart attack.'

'Sorcery, more like.'

'You don't believe in it.'

'I don't. But that doesn't mean it doesn't happen.'

He takes a deep breath, prepares himself for the argument that's brewing, but Laedi puts a stop to it. She gives Bili a warning look and sends her to the kitchen for more beer.

Laedi's house is full of people staying for the celebrations. Too many faces, he can't get their wide web of connection sorted out – it's enough to know they are her relatives from the Highlands. She sends the fares, she buys the food, and they fill the kitchen, thick with the smell of cooking. Tamba is there – he remembers her, *of course* he remembers; the soft touch of her hand, her wide lap, her comforting presence, lying beside him when he couldn't sleep. Tamba and Bili. He'd sleep between them, and in the morning Tamba would prepare cold yam and lemon water. Now she fusses over him, 'Ah, Jericho, so big, so strong, you came back to us.' She brews Highland coffee for him, not the Italian coffee Laedi buys from Australia.

With Laedi's relatives, there's no room in the house for the young men from the mountain, Jericho's *wantoks*, who have walked over the Kokoda Track with their peanuts to sell. Young Albert is offended that there's nowhere for them in this reward of a house. He is sulky. Jericho doesn't know how to remedy the offence, apology adding to his woes. He has no idea how many are coming, or why. He doesn't know whether the peanuts and the celebrations are enough to bring them. Or whether it's him, the investment, they are making the long trek to inspect.

'It's not so far,' Young Albert says. 'Australian tourists, they make big work.' He mimes them gasping for breath, struggling along the track under the weight of their packs. 'For us, it's like a road. The ones coming, they do it often.'

'How often?'

'Some time. Some time.'

'What shall I do?' Jericho feels his voice thin and pleading. 'Where will they stay?'

'They stay at the settlement. *Wantoks* there.' Young Albert grins. 'It's okay. We'll go to the market, buy fish and beer.'

Vertiginous is the word Jericho uses to describe the state he's in, spinning from the strange new perspective that arrives with the boys from the mountain. Boys, they call themselves, and that's how they seem to Jericho in their ragged clothes, pulsing with unpredictable energy. He is wary of them, and of the bearded man who arrives with them, whom he takes to be an emissary from the chiefs with messages of welcome. His uncertainty before this next array of kin he does not know has him precarious and afraid of falling. He cannot answer their questions, or understand the language that was once his, so he can't gauge what they want, and as a result he buys too much beer. The boys are drunk on three bottles, and so is Jericho. Young Albert watches with frank disapproval. He takes Napo, the bearded one, back to his family in Gerehu, the suburb out past the university where he lives, leaving Jericho in the settlement with the boys. He is too drunk to mind. Besides, he is making a friend of Presley, who wears his baseball cap backwards and who knows how to rap. He works at the post office in Popondetta and speaks English after a fashion. Unlike the others, his clothes are sharp. Cheap, but sharp. He draws Jericho a map in the dust, a family tree – except his grows up from the ancestor roots – and there they are, his mother's brothers, five of them, sturdy branches growing up, and tucked behind them, not yet strong enough to make branches of their own, are his cousins. At least, he thinks that's what they are, and their children: a great array of names. Napo has his own branch as the eldest son of Janape's eldest brother, and his sons and nephews are among the boys crouched around Presley as he draws the tree in the dust. They grin when he calls out their names. Jericho, the child of the mountain, the singular child with his singular skin, is surrounded by kin. Test his DNA and he'd be in a great pool of sameness.

Life in the settlement has taken him by surprise. He'd expected to find the open-mouthed scream of German expressionism. Instead, he finds women sweeping the ground outside rough houses, worn shirts washed and hanging on a line strung between trees. The settlement they're in is on the edge of town, near the airport, a shanty on marginal land, one enclave among many for the thousands who come looking for work and adventure and end up in these tacked-together places. It's not as bad as Jericho imagined, not as bad as the stories he's heard. There's corn growing, rusted-out cars, chickens scratching at a pile of rubbish. Even that is picturesque. There's nothing *African* about the settlement, by which he means nothing as swollen-bellied and grinding as the TV screens make out. That's starvation. This is poverty, and though he wouldn't want it for himself, in the midst of

song and string band, and with too many beers in him, he enjoys
the sense of being part of it and becomes sentimental about a life he
doesn't need to endure. He takes the guitar, there's a round of cheers,
and he dances until at last he falls asleep next to Presley on a hard mat
– too tired to dream, flat-out among the boys, his kin. In the morning
he finds that nothing has been pilfered from his pockets. He's yet to
see a fight that's anything like the fights Simeon has described. Stay
out of the settlements, he warned, and when Jericho tells him of the
songs and the girls and the taro roasted in the fire where the women
cook, Simeon is not convinced.

'Come with me,' Jericho says. 'See for yourself.'

'Nice try,' he replies. And then, 'You'll learn.'

On the day of the independence celebrations, Jericho relinquishes the
seat that's been reserved for him with Laedi and Bili, instead squeezing into the stadium through a hole in the fence with the boys from
the mountain. They're wearing the shorts he bought them at a trade
store, and he's wearing the same. He's on the upswing, no longer an
imposter – *authentic*, he thinks – as the sun beats down through the
long wait, and a slow, resentful clap starts up until Somare arrives,
very late.

Jericho is part of the wild applause as the pageant begins. Hundreds
of schoolchildren tumble into the stadium in an acrobatic display of
mountains forming. He cheers the first ancestors as they draw fire
from the earth, and he roars for the coming of the sea people in their
canoes and *lakatois*. There's a louder roar yet for the coming of the
white men with their flag. Jericho spins back to his other self, astonished by the cheers that ring out for the big war with the Japanese,
and the native bearers who carry wounded soldiers, their faces painted
white on the rollicking stretchers that circle the ground. Something
queasy happens in his stomach as an Australian woman from Laedi's
department stands in a cart and reads a poem about the fuzzy wuzzy
angels who, 'Though their skins are surely black,/Have proved the
whiteness of their hearts/On that Kokoda Track.' But cheers are in

the crowd, and in the air, and he rejoins the applause until his throat is hoarse, as squadrons of dancers, plumed and painted and rival-rous, spin into the arena, each group out-dancing the last. Of all the applause, of all the cheers, the greatest is for the Christian missions, the priests who cross the stadium with their crucifixes and their bibles. Bigger even than independence and the bird of paradise flag, though it gets a roar, sufficient to lift Somare's heart when he walks into the stadium as 'the chief, the father of the nation'. The appearance of God in paradise, Bili says afterwards. She says she's the only person in this whole damn place who isn't a Christian. Even Simeon says he is, sort of, though he never goes to church.

'Jesus,' Presley says, 'good man true,' and he leaps in applause. 'He die on a tree. Very good. He die for PNG.'

When the celebration finishes, Jericho walks in the singing crowd back to the settlement, where the pageant goes on, every scene re-enacted and embellished. Jericho takes the part of Captain Moresby sailing into the harbour – though he hasn't read the account Laedi left for him – and that evening he feels at one with the boys who tumble as mountains, drop dead on the ground as wounded soldiers and rise to become missionaries. It feels good, sitting there on the ground chewing that foul-tasting betel, aiming his own globules of red spit, his lips and tongue numb. Napo takes a turn as the first ancestor raising fire from the earth, and Young Albert lights a cigarette, trans-forming himself into a politician, his pockets full of cash.

It is a good night: fun, raucous, a few fights, nothing much, until the beer runs out and the steam they brew appears, and the police arrive in a blaze of threats and noise and flashing lights. Jericho doesn't know what it is that they want – nothing, it seems – but there's shouting and lining people up until, just as suddenly, they leave. Everyone sinks into despondency, the steam they're drinking is evil stuff, made of bad thoughts; fights begin, the old people grum-bling that it wasn't like this when the Australians were here. Even Young Albert is praising the order of colonial times, until Presley says, no, they were no good, remember, they called us *bois*, the elders and the chiefs, and they took what they wanted, bastard Australians, and now they're trying to get back, still bullying us and taking our trees.

He lies down on the ground and goes to sleep, but before he does, he opens his eyes, squints at Jericho. 'You go to your house now,' he says. 'Go with Young Albert.' He chuckles, a dark, ominous chuckle – Jericho has never heard its like – and closes his eyes.

Jericho walks down the road with Young Albert, who stops a truck that drops him in town. He limps back to Laedi's feeling sick. The steam is burning a hole in his gut. The road up the hill to the house is steep; he thinks he won't make it before the diarrhoea strikes. Lights shine on the dark water of the harbour, and the sight of them brings him a faint memory of starry nights he's known in another existence, lived mainly on canvas.

The house is quiet. Laedi is still at the official reception. There's no one there except for an old lady in the kitchen. She gives Jericho a yam. 'Good for *watershit*,' she says.

THE NEXT MORNING YOUNG ALBERT AND NAPO ARE AT THE GUARD post outside Laedi's house. They've come to talk business. Jericho's head aches. He makes coffee, real coffee, and they look doubtfully into their cups, spoon in the sugar. '*Bisnis*', they say. The guesthouse. The chiefs. Young Albert has his business plan out on the table.

Jericho looks at the rows of figures. 'It won't work,' he says, as blunt as that, and Young Albert fixes him with an unblinking gaze. Napo leans across, and in a low voice says something that Jericho cannot understand, though he sees – he thinks he sees – disdain in those watchful eyes.

Young Albert nods, then tells him again that the chiefs said he would return, this time adding that now there will be prosperity on the mountain, they will have money for blankets and lamps. Now they will grow cash crops like vanilla; the price of coffee will go up, and they will install a radio phone. Young Albert smiles a wide smile. 'We finish with peanuts now,' he says. 'Peanuts are no good. Big work, small money.' There is a buzzing sound in Jericho's ears, as if his head is full of night insects. He says nothing. There is nothing he can say.

Young Albert watches as Jericho goes for aspirin, brings water and fruit to the table, a loaf of bread, a jar of jam, to compensate for his weakness, his incapacity, his guilt.

It is then that Young Albert tells him, again, about the war and the Australians interrupting the initiation, taking the boys to work on the Kokoda Track. There was no choice, the police marched them down the mountain with their guns. And he tells him about the Japanese who came from who knows where, an empire from the sun, and afterwards, when the big fight was over, about the Australians walking down to the coast, landing their planes and driving their jeeps, shouting out to everyone that they were *masta* again. And how they captured the men who'd worked for the Japanese and marched them to a special place where they killed them dead. The Australians had a machine for killing men, Young Albert tells him; the father of one of the chiefs saw it when he was still a boy, down on the plain with his uncle. He tells Jericho how he is related to this man who saw the machine, and how many children he had, and which of the children live still, and how many children they have, all the way down until they reach the room in Laedi's house where the relatives to the witness of this machine sit. It was kept, Young Albert says, at the top of a small house. The Australians walked the men to be killed – Orokaivan men, all of them – up the steps to the platform of this house. The machine came down on top of them, round their necks like a large pair of scissors. When the soldier pulled the lever – Young Albert demonstrates with a hefty yank – the head flew sideways. Dead.

'Did the Australians hang collaborators?' Jericho asks Laedi.

'Some,' she says, 'but not in public.'

Simeon says it's a metaphor and there's no point getting into statistics, or explanations of hanging. Anyway, is rope better than giant scissors? 'It had the effect they wanted,' he says. 'What did you do? Don't tell me: you agreed to do business, any business. You'd agree to anything after that.'

'Vanilla,' Jericho says. 'I've been reading up on it. It should grow at that altitude, and I think I can afford it. Only it takes seven years to mature.'

Simeon laughs. 'White man,' he says. 'White-man guilt.'

That night Young Albert takes Jericho to his house in Gerehu, where his wife and her sister and his mother have cooked a large feast. The room is small and full. The paint is old, and the windows covered in tough wire. Mats are spread out on the floor, and Jericho is invited to sit. Small children push their fingers into his hair. 'Like yours,' he says, and they shake their heads. '*Hapkas*,' they say. Young Albert's old mother shoos them away, and sits beside him stroking his arm, murmuring in the language he cannot speak.

'She is the sister-cousin of your mother,' Young Albert translates. 'She says it is good you are here – a man must return to his place, know his kin before he dies.'

'Tell her,' Jericho says, 'I am sorry I do not speak her language.'

'It's your language too,' comes the reply. 'No good for a man to lose his talk. Lose his talk, he lose his mother's bones. Grave, she means.'

'I am sorry,' Jericho says again.

'It's okay,' Young Albert says, and the old woman speaks again, her hands patting the air and coming to rest on Jericho's arm.

'What does she say?' he asks.

'It is a long time before you die. You will learn to speak again.'

The meal is large and generous: great bowls of sweet potato, fish from the market, watermelon, tomatoes. Children lean towards the food, and the women hold them back to let the men, the visitors, take theirs first. The boys are hungry from the nights in the settlement. After the first plates of food are gone, everyone speaks at once. Jericho hears snatches of many stories, and deep inside him a kind of joy, such as he has never known, rushes at him in this hot, crowded room without a fan whirring overhead. It's a feeling unknown to him in London, being a part of a clan, but even as he takes a breath and expands, he hears the words *bisnis* and *resort* and *vanilla*, and feels himself shrink as the spinning returns so fast there's nothing left of him but a tiny speck.

More food arrives on the table – eggs, pineapple, biscuits – carried in by a young girl, maybe twelve, thirteen already, with shy eyes the exact colour of his own. She could be a sister, even a daughter. Something tender rises in him, a flood of imagining, of Bili as her mother, the same almond eyes, the same skin, soft and brown, not yet hardened by the sun.

The glow of belonging returns. Kith and kin. Blood of my blood. Union. *Union*, he thinks in the midst of his kin. There is no union. Just strangeness and wanting. Suddenly he wants to lie down, escape into sleep.

Later that evening, when at last the children have fallen asleep and the house empties, Jericho goes back to the settlement with Presley and the boys. The roads are full – cars, trucks, people walking – as if the whole town is going somewhere. They come to the fork in the road where he could turn towards the harbour and Laedi's house, the comfort of his bed. He hesitates. The revolving door in his head, or his gut, wherever it is, turns from the knowledge that he should care for himself and leave, and round he goes, one of the boys again, wanting to be like them, liked by them. So he walks on with them towards the settlement. The pubs and hotels are shut. There's nowhere to buy beer, the government closes everything down when the town is full and there are holidays and celebrations. As they walk, he realises that the movement around them is aimless. No one's going anywhere, just circling about, retracing their steps, moving again, following another rumour of where the steam is. They pass scuffles and fights. They get a lift on the back of a truck. Grit blows in their eyes as they grind up the hill near the airport. The lights for the runway are off. It's late.

He should have gone home. *Home.* Even the simplest of words disorientates him.

At the settlement there's more of the steam that comes in the misshapen bottles that made Jericho sick the night before. He knows he's made the wrong decision, but he's there now, and when the bottle is passed to him he drinks. The mood is surly, there's no taro in the fire tonight, there's no string band, no ukulele, no dancing. Groups of men are smoking in the shadows; there is something aggressive about them, and they don't call over. Jericho feels sick, walks to the gutter, tries to vomit – the steam, he supposes – and when he returns, two girls have appeared, he has no idea where from, with swollen faces and blood on their legs. A woman comes out of one of the shacks. She yells at the men smoking, there are shouted accusations and boys he doesn't recognise come running into view. A fight starts. When the police arrive, Jericho thinks it's because of the girls. A boy is being thrashed; another man swings a belt at the girls. The police do nothing to intervene. The girls are yelling, the police are yelling. It's nasty this time. Sirens, guns, spotlights. There's been a hold-up on the road and a man was shot when he tried to reach behind his carseat for a gun. Jericho doesn't know what's happened. He throws up right there, and this time his head really is spinning, and his ears are roaring. He throws up again. Everything is in slow motion. His gut gives a dangerous gripe as he is hauled to his feet by the police. He feels the motion of the police truck. He lies on the jolting, moving floor and feels the release of shit on his legs. Blankness settles around him.

He remembers nothing, nothing at all, when he wakes on a concrete floor. He can smell the stink of himself. There are stinking bodies asleep around him. He has no idea who they are or why he is there, and this time, when it might be a scene from Käthe Kollwitz, he doesn't think of art. He looks at the bars and sees he's in a cell full of people. More like a large wire cage than a cell. Beyond the concrete yard outside he can see faint light. Dawn maybe. His head is throbbing, he wants to pee. He can hear someone across the cage piss into a drain. Is it a drain? A bucket? He raises his head. There are more people in the next cage. He sees Presley's head, he thinks he sees Presley's head. He hears voices, and doors clanking as nausea drifts back over him. He turns, the floor hard on his hips. A pair of familiar shoes is standing next to his head. He looks up and Bili is yelling at him.

'Have a good look round,' she says. 'Is this where you want to end up?'

Napo is standing beside her. His face is long and sorry.

'Get up,' Bili says, and he struggles to his feet. He looks for a tap. There isn't one.

Bili's done whatever it is she had to do to get him out. And the others, all of them. There are no charges, but the boys from the mountain – and Napo, who wasn't even there when they were arrested – must leave that morning, back over the Kokoda Track. All of them. That's the deal. As they come out of the cages, they stand in the concrete yard rubbing their eyes while a police sergeant shouts at them. Their heads are no better than Jericho's.

'It can't have been too bad, if they didn't charge us,' Jericho says. He's in the ignominious position of having to sit on an old towel in the back seat of her car.

'You know nothing,' Bili says. Her jaw muscles are set grim.

Outside the window, the hills are glowing a pale orange in the early sun; as they come over the saddle to the harbour, the water glistens, calm and beautiful. Out on the horizon there's a low band of cloud. Through the windows, open against the smell of him, Jericho tastes a tang of salt in the breeze.

'You owe me one,' Bili says as she dumps him at Laedi's door.

JERICHO RETURNS TO HIS BOOKS. WHAT ELSE CAN HE DO? HE SKULKS out of sight at the back of Laedi's house, avoiding everyone. Even Simeon makes a joke of it – 'Hey, shitman' – and when he's finished every le Carré in the house, he takes a deep breath and goes back to the beginning. Whose beginning? Bili's voice is lodged in his head. A beginning, the beginning of this hot, stifling town.

At the back of Laedi's house is a slab of concrete, two laundry sinks, an old laundry copper. Below the slab is a small stretch of grass where washing is dried, before the wall of the garage next door. There's an awning over the copper and next to it, in the shade, a hard seat. Sitting there one morning, Jericho reads that when Captain Moresby sailed into the harbour in February 1873, he found 'well-fed, contented-looking people'. Ships had been seen passing out to sea beyond the reef, but the *Basilisk* was the first to find the deep passage into the harbour, and when it did, the canoes came out to take a look. Captain Moresby invited the men aboard, recording in his log that they took great interest in everything, bringing out 'rushes carefully knotted together' with which they measured the decks.

In exchange, the men from the canoes invited the captain and his men to a large village consisting of 'two rows of well-built houses separated by groves of cocoa-nut trees' on the edge of the harbour. During their five days anchored in the harbour the captain and his men 'visited often'. The women 'seemed to busy themselves much in pottery', Jericho reads, 'and moulded clay into large globe-shaped jars, which they baked slowly among the embers of wood fires'. He reads a description of 'a vegetable porridge' cooked in one of these jars, 'with cocoa-nut finely shred over it'. The captain 'found it excellent'.

At the villages the captain visited, 'the men liked to hold our hands as we walked through', but they didn't want the strangers going into their houses. 'If we pressed the point they yielded in this, and awaited us patiently outside.' Melanesian courtesy, Laedi would say, but Jericho is angry with the people of that long-ago village for being so polite. So credulous. Even after this intrusion into their houses, they offered fresh green coconut to the captain and his men.

While in the harbour the men from the ship were also taken inland to hill gardens. 'All the valleys we travelled over were covered with rich grass, shoulder high, and had we possessed an army of Irish scythes, and an English market, we might have cut down our fortune.'

On the hard bench at the back of Laedi's house, Jericho makes a huffing grunt. Is it in the English gene to turn even grass to profit? He puts down the book, creeps past the buckets and mops at the back door – he can hear the women cleaning inside singing out to each other as they work – and looks down to the harbour, where cranes are working on the wharfs.

'You want tea? Soft drink?' One of the women is standing at the back door. Jericho shakes his head and she comes over. 'No good sitting here,' she says. 'You strong man yet.' He shakes his head again, and wishes her away. Her kindness is a salt.

His mood is dark as he starts on the next account of the trading post that is named after Captain Moresby. It makes depressing reading. Just short of twelve years later, when Commodore Erskine sailed into the harbour to claim the south-eastern portion of Papua as a British protectorate, it's a very different picture. On board HMS *Nelson* was a journalist from the *Sydney Morning Herald*, who reported on quarrelling natives, and men thought to be chiefs 'destitute of clothing'. Port Moresby, by his account, was a wretched place. Twelve years of planters and traders and missionaries, and the village of well-built houses separated by coconut groves had become a place of poverty and previously unknown forms of sickness.

In recognition of their protection, a ceremony was held in which 'gifts attractive to the native eye' – a tomahawk, a knife, a coloured shirt, a piece of cloth and twist tobacco – were given out to each of the men thought to be chiefs, who were grouped with the officers for a photograph. The faces of the old men are sad and bewildered. Their 'protectors' hadn't even managed to discern that they were elders in a clan system that has no chiefs. Even so, Commodore Erskine raised the British flag in the 'fervent hope' that it would be to the people of 'this portion of New Guinea the symbol of their freedom and their liberty'.

Something inside Jericho gives, and he can no longer sit. He stands, takes a few steps, falls on his knees in the sparse grass beside the washing. He thinks of Aaron, the strong father of long ago who stood with him in the saltwater until he found his strength and could kick off with his feet, until he learned the way of this strange new water so different from the rivers that came from the mountain. 'No need to be afraid,' Aaron said, teaching him to hold his breath and sink down under the water. Under they'd go, his hand in Aaron's, and they'd open their eyes to see the shells and tiny coloured fish.

He thinks of Aaron on the beach below Bili's flat, where now no one can swim because of the pollution. There are concrete barricades in front of the trees where Laedi used to park after school. He thinks of the fjords, a fleeting moment of sunshine, Aaron lifting him out of the water into the sparkling air, and the dream that must be memory, dark and green and menacing, closing in. In this dream, this vision, which can come upon him asleep or awake, there is no Aaron, no order. Swaying giants bend down, dropping water and saliva on him, they smell rank and sour, and he cannot hide his face. He rolls into a small ball like an insect and Bili is rolled up with him, her breath salt-sweet. Above them the giants who once were orderly are fighting each other, large as trees. There is noise and rushing water and no one to carry him across. Bili wraps her arms tight around him, but underneath the fighting and the shouting all is still and silent, there is no air, and somewhere, he doesn't known where, Aaron floats in that silence, head down in deep green water.

Under the drying sheets, Jericho raises his head a few inches. He remembers Rika's story of Aaron beaten by the white men in balaclavas and left bleeding, face-down in the grass. That's one story she tells, when she tells anything, which is rare. 'They beat me into him.' A kind of perverse pride. 'They beat us together.' Aaron got up. He crawled to the road. He stood proud in the town. He stood like a man. And here is Jericho lying under the washing for no better reason than he's made an arse of himself in front of Bili. It doesn't help to pity himself consigned to a life of exile.

He rolls over, looks at the patch of blue above, between the drying sheets and the next-door garage. Something in him gives a small laugh. He gets up, goes into the house, walks along the passageway to the kitchen. 'Ah, Jericho,' the women say, 'good one,' and he sits at the table with them, drinks tea and eats bread. They are talking about the wedding of the daughter of the woman who comes from Hanuabada, down on the harbour, the village that gave Captain Moresby his vegetable porridge.

Later that afternoon, Jericho stands on the veranda at the front of Laedi's house and considers its colonial origins. He thinks of the civil servants drinking gin on this veranda and the curfew that forbade 'natives' entry to the town after dark. He is ashamed. Ashamed for the blood he shares with Commodore Erskine, or, if not blood, then heritage and culture. And he's sickened by his own cowed behaviour, his irresolution, his snivelling self-pity.

He goes inside, finds the number Laedi has given him and rings Milton.

'Please,' he says, 'I'd like to come over and visit you for a few days.'

Milton does not sound surprised. Has Laedi worded him up? Probably. 'It's time, eh?' he says.

From the Martyrs School where Milton teaches, the mountain will be in the line of his sight with nothing to obscure his view.

THE JERICHO ROAD

On Milton's shelves, Jericho finds a row of James Baldwin paperbacks. The paper is yellow and flaking, the covers have warped, the glue of the binding has been eaten by cockroaches. It's not the climate for books.

Still, the pages are readable, and while Milton is teaching over at the school, Jericho sits in his house and reads. He chooses the slimmest, the most thumbed, with a corner turned down.

'They've got the world on a string,' he says when Milton comes sloping back up the hill.

'Ah,' he says, '*The Fire Next Time.*'

'I expected it to be angry.'

'He knew angry, every step of it. Took me a long time to learn that a writer can't write angry without knowing what anger does. Then he can write. Then his words are true.'

'I've read you angry. That first novel.'

Milton ignores him. 'I've seen a lot go down on anger. I nearly went down myself.'

'Martha told me.'

'Ah, Martha. You saw her?'

'Yes, in Sydney, on the way through. We talked about those early days when I came to live with Rika. My mothers.' He laughs. 'On that platform of yours.'

'Theirs, you mean. They loved it – thought we were all one big family, a new kind of clan.'

'Weren't we? I remember it – everyone there, the meals. Bili's games, all of you talking. It was comforting.'

'It was. When I came back from Melbourne, oh, I was angry. I'd sleep there all day, and at night Rika and Martha cooked, and Aaron got Sam and Pete talking like Melanesians. Yeah, I liked it. They were friends, looked after me. I *thought* they were friends. But when it all went wrong here, they left, the whole lot of them.'

'Were you angry?'

'We hated them for it. We'd read Baldwin, caught his way of thinking. Rufus Scott, all of us. No, that's not true, there were a lot of us figuring out how to get that string working for us. Get it from the *masta*, reel in the money.' He made a sound that might have been a laugh. 'The ones who didn't . . . Well, here we are.'

Where they are is in the living room of Milton's house, in the row where the teachers live, set back from the school buildings, the classrooms and dormitories. It is the lunchbreak, and over at the school students are milling around, the girls sitting under the trees, the junior boys chasing each other.

'You still teach Baldwin?' Jericho asks.

'Sure I do. A foundation.'

'They still want to be Rufus Scott?' He gestures across to the school, which they can see from the table where they sit by the window.

'Some do. The angry ones.'

'Like you? They want to write? Baldwin Rufus?'

Milton scowls. 'It's different for them,' he says, sinking into thought. 'No opportunities to write. Anyway, look at me. They see it's useless. They don't hate the whites the same way. Well, they hate them, but it's like the weather – nothing they can do about it. They hate the politicians, that's who they hate, their own skin. They read, they're smart, they see who gets rich. Their parents work the oil palm, some have their own blocks, bring the palm to the road. The contractors collect it, the companies drop the price, or delay paying, or don't pay, and when their fathers and brothers go to protest, what happens? Who ends in jail? They do.'

It's a gloomy picture he paints. Laedi has warned Jericho not to take everything Milton says for true, he'll always see the worst. He thinks of the work Bili does, her friends in the NGOs, the people who work against corruption. Laedi has some in her department.

'Laedi says there are good things happening,' he says. 'I meet people in Moresby.'

'Sure, there're good people. There are some here, at the school. In town. Brave people, like Bili. I worry for that girl. Too brave. Always was.'

'She's tough,' Jericho says.

'You here for her?'

What's Laedi been saying? A prickle of sweat, or is it shame, runs along Jericho's spine. 'I suppose,' he says. 'Partly.'

There's a pause and Milton gets up, takes Jericho's mug, puts the kettle on the gas. There's a refillable tank secured against the outside wall.

'Did Aaron love Rika?' Jericho asks.

Milton rolls a cigarette, frowns. 'Love?' he says. 'I don't know. She was in him. She had him hooked.' He pauses. That frown again. 'Yes,' he says, 'I guess you'd say he loved her. He wanted her near him. Wanted her all the time.'

'And the baby stuff? Rika told me once that Aaron thought there was something in her that rejected his sperm.' Jericho had gone over to Paris to see her – she was living there, escaping Oxford. They'd had dinner, it was late, one of the few times she spoke of it. Really spoke. In the morning, when he asked her again, she insisted she'd never said it. That *he'd* never said it. The occasion comes back, and with it the frustration, the questions not answered, the pained look on Rika's face. And, though he was in Paris, though he'd come over especially, still she went to her studio; you can't disturb her in the studio, always the bloody studio, a rule from his childhood. He'd pounded the streets, furious, ended up in a bar in the Marais, and went back to London early.

'That's Baldwin again,' Milton says. 'Slam that white womb, again and again, and the fear somewhere inside that it was mocking him, mincing his sperm, chopping him up.'

Down at the school a bell clangs. Milton gets up, gathers his books. 'Remind me to tell you about the time they came to the river and there was a snake,' he says.

He sets off down the path, and Jericho watches as some boys run towards him. They love him. Jericho has sat at the back of a class, and heard him through the windows. He's seen the performer in him as he recites poems and the children perform them back. It's Derek Walcott at the moment.

Alone in the house, he takes another book from the shelves of rough planks that Milton has built. Baldwin again. *Another Country*. Jericho's never read it. Mildew has formed behind the shelves, large black blooms of it. The concrete floor is damp, staining the woven mats, and the paint, long past its prime, is flaking. The house of an intellectual, Jericho thinks, and then doesn't know what to do with the thought, which began with Leonard's book-lined study, and peters out to nothing.

He gets up and stretches, and when the school quietens and the classes begin, he walks down past it, skirting the classrooms and the offices, and takes the path to the river. He walks upstream to a place where the older boys swim. There are signs of them everywhere – clothes laid out to dry on rocks and branches, sly cigarette ends, an exercise book – but he is there alone. He takes off his clothes, wades into the water, feels the current and the sun on his skin. Above him, a ripple of thin cloud against the blue, the whisper of trees. Birds.

There's a voluptuous feel to the water as he dives under, holds his breath, comes up, sits on a rock, lets the water tumble between his legs. His body is strong and confident. But inside he is roiling. This water comes from the mountain; its streams are headwater tributaries. Yet his thoughts are not of that – of the future, of where he is headed – but of Rika, and the past. The years she stayed in Oxford while he was at school, and the flat she kept not far from Leonard. Jericho knew she was only there for him, and whenever she went away for work – to London, to Paris, to New York, and he could stay on with Leonard – oh, the relief of it; the quiet ease, and the knowledge that this man was the one fixed point in his life. He wouldn't want to go back to Rika's, and Leonard would say, 'It hurts her if you don't.' So he'd go, learn not to hurt her. 'Did you bring me back to England to please Rika?' he asked Leonard, and always the same answer. 'I brought you back because I am your father.' And Rika? 'For her too. She'd become your mother.' Had she? She came to parent nights. He called her Mummy. And there in the river he remembers back to the school in Oxford and the boy who said, 'She's not your mother. Your mother's black. *Nig-nog.*' The shame of it. Not that she was black, and him too – it was the 1970s, after all – but the shame of teachers overhearing, and the whole class sat down to hear the talk about equality and the colour of our skin, the great rainbow of mankind, when everyone knew that the boy who'd said it was an idiot. And fat with thick glasses. Pebble eyes. That was worse than nig-nog. 'Nig-nog, have a snog.'

There's a boy watching him from further down the bank. When Jericho sees him and waves, he shoots out of sight, back towards the school. *I won't tell,* Jericho wants to shout over the tumble of the river, but there's no one there to hear him, just a slight movement in the trees.

He lets himself into the water again. On the far side of the river the current is strong and it sweeps him round the bend, away from the pool where the boys swim, before he can get back, climb out on the rocks and pick his way up to his clothes. He lies on a rock watching the river flow past, and thinks of a friend of Bili's in Moresby who told him about the junction of two great rivers near where he comes from in the Highlands. The smaller of the two – which is large enough for them to have to make rope bridges to cross – is stopped by the flow of the bigger river, which is so fast, so dangerous, there's no getting across it at all. You can swim at the junction, this man said, for the water from one river is stopped by the force of the other.

It's as calm as a swimming pool. 'Where does the current go?' Jericho asked. Was it tugging away underneath? Bili's friend, who works for an NGO, laughed and said yes, maybe, but swimming across the smooth surface you'd never know.

Jericho doubts that this is true, but he likes the image. Milton says life's a road not a river. He called that first novel *The Jericho Road*. The one about Baldwin Rufus. Last night, Milton told him that Martin Luther King had spoken of the Jericho Road in his last speech, on the night before he was assassinated. It took the Good Samaritan, 'a man of another race', to risk his own safety by stopping to help an injured man on a dangerous road. 'A dangerous road' the Jericho Road; steep, with sharp bends through ravines on its climb up to Jerusalem. Dr King had driven it himself. What happens, he'd asked, if we don't stop to help those who are injured, or in need, especially when they are left to die on a road 'conducive for ambushing?' A good question, Milton said.

Jericho was sitting with him at the table by the bookcase. He'd taken the novel out during the day and it was there on the table with them. *The Jericho Road* with its black and red cover of an angry mask. Jericho has never read Martin Luther King; he'll look up the speech when he gets back to Moresby. It was April 1968 when he was assassinated, the month Leonard and Rika arrived in Port Moresby.

Milton told Jericho that the point of the story for him wasn't the Samaritan. It was the road and how we walk it. That was true for independence when he was writing the novel. It was true of Baldwin Rufus and his failed rebellion. And it's true now, for each of us. The road we walk is the road we make. Lying on the rock, Jericho thinks about it. Was Milton warning him to be careful of the road he makes for himself? As if he could. He can't see anything resembling a track, let along a road. Roads. Rivers. Nothing is any clearer, and there in front of him, if he lifts his head from the rock where he's lying, the river is tumbling past. There's no uncertainty about its direction. Over at the school he hears the clang of the bell and the voices of children between lessons.

*

He goes back to the house, which is quiet during the day. The last of Milton's boys are at the school, and Meg, his wife, is at the hospital, where she's a nursing sister. A woman comes in and sweeps, a relative of Meg's; she washes clothes and goes again before Meg arrives back late in the afternoon, long after Milton has returned from school. When Milton hears her old Toyota station wagon come grinding down the school road, he goes inside, turns on the gas, fills the kettle. He smiles. Well, for Milton it's a smile. Smiling's not something he does much, as if the past has stamped him so thoroughly he can't let a glimpse of smile show, it'd shake the edifice. But he's happy, as far as Jericho can tell. Or if not happy, then content. Or if not fully content – Milton will never be that – then with Meg he is content.

She is a large, comfortable woman. She's from this area – Orokaivan like Milton – but while he's skinny with no meat on him, she's large enough to envelop him in her rolling breasts. It's not a thought Jericho pursues. They're so different, Meg and Milton, that he finds it weird to think of them married. But they dote on each other in an offhand kind of way. He follows her with his eyes, and looks away if he catches Jericho watching. She treats him like another of her children. Jericho finds her easy to know, comforting, it's all there on the surface, or seems to be. With Milton, whatever is going on underneath is out of sight. You feel it, but you don't see it. Jericho rereads his poetry from years past, slim volumes at one end of the shelf, clamped together by the damp, not opened for years. There's one that gets snagged in his dreams that night, about being at the bottom of an abandoned water-well, crawling downwards for eternity to some great waiting underworld, and white girls looking down at him, all inviting voices and silky legs, and the image of a man, whom Jericho takes to be Milton, alone and writing when the wind has blown down the walls and torn off the roof.

Jericho wakes at first light. He's in a room with Milton's boys. They are snugged down under the sheets. The room smells of farts. He goes outside, washes his head under the cold tap. Inside, Meg has the kettle on and she gives him a cup of sweet, powdered coffee. He never thought he'd come to like it, or milk from a tube, but he does, sitting there with Meg. Outside, through the open door, the sun is turning everything gold: trees, river, even the roof of the school.

If Jericho is careful where he walks, he can avoid seeing the mountain from the school, it's hidden by the rise of the hill and the forest. But when he drives into Popondetta with Meg, he can't avoid it, out there to the east, its peaks swathed in cloud as if deliberately keeping itself from view.

'It's the season,' Meg says. 'Rain up there. Pneumonia.'

'Do they come down?'

'Not when they're ill. If they're old, they think it's because their spirit is tired and their time is up. Every rain season, some of the old ones go.'

'And the young ones?'

'They might come down. But habits are strong – it's a big problem for us at the hospital. It's the same everywhere here, they don't believe you can die during strong life unless there's been sorcery, or they've upset the ancestors. It takes some other kind of power to kill you after you're no longer a small child whose spirit's not yet taken hold, or very old when it becomes tired.'

When they arrive at the hospital, Jericho asks about Tobias and what it was like back when he was brought down from the mountain as a child. Meg wasn't there then. She came later, when Tobias was director; 1980, she started, so she was there when he died. She says it was jealousy that killed him, still a young man. 'His relatives were angry because he didn't give them big money, and his colleagues because he stopped them taking hospital money. It killed him, all that bad thought. One day he died, here in the hospital. I was a new nurse.'

'What, he just dropped dead?'

'One afternoon. He was tired, said he'd sit down, went to the small room the doctors used. An orderly found him dead in his chair.'

'Sounds like a heart attack.'

'Maybe. He was young yet.'

The hospital is run-down, the wards are cramped, outside on the walkways there are families preparing food for their sick ones. Jericho walks around, trying to picture himself as a child. He's been told the story of being brought down by Janape, of sitting under a tree with her, waiting to see Tobias, waiting all day until at last Tobias noticed them, took them into the hospital, to his house, where Jericho saw his books and took one from the shelf. It was another of the stories Rika told, a set piece rehearsed over the years. As a child he corrected her if she got a word wrong. Now he wants the version that hasn't been rehearsed. He looks at the tree where they sat and waited. He supposes it's the tree: it's dusty, it doesn't shed much shade, but there are women and children under there. He turns away from their patience, their subservience, from so much waiting. They can't tell him anything that will answer the questions for which he can't form the words.

He goes back into the hospital. Meg is in the outpatients' room, which is full of women and crying babies. An old man sleeps on the concrete floor. Jericho thinks maybe he's dead, then sees him move. He should be on a mattress, but there are not enough. Some of the beds are a metal frame with pandanus mats. Even mattresses are stolen. The storeroom has steel bars around it like a vault, and still the keys fall into the wrong hands and the morning comes when Meg opens the doors and there is no antivenom for the snakebites that come in week by week. It makes big money on the Asian market.

Popondetta is a dispiriting town. It spreads out around a grid of trade stores that sell their goods through hatches protected by heavy wire. The streets are filthy, with garbage piled up in small hills that have to be negotiated, along with the women who set out a cloth with their wares for sale. Single cigarettes, betel and *daka*, plastic packets of lime, string bags made with trade-store nylon, garish colours. It's flat and hot in town, under every tree there are people waiting for the PMVs and trucks that rumble in from the villages depositing more people. Wherever you look there seem to be people waiting. Jericho buys the things Meg has listed – cooking oil, rice, sugar – returns to the hospital, then walks over to the post office to see Presley. He's busy inside and Jericho goes round the back and waits until he comes out, his basketball cap in place, a snazzy red and white shirt.

'Hey, brother,' he says, slapping Jericho's hand in a high five. 'That steam. Man.' He puts his hand to his head and staggers a few steps, looking just as Jericho felt when he hauled himself to his feet in the cells.

'How did you get back that day, ill like that?' Jericho asks.

'We didn't.' He laughs, takes out his tobacco, rolls a cigarette. 'They put us on that truck, okay, up to the start of the track. We walked out of sight and went to sleep in the bush.' He hands the tobacco to Jericho, who shakes his head. London man. 'Two nights, then our heads could see again.'

'The others? Where are they now?'

'On top. They go home to the village. The chiefs got angry. They used up all the peanut money. None for the village. Now they must grow more and come to the market here in Popondetta. Not as much money here. For Moresby it is better, but then the money goes. In steam.' He slaps Jericho's hand again, dances a little jig. 'You go up the mountain, eh? Big walk!'

'Soon,' Jericho says. 'Soon I go. Maybe.'

'You white man! Soft!'

A few days later, Napo turns up at Milton's house. He has Obi with him. They come down the road on their wide, calloused feet, and wait under a tree until Milton comes up from the school. 'Milton,' they call. 'We come.'

Jericho is asleep inside, Langston Hughes open beside him.

'Lazy bugger,' Milton says when he comes into the house. 'You've got visitors.'

Jericho gets up, shakes himself awake and goes outside to face Obi, whom he hasn't seen since that visit with Leonard when he was fourteen and full of resistance. As Leonard's translator, Obi would have been witness to Leonard's anger at his *gracelessness*, his rudeness and turned face, the long hours spent hunched in his sleeping bag listening to music. He was there when Leonard confiscated his Walkman. 'Enough,' he'd said. 'You're to get up now. At once.'

'Ah, Obi,' Jericho says, shaking his hand and Napo's. 'A long time. I behaved badly. No good at all. I am ashamed.'

'You were young yet,' Obi says. Like Napo, he has a thick beard. 'You are a man now.'

'A good man,' Milton says as they go into the house. 'You'll see.'

'You are here,' Obi shakes his hand again. 'You are welcome.'

Jericho puts the kettle on the stove, spoons powdered coffee and sugar into the cups, and while they wait for Meg to come home and the boys to return from the school, where they are doing prep with the boarders, or are meant to be, and not swimming in the river, or climbing up in the bush to catch lizards, they sit at the table and Jericho feels the old anxiety knocking at his chest.

'Any trouble on the road?' Milton asks.

'*Nogat*,' Napo says. 'All is good.'

Obi is looking at the *Post-Courier* on the table, a few days old, with a story on the front page about a confrontation between landowners and the government over a nickel mine that's planned for a river to the north-west. Inside he finds a photo of Laedi opening a community centre in Madang.

'Laedi,' he says. 'She is not corrupt.'

Jericho is not sure if it's a question Obi is asking, or a statement. 'No,' he says. 'She's not.'

'In Popondetta,' Obi says, looking at Milton, 'there is much corruption.'

Again Jericho doesn't know if it is a question or a statement. Obi doesn't come down much any more, he is telling Milton, and he's taken his sons out of high school in Popondetta. Even with Leonard's help, the money is too much, and they learn bad ways in the town.

'They should come here, to Martyrs,' Milton says. 'Out of town.'

'They catch the PMV. It is better on the mountain.'

'They need education too,' Milton says, and Obi sighs.

Napo starts to talk of Port Moresby, and visiting Laedi's house with Young Albert, telling Milton about the bark-cloth on the wall; how, long ago, it was made by Nogi chief. Jericho knows where this is heading, but before Napo gets to the question of *bisnis*, he is saved by the sound of Meg's car coming down the road, rounding the corner and stopping in front of them. '*Ai, ai.*' Milton goes in, puts the kettle on the gas ring, his daily contribution to the domestic economy, and Jericho goes to the car, offers to carry Meg's string bag full of vegetables from the market. But no, a man doesn't carry a woman's *bilum*. Meg heaves it onto her head and goes inside.

The next morning, Napo says, 'You come to the mountain. The chiefs, they wait.'

Jericho does not know if he means now, or later sometime.

'Now?' he says, before he has time to compose a better answer.

'It's okay,' Napo says. 'All the same.'

'I mean,' Jericho says, 'first I must go to Moresby.' The Collingwood Bay case is finally to be heard in the national court. He's promised Bili he'll be there. It was back before, when he made the promise, but he wants to keep it. Like she said, he owes her one. And himself. Besides, he met the landowners, and was in the court with them last time the case was adjourned. He watched Jacob sweep out, and saw the emotion in the eyes of the elders when proceedings were postponed again: the indignation, the disbelief, the *fury* that they have to fight like this to save their own land. Not someone else's land. Not disputed land. *Their* land. Jericho had been round the hotels with them while they sold the tapa cloth hats made by the women back in the village to raise money to pay the lawyers. And now, after four years of waiting, at last there's to be a full hearing. The date is set, and this time they'll get the fight they've been waiting for.

Napo's face has gone still. He speaks to Obi in the mountain language Jericho no longer understands, and Obi's face takes on the same immobility. Jericho doesn't know why it is Napo making the request, not Obi; maybe because he's the elder of the two, and the son of a chief. He doesn't know how to ask, but he knows from the low rumble in his gut that he has got this exchange wrong.

'All what is going on?' Meg says, bringing sweet potato to the table. Milton's grey head has sunk down into his chest, Chinua Achebe on his lap ready for his matriculation class.

'Jericho,' he says. 'He must go to Moresby for Bili's case.'

'So?' Meg says.

'They want me to go to the mountain,' Jericho says. 'Today maybe.'

'Today,' Meg says to Napo. 'No good today. How is he to buy fish and rice, kerosene to take to the chiefs? Gifts. He cannot return without gifts. Much work to be done. Do you have a house for him? Are you ready? Obi, you know there is much preparation to do.'

'He is here today,' Obi says. 'First we take the PMV to town. He can buy kerosene there.'

Something in Napo's face has tightened. 'He goes to Moresby,' he says to Meg.

'He goes to Moresby. He can come back. The planes, they fly every day. Okay?'

'Okay.'

And then to Jericho, 'So, you set up the date. You tell them when you will arrive. You say which day you come back. I will drive you to the end of the road. They will meet you. Okay?'

'One month,' Jericho says, plucking a date out of the air, and once it's said, he knows it can't be unsaid. *One month.*

Milton is looking into his lap as if he can read the words through the covers.

'Okay,' Napo says. He is smiling. 'Very good. All the same. We tell the chiefs. One month. We will wait for you. The end of the road.'

'Good one,' Meg says. 'Okay, Jericho. It's up to you now.'

That afternoon Milton has no classes to teach. He comes across from the school with a letter for Jericho.

'This came,' he says. It's from Bili, addressed care of Milton at the school.

'Just because you said you would,' she writes, 'don't think you have to come back for the case. Better you get things settled. No expectations here. Bili.'

'Bad news?' Milton asks, watching him read.

'She says not to bother to come for the case.'

'She's proud. Always was. She's hardly going to ask you to come.'

'She didn't need to tell me not to.'

'Probably means she wants you to. Getting in first, in case you don't. She was like that as a child. Ferocious when she was fighting for someone else. When it came to her, she'd refuse help. On her own, shoulders back, didn't matter what happened.'

Jericho sighs. Oh, Bili. Why do you have to make it so hard?

'Come,' Milton says. 'I'll show you where my village was.'

Having known his own share of shame, and given to gloom, Milton doesn't attempt to cheer, or advise, or offer wise words. About Bili, or about the mountain. All he says is that they, the two of them, are on a pivot, and there are people who'll never understand what it's like exactly, or even a bit. 'We're not just *hapkas*, that's one thing,' he says, and anyway he isn't. 'We're *existential hapkas*.' He's made his own language for it. As they walk on, the trees become sparser. It's like being inside a Max Ernst painting, Jericho thinks. Looming figures greet Milton, and cut on through to their village, or their plots of oil palm.

After a while, they come into gardens again. On the opposite hill, on the other side of a small river, the oil palm begins. As they follow the rise and fall of a path that borders the gardens, Jericho reminds Milton of the story he was going to tell.

'What story?'

'Rika and Aaron. At the river.'

'Ah,' Milton says, and walks on, head down, frowning that frown. Jericho's come to understand that it means he's thinking, or, more likely, remembering. 'Yes,' he says at last. 'I was living out there, in a shack, back before independence.'

'I've seen photos,' Jericho says.

'Rika's?'

'Of course. A whole gang of you. Long hair. Flares. A bong.'

Milton makes a noise that might have been a laugh. 'Yeah,' he says. 'At weekends they all came out. From the arts centre, everywhere. Cooked fish on the fire. Got drunk.' They walk on, and Jericho waits. He's learned not to push. Several minutes go by, and then Milton starts again.

'If Aaron and Rika came, it'd be late in the day. Aaron worked hard. Saturdays, Sundays, no difference. On this day they arrived late as usual, not long before dark, and Aaron went down to the river for a swim. Rika had a whole lot of food and stuff, she was busy with that. Then she went to the river. We were sitting around outside, and watched her go down the path, out of sight. A moment later she was screaming, loud enough for someone to be dead.'

Milton goes quiet again. 'She saw a snake,' he says eventually. 'It slid into the water from the other bank. She was standing on the rocks and called across to Aaron to get out, but he stayed in the water. He turned and watched the snake with its head held up, then moved to let it pass behind him.' Milton makes a graceful gesture with his head as if watching the snake. 'It slid up onto the bank upstream from Rika and disappeared. We rushed to the river. It was almost dark by then. Sam thought he'd been bitten, Rika was making so much noise. Aaron was sitting on a rock with his arms and head hanging down. Didn't matter how much we said land snakes don't bite when they're in water, Rika kept saying he'd let fate come up close, left himself open to danger. She was angry. First she was angry, then she was silent. That closed-off silence that once fascinated us had turned against him.' On Milton's face is Aaron's bewilderment. Jericho recognises it. The hurt when you're on the wrong side of Rika's silence.

They walk on, back into the trees, and more minutes tick by. All Jericho can hear is the shrilling of cicadas.

'Then what happened?'

'Nothing.'

'Nothing?'

'Nothing I remember.'

'So what does it mean?'

'Mean?' Milton stops, turns to Jericho, and puts his hand on his arm. 'Englishman.'

'Do you mean they were fated?'

'Fate? No. They were bound. Bound tight.'

'Not destined? "Into the depth of massy green?"'

Milton's face creases. 'You've been reading too much poetry.'

'*Your* poetry,' Jericho says, and he too falls quiet. 'So was Rika right, then?' he says after a while. 'It was the work that killed him?'

'He *loved* the work.' There's a note of exasperation in Milton's voice. Slight, but Jericho hears it. 'It mattered to him that he did it. She never understood that. Or if she did, she resented it.' He looks down, then turns to Jericho again. 'She was jealous,' he says. 'And she'd never admit that.'

'Jealous of what?'

'Of the pleasure he took in it. The recognition. Being at the centre of things. Part of history. It was like a drug. For all of them. A perfect drug, as they were certain, despite it all, that they were on the side of right.' He smiles, an ironic, sorrowful smile. 'Power. Don't they say it's an aphrodisiac?'

'A rival love,' Jericho says.

Milton shrugs. 'A rival power,' he says. 'A rival road.'

They've been walking for an hour, more, when they come out of the trees again, onto a side path that leads to the overgrown clearing where Milton's village once was. Clouds have come over, blotting out the sun. It's gloomy, a desolate, forgotten place. Milton looks up at the sky.

'Rain?' Jericho asks.

'No. On the mountain.' Milton gestures behind him. 'Not here.'

The ground is hard and dry. Weeds, strangling grass, the remains of house poles sticking up through the wreckage, an old fence and the bush growing in. A few hundred yards on, the plantation begins, covering the land that once belonged to his clansmen. Gone, before independence, before the constitution. Before the court cases.

At the edge of the oil palm, it's eerily quiet and dark. Anyone with any claim to land has moved further inland. The rest are in the settlements round the edge of town. *The scrap heap*, Milton calls it, a term he says he learned from Leonard, who said it of himself when he came off the mountain.

'It's gone,' he says. 'The life we came out of. All that's left is a shadow, and that's no good for a Melanesian man.'

'Couldn't you say it's the existential reality, and it's made you an artist?'

Milton makes a huffing sound. He doesn't believe in redemption; Meg does, but he doesn't. 'If the village is buried in you somewhere,' he says, 'how do you turn that loneliness into art?' He doesn't write any more. Or won't, Jericho doesn't know which. He reads. And he teaches the boys to read. Not to write. The younger teachers do that. 'Time to go,' he says, and they cut through the trees and tramp back along the road to the school. Where the mountain should be, all Jericho can see is cloud. In a month he'll be up there.

'The Jericho Road,' Milton says. He laughs, and punches Jericho's shoulder. It's the first time he's heard him laugh. A proper laugh. 'The Jericho Road,' he says again. 'We're all on our Jericho Roads.'

BILI LIVES IN HER TOP-FLOOR FLAT OVER A CLIFF WITH GUARDS ON the main door because of the threats against her. There have been too many of them, and Laedi insisted. That, or come and live with her behind the security of her ministerial guards. She might be single, Bili says, but she is too old to live with her mother, and, besides, she needs her own place. After another nasty incident – *Yu laik lukim tumora?* Do you want to see tomorrow? scrawled on her door, and her dog dead on the step – she left her old house with its lemon trees and familiar neighbours and moved into her cliff top eyrie.

So it is a shock for her to wake on the morning that the Collingwood Bay case is to start and find her laptop gone. Has she hallucinated working on it late into the night? Was she so tired that she forgot to put it in its case ready for court? She has an early meeting with the barrister who's come up from Sydney. Nothing has been tampered with, nothing else has been touched – no broken door, no open drawers. Nothing except the laptop, which has vanished.

She hasn't been hallucinating. Her mind has never been more focused. This is an important case in the national court, it could become a precedent, and she can't afford a slip. She knows the counsel Jacob has brought up from Brisbane; he is aggressive, and he is good. The stakes are high. The evening before, she had an early meal with the landowners. They were on edge – too many times they've been disappointed, with the case adjourned because Jacob and his lawyers have found another way to delay. No, she told them, this time no delay is possible. Tomorrow at last you will be heard. All the arguments. All that has happened. Everything will be heard. Then she'd left, not staying to talk more. The old men frowned, until she said she must work, prepare for the court. Then they took her hand, bowed their heads. Thank you. *Tenkyu tru.*

Jericho stayed with them. 'Will you be okay?' he asked her. 'Would you like me to take you home?'

'I'll be fine,' she said and squeezed his hand, a soft small squeeze, but he took it as a softening, a gesture. 'I'll be fine. You stay here with the landowners. They need your support tonight. I don't.'

Need. Would Bili ever admit to a need? To needing him? He's come back from Milton's despite her letter, hoping Milton was right and secretly she needs him. Sure, she's had him running around since the barrister arrived, ferrying the landowners, or making tea for everyone. He's been busy and it's help she needs, but nothing he's done couldn't have been done by someone else. No particular need there. She let him cook dinner one night, but only once, and she was distracted, eating with the laptop open beside her, going over, and back over everything. 'What have I missed?' she asked, and it was not a question he could help her with. He was grasping at another thin reed. He had a beer with Simeon the night he got back from Popondetta. He told him the whole story, about Bili telling him to not bother coming back, and Napo arriving, and not going up to the mountain.

'You should have called her bluff,' Simeon said. 'Jump to Bili and she'll make use of you.'

Is it use? Is it need? He doesn't ask if it is love. He doesn't use the word any more, not even to himself, not even at night. It is too ragged. Either that, or the idea of love, what the word is meant to mean, has emptied out into the songs he can no longer listen to. He'd settle for the balm of need, even a little of it.

On this morning of the case, Jericho also wakes early. The first glimmer of light is showing on the harbour when he goes into Laedi's kitchen. Tamba is up. She is in Moresby for a visit. She has the kettle on. Jericho opens the fridge. Eggs are a good idea on a day like this. He is standing at the table looking at them, thinking *boiled? scrambled? fried?* when the phone goes. Early for Laedi's office. Boiled. It's easier.

'For you,' Tamba says, and hands him the phone. 'It is Bili.'

'Jericho.' For a moment he doesn't recognise Bili's voice, it is so strange and strangulated. 'My laptop. It's gone.'

'Gone, how?'

'I don't know.'

'Did someone break in?'

'No. No sign.'

'Did you ask the guard?'

'Benson has just come on. He said nothing was reported.'

'Who was on last night?'

'Davis.'

'Do you know him?'

'Sure.'

'He's okay?'

'How can I know? How can I know anything?' Her voice is rising. 'Stop asking questions. Can't you just *come*?'

Sweet words. In any other circumstance, they'd be sweet words, and actually, though he doesn't like to admit it, even in this circumstance they are sweet.

Laedi is in the hallway behind him when he puts down the phone. 'What's happened?' she asks.

'Bili's laptop. It's gone.'

'Jacob. It'll be Jacob.' She picks up the phone. Jericho stands there and listens. It takes a while to get through. He must have minders. Staff.

'Good morning, Jacob.

'Yes it is, very early . . . A strange thing, Jacob, most strange. Someone got into Bili's flat last night . . .

'No, of course. Did I say I thought it was? But with you owning the block next door, maybe one of your men saw something. Perhaps —

'Yes. Yes. You too.'

Bili will be ropeable.

'It'll come back,' Laedi says. 'They'll have got what they want by now.'

She hands Jericho the car keys and by the time he pulls up outside the flats, there is Benson the security guard talking to the guard from next door. In his hand is a laptop.

'Found it down by the gate,' the guard says. 'Benson here tell me. *Sori tumas.*'

'Who gave it to you?' Jericho is sharp.

'No one, Jericho Mister, I tell you true. I find it by the gate.'

'And who sent you to look by the gate?'

'Nobody. Nobody say. I walk about, that's all.'

'And do you usually go walking about when you should be on the door?'

'I go talk to the boys on the gate.'

Bili comes down the stairs and joins them at the door. 'Don't shout at him,' she says. 'He didn't do it. He's just been told to pick it up.' And then to the guard, 'It's okay. *Tenkyu tru.*' The guard slopes off next door and Benson shakes his head. '*Sori tumas,*' he says again.

'Can they get in from next door without you noticing?' Jericho persists.

'Maybe,' Benson says. 'If the door is open. Down below. Where the machines are. Air conditioning, all something.'

'We don't have time for this,' Bili says, and walks out into the bright light. She is dressed in black. Her hair is pulled back, severe. Jericho sees a vulnerability he hasn't seen since that visit to Oxford when Bili, dressed in her best, was waiting for Don. The time he had forgotten and was instead on his way to London to see the Algerian journalist who was about to become his third wife.

The barrister from Sydney is a small man, of modest appearance. Pale hair and wire glasses. He came off the plane the morning before with a battered leather briefcase, and shook Bili by the hand. 'How's it going?' he said, mopping his brow. 'You well? You look well.' He'd worked for her before, knew the country, liked it. Liked the people. Liked her.

'We'll win this case,' the barrister said. 'We should win on the documents, but if we need to, we'll call the landowners. Here.' He pulled a pile of papers out of his briefcase. 'I've read their statements and these are the ones I think are strongest.' He had a list of four he wanted to interview that afternoon. Forgoing lunch, Jericho got up, left Bili with the barrister and their sheaves of paper and went to find the landowners. There were twelve of them, elders of the clans, some of them with grey beards and gnarled faces, others younger, recently called to their position, men in the prime of their authority.

They were staying with their *wantok*, the clerk in the forestry department who had first found the documents and alerted Bili to what was happening.

The clerk's uncle was one of the men assembled in the small house in Gerehu when Jericho arrived to find the four the barrister wanted to interview. The uncle was one of the younger of the elders. His hair had only a whisper of grey. He had recently returned to Collingwood Bay after years over in New Britain working for one of the large importers. He'd seen what happened when villagers lose their land, and what happened when the first flush of money had gone and they had to beg garden land from others. When they were reduced to rice and tinned fish. And he'd seen what happened to the land when it was planted with oil palm. Sitting with the older men, cross-legged on the pandanus mat, with his shirt buttoned up to the neck in respect for the barrister, this uncle was mournful. He knew the arguments for development. What did he have to offer the young who go to town and see only what they do not have? He knew the benefits of a tin roof, and a tank of water. He knew the shame of young men who went into town and felt they were of no account, but he had no answers. He knew only that they must fight for their land, that foundation and heritage. Without it, there would be true poverty. He wanted to ask the lawyer about these things, he said to Jericho. The barrister come from Sydney. The man they were paying by the work of their women who sewed the tapa cloth hand bags and hats.

But the uncle's name was not on the list Jericho brought. The creases of his face lengthened. Jericho recognised in him the hard sorrow of being up against questions that could not be answered, strung between the imponderable and the impossible. Still, when he walked to the car with the first elders on the list, the uncle was there with them, and although Jericho knew the barrister would have nothing to say in answer, he did not deter him.

In court, Jericho sits with the landowners on the blue benches of the public gallery. The barristers file in. Dressed in wigs and gowns, their little white bibs, they could be in the law courts in London. The court is air-conditioned, almost cold. There are no windows, no sounds from outside. The solemnity pleases the landowners. Their barrister sits at one end of the bar, on the left-hand side facing the judge's bench. Bili sits behind him. Another lawyer, *pro bono* from the university, is beside her. The barristers for the other side sit further along to the right. Jacob sits behind the barrister for the company. With him are three lawyers from his office, and solicitors from the government. The landowners can see that the stage is set for a fight that may yet be worthy of its name. Their backs are straight, they hold copies of their statements. Their *bilums* are neat over their shoulders. Ready.

The tipstaff calls the court to silence and the elders rise to their feet, their eyes alight. The judge comes in, a tall man in his robes and wig, from Milne Bay – they recognise his skin. He trained in London, Bili has told them, and they can see the standing of his person by the way he walks. An upright judge. Bili has said, others too, that the judges of this court are not corrupt. 'It's our great strength,' Laedi says. At last everyone sits and the proceedings begin. There's legal talk, formalities the landowners don't understand, and nor does Jericho. He is no help when they turn to him for explanation. The barrister in front of Jacob stands. The company will not be contesting, he says. The landowners murmur. Did they hear that right? The second barrister, on behalf of the Registrar of Titles, asks for another delay. There is low moan from the landowners. They are here to fight, white-man style. Bili has persuaded them that in the new world, this is the way to fight. The clerk at Forestry has persuaded them. Are they to be cheated again?

What kind of fight is it if your adversaries won't fight? Their barrister stands to oppose the request for delay. The judge allows the matter to proceed. But still it is no fight. There is no dispute to the landowners' application that the leases be cancelled. The affidavit material is accepted in the related matter that concerns the forestry department. That is all. The elders murmur. They cannot believe that already it is over. But the barristers are closing their papers, and everyone is on their feet. The judge, with his stately walk, leaves through his own door. The barristers turn to talk to the lawyers behind them. They pack up their papers. Jacob nods to Bili and the barrister from Sydney. He shakes the hands of the barristers at his end of the bar, speaks to people in the public gallery. You'd think he'd won by the way he leaves the court. Jericho calculates the cost of his suit, his tie, his shoes. The very model of the successful lawyer, he'd not be out of place in Melbourne, or London.

Jacob. Did anyone understand Jacob? Nothing about him made sense to Jericho, from the past or from the present. He'd asked Milton about him, but all he got was a story about a school trip to Sydney during their last year at Martyrs. They hadn't liked it, being in a white city. The host boys were snide, the teachers assumed they didn't know how to use a fork. The night before they left, four of them walked from their hostel to Kings Cross. The streets were wet and there was a sharp wind, their first experience of cold. In the Cross, with its bustle of people, girls leaning in doorways smoking cigarettes, derelict men drinking on the pavement, the boys walked to the end of the strip and back. They listened to the pulse of music that was spilling out into the street. They read the signs. A strip club. Naked white women, that'd be something to see. Milton and the others wanted to go back to the hostel. They were cold and the doorman had told them he closed up at midnight sharp; if they weren't in by then, they'd be sleeping on the pavement. But Jacob went up to the man at the top of the stairs and held out the money he'd collected from the boys before they left the hostel. The man wouldn't take his money. Wasn't it good enough? Jacob asked. Money in black hands? And the man had laughed at him. Nothing wrong with the money, he said. Just not enough of it. Your first time in the city, eh? You won't get a girl that cheap.

Milton had laughed, remembering Jacob walking back down the street in the rain. That wouldn't happen again. Next time he'd be in a car and there'd be a driver, and when the car stopped at the top of the stairs, the white-trash bouncer would come over and open the door. 'Sir,' he'd say.

'Did he go back?' Jericho asked.

Milton didn't know. 'Doubt it. He'd have gone back to the Cross. He'd have had a driver. But not to that joint. Wherever he goes now, it'll be where the rich men go. The politicians, the lawyers, the brokers.'

And there he is in his smart suit, talking to Bili's barrister, shaking his hand, touching her on the shoulder. Jericho sees her bridle, a smile that's not a smile, and Jacob sweeps off down the concrete ramp towards the carpark. As he passes the landowners and sees Jericho, he comes over, hand outstretched again. The landowners turn their backs.

'So you've come back, eh?' Jacob says. 'Welcome. Let me take you to lunch sometime. I hear you're looking for clues to the past.' He smiles, hands Jericho his card. The driver opens the door of the car, and Jericho is left standing there like an idiot, not having said a word.

The landowners have retreated to the shade of the avenue of trees that leads to the court. They are muttering, their heads in close together. The uncle is writing something on a sheet of paper. A statement of thanks to the barrister. They want to read it to him. They want to prepare food and thank him. He shakes their hands one by one, explaining again that the case collapsed because the other side knew they were strong, fighters yet, and the land was theirs. He'd like to stay, he says, he has much respect for this place, this beautiful place, and you people. But if he stays, it costs more money. Enough tapa cloth hats, he says, and they laugh with him, though their eyes are disappointed.

The barrister looks at his watch. 'I'm in time for the plane today,' he says. Bili's assistant is on the mobile fixing it. The car is waiting, so the uncle steps out into the sun and reads the statement:

> We are indeed forever indebted to you, or as lawyers would put it, we carry a perpetual debt not only at this present but for as long as our land remains with us. Our land is our birthright. We are born into it and die into it. Land and our continuity are two in one. They are inseparable.

That evening the landowners come to Laedi's house. Jericho cooks sausages on the barbecue. Bili hands round beer and Coca-Cola. They try to make the occasion celebratory. They have won. The land is saved. It cannot be logged. The uncle makes another speech, this time thanking Bili, but frustration fills the air around them. The next day they will fly over the ranges to Collingwood Bay and take the news of their victory to their people. There will be dancing and feasting. But something inside the old men knows that a power has been unleashed. They've seen it raw, and they do not trust that it will not come their way again. That night, and for many nights to come, the elders will dream bad dreams. One dreams of a large iron ship at anchor off the beach of the village, another of rafts loaded with logs. Another dreams of a wounded forest boy standing before a bulldozer, trees with sap of blood.

That evening, Bili is exhausted. Between court and the barbecue, while Jericho stayed with the landowners, she went back to the office. She had to arrange for an injunction to be served on miners who are encroaching into village land on a river to the north-west. She too is dispirited at the endlessness of it. One victory, and it's no more than a pebble saved from the tide.

Jericho has learned enough not to tell her she's feeling that way because she's tired, she's been working too hard, no rest for weeks. He doesn't say what he fears about the impossibility of mediating between two cultures, two ways of proceeding, that this is less a victory than a stay of execution. Even Laedi says the country must come into the modern world, that its minerals and forests offer possibilities – they can't be locked up for ever.

'Stay here,' Laedi says to Bili when the landowners have gone. 'After last night you should stay here.'

Jericho sees a glint of tears, or thinks he does, but Bili shakes her head. If she doesn't go now, when will she go. Will tomorrow be safer?

So Jericho drives her back to the flat and gets out of the car with her, rides up in the lift.

'Shall I stay?' he asks.

She nods. He thinks it's a nod. 'If you do,' she says, 'you're not to make anything of it.'

'Promise,' he says.

But it is a lie. He makes as much as he can of anything she gives. He takes her to her bed, and while she lies still, he traces every vein in her body, every crease, every dip, every rise; he lets his fingers move gently, and when she does not stop him, he feels her soft and moist and open, the mysterious, miraculous stirring under his fingers, and he feels the pulse of her, the taste of her as she comes. When the tears seep between her closed lids, he tastes them too. She raises her mouth, taste on taste, and her hand guides him into her.

'Are you sure?' he murmurs. 'It's not an exchange.'

'I'm sure,' she says.

Afterwards he thinks, *sure of what?* That one exchange? Of him? He has the sense not to ask.

ANCESTOR GIFT

 THE DAY COMES FOR MEG TO DRIVE JERICHO TO the end of the road.

They leave the school early, before classes begin. Boys are milling around, peering at the *kago* that has been squeezed into the back of the station wagon: kerosene, rice, tinned meat; blankets and wet-weather gear; buckets, tarpaulin, rope; torches, nails, batteries, tobacco; as many *Time* magazines as Jericho could lay his hands on – a request from Obi – and a bottle of rum for emergencies; a box of medicines from Meg.

'That'll set you up,' Milton says as Jericho secretes the rum at the bottom of his pack. And then, through the window, his voice morose: 'If it gets too hard, you can come back early.' He waves the book in his hand as Meg coaxes the car into life.

At the end of the school road, she turns inland, towards Kokoda. She leans forward as she drives, rarely out of third gear, easing the car over gullies and creeks where rain has washed the road away, up onto the verge to avoid the vans and utilities that come hurtling towards her, their human cargo clinging on at the back. She leans out of the window, shouts at the exhaust fumes that blow across the road. 'Too fast! You want to die yet?'

Their progress is slow. They are flagged down at villages, sometimes for nothing more than to say hello, once to wait while a child is sent for a pineapple. Another time, it's to see a woman with a scrunched and fevered baby, then an old man wheezing pitifully. Meg says she'll pick them up on her way back. 'You be ready now.' She gives the mother a cloth to sponge the baby, cool the fever.

'Will it be okay?' Jericho asks. 'Should we go first to the hospital?'

'I'll be back soon enough,' she says. 'You have a long walk, remember.'

'What if the baby dies?'

'Babies die all the time.'

He is about to protest when she says, 'Don't worry. This one won't.'

On they drive, until they turn to the east, following a small creek through a village, along the edge of a garden. The road dwindles to a track, then peters out into a narrow path. Meg stops the car; the engine gives its usual shudder and hisses quietly. There's a moment of silence before they hear the crash and whoop of people running through the trees towards them: Jericho's kin from the mountain coming to meet him, with Obi in the lead.

'You can drive further yet,' he says, shaking Meg's hand up and down. 'We can cut a road.' The men have their bush-knives out of their belts, already hacking at the edge of the path.

'No further,' Meg says. 'You'll have to walk.'

The walk. The climb. Jericho remembers it from when he came back with Leonard. The airstrip was still there then. He hadn't had to do this first part, but every muscle in his body knows what lies ahead. Two hours, they say, to the village by the old airstrip; not far, but hours are notional when the day is measured in the movement of the sun. The *kago*, heaved onto backs, takes off along the path, vanishes into the trees. Jericho keeps what he thinks is a good pace with Obi and Napo, the path rising and falling through the foothills, past gardens, small villages. Two hours pass and they are at the river, that's all, at the border where the mountain begins. The water is deep, chest-high, running fast. Jericho lets Obi steady him against the current, and though Obi smiles, calls him brother, it is a small humiliation, a reminder, if he needs one, that he might be from the mountain but he is not of it.

The path that rises ahead is steep. Valleys fall away to the side. Some are planted as garden; he recognises the wide leaf of banana, the tangle of yam. Another slope is planted with coffee, left untended since the price dropped and the road that was promised, through to the river, was abandoned before it was started. Jericho wouldn't have known it from regrown forest were it not for Obi's commentary. On every side he is pointing things out – plants, rocks, ridges, the birds whirring above them, a spider, a trailing vine – giving everything its mountain name, slowly, repeatedly, as if he has taken on himself the task of educating this returning *hapkas* brother. His words ping in Jericho's head as they climb.

The sun is in its slide down the sky when they reach the village. Mauve-grey clouds are rumbling overhead as they walk across the airstrip where Jericho and Leonard landed all those years ago. It's been closed for some time and saplings are poking through long grass. The aid post with its tin roof is still there, but the doctor has gone. A rusted tank turned on its side is being used for a cooking fire. Two men come out of a house. Jericho thinks it's to greet them, but there is something surly and impoverished about them, and inside, out of sight, he can hear a child crying. More men appear. They shake Jericho by the hand. 'You bring plenty *kago*,' they say, and he doesn't know if it is disaffection he hears in their voices, or envy. Or a comment, that's all. The boys take it on up, they say. They gesture up the mountain, which has vanished under the clouds.

A teacher comes across from the school to greet Obi, and he walks on up with them to the village where the children from higher up stay for school. The first of the mountain villages.

'Was this village here when I came before?' Jericho asks. He has no memory of it.

'It was small then. Now it is bigger. You and Leonard walked to the next village.'

'Above the waterfall?'

'The same,' Obi says. 'Tonight we stop here.'

He looks up, towards the rain clouds gathering ahead. Most of the others have gone on, taking the *kago* with them. There'll be no sleeping bag for Jericho tonight, no camping mat, no mosquito net. But a few have waited, and men from the village are gathered to greet him; the atmosphere is almost festive. The women are cooking on the fire, they dry his socks, and the night proves not so bad. The schoolteacher has a guitar, the village men talk, a river of sound in the heart language he once knew, and after that walk Jericho could sleep anywhere. He dreams of blind pigs. It's a story Leonard and Rika both tell. A set piece, a reminder that darkness can lie side by side with beauty.

At dawn the next morning, after a quick meal of cold sweet potato, they say goodbye to the teacher, shake hands with the women, and are on the road again, accompanied by some of the men from the village. They are carrying their *kundu* drums and feathers. Jericho's feet are sore. He is stiff and tired. Mountain man, what a joke. Following Obi, he thinks of Rika climbing up to tell Leonard she was leaving, breaking his heart. Yes, she broke his heart, Leonard never tried to conceal it, but a broken heart is not such a bad thing, he'd say, it means you have loved; the parts can reassemble, and in the cracks and breaks we reshape ourselves. 'No, I don't blame her. I regret every day I didn't spend with her, but I don't blame her. I regret nothing of the changes it brought – how could I, when it brought me you?'

All this Leonard says, speaking in Jericho's head, his voice keeping time with the rhythm of his feet as he climbs. And all the while the great trees rise up and through the high canopy, wisps of cloud over a pale sky. This is the land he was born to, alive in his dreams, and here he is, returning as a stranger who cannot find the path to bring himself home.

He walks on, ceasing to think, and when he has given up all expectation of arriving anywhere, ever, they come down the ridge to the river beneath the village. Through the trees, he can see sun playing on the water, women washing vegetables and babies sleeping in *bilums* hanging from low branches. Young boys come splashing over to greet them and, without pausing, Obi runs up the waterfall path to the village. Jericho crosses the river, sits gasping on a rock in the sun, shaking hands, laughing, remembering. Yes, he remembers this river from last time, and climbing up the rocks with the boys. 'Is the pool still there?' he asks the children who crowd around. 'Big pool,' they say. 'We take you.' Later. Later. The women have gone up the path, calling the children to walk with him. Jericho lets them gather him up, show him the path, how to keep his step on a waterfall. Halfway up, when he hears the drums, each with its own voice, something moves low down inside him. At the top, where the ridge flattens out, they are in an ordered world of paths and hedges, planted gardens. Just as in Leonard's film, though it was black and white, and this is *fauve-ish* in its colour, vivid after sombre hours beneath the forest canopy. All around he sees flowers, and trees laden with fruit.

At the entrance to the village, a large bark-cloth hangs across the gate, a jagged line of painted mountains moving in the breeze, and in among them the words *ROVANE* and *JERICHO*. Somewhere at the back of his eyes, Jericho feels the sting of tears as the bark-cloth is lifted and the dancers welcome him in. A sea of faces, a sea of hands, familiar, strange, he does not know. The inside of his head is dancing, beating to the drums, as he crosses the dance ground, shaking hands, leaning towards the faces that lean towards him, breathing the next breath. And then his feet remember. They pick up the rhythm and dance him into the village.

THE GUESTHOUSE WHERE HE AND LEONARD STAYED HAS GONE. ALL that remains are indentations where the house poles were. Instead, he is to live in a small house next to Obi's, near his uncles, Napo and Boja. '*Gutpela*,' Boja says, sniffing at him, grinning with his red stumps of teeth. An amiable man, he tells Jericho the names of the boys and men who gather round. These are Janape's brothers and cousins and nephews. He finds it hard to speak the name of his long-dead mother, who succumbed to a fever and died in the night when the moon was full and the rivers in flood. What was her story? It is not a question he knows how to ask. Maybe she gave him an answer when she sang to him the night before she left him with Rika and returned to the mountain. He doesn't know if he remembers her lying beside him singing, or if he's made a memory from the tales he's been told. There is nothing coherent about the memory, if memory it is, just rumblings, like an ache. She has no face but the face of a photo-graph. She has no smell, as Leonard has, and Rika. And Bili. Espe-cially Bili. Even as a child he liked the smell of Bili. Stringent, not sweet, like citrus, a touch of salt. Has he folded Janape into Bili, as Laedi suggests? Has he mistaken one smell for another?

The house for Jericho consists of one room and a covered platform. The room is dark, but in deference to the new ways there's a flap he can push up with a stick and open like a window. On the floor of the platform are woven mats and on the wall a covering of bark-cloths. They are at once like the mountain peaks that hang in Bili's apart-ment, and the curled hook of the vine in Laedi's living room, but also different. It's as if something has moved in them: there's a different delicacy, the markings are finer, more exacting, more *modern*. Is that a word that makes any sense on top of this mountain? Why not? Many of the younger ones speak some English, and books are prized. Obi keeps his wrapped in bark-cloth against the mists. The *Time* magazines are passed between the young men who go to Popondetta and have seen the images on the big screen of the towers falling in New York and the soldiers in Iraq. They ask Jericho about America, and want to know everything he saw there. They know about the world beyond the mountain, and beyond Papua New Guinea, and they want to be a part of it, not in a job like Young Albert, or in the post office in Popondetta. It's not just that they are poor, with no money for tarpaulins, or lamps, or radios; they want to be of account, and they want the mountain to be of account.

From the first day, the question of *bisnis* hovers in the air. How are we to make money? How are we to be known? How can you, our *hapkas* brother, help us? They have seen tourists walking the Kokoda Track. If they walk there, why not here? Jericho tells them that Australians walk the Kokoda Track because of the soldiers, their own people, dying there in the war. There's no reason for them to climb up here, no myth to cast light on the forest floor. They're not interested in the mountain, that's the truth of it.

'Let me think. Give me time,' Jericho says. 'First I must learn the mountain ways.'

Every day of that first week, Jericho has to force himself not to run back down the mountain to Milton. The thought of Bili is enough to stop him – the scorn on her face – though in truth it's an impulse that is more in his mind than a real possibility. His head is a jumble of impulses that run against each other. He takes out the photo he has of Rika standing beside the ground-spider cloth with its sun-ray legs. He had it blown up in a shop-front lab in London – Rika would never approve, but that's what he did – multiple copies, which he gives to the *duvahe*.

Nanaji has died, and in his place is another old man, whose mind is sharp though his eyes are rheumy and his knees pain him when he walks. When he goes, Napo tells Jericho, Obi will be chief. The clan will choose Obi, he says, confident of a consensus before its time has come. The old men look at Rika in the photograph, and at the cloth, the talk going back and forth; Jericho doesn't understand what they say. When he gives a copy to Lilla, something about the way she smiles makes Jericho smile. As the chief of his clan's women, she was first in the line of women to welcome him to the village. He recognised her at once, though twenty-two years have passed since he'd seen her; something about her high cheekbones and dark eyes have merged into the image of Janape from Leonard's photos.

The painting is in New York, the young men ask, for all to see? All who visit Rika, Jericho replies. And all who see this photo. It was in a magazine, he says, the same as *Time*. The old men tut and shake their heads. The young men clap their hands together. They pull him into the future, while Lilla talks of the past, and Rika's visit, all that she learned from old Nogi chief, who is dead now, and gave Rika the cloth, a gift from the mountain to take into the world.

The next day, Boja takes him round the dance ground. The *amorire*. Jericho loves that word, so close to love, soft, easy on the tongue. This is where Leonard stood to film, Boja says. Jericho doesn't want to hear about the film, he's spent hours in Leonard's study, back and forth through every foot of film. He needs to escape the film. He had thought he wanted the past, he thought that was why he came, but as Boja continues his tour, and the sun rises into the sky, and the young men go to the gardens, he finds he'd rather be with them in the hard work of *now*. But each morning of that first week, Obi has a plan for him. He takes him to the boundaries where village land ends and hunting ground begins; he shows him where the river can be crossed, where the sago trees grow that are used for thatching, and where the trees they cut for cloth can be found. He walks him fast, teaches him the names of bush plants and caterpillars, nuts and spider webs. And again Jericho hears the story of the war, of the initiation interrupted, and the eruption of the volcano in 1951. He learns the names of the chiefs who climbed to the rim of the volcano, where the heat turned their skin white.

In this way a week passes, then Obi returns to work with the men – Jericho's cousins – who are clearing a garden an hour's walk away. They set out with their bush-knives and axes, and when Jericho asks if he can join them, Obi says, 'No, it's okay, we are going to work, no need for you to come.' So he stays behind *like a girl*, hanging around the village with nothing to do but listen to the chatter inside his head. The next day he picks up a bush-knife and, without asking, he accompanies the men. It is hard work, hacking at the forest, digging out stumps; his arms ache from it. The ground is uneven, a steep slope to a river. He doesn't stop for the pain, the ache in his shoulder. Obi's wife, Doris, gives him a leaf to rub into the blisters. He wraps a cloth around his hand and returns to the garden the next day. He thinks he sees respect in the way the men look at him. He forces himself on. The work moves to the cleared soil, and Jericho takes off his boots, barefoot like his kin, feels the muscles of his feet and the earth between his toes.

When they stop for a smoke and sit along a fallen tree trunk, Napo's eldest son, his cousin Hector, sits beside him, puts his foot alongside Jericho's and laughs. Jericho's foot is slender compared to the splayed shape of Hector's mountain foot, which has walked unshod for more than thirty years. Hector tells a story of a white woman he saw in Moresby, when he was there, long ago, at the city mission. She had little tiny feet, this woman, like pig trotters, and high heels, and over she went and couldn't get up. The police were called, and a van carried her away. Hector slaps his thighs at the memory of it, and everyone laughs, Jericho too.

'How long for these to become mountain feet, do you think?' he asks, looking down at his toes.

'Long time yet,' Hector says. 'You stay with us many years. Then you have mountain feet.'

When it comes time to return to the village, Jericho ties his boots together by the laces and slings them over his shoulders. Obi frowns and tells him to put them on.

'They've been working all morning,' Jericho says.

'For the forest, they are no good,' Obi says. 'Too soft.' He lifts his foot and shows the tough under-skin, like a leather sole.

So Jericho sits on the ground, wipes the mud from his feet and pushes them back into the boots. But something has shifted, and he knows it.

That afternoon, Hector comes onto his platform, lies on a mat, rolls a cigarette and asks Jericho about his life in London. White girls, are they white all through, inside too? Has Jericho lain with them? He has? *Yeah!* 'It's good that you come back, cousin-brother,' he says.

When Hector leaves, Jericho looks out as mist blows in. The chatter in his head has slowed. Maybe it's the effect of hard work, this unaccustomed feeling of stillness. It returns again the next afternoon, and the next, whether it's mist or sunlight that fills the space between the mountains. As the days pass, the air around him seems to lighten, as if a veil is lifting. Snippets of language return, submerged sediments lift up.

And as if Obi has grasped the metaphor of digging down, he and Napo take him into the forest, along a spur where only men can walk, until they reach a high cliff that leans in, blocking the sky. At its base, there is a large hole dug deep into the ground. The *ujavue*, where long ago initiations took place. The nest where boys went to become men. Jericho has imagined somewhere snug, *cosy*, and here is a dark, damp hole. There are rocks and tree roots at the bottom, the bones of animals that have fallen in. 'Long ago,' Obi says. 'Before we were born. The chief was a small child when the *ujavue* finished.' His voice is apologetic. 'Old practice from before. Long ago, we stop.'

Jericho knows of the *ujavue* from Leonard; he's made a story of it, which he's told many times in London. The director of the gallery where he works told it at his farewell party. 'So Jericho's going off, back to his roots, literally it seems, for where he came from young men are taken into the forest to live in nests under the ground for a year. And when they emerge, the youngest perches on the shoulder of the eldest and pecks his way through the roof. Boys hatched as men! It could be an installation. They go in soft-skinned and come out tattooed warriors.' The director paused for the laughter. 'We're sending a man, a fine man, an excellent curator, and we hope that when he's hatched he'll return to us.' Standing there in the forest, Jericho remembers it all, the applause, the clink of glasses, the girl he took home that night, her hand on his arse, her posh voice shouting over the party roar. *A-maz-ing.*

He looks down into the ground and everything sinks. The ancient sediment. The heavy veil. His ponderous metaphors. The muscles in his stomach. All these years, he's imagined a *nest*, a warm cocoon, and the forest soft and feathery overhead, not this grim darkness and the cliff rising up. No sunlight, so that the bodies of the boys would soften for the tattoo.

'How could boys live down there all that time?'

'This is an old hole,' Obi says. 'On top, a roof. Inside, plenty of leaves. The chiefs camp on top, they build a small house, they make a fire.'

'And food?'

'The women leave it.' Napo gestures, back behind them.

That night, when he returns to his house after a meal on Boja's platform, after the other men are asleep, Jericho surreptitiously opens the bottle of rum secreted at the bottom of his pack and takes a swig.

He is on the mountain.

IT IS AFTERNOON AND LILLA IS STANDING AT THE STEPS TO JERICHO'S platform, calling up to him through the white feathers that fall across her forehead. Beside her is a young woman. He recognises her, clan-kin but not a sister, one of the girls from a family who lives at the other end of the village.

'Come up, come up,' Jericho calls, rousing himself from a nap while the village is quiet after the labours of the morning. Hector, dozing on another mat, wakes with him.

'Nelly, here,' Lilla says, indicating the girl, 'she comes to learn the medicines with you. You will show her, okay?'

Nelly blushes and puts her hand to her face. She is not yet married, with the shy look of the girls who follow Jericho with their eyes, then giggle and run away when he tries to talk to them.

'No one much is sick,' Jericho says. 'Not many come for medicine.'

'Nelly will show you.' Lilla gestures towards his boots.

Putting his boots back on is not what he wants. Or a medicine run. Hector rolls on his side, grins, *white-foot man*, rolls a cigarette. Lilla is looking through the box to see what Meg has sent. 'This,' she says, taking out antibiotics, antimalarials, paint for tropical ulcers and boils. Nelly puts them in her string bag. 'She must learn,' Lilla says. 'Come.'

She leads the way to the far end of the village, to a group of houses where the ridge drops away, close to the forest. In one house an old man with a watery cough is sitting beside his sons. In another, a woman with a fever lies glazed and grey. He reads Meg's instructions, gives one lot of pills to the man, another to the woman. Lilla calls the children, all of them, and Nelly lines them up, all shyness gone, calling back the ones who run away, making them show the ulcers on their legs. She has a tight hand around the wrist of the small boy, who's reluctant to show Jericho the sore in the crease of his groin.

'Every day,' Lilla says.

And indeed every day, late in the afternoon, after he's returned from the garden with the men, or from Obi's educational tours, after his smoke with Hector, his nap, Nelly is waiting at the steps. She takes him to houses where people are sick. The woman with malaria recovers, the old man doesn't. He rattles and wheezes in the dark, refusing to come out of his sleeping room. His sons shake their heads. Jericho asks Obi to send someone down with a note for Meg. 'How do I know if it's pneumonia, or TB? What shall I do? He's too sick to walk down.'

He already has a letter to Bili ready to go down to Meg and Presley at the post office. He adds another page about Nelly and the medicine run, the strange sense of replay with her in the role of Janape, which is not a comfortable transposition. He thought he was here for the past, he tells Bili, and finds it's when he forgets the past, and they do too, that it's best. The worst is when they go galloping into the future. There's been no talk of the guesthouse for a while, he says, 'fingers crossed'. He stops himself from saying he hopes she'll come up here one day, see the mountain with him. Instead, he writes that she is with him in mind, he talks to her every day. 'I'm not sure when I'll be back. It feels important to stay. Or rather, that if I don't stay I won't have done whatever it is that coming here is meant to do.'

'What happens when people get really sick?' he asks Nelly at the end of another run. 'Do you go down to the aid post?'

'Sometimes,' she says. 'A long way.' She smiles, a shy, unguarded smile. 'We walk to the road, catch the PMV.'

Nelly finished grade six at the school near the old airstrip. She speaks in English as Jericho asks about her time there, and yes, she says, at school she liked reading, and the map of the world. She has seen England there, an island like Papua New Guinea but one that sits up, like a queen. 'Here,' she says, 'on the map we are a bird.' As if she's conjured them up, a pair of sicklebills fly past and into the trees. She laughs, her soft, pretty laugh. But when Jericho asks if she'd like to go on, become a nurse maybe, or a teacher, her face clouds and she falters on the awkward words of the new people's language. She changes to their mother tongue, slow and soft, and says that this is their mountain. She stops and looks around her as if that is answer enough, and smiles a smile that is in every way different from the smiles of girls in cities. They are crossing the *amorire*, and Jericho looks with her over to the houses, to the pathways that run between them and across the valley to the high peaks of the mountain.

That night he is peaceful, and in the morning he doesn't check his diary to mark the dawning of the next day and the passing of the next week.

Another afternoon, after two days of sudden rain, when they have visited the old people who are wheezing from the cold, Nelly asks Jericho if he'll come to see her mother. They are walking slowly, enjoying the sun.

'Is your mother ill?' he asks.

'No. She paints for you, that's all.'

They take a path past a small garden, onto a spur where a cluster of houses looks out towards a peak that is not *Huvaemo*. No, Nelly says, this peak is not a volcano. It's a word she learned at school, she tests it in her mouth, *vol-ca-no*; yes, he says, very good, she has it right. She smiles, and tells him that this peak is safe inside, it is the ancestor peak, where the first two ancestors came from. They came out from deep inside the mountain. 'The man gave the woman a baby,' she says, 'and the woman gave the man the cloth. You know?'

'No,' he says. He's never heard this story. Did Leonard not know it? 'Will you tell me?'

She shakes her head. 'Lilla,' she says. 'Lilla must tell.'

At the house, they find several women painting, with children crowded round them, leaning against them, watching. Nelly's mother is sitting with her legs out, straight in front of her. She has a cloth folded on her knees and is painting an elaborate grid of black lines, cut by intersecting triangles. Beside her, younger women are painting a cloth laid out on the ground, flat between them. The black pathways have already been painted, uneven rows of semicircular shapes. 'The tusks of pigs,' Nelly tells him. 'Money.'

Money. Always money. Jericho frowns, but the young women are laughing – a man come to sit on the platform. 'Brother-cousin, white-man visitor.' He asks Nelly's mother about the story of the ancestors who came from inside the mountain, and there's another ripple of laughter, more hands to faces. A small girl is sent to find Lilla. Nelly's mother pats the mat beside her, clears the children with a flick of her hand. Jericho sits watching. The women return to their work and the soft murmur of their voices brings that old familiar sensation some-where around the region of his heart; he's always thought of it as an ache. But today there is no threat of tears. Surrounded by women – Hector will laugh at him – he feels soft, liquid all the way through.

'Okay,' Lilla says when she arrives, quietly beside him. 'Okay, you learn.' She is talking in their language, and he understands that she will talk to Obi and the other chiefs. Then she will tell him the ancestor story. When he is ready.

The following afternoon Jericho goes again to watch Nelly's mother paint the cloth that is to be for him. Long and thin, a loin-cloth for him to dance in. This time he has a notebook with him. More children are crowded onto the platform, they take his book, turn its pages with care, and after a lot of whispering, Nelly tells him they'd like to draw in it. He hands over his pen and they lean into the page drawing – first one, then another: a plane flying in the sky, a tree with its roots down into the earth, a *kundu* drum, a snake.

Underneath, Nelly draws the design of the vine. 'First the girl learns this. The vine,' she says.

'And a boy?'

She draws two concentric circles. 'There,' she says. 'The number one tattoo. Long before, it was tattooed on his belly. The sign of a mountain man. See, my mother paints for you.'

On the cloth, which her mother holds up, at the junction of the lines that form the grid, are the bellybutton circles, perfectly placed.

'A gift for you,' Nelly says, speaking for her mother, who laughs and pats Jericho's arm as he thanks her. '*Ai, ai*, Jericho.' Then she gestures to a woman who's sitting back against the wall in the shadows, rubbing a twisted foot. She's a thin woman, scrawny; her ribs show under empty breasts that hang low.

'Her foot,' Nelly tells him. 'It broke. Long ago when she was young yet. Now it pains her. Every day. See. You look. '

The woman unwraps a cloth from her foot. It is twisted over onto one side and where the skin is bunched up on itself is an angry, weeping sore. He paints the sore with red antiseptic liquid and squeezes anti-biotic cream into it. He gives her codeine, and the next day she asks for more. He can paint her foot each day, but even Jericho knows she can't have codeine every day. Besides, there isn't enough. He sends another note down to Meg, and to Bili. Nothing has come back yet. He tells Bili about dressing the putrid sore on the woman's foot.

At home – *home*, how easily that word comes – in London, he has to lie down for a blood test, otherwise he faints.

'Do you want Nelly to come to you tonight?' Obi asks when he stands up late one evening to return to his house. Jericho is shocked, though he's been told that's how it happens.

'Be careful,' Simeon warned.

'I thought you wanted me to marry a mountain girl,' Jericho replied.

'Nah! You don't have the sense. But if you try one out, be careful. They'll want your balls.'

After the offer of Nelly, Jericho is cautious. He sees her blush when he looks at her. He can't deny that the thought of her sweetens the nights. They are long – twelve hours – time bifurcated between light and dark. Kerosene is heavy to carry, there are few lamps and they cannot be lit for long. It's impossible to read. He's brought Conrad and Stevenson; both are wrong. He doesn't want the ugly face of colo-nialism, he doesn't want Pacific dreams. Not now. Not here. After dark, he listens to the talk amongst the men before they fall asleep:

adventures in town, prowess in hunting, conquests in love. Though he has learned how to joke with them, after the offer of Nelly he finds himself edgy and critical. When the talk returns to the smouldering feud with the low village, he snaps. 'Why don't you have a feast and make up?' he says. 'Why have a fight with your own clans? It'd make you stronger against the people down below.'

'No good,' Hector says. 'Down below, they are angry. They gave up their cloth, joined the mission.' He laughs, makes the droning sound of prayer, then lifts his arms and rolls his eyes in imitation of a preacher. 'They think they win that way. Ha!' He laughs again, slaps his hands in the air. 'They upset the ancestors and now you come. Ancestor gift. Yeah!' He puts up his hand for a high five, but Jericho isn't playing.

'No,' he says. 'I'm not an ancestor gift. Just a man, all the same as you.'

Obi has put up a warning hand. He has a bible and leads the prayers on Sunday. Whatever it is he says to Hector – too fast for Jericho to understand – Hector does not reply.

'So why did you people up here keep your custom? Your art?' Jericho asks. He might as well stay serious.

'It was necessary for the mountain,' Obi says. 'The chiefs heard it from the ancestors. Then Leonard came.'

'Did the ancestors *say* Leonard would come?'

'We knew.'

'What about Don?'

'A trick. He was a trick.'

'How do you know Leonard wasn't a trick too?'

'Because of you. Because he gave us you.'

'I thought you gave me to him.'

'We did. The chiefs did. We gave you to Leonard so you grow on his land, in his place. We wait for you to return.'

'And if I didn't?'

'You did.'

'Anyway,' Jericho persists, 'you gave me to Rika.'

'We did not know how to find Leonard. I knew that she was in

Moresby, I knew that Aaron was a good man. Leonard was in England. Too far to come back.'

'But he did. When Aaron died he came back.' He came back to get Rika, to get him. His first act as a father.

Obi shakes his head. 'No good Aaron died. He was a good man. He would make good government.'

Jericho sticks to the main point. 'When Leonard came back and talked to the chiefs, did you see him?'

'Yes. He came to Popondetta. Two days he was there. The chiefs come down. Big talk with Nanaji.'

'Some people wanted me to stay in Moresby, go to school, become part of the government. Nanaji didn't want that? Nanaji told Leonard to take me?'

'Nanaji decided. Leonard is not a man of government. He is a man of good spirit. Better for you to grow on his land.'

The relentless logic sews Jericho up. Just when he'd begun to feel at ease, the past loosening its grip, he is back in this neat, tight bind. The question buzzing in his head is how does he give what is necessary when he has no wealth to give? Should he have left them to their disappointment and never have returned? Maybe they'd think he'd been stolen by someone along the road.

He thinks of Bili as he lies in his damp sleeping bag that night. He closes his eyes, but her face is imprinted somewhere deep inside him. Then another thought snaps him awake: was Janape offered to Leonard as Nelly was offered to him? Would Leonard have agreed? Surely not. He tries to imagine the scene, a little film playing in his mind, but Leonard doesn't fit. Jericho contemplates the version he has lived with all his life, a tender love affair given brief expression. Was it nothing more than a story – a *romance* – adapted for the culture that taught him to read? Could it have happened like that here? He doesn't think so. How could Janape be away for a night from a house of sisters and mothers without being noticed? Besides, Leonard knew that her absence would be taken as a form of betrothal. A surreptitious quickie? That also goes against everything he knows of his father. He's back to the uncomfortable thought of an offer. He doesn't like it, but it won't be extinguished. He gets up, finds the rum bottle and in the dark of the night sits on the platform.

He thinks of Janape returning to the mountain. He's thought only of her sorrow, imagining her as she left him in the house with Rika, another imagined scene from the story of his childhood – the bereft and weeping mother stepping onto the plane that takes her over the mountains into the dark of loss. The sacrifice of the woman who relinquishes her life so that her child can inherit the world. Sitting on the platform, watching the silvery moon, he thinks with a small lurch of the heart that it mightn't have been like that at all. Returning here could have been a solace, more than a solace, a return to a centre, to the great breathing presence of *Huvaemo* and the ancestors and the clans. Her son, gift of the ancestors, could go with his father and see the new places of new people, but she belonged with the old people, with roots to hold the land steady. He imagines her sitting as he is sitting now, her sisters asleep behind her, and it comes to him that loss and contentment can exist together, one with the other.

THE PATH TO THE VILLAGES HIGHER ON THE MOUNTAIN TAKES THEM past the garden they've cleared, to the borders of their clan-land. As he walks with his brother-cousins, the forest beyond no longer seems impenetrable *jungle*. Jericho can't read the sky as Hector does, and he can't interpret the passing of birds or the change in wind. But when he walks, he sees trees with names he knows; he sees the shapes and colours of the bark-cloth, and however much the path turns, he knows where *Huvaemo* is. He no longer needs a hand to haul him over a ridge; he no longer soaks himself in the rivers and creeks that tumble down the mountain. He splashes his face with the others, replaces his cap and walks on.

Two hours pass, and he begins to tire. Two more, and he's trailing behind, first with Obi and Hector, then with Obi. Patient Obi. Ahead, Hector is smoking on a ridge top with the other men, and when Jericho comes into view, they stand and shout down to him. Town man, they laugh, not unkindly, sharing the joke, running on down the path, disappearing through the trees. And there they are, waiting in the sunlight at the next river. 'Ah, he comes! Brother of ours! *London man!*' Jericho's smile wears thin. He knows Leonard and Rika both came up here but he gives them no thought. There is no thought to give, just the placing of his feet, one after the other, as if he's in the control of some other force, and all he consists of is unceasing movement.

When the sun is full overhead, they stop for a smoke, all of them together. They sit on a high outcrop of rock, and the men use their cigarettes to burn the leeches from their ankles. Across the valley is a scarp of bare rock. They can hear the sound of a river crashing below. The village they are heading for is across that rocky chasm, daunting as a Kiefer landscape.

'It's okay,' Hector says to Jericho. 'I'll show you.' He stays beside him as the path narrows to a ledge above the river that foams white across the rocks. The path winds down, steep and precarious, until briefly it becomes level with the river, which smooths out into a bowl. There is a plump bank, a stand of trees, boughs hanging out over water that is fast-flowing, but no longer savage, before it tumbles again. They cross, one by one, single file, wading chest-deep into the current. Jericho's hat disappears, washed from his head. Hector grabs it, puts out a hand and catches Jericho as he loses his footing. 'White-man boots,' he says.

On the other side, even the boys of eighteen are too tired to joke. They look at their feet, rub their ankles. Under the trees the air is cool. Jericho's head aches and there's a faint shudder in his legs that he can't still. He looks up into the branches and sees spots of colour. He points. 'Orchids,' Hector says, and Jericho registers that he is in a small oasis, a resting place. Above the sheltering trees and the flowers, the cliff rises to rock again, trees dwindling to the few that cling here and there, until, way above, the forest begins again. There are no clouds this day. A few gather around the highest peaks and though *Huvaemo* is nearer, and they are higher, still it is far. They begin the hot trek up across rock. Napo's feet are bleeding. When they reach the forest, he wipes them on soft leaves. The roar of the river is gone; above, the familiar whirrings and rustlings of the forest.

The village is on a high ridge, with a path up to it that strips the waterfall ascent of all challenge. A thousand feet, Jericho reckons, as he climbs into the song of the *kundus*. At the top, rather than open out like Obi's village onto what is, now Jericho comes to think of it, more a small plateau than a ridge, this village occupies a narrow area of flat not much larger than a football pitch, the earth dropping away steeply on all sides. Beyond, an amphitheatre of peaks.

When the gate opens, they are welcomed in by dancers holding banners of bark-cloth that move in time to their steps. Everything seems large. The plumes, the headdresses, the size of the ceremonial hangings, the peaks of the mountain. Was he here as a child? Is this where the giant people of his dreams come from, with their hoofed feet? Round the ankles of the dancers are small skirts of grass and herbs, seeds that rattle and sing. He takes off his boots and his legs tremble as he circles the dance ground, his mind a blur, given over to sensation – the feel of the earth – following the dancers, his feet advancing and retreating to a rhythm as deep in him as his heart, until at last he is sitting on someone's platform. For a moment it looks as if he has six toes. One of them is black. Hector holds a cigarette to it, and they watch as the huge, full leech falls, oozing blood. 'Ah, man,' Hector says. 'Boots are good. Next time you bring them for me. Brother, man.' Tobacco is passed around in a bamboo pipe as the light fades, turning the peaks soft, a bluish lavender. Jericho lies back on the mat and slips towards sleep.

Obi prods him awake. The old chief Nelson is sitting cross-legged beside him. Earlier he stood in the dance ground on a raised pulpit of saplings, talking fast, too fast for Jericho to get the words, but he understood their meaning, heard the voice of welcome to this next village of the mountain, source of life and art, walking and learning, walking to hear, walking to see. *The ancestors give us Leonard. We give you to Leonard. And now you return. Ancestor gift. The child who left us, who we called Jericho, has returned, the man who can make a great noise, blow down the walls. Jericho, the name from the ancestor story of Leonard.* And now the *duvahe* is sitting here, murmuring quietly to Jericho, his pig's tusk necklace hanging over the folds of his chest. His eyes are soft. '*Ai*, Jericho. You are here. *Rovane.*' Tears stream over the ancient ridges of his face.

The next morning Jericho wakes early and goes for a pee. He stands at the edge of the village, which is also the edge of the ridge. There are wisps of cloud in the valley, and birds of paradise in the trees. Their plumes are a darker red than those he's seen in the forest below. They fluff out their tail feathers, preening, it seems, just for him. He walks quietly towards the house so as not to disturb them, and asks Hector their name.

'Bird of paradise,' he says, unimpressed. He rolls over and goes back to sleep.

For Jericho this village is a paradox – so rich and so poor. There are no lamps up here, few plates. Abundant meals from abundant gardens are eaten off banana leaves. Water that runs fresh from the mountain is heated in bamboo. Nails are few, but houses are well built and their platforms generous. The children wear rags for cloths but there are few sores on their legs. That morning, the air is cool, the sun slants onto houses. The first fires are being lit, smoke drifting from the roofs. He breathes in, tastes the mountain air. This would be the village for ecotourism, if you could parachute the tourists from a plane passing overhead. Even the flowers on the trees are different. So is the bark-cloth hanging on walls and worn by the women as skirts. The cloth is paler than in Obi's village and there are fewer of the intricate workings of designs from the forest he's become used to: vine and fern, bush snail and the backbone of river fish. There's a boldness of intersecting lines, as if the underlying sinews are made present. For the first time Jericho wishes he had Leonard's film with him.

'Did Leonard see this cloth?' he asks.

'The same,' Obi says. 'He came to this village. Ask Boja. Plenty of filming in this village. Then he went back. He did not go on top.' His head gestures to a peak that is clear above the morning cloud.

'There's a higher village?

'Small village.'

'Is the bark-cloth like the bark-cloth here?'

'More different,' Obi says.

'Can I see? Will we go there?'

Obi jerks his head in another direction. 'We go to a village that way. Big village.' He shouts over to the women in the cookhouse, and the reply comes back. Yes, the women from the top, they will come.

And sure enough, some days later, there on the grass are three women with long dreadlocked hair. When Jericho goes over to greet them, he sees that it's not hair that's plaited. It's bark-cloth. Rika can't have seen these women or she'd have photographed their strange and beautiful locks. Texture. It's what she's become famous for. Edges, shadows, erosions.

'Do all the women wear their hair like this?' Jericho asks.

'Some,' Obi says.

'Can we go there?'

'It is not a village for visitors,' Obi says. 'The first ancestors lived there.'

So he is a visitor? Oh well, Jericho thinks, I suppose I am. A visitor, a brother returning, not yet returned. He looks at the dreadlocked women. Their language has the sound he's become accustomed to, the same music, but its meaning slips his grasp. On the cloth they wear are large squares, long wide pathways, pyramid-shaped mountains. He looks carefully. The designs are cut from another cloth, sewn on, a form of collage, like Rika's ground-spider; the first he's seen. Same technique, different design, a very different effect. There's something about these bold shapes and the way they're placed on the cloth that reminds him of the constructivists. Malevich's squares, or Popova perhaps. A ridiculous thought, the sensibility is quite wrong. *Stupidly* wrong. They are something else entirely, unlike anything he's seen, but for all that there is something about them that is *modern*.

Standing in the morning sun with these bark-cloth women, Jericho is startled into a thought, and he can't imagine why he hasn't had it sooner. Here is the mountain's wealth. Here is how he can help. Their cloth is art in any terms. It's contemporary, it's bold, and it's beautiful. And it's *unknown*.

'That cloth,' he says to Hector. His training has not equipped him for this. He raises his hands in a question, and something in Hector's demeanour changes. His face sharpens, without the teasing edge, as he tells Jericho that the cloth that is cut to make the village designs isn't painted. Its colour comes from being soaked in mud. It's the old way, before the ancestors found the dyes. Once, it was done in every village – their grandmother, Nogi, made cloth that way. But now there is less knowledge, and when the old *duvahe* women die, who knows if there will be more. The young women say it is too much work, the bush-string is stiff and the bone needle hurts their fingers. That afternoon Hector does not joke. He has thought a lot about the future of the cloth. When he was in Moresby he saw the bark-cloth from other tribes that was sold to tourists. Young Albert wanted to bring mountain cloth, make hats, cut it small, then sell it to the tourist shops. The chiefs said no. They were right, Hector says. It may make a small *bisnis*, but the cloth here will die, no longer for the mountain. Down below, on the flat, the Orokaivans sold their cloth, and now the trees are gone. No cloth, no trees, no art. That's why the chiefs like ecotourism. The tourists will come and look. They will learn about the mountain and take their talk of it back to the place they come from. That way, the mountain is known, and it stays safe.

How would you feel, Jericho asks him, if we made a different business with the cloth and sold it in London, or Australia? Not to tourists for a little money, but for people who understand art from all over the world. In his gallery in London, sometimes they have exhibitions from India, or Japan. Not just white-man art, the bright-colour art Hector has seen in *Time* magazine, or the empty designs he saw in the lobbies of hotels in Port Moresby. There's a seriousness about Hector when it comes to the art, a thoughtfulness that Jericho hasn't seen before. 'Nogi was my grandmother,' he says. In Port Moresby he went to the museum, saw the cloth from other places in Papua New Guinea, cloth from their neighbours in the ranges, from the coast down below. Old cloth from long ago. He talked to the guard, who didn't know how the art was chosen, or how it came to be there. It was a dark place, no one looking, and the electricity off. Even so, their art should be in the museum. Hector felt the insult of its absence, and so did the *duvahe* when he told them. It is a sorrow that the mountain is not known and respected. He asks Jericho about museums in other places, and who would buy their art, what they would do with it, and who would see it. He thinks about the trees, and all that the young women must learn, and the work of keeping the cloth dry and safe, and the pride that could return to them.

Would the *duvahe* be open to the concept for a *bisnis* that is taking shape between Jericho and Hector?

'We try Obi first,' Hector says. 'Brother-man.'

'Obi?' Jericho says when they are standing alone at the edge of the village. It is dusk, they are watching birds of paradise display in the trees along the lip of the ridge. Obi is telling him their mountain names. 'If we want to start a business, how would you feel about making bark-cloth to sell?'

'We use the cloth.'

'I know. Could you make more? Would the women want to?'

'Who would buy? No tourists come. The chiefs like eco-tourism. Last year Young Albert visited and speaks to the chiefs. Tourists walk here, we dance for them, build a guesthouse, they like our birds, the river, we tell them *kastom* stories. They pay big money.'

'How big?'

'One hundred kina one night.' Forty Australian dollars. Fifty, at most. Twenty pounds.

'And how many can you have here at once?'

'Young Albert said a guesthouse for six. Eight maybe.'

'Do you want the place crawling with white people? Making trouble with the girls?'

'The girls can stay in the houses. They come for one week, Albert has the *bisnis* plan. Then they go, and another come later, maybe after a month.'

'You're not going to get white people walking up here. It's too far. Too hard.'

'Our villages are clean,' Obi says. 'Not like the Kokoda Track. I have been and looked. Plenty of *tauba*, they wear boots the same as yours, they have sticks to help them. They walk. The villages sell them *kastom* goods. There's rubbish on the track. Mud. Here,' he gestures around him, 'look, it is clean. No rubbish. No *raskols*. Young Albert says tourists like clean houses. If you like, maybe we can sell them some cloth.'

'And if the people at the old airstrip get jealous? When they know you have money, and there's trouble on the road?'

'We take security guards.'

'Obi. I'm sorry. I wish I could persuade you. It's not going to work. It's dangerous. It's too difficult. And the money is not a lot. Just a little and you must do it again and again, and what if bad people come up here and make trouble? Bad white people. There are plenty. Or men from the airstrip come up here and burn down the guesthouse? What then, if the tourists are coming?' Obi shrugs.

Jericho goes on. 'And if you sell them bark-cloth, how much would you charge?'

'Fifty kina maybe. Sixty?'

'That's crazy.'

'Albert says they sell cloth, other cloth, in Moresby. If it is a hat, then maybe forty kina. On its own, cloth that's all, maybe less. He says it is not big money. Tourists like shields from the Highlands. Or armbands from the Trobriands.'

'It's too little. Much too little. Your cloth is art. You say so, the chiefs say so. *Our mountain, our art.* Its your wealth. And no one else can do it. Plenty of people can do guesthouses, all the people along the coast, on the islands.'

'You don't like ecotourism.'

Jericho sighs, fights back frustration. 'Your villages are rich, you know that. Do you want them to turn into villages like the ones on the Kokoda track, with white people walking through and too much money for the young men and not enough for school fees and the old ways going?'

Hector has joined them, squatted down beside them, chewing tobacco. 'He talks *tru*,' he says. 'He can't stay here for the guesthouse. Soon he goes.'

'I have work in London,' Jericho says. 'I have to go back to it. It's where I earn money. Without a job I can't help you, and Leonard will be old soon. We must find a way that Hector and I can work together, with you – all of you – when I'm not here. When I'm in London.'

'A long way.' Obi's voice is doleful.

'Yes. A long way. But other opportunities. In England, in Australia, people like to buy art, beautiful art, with stories of the place it comes from. They buy art from all over the world. Africa. Asia. They pay big money. Hundreds of kina.'

Obi whistled. 'For cloth?'

'Maybe. See? It's a different way of thinking.'

'We must ask the chiefs.'

'First, can I look at all the cloth, talk to the women, take photographs? With Hector? Would that be okay?'

The chief of painting, a squat woman with tattoos on her temples and a pierced septum, welcomes Jericho and Hector onto her platform. Yes, she says, they can see the cloth. She has asked the women to bring it, and there they are, sitting behind her on the platform, crowding around the steps, with cloth folded in their *bilums*. They unwrap babies to show the swaddling cloth and begin to unfold their paintings in a great pile on the floor. Obi shouts across to a group of boys playing a game with stones under a tree. He tells them to rig up lines of bush-rope on the dance ground so that the cloth can be displayed. With it swaying in the early morning sun, Jericho thinks of Rika and the *Surrealist Map of the World*. He'd liked that story until he told it to Bili, in London that disastrous time. 'You expect me to applaud the surrealists for claiming a place they never bothered to visit? Cheer them for making New Guinea large enough to be visible in Paris?'

He packs the thought away and returns his attention to the work at hand. There is much to be done if they are to make a record of the art that is here in the village. All day he and Hector are busy, measuring cloth, photographing it, taking notes. Working beside his cousin, Jericho is happy. Or rather, he thinks that the state he's in is a form of happiness he's not encountered before. He knows the pleasures of a day's hard work, and he's enjoyed working with others. But this is different. As if the work he does in London has, on this day, become fused with his life here. The equipoise of art. Where does that come from? He can't remember. It doesn't matter. Today, now, somewhere inside him a new shape is forming.

Hector is adept with the tape measure. He draws up a sketch of each cloth, writes in the measurements and the names of the designs. He asks the artists when they use a stick to paint, when they tie grass to the stick and cut it to make a brush. He asks them where they make their paints, and from whom they learned the designs. He makes notes for the chiefs.

'How much school did you do?' Jericho asks.

'Grade eight.'

'You didn't say.'

Hector laughs. 'You think I am a bush-man, that's all. You're like Captain Cook. White-man boots, same as yours, they come up higher.' He marks the place on his leg from the pictures he's seen, and laughs some more. 'Captain Cook!'

Jericho puts an imaginary telescope to his eye, as if surveying the horizon.

Other young men arrive to help, some with pencils of their own, yellowing exercise books. Hector sets them to work, and all around him on this bright morning there's a clean, focused energy.

Among the faces bent to their task, he sees the shape of his own nose, the curl of his hair, the set of his eyes. A strange experience after living all his life as a face that has no reference point. Are you Indian? African? Jamaican? No, I'm Melanesian. What? Where? After a life of that, it feels good to find himself among faces that are like his, among people who can fix him in generations going back, to look around and see familiarity. There is even a woman who, at a certain angle, has a look of Bili. She turns and the hallucination fades. No, nothing like her. Brenda is her name. Six large hangings are hers. She has the sweeping line of this village, and the intricate cross-hatching of Obi's village. His village.

'Yes,' Hector says, 'her mother is there, in our village. She married here, in this village.'

'You have both,' Jericho says to this woman, Brenda. 'Two village wisdom.' She laughs, and he glimpses Bili again. The set of the forehead, maybe. Something about the hair. But her skin is darker than his. Darker than Bili's. She doesn't look *hapkas*.

'What is the name of your mother?' he asks her.

'Josephine,' she says.

'You know her,' Hector says. 'You gave her medicine. You talk to her down below. She has the bad foot.'

Yes, the woman with the twisted foot. *Josephine*. The connection clicks in his mind.

As he and Hector work on, the thought presses at him: Brenda and Bili. He doesn't know what to do with it. He hasn't been able to send word to Bili since he's been up here. No one has gone down to the road. He will write a letter tonight and ask Obi if it can be taken down to Meg, or to Presley. He needs to write to her anyway. The more the *bisnis* takes shape in Hector's mind, and in his, the more he realises the scope of what it will entail. It will need a structure. A co-op, perhaps. An arts centre. He has no idea how such things are established. There must be procedures and precedents. Bill will know; he can't do this without her.

A small girl arrives with a pineapple. Hector slices it with his bush-knife, looks at the sky, a flock of birds; the small girl points upwards, over the peaks. Rain is near, she says, though there are no clouds. They work on into the afternoon, until the women pack up the cloth, fold it into their string bags and return to their houses as the clouds rumble in overhead.

'Josephine is married to Hunter, yes?' Jericho asks Obi as they walk back through the village to Nelson's house. 'Josephine all the same as the trouble with Don?'

Obi looks reluctant. 'The same.'

'And Brenda here, her number-one daughter? Number-one child?'

'The same.'

'Could she be Don's child?'

'*Nogat*. She's Hunter's girl.'

'When was she born? Same time as me?'

'Before. A little before.'

'There you are. She could be Don's.'

'No. Josephine, her mother's blood made her.'

'The timing's right,' Jericho says.

Obi is silent.

'Look at it this way,' Jericho says. 'Don and Josephine. For many weeks Josephine went to Don. The village was upset. Nanaji was angry. Leonard made a settlement. He told me.'

Obi remains silent.

'It could easily be that the baby came from Don. I came from Janape, and she went to Leonard one time only. Before Leonard left. One time, maybe two?' He turns it into a question.

'Janape did not go to Leonard.'

'What do you mean?'

'She did not go to Leonard. She was not sent to Leonard.'

'But she went, didn't she?'

'No, she did not go.'

'They didn't have sex? Is that what you're saying?'

'They did not lie together.'

'Of course they lay together. How else would I be here?'

'You do not understand.'

'Yes, I do.'

'Leonard made you.'

'That's what I'm saying. With Janape.'

'He makes you as an ancestor gift. No lying together.'

'That's ridiculous.'

'It's true,' Obi says. 'In the new world they think the baby is made only with semen and blood. It is not so. In our world it is spirit that makes the baby. Spirit comes from the ancestors. From the mountain. It is always so.'

'You don't think you're getting muddled up between the old stories and the new ones? Bible stories?'

'You grew on Leonard's land. You have much to learn of the mountain.'

'I sure do.'

Jericho is unaccountably angry. He walks over to the edge of the village and looks down at the trees. The night before, he'd walked out there with Hector, and there below them were trees alight with fireflies, flickering on and off in unison, like Christmas lights. For a few seconds, maybe thirty, maybe more, they were all on. Then off. Then on again. Then off. Synchronised within each tree and between trees.

'Now I believe in magic!' he'd said.

'Fireflies, that's all,' Hector said. 'It is always like that.'

A magical place, and now, today, before the earth has had time to make its daily move around the sun, he is cursing those same qualities. What seemed magical last night, today is credulous and self-serving. What has he walked into? An ancestor gift. Well, that has him shackled. *Hapkas* nothing. As if it isn't enough being born between two cultures, now he's a gift from some mythic entity; a virgin birth, no less. Is that really what they think? Is it concocted as a trap? Surely not. These open faces. Open, yes; and yet always something behind, beyond, something unknowable.

He wants Bili. That glimpse, that apparition has him aching again. She'll know. She'll know how to make a picture of these pieces.

Bili. His stomach gives a cramp of longing.

That night, when he lies down to sleep, the rumbling in his gut becomes louder and the brooding returns, the unanswerable questions. He's planted a seed, and he has no idea if it can grow. And if it does, what will be the consequences? He feels afraid as the talk goes on and the hopes of the young men rise, and the chiefs remain silent. Will they embrace the selling of the cloth? Will they say, 'No, the cloth, it belongs to the mountain'? Will they save him and Hector from this folly?

All night he lies awake beside the sleeping form of Hector. He hears the rain start. The hours wear on. There is nowhere to go but out into the rain. There is no latrine in this village. Last time he went for a shit in the bush, he'd hardly finished when a pig, a *blind* pig, scooped it up and ate it. That was a bad moment, not something he wants to think about as he goes out into the rain and the dark now. He finds a place he thinks is away from the paths and the *amorire*, and with nothing to listen to but the hammering inside his head, he deposits the watery, stinking substance that gushes from his bowels.

At dawn, when the first cockerel crows, he falls into a fretful sleep, brought out of it by Hector beside him with water in a bamboo container, and a dry yam.

'It's okay,' he says. 'You are not alone. Mountain man.'

THE MOON IS CLOSE TO FULL WHEN THE CLANS FROM JERICHO'S VILLAGE arrive for the dance which will go from the next day's dusk to the following dawn. The large contingent comes up the steep path at a run, the men with their drums, the women with switches cut from the bush, which move above their heads in time with their step. All afternoon clans from other villages arrive at the gate to the village, their voices joining the singing and the *kundus*, until the ridge dance ground is so filled with movement that Jericho fears the outer circles of dancers will fly off its edge. The clans of the host village, who have been preparing for days, dance in welcome. Jericho takes his place beside Hector, circling the *amorire* until the movement stills and the formal welcome of the chiefs is finished, and the men who've made the long journey from distant villages lie on the platforms built to shelter them. The tempo of the afternoon changes as large earth ovens are filled with sweet potato and yams. Hector and Jericho walk across to the gatherings of women from their clan. Nelly is there with Lilla, and they come to meet them with Hector's wife, his children running ahead. *Ai, ai.*

Lilla leans to Jericho and smiles. 'Nelly,' she says. 'She will marry soon. Boja's grandson. Leonard's namesake.'

'Ah,' Jericho says, relief tinged with regret.

The next afternoon, Jericho dresses in the loincloth Nelly's mother made for him, and the heavy headdress Hector has helped him prepare, sewing the white feathers to the black, attaching them to the wooden frame, ready for this night. Jericho is paired with Hector, and he understands that it is an honour to dance with one so strong.

He also knows it is a test. Only the strongest men and the strongest of the women can dance the full twelve hours from dusk to dawn. Hector has done it before, and with all the chiefs present, every one of them, he says that Jericho must let them see that he is strong – a man of the mountain. Such a man, he says, will surely be trusted to carry the cloth to London. Or rather, Jericho thinks, is it that a man who dances the mountain from dusk to dawn cannot walk away and never return? He slaps away the thought and limbers up as if for a cross-country run. He remembers them from school, the hours of running, the exhaustion and the achievement.

But cross-country running is nothing to the dance that lies ahead. At dusk hundreds of dancers circle the *amorire*: old men, young men, old women, mothers with babies on their hips, small children dancing in pairs. They fill the *amorire*, each clan with its line of dancers, crossing the ground in step, circling out from each other, and re-forming to circle again. And all the time the *kundus* mark the beat. The belly-button tattoos of Jericho's loincloth mark him as a mountain man, and in his place beside Hector he feels exactly as he is: participant and witness. Around his ankles are small ruffs of dried grass and in his armbands are pungent herbs. On his head is the cumbersome head-dress he wears with a sense both of pride and fraudulence.

For the first hours, he keeps abreast of Hector, joined with him in a dance that becomes increasingly mesmeric. By midnight, somewhere in the middle of the long twelve hours of dark, many of the dancers leave the *amorire*; they stand at the side, lie on the platform, or sit on the ground watching. Jericho dances out for water from a gourd, a stick of sugarcane. When he lingers, Hector waves him back and he returns to the beat of the drums. The moon is bright, the dancers cast shadows on the ground.

After another few hours, only the strongest of the dancers remain. The dreadlocked women are dancing with capes of bark-cloth hanging from their shoulders. The hours go slowly, the *kundus* slow the beat, and Jericho goes out again for more sugarcane, cold water from a gourd. He wants to lie on the grass and sleep, but he sees the chiefs on their platform watching as he hesitates, and Hector makes a circuit of the *amorire* alone. When Hector comes level with Jericho, he dances out, takes a stick of sugarcane, leans in towards Jericho. *Do not fail me, brother-man.* The outline of *Huvaemo* is clear against the night sky. The white feathers shine, the anklets of dried grass rustle in the moonlight. Jericho removes the heavy headdress, hands it to Napo and returns to the dance.

More hours pass. Jericho loses all sense of time, until there is nothing of him but the rhythm of his feet. The dance takes him over, and in so far as he remains capable of thought, he thinks it is not they who are dancing the mountain, it is the mountain dancing them. Hector's back shines with sweat. It is the force of his will that is holding him to the dance. Jericho can feel the sweat on his own back. His bare feet ache, they feel swollen, the size of serving plates, and still he dances on, through another barrier of exhaustion, through the long, dark hours when he is no longer sure if he's himself or has become another, until at last the sky begins to lighten. Napo comes towards him with his plumes. The *kundus* hasten their beat now, led by Hector's drum, and still they dance. There can't be more than ten left in the *amorire*, though Jericho is in no state to count. People coming down from the platforms are singing, children who have been asleep are woken, and when the first rays of sun come round the edge of the peaks, there is shouting of thanks, the dance ground fills again with dancers and the crescendo of drums. Hector and Jericho dance out, over to the platform where the men from their village have hung their headdresses. No drug, no night awake has done to Jericho what this night has done – removing all thought, all mind, until he is pure rhythm, the beat of his feet on the ground. The *kundus* have stopped, the dancing has ended, but still he feels the pulse in his feet that continues in another sphere of existence.

All that day he and Hector lie on the platform. Food is brought. Girls come with fresh water from the spring, yam and baked banana are laid out on large leaves. A pineapple; Jericho eats chunk after chunk, its sweet juice a balm, and as the sun rises into the sky, he begins to return to some sense of himself, whatever it is that he now is, and falls asleep.

When he wakes, Lilla is beside him. 'Ancestor gift,' she says. The word she uses for *gift* is soft, different from the word Obi uses; more like spirit, he thinks, listening to this language that comes back to him and eludes him all at the same time 'Ancestor gift,' Lilla says again, and Jericho shakes his head.

'No,' he says, 'not an ancestor gift. Just a man, that's all. Look. A man who can get sick.' He puts his hands on the hollow of his stomach.

Lilla smiles. 'Dance spirit,' she says, and he drifts back to sleep.

When he next wakes, she is still there, a strong, calm presence. Like the mountain.

'Janape and Leonard,' he says, and she makes a soft cooing sound, letting her fingers twine around each other. 'Obi says they did not lie together. Maybe not.'

'Men do not always understand,' Lilla says.

'So Janape lay with Leonard?'

'They lie. They lie very quietly. Soft. Soft baby spirits. Leonard gave the baby to Janape, she grew the baby inside her. The same as always.'

'Nothing to do with the ancestors?'

'Ancestor spirit, that's all. The ancestor spirit brought Leonard, brought Rika.'

'How? I mean, why them and not the others who came?'

'Look,' she says, pointing across to the clouds gathering on the high peaks. 'It's like the cloud. It lives on *Huvaemo*. Sometimes you see it. Sometimes it comes down and catches all of us. Sometimes it is spirit, and like the rain, sometimes it is the mountain that sends it, sometimes it is something else – it comes from somewhere else. But when it is ancestor spirit, mountain spirit, we know. We know when Rika came, she was for you. She and Janape were like sisters. Janape's baby is all the same as Rika's.'

'Did Janape think that? Did she think that me going to Rika was the same as staying with her?' He can hear the terseness in his voice.

'She was sad. A little sad. She knew.'

'Knew what?'

'You must go. She is sad, and you must go. The mountain wanted it.'

So it *was* her duty. All that dancing, and here he is back in the same tangle.

'When did she get sick?' he asks. 'How soon after I left?'

'A little soon. When she come back from Rika's house. From Port Moresby. The plane maybe make her sick.'

'Is that why she didn't go to Popondetta when Leonard came to talk to Nanaji? Did you go?'

'No. I stay with Janape. She was sick. Big fever.'

'Did anyone tell Leonard? He could have taken her to Moresby. To the hospital.'

'She did not want. It was *kastom* sickness.'

'She knew about medicines.'

'Sometimes medicine is good. Sometimes, no good.'

'Were you with her when she died?'

'Yes. She die quietly.'

'When?'

'After Leonard left on the plane.'

'When he took me to England?'

'All the same. She die, release your spirit. Let you go to Leonard's place.'

Tears are sliding across Jericho's face and he does nothing to wipe them away. They come silently, without sound or movement from the body.

'The dance,' Lilla says. 'The dance brings tears, often it is the same.'

'I'm not surprised,' Jericho says. 'Big work. I don't know how I did it.'

'The spirit of Janape helped you.'

Jericho is not so easily comforted. His Englishness has returned and does not believe in spirits.

Lilla puts her hand on his chest. 'Here,' she says. 'Janape is here. Listen and hear me.' She takes a cloth from her string bag, spreads it out beside Jericho. She has come to tell him the story of the first ancestors who came out of the mountain, high on the peak where the water runs hot.

There were two of them, a man and a woman, but the woman did not have the birth canal that could bring forth children. So the man cut the cleft in her body, and in return, she went into the forest and cut the first tree. From the wound in its bark, she made the first cloth, which she gave to the man, her husband, in gratitude for the power he gave her, and the children born to them. This originating exchange, Lilla is telling him, brought to life both babies and their art. On the cloth beside him, she has painted a large pyramid mountain of solid black, with a triangular section at the top left unpainted. Inside are two small beings, the first figures he has seen on any cloth.

'You take the cloth when you go,' she says. 'It is good.'

'So you chiefs have decided?'

'We think much on this yet. Last night we watch you dance. Today I tell you the first story of our ancestors. Tonight you and Hector will come and sit with us, all the chiefs together.'

Oh, oh, oh. Jericho is raw, all the way through.

'Come now,' she says. 'You must eat.'

He gets up from the mat, tests the strength of his legs. With Lilla beside him, he steps out into the afternoon light and sees the smoke rising from the earth ovens. Tonight there will be a feast of pig.

JERICHO DOESN'T KNOW HOW MANY DAYS HAVE PASSED SINCE HE came up to this high village. His watch has sunk to the bottom of his pack, and he's long since ceased to think of it. Something has shifted so that he no longer feels himself on the end of a very long rope, as far away as it's possible to be from his life in London. Even from Moresby and Bili. Or Milton and the school. For these past weeks, he's come to glimpse himself at the centre of something, with time and distance rippling out, not in a line but in some sort of rhythmic, circling movement.

And now, when at last he's dropped into mountain rhythm, drifting with the days, breathing in and breathing out, Obi says they must return to their village. The moon will soon be full again and the chiefs will tell the gathering clans about the *bisnis*. Jericho already knows their decision, and their conditions. After the night of dance and the feast of pig, he and Hector sat with the *duvahe* on their platform. Lilla was there, the youngest of the chiefs, and Obi, a chief-in-waiting. A small hurricane lamp was lit for the occasion, casting shadows on their faces and the cloth that hung from the walls. Yes, the chiefs said, there can be a *bisnis*, the cloth can go with Jericho, but the *duvahe* must agree on each cloth that leaves, and each story that is told. And before they speak aloud to the clans, Jericho and Hector must tell them how they will be sure the mountain art and its stories will not fall into bad hands. Copyright law is not easily explained, but the chiefs know of Laedi and her lawyer daughter who got Jericho and the boys out of the police cells. It is not an event Jericho wishes to recall, but Hector, not having been there, has no such qualms. 'Bili has a strong spirit,' Napo told them.

Jericho's letter asking for her advice was sent down to Presley, and Obi has now heard that men returning from the market have left a package for Jericho in the village below. So in the early light of dawn, Jericho straps on his boots for the walk down the mountain. At the river that runs beneath the rocky scarp, they wait for the people coming from other villages, and the dreadlocked women from theirs, the only village he has not been taken to visit. With the artists and the chiefs and the men and the children, all together maybe two hundred people are in the long line that snakes through the forest. The steepness of the ridges no longer alarms him. He keeps pace with Hector. With every step, even in his boots, he can feel the mountain pressing up through the soles of his feet.

Clouds are rolling over when, at last, they reach the village, and they are greeted with green coconut milk to drink. Jericho goes onto the platform of his house, opens the door to his sleeping room, changes his clothes, looks at his sleeping bag and camping mat as he might his own bed after a long flight, and is *pleased*.

Obi's sons come walking towards him carrying the parcel. Inside is a packet of the tea he likes from Bili, and a volume of Langston Hughes from Milton. 'You might need reminding that there's a world here waiting!' Milton writes. There's a box of medicines from Meg and instructions for his and Nelly's patients. 'No,' she says, 'nothing can be done for Josphine's foot. It has been that way a long time now.' He sighs. Yes, he needs reminding of the unequal world. Bili's letter is in a thick envelope with just his name.

Hey mountain man,

You okay there? Long time you been gone. Ah. Yes, I notice.

I'm in town, two days here, working for the small block-owners against the oil-palm factory. They bring in their palm fruit, it's months now and still the processing plant hasn't paid. Every excuse, usual story, and powerful men are shareholders, usual story, so when the block-owners protest, the police are sent in. Smashed windows. It gets called a riot and a bunch of block-owners land in the lock-up. Dealing with that too. The case against the factory won't come to court. I'm rattling sabres. Leonard taught me to say that. He rang Laedi last month, glad to hear you're on the mountain. He's thinking of coming out. As it's thirty years since Aaron died, if you're going to be here for a while yet, he says maybe he will come, we could go to the fjords, all of us together – remember Aaron. A Leonard idea. He must know your plans. Melanesia man!

I've written out a letter for the chiefs. A structure is easy enough. And business registration. You should bring Obi and Hector over to Moresby while Leonard is here. We can do the paperwork. Maybe I'll have to come up there with you, talk to them myself. They're right to be concerned. There are a lot of cowboys in this town. Then I can meet this woman you say looks like me. Not everyone is *hapkas*, you know, and just because you're getting the hang of it, doesn't mean you should see them everywhere.

I'm at the hospital with Meg, writing this. She drove me out to the school yesterday evening. I stayed there – a relief to be away from the block-owners. Milton says you're okay, doing well up there. Some boys have been down with peanuts. Your notes to Meg, medicine man. Milton says yes, the fjords, okay, he'll come, see Leonard again. Very Milton.

I'm sending this tea up with a message from Meg. They're waiting for someone to come through to collect it. Some men are at the market with their peanuts. Hope it arrives, this letter. You come back, eh. *Mi laik lukim yu.* See you soon, I hope.

That's enough. *Em tasol,*

Bili

Well, he thinks. And then, with a jig that rocks the bamboo slats of the floor, he says 'Yeah,' and in a high five slaps the hands of Obi's boys. Yeah, they echo. *Yeah!*

THE FACE OF THE DAY

MARTHA DIDN'T THINK SHE'D SEE THE FJORDS AGAIN, and when Jericho's invitation came, she hesitated. Going back without Pete would be hard. She hadn't returned, even to Moresby, while he was alive. He made his field trips alone, while she remade her life in Sydney. She'd see Laedi when she was down in Sydney, and Wana occasionally; Bili not often enough. But yes, she would go, for Jericho's sake – of course – and also for her own. It was time she faced up to the past and made her own reckoning with it.

Since Jericho's visit, she'd found herself back in those years, waking most mornings to memories ignited by the surge of love she'd felt for him at their lunch by the harbour, and again the next day when he came to her flat. She'd made a cake for him and they'd talked by the window looking over the park. After he left she'd taken out the box of photos, most of them Rika's, that had been untouched at the back of a cupboard. Pete joked sometimes that they should sell them, make some money on her, but they rarely even looked at them. There was years of dust on the box. The only photo they'd kept in view – framed and on the wall – was one of Pete with Aaron and Milton out by the river. In it Pete and Aaron, in very short shorts, were about to swim; Milton, still in a shirt, was on the rocks with his ukulele. Aaron was smiling into the camera. 'So young,' Jericho said, taking it off the wall, bringing it to the light of the window. 'And now only Milton is alive.' Pete went with a heart attack, four years ago.

Martha has one night in Port Moresby, and she stays with Laedi. Leonard isn't there. He's gone to speak at the university in the Highland town near where Laedi was born and Simbaikan lived until she took herself back to the village to die. Leonard is to fly across to the fjords with Laedi at the end of the week, Martha going ahead on the flight that stops at Popondetta, where Milton will join her. They'll have two days alone with Bili and Jericho, who are to meet them there from Collingwood Bay, where they've been with a German television crew, making a documentary on logging in the Pacific.

In Laedi's house with a view over the harbour, Laedi takes the chair with its back to the window, and although Martha watches the sun set over the mountains, it's their platform in Hohola that is vividly before her. The houses have gone, Laedi says, under the freeway. Maybe just as well – erased, like their lives there. On the sideboard is the photo of Bili and Jericho as children on a branch hanging over the fjord. When Martha looks at it carefully, she realises Rika must have taken it on that last visit, just before Aaron drowned. Laedi nods. Even so, she likes it, she says, it captures something of how they were as children.

Would it have been better, Martha asks, if Jericho had stayed with Laedi; if she'd raised him with the girls? It's not a question that makes much sense in the face of life as it has transpired. 'An opportunity lost,' Laedi says, her voice brisk. Having had Jericho in the house with her, abject with self-pity, pining for Bili, she sees him as untethered. 'No ground,' she says and her expression is so like Simbaikan that Martha laughs.

No ground. Was that it? Do any of us have ground, us transient ones? How could Rika give Jericho ground when she'd lost the ground she thought was hers? Laedi saw her in Oxford. She was good as a mother, but her mind wouldn't stay with the daily grind of school projects and uniforms and cakes for the weekend; everything about her leaned towards the next escape, camera at the ready. Leonard was the consistent one. Isn't he ground enough? *Father ground*, Laedi says. *English ground*. Papua is Jericho's mother ground and how could Rika be that when she looked to him for ground a child could never give.

Martha keeps her thoughts to herself. She doesn't say that when the end came, the question of her relationship with Jericho was never raised, and that now it presses on her. Hadn't she been the third Hohola mother? She knows it's a vanity to think of herself in those terms, no matter how many school runs she did, or baths she gave, no matter how her heart swelled with the pleasure of it. 'We'll have one of our own,' Pete had comforted, as if one could be had in place of another. But his widowed mother was an invalid, and Pete her only child, and Martha was teaching at one of the new universities in Sydney. So they put it off 'until there was time', by which they meant until his mother died and Martha had tenure. By then she was not far from forty and a child was not to come.

'How was Jericho when he got back from the mountain?' she asks Laedi.

'Oh, much better,' Laedi says.

'The art project? That'll be grounding. A good fit with his life in London.'

'That's what Leonard says. He seems to think Jericho is in *excellent form*.' Laedi laughs as she catches Leonard's inflection. 'It's true, despite everything – and I can tell you there's been a lot – he's come through well. Though personally I think it has more to do with Bili taking up with him again.'

'That's so good,' Martha says. Jericho had given a hint of it on the phone. He didn't want to say much in case he spooked it.

'It's been inevitable for years,' Laedi says. 'And if they don't get a move on, she'll be too old for a child.'

'I thought Bili didn't want one.' Martha remembers her, insistent from the age of sixteen that she wouldn't have children.

'She will with Jericho,' Laedi says.

When Wana arrives for dinner they sit at the large table, just the three of them at one end, and talk of New York, where Wana was ambassador to the United Nations for many years. At first she'd seen Rika whenever she came over from Oxford, but the past was so hedged about that they went to films and exhibitions to avoid it. Later, when Rika moved to New York, they spoke mostly of politics. This evening, it is politics again, and when Martha raises the past, Laedi and Wana slide off it, not because they are avoiding it, but because for them it is long gone. Although they ask Martha how she is managing without Pete, and are interested in the few small books she's written, including the one about the colonial traveller who lived in a house not unlike Laedi's, for them the present is more powerful, and they are back to the shifting alliances and deals that make up the politics of the fracturing parties, which are doing what they can with the parliamentary system imposed on them.

Martha does not feel offended or neglected. She had great affection for these two women she knew as girls. We become more ourselves as we grow older, she thinks, watching them: brisk, pragmatic Laedi and studious Wana, who's lost her hourglass figure. She wants to ask her how it was when Sam took a job in Melbourne, where he now has a family of boys. She wants to know how it felt to be the post-modern, post-colonial woman who flew between New York and Port Moresby. She doesn't ask, any more than they ask how it is for her, a widow with no child.

When the talk returns to Rika and her many successes, Martha admits to the mix of fascination and envy that she feels when she looks at Rika's portraits of Louise Bourgeois and Lee Krasner. Her *Artists Series*. 'What a life Rika stepped into,' she says. 'I have to Google her to keep up.'

'She's not happy,' Wana says.

'Happy!' Laedi says. 'That's not the important thing.'

She doesn't say what the important thing is. The woman who works in the kitchen comes in with a pot of tea and a platter of fruit.

'Thank you, Kara,' Laedi says. She doesn't drink coffee at night. Nor does Wana. They have to be up early. For their work which, Martha supposes, *is* the important thing.

Martha sleeps in Jericho's room. She doesn't snoop exactly, but she touches the clothes, looks to see which books he has, resists the note-books with his handwriting, the small pile of letters from Bili. On the table he uses as a desk, there's a letter, face up, from the director of his gallery in London, attached to a pile of papers, brought by Leonard, she supposes. The director welcomes the idea of an exhibition, if the work is indeed as Jericho describes.

That night, her first in Papua New Guinea for thirty years, Martha barely sleeps, propelled back to those terrible weeks after Aaron's death when Rika clung to Jericho, and he had to be rescued from her grip. *Jericho*, Rika would weep, *at least there is Jericho*. Aaron's gift to her. Martha went to see her in the hospital, and when the nurse let her through the door, Rika had said, 'Why are you here? Always nosing about. Can't you leave me alone?' They never really spoke after that. Not properly. Martha sat beside her in the ward, but Rika would turn from her, and Laedi said it was better if she didn't go. Rika didn't say much when Laedi was there, and Laedi didn't pass on what she did say. But it was clear that if Rika couldn't stay, she wasn't letting Jericho stay – as if he was hers to keep, or let go. When Leonard arrived from England, the doctors allowed him to bring Jericho for a visit. After that she spoke to Leonard, until at last he persuaded them to discharge her.

'Come home,' Leonard said. Home? Where was home? Where was there a home for Rika? For Jericho?

FROM THE WINDOW OF THE PLANE THE FJORDS COME INTO VIEW AS green fingers of land extending into clear blue water. At their tips a rim of pearl billows into turquoise reef. The plane circles over a line of outer reef, returns to land, swoops in low, disturbing the sea birds. The rise of the runway is just as it was, a bump of wheel on grass, and the plane comes to rest in the place where, at the beginning of 1976, they'd landed to celebrate the first New Year after independence. Ten days later a bowed and silent Rika was put back onto the plane, leaving Aaron behind, buried in his ground. That day the air was filled with high, crying wails, but as Martha steps off the plane on this day, the past is overridden by the beauty of the place, the glittering sun, the familiar physique of the fjord people, grown into a new generation. Waiting on the strip, instead of the kiap, is the manager of the resort in which they'll stay until they go to the village – a rugged Australian just old enough to have been born and schooled there before independence, one of the few who renounced Australian citizenship in order to become a Papua New Guinean, and for that alone Martha likes him.

'Resort' gives the wrong impression. The government station was sold off after independence, at first as a place for divers living in the old dormitories. Slowly the ramshackle buildings were added to and resold – to the consternation of Giwi's clans, who never had this in mind as they watched the fence go up around the wide verandas, and a terrace appear above the path down to the jetty. Martha tries to work out where the kiap's house used to be, but nothing looks as it did. It's as if someone has come in and rearranged the puny structures.

To Martha's eye, they've rearranged Milton as well. The shape he makes in the air has changed: no longer a skinny silhouette of sharp angles and rapidly raised arms, instead a slightly rotund shape, a downward pressure in the air. His hair is greying. His gait is slow. Even so, she recognises him at once when he comes across the strip at Popondetta to join the crowded plane – a twin otter – for its flight along the coast. He climbs in and sits at the back near the door, calling hello and waving to Martha in her seat at the front.

'Well,' he says when their bags have come off the plane and they're walking over to the resort, and have had time to embrace each other. 'You look the same, Martha. Handsome. You told me once that was the word for women like you. Well, you're still handsome.'

'Older,' Martha says.

'True,' he says. 'We've seen a bit, you and I. And here we are with more to see.'

They are on the terrace that hangs out over the steep cliff-path down to the fjord, where a small wharf has replaced the jetty. The water is still, a canoe comes into view and glides in under the trees.

'So where are Jericho and Bili?' Milton asks Jim, the manager. 'Weren't they to meet us here today?'

That had been the plan, for them to come here with the German television crew as soon as they were finished in Collingwood Bay. Approaching in the plane, Martha had looked across to the wide scoop of land continuing into the distance, east from the fjords. An uninterrupted tract of forest, saved by the landowners' resistance, and Bili's tenacity. The crew are booked to leave the fjords on the flight that will bring Leonard and Laedi in two days' time.

'They're held up,' Jim says. He spoke to Bili on the radio early that morning. The dinghy has arrived, but they have a sick boy with them and can't leave until the elders decide what should be done. Bili wants him taken out to Moresby. The family says it's sorcery, and they don't want him leaving their land. There might be a delay while it's decided. Bili, Jim says, is very determined.

'Tomorrow?' Martha asks.

'Hopefully,' Jim says. Then someone calls, and he goes off, always busy, leaving Martha and Milton alone on the terrace.

Neither of them entirely welcomes the prospect. Thirty years is a long time and, as Martha learned in Moresby, the ease of youth doesn't necessarily translate into ease now. In a strange way, old familiarity adds to current unease. They watch two parrots on the railing. The female, glossy in green and red, takes the chunk of banana that's been left for them. While she pecks at it, the male bats her aside and takes it. She acquiesces, turns her back, droops her head. The male ignores her, finishes eating and flies off. *Shreeesh.* Martha laughs. Milton doesn't.

'You know Jericho's been to stay with us at the school,' he says.

Martha nods. 'How did you find him?'

'There's a lot of Leonard in him. At least, that's what I thought at first, and that it'd be best if he could accept that England is where he belongs. But I came to see I was wrong. It's not just out of curiosity that he asks about the past, there's a part of him still tied here.' He turns towards Martha and the awkwardness eases. 'He was on the mountain for a long time. When he came down he was different.'

'Different how?' Martha asks.

'More Papuan. Less English.' He frowns. 'He and Hector were like this.' He holds up two crossed fingers.

'Who's Hector?'

'A cousin. The son of one of Janape's brothers. He was at school at Martyrs. Smart boy, when he wasn't playing the fool. He should have stayed on, he could have made a contribution. I tried to get him to think about government, but he'd make a joke of it and crinkle his hands as if he was counting the money. He went back to the mountain.'

'A successful return then,' Martha says. 'Selling the bark-cloth sounds a good idea. I gather Leonard is optimistic.'

'It's already walked him into trouble.'

'What sort of trouble?'

'He was held up on the road. Didn't Laedi tell you?'

Martha's heart gives a bump of fear. 'Guns?' she asks.

Milton shakes his head. 'More a confrontation. Young men. They'd been sent to tell him that the bark-cloths Hector had sent down to Presley had been stolen. Presley's door had been broken down the night before. They'll steal these next ones too, the young men said, indicating the ones Jericho and Hector were carrying. "You pay now," they said. "You keep the cloth. Ten thousand kina." A ridiculous amount. Jericho turned out his pocket, showed them it was empty. He didn't have a key card. They took his wallet, cursed, thumped the ground with the clubs they carried. Jericho held his nerve. Or Hector, more likely. Obi was with them and said, okay, we go to the school, find Milton, we'll negotiate, and the young men – who knows why – said okay, we will tell Milton. Maybe they thought they could get the money from me.'

'So what happened?' A note of injury enters Martha's voice. She hasn't been told any of this. 'Did you sort it out?'

Milton gives one of his gruff almost-laughs. 'No. Not me. Meg. She knew one of the boys, had nursed his mother. She roused on them, and told them they should be ashamed. They went away and we locked the bark-cloth in the school office. We thought it was a try-on. Too inept for a shake-down. But a couple of days later Meg was stopped on the road. It was a foreman from one of the oil-palm plantations, married to a woman from the village near the airstrip. Warned her off. He frightened her, and Meg's not easily frightened.'

'So, it's not just young men from the airstrip,' Martha says.

'No. There'll be someone behind it, using them. The bark-cloth that was stolen from Presley was dumped at the school turn-off. Some of it had been slashed and dumped in oil.'

Milton consults his hands for a while, as if to say that's enough talk for now. He pulls himself up out of the chair and says he's going for a walk, into the small township, and to the school. The head teacher had been a student with him, long ago when they were boys at Martyrs. He invites Martha to go with him, but she is perturbed by this story. So she stays on the terrace alone with her thoughts, and this sweet air. Judas perfume, Pete used to say, the treachery of paradise, the sweetness that leads you into the forest, where the smells are acrid and moist, the ground treacherous. She thinks of Pete with his head slumped on the table when she came in from the shops. She knew as she put the key in the door that something had happened. The air felt dead, even before she called out and nothing came back. He'd been reading the paper. And now here she is, *alone*, without him, looking into the deep green of the fjord.

It is late in the afternoon when Milton returns to the wide veranda where Martha is reading under the fan. He has the head teacher with him, a fjord man who's come back to teach at the middle-grade school after many years at a senior high school in Moresby. Milton orders him a beer and raises his eyebrows at the resort's prices. They sit with Martha in the wide wicker chairs, reminiscing about their careers. Milton tells a story of a student of average ability who became rich and sent his son, also of average ability, to Martyrs, where Milton had him for Literature. He was a lazy boy who never read the text and copied the essays of other students. He was no better in other classes, and one day Milton took him for a walk along the road, spoke to him about the riches of literature and the possibilities of life ahead. To no avail. When he failed the year, his politician father arrived at the school waving a fistful of notes, demanding that the boy's teachers, including Milton, give a distinction to his lazy bully of a son, who boasted that he need do nothing, for his future didn't depend on grades. Milton asked the father if he remembered *Another Country*. The father didn't. Everything he'd learned in Literature had been a waste of time, no use to anyone. *Literature* doesn't make money. Look at you, he said to Milton, and Milton nodded. Yes, it was true, but unlike Rufus Scott he, Milton, was alive, when he could as easily be dead, burned on the anger and arrogance of youth. Taking advantage of the politician's faulty memory and bad reading, Milton drew a moral tale of boys who burn up in insolence and end up dead. When the boy returned the next year to repeat the grade he failed, Milton put his chastened behaviour down to the power of literature rather than the refusal of the headmaster to make a deal, or even the beating he suffered at the hand of his father.

Milton has lost none of his power with words and, listening to this story, Martha relaxes. The past recedes as she returns to 'the face of the day'. That's what Malinowski recommended when the frustrations of fieldwork got to him. It was a phrase Pete used, a way of getting through bad days anywhere, through interruptions and demands, disrupted plans. 'Trust the face of the day,' he'd say, which was not much help on the day he died. The broken face of her life was how it felt.

That evening, Martha and Milton have a bottle of red wine, on her account, which she can't afford. Neither can he. She makes the white gesture and feels herself in a false role. The awkwardness between them returns, and with it a dismaying familiarity, as if they know its contours and origins, which she supposes, though she's reluctant to admit it even to herself, must have to do with the colonial mind they grew up to, a residue that stays with them even as they lay it aside. Or maybe it's just personality. They both live too much in their heads. Milton says often enough that he prefers the company of fictional characters, and Martha says she's rarely happier than with a book, though it's not entirely true. Or even true at all. Which is why that long-ago time with Rika and Laedi changed her mind as well as her heart, and why those years in Hohola live on in her, despite everything, as more than memory.

To avoid the dangers of that terrain, she asks Milton the question Pete would have asked if he'd been there. Did independence come too soon?

'Helpers not rulers,' she says. 'Isn't that what Whitlam said when he was determined to *divest*?'

'That was the thinking of the day,' Milton says. 'We wanted independence. We wanted freedom. They are very great words we learned from you and we wanted to remake them in our own image. That was our ambition.' He makes a gruff, huffing sound. 'Those of us who didn't have to deal with the day-to-day reality of it, and the power-play and the money and the foreign companies, and the tight rein of Australia. Aaron was right, we knew nothing – all ideas, no responsibility.'

He shakes his head and an aura of sadness descends on them, a heavy sensation as if the air has thickened, although the fan is moving above them.

Ruminating. That's another thing that's changed about Milton. The young man who sparked with words has become a *ruminator*. He has a way of sinking down into himself and thinking, or remembering, *ruminating*, before he rises back up onto the sweeping plain of words. And when he gets there, he's lost none of the flair he had as a young man.

In her bag by her chair, Martha has a volume of Milton's poems. She takes it out and puts it on the table between them. Milton looks down at his hands, but when she reads a short passage about a hut on a river, he smiles, and they are in the memory realm that feels more real to them both than the pleasant comfort of this resting place. Milton is back with Aaron, out at the river, the last two awake by the embers of the fire. The poem sets the scene, Martha can see them as clearly as the chair where Milton sits. Martha leaves him there by a long-extinguished fire until he rises up again and his eyes lift to hers. They, too, are sad. Large, brown, and sad.

'"Milton brother," he said to me,' Milton says, '"I am afraid. Why is it I am afraid?" I said it was too great a task. Was it the last trip to Canberra, the big cut in the budget? He said no, though he was afraid for that. But that wasn't the fear. It'd take courage to bring the country through to a real independence and not a new form of dependency. We couldn't manage without money from Australia. We still can't.'

He is quiet again. Out in the dark they can hear frogs croaking, someone singing in the kitchen. Lamps glow along the edge of the veranda. The mosquito coils on the floor aren't enough to keep every mosquito away. Martha rolls down her sleeves.

'We sat by the fire in silence for a while,' Milton says. 'I was chewing a lot of betel in those days. Then Aaron said again, "Milton, brother, why is it that I am afraid?" I didn't know. I had every reason to be afraid – my life was in tatters. I was refusing to make anything of it, refusing to join the new class that was making money. I had no wife, no home, no money. But I wasn't afraid. Morose and angry, but not afraid. I thought we'd muscle through, I thought we'd be safe as long as enough villages remained safe. That was my mistake.

'Afraid how? I said to him. What colour this fear? I asked him. What shape? What feel? Where does it come from? Go to?

'"It's the colour of green ginger. It's the shape of a metal coil. It's the feel of sorcery." I believed him. I still believe him.'

'You do?'

'Well, no. Not with all of me. Not with the part of me that sits here in the white man's resort with you. Not with the part that waits for Leonard and Laedi. The part of me that knows the villages down here, that knows the magic worked in these fjords is strong yet – that part of me, yes, it knows. The part of me that waits for Jericho and Bili and is afraid for them.'

'Isn't sorcery the reason that's there when there is no reason?' Martha says.

'How western you are, Martha. Reasons. There are no reasons. There are mysteries. There are things that happen for the reason of happening. And there's magic. Do you look at these fjords, these still waters, and not think that in the deep water there is a force that could bring you down? Do you think nothing lives down there but mackerel and squid? In the caves and holes that go into the seabed, under the ledges?'

'You're an inland man. You don't like water. It makes you suspicious.'

'Ah, Martha. Even you talk of mystery.'

'The mystery of the human heart,' she says. 'That's what I call a mystery.'

'So is death.'

'For death there is a reason, you know that. A heart attack down there under the water. A sea snake.'

'There was no mark,' Milton says.

'There was no autopsy.'

'There was no reason. It was time. Aaron knew. Rika knew long before. It was made to be time. There was a force at work. Strong force, no matter what you call it.'

'Angel,' Martha says. 'That was Rika's mistake. She should never have told Angel.'

'They knew anyway. They didn't know how, but they knew she'd done something to stop a child. All Angel did is tell them what.'

They are on uncomfortable terrain, and while it doesn't embarrass Martha, it does him – this matter of Rika's infertility, and Angel's betrayal when she told the women in the village about the coil inside her, *drilled up*, mincing the sperm, killing the spirits of babies. So Milton slopes off to bed with an apologetic half-smile, leaving Martha alone on the veranda with a bill to sign.

BILI AND JERICHO ARRIVE LATE THE FOLLOWING AFTERNOON. MARTHA has read her way through another morning of waiting. The sky is overcast, and Milton is down on the wharf when the dinghy comes into the fjord, but it's not until they're at the bend on the way up the hill, Milton hollering to her on the terrace, that Martha sees they've arrived and hurries to meet them. The clouds are darker, and the first drops of rain are splattering onto the path, and there, striding ahead, is Bili. She's taller than Martha remembers. Her hair is tied back in a knot, and she has a small canvas pack on her back. There's a lot of her grandmother in her – wide mouth, prominent cheekbones, large, slightly hooked nose – but where Simbaikan walked with a determination that had her all knees and angles, Bili walks with the confidence of a modern future.

'Martha,' she says, her eyes alight. 'You're here.' A long hug lifts Martha off her feet.

'It's so good to see you,' Martha says, and they're hugging, and the spots of rain are getting bigger, and happiness is welling in Martha, when Jericho rounds the bend. Milton's right – something's changed in him. She can't tell what, except that the city-smooth edges have gone. His boots are worn, the colour of earth, and he smells of wood smoke and fish. He has Milton by the arm, coming up the hill, and when he stops to greet Martha – another hug, another kiss – Milton puts his hand on her shoulder and says, 'Old friend, these *tupela* have come for us,' and they walk on like that, at ease again.

At the top of the hill, on the open space above the airstrip, the councillor, who's been waiting for news of Bili's arrival, shakes her hand as he makes his welcome speech. People are gathering round as he recalls the last time she was here, in the fjords, when pirate fishing ships were dropping their nets off the reefs that are as much a part of their heritage as the forests that have vanished under the rain. Since the boats have been back in Collingwood Bay, the councillor has many questions for Bili. His wife has a pineapple for her, and his children have come from the school to shake her hand.

'Do you want to go inside?' Milton asks Martha, and she can see that it's he who wants to go in, but can't abandon her to the wet. All either of them have is a banana leaf to hold against the rain. 'You go,' she says, but he shakes his head and they go in together, and by the time they've met the German television producer, the sound- and cameramen, the rain has stopped as suddenly as it started. Sun glints on the puddles, steam rises from the grass, and bright rays of sun return the fjords to their massy green.

Jericho is the next to come into the resort. He puts down his pack, drinks a bottle of water, looks around at the bar, the wide veranda and wicker chairs. 'Straight from Somerset Maugham,' he says, and Martha can't tell if it's disapproval she sees cross his face, or relief. He takes off his boots, and is talking of a shower – the Germans have already gone for theirs – when a young man with dreadlocked plaits appears.

'This is Archie,' Jericho says. 'From Conservation Melanesia. He came up on the dinghy with us.' Archie has been in Collingwood Bay because of the pirate ships the councillor is talking to Bili about. They were fishing off the reefs in the bay. It was a provocation, Archie reckoned, because one of the men who was a principal in the company that had wanted to log along that coast and then plant oil palm also has an interest in the ships – which are registered in another country and shouldn't be in these waters at all.

'Bili got an injunction against them,' Archie says.

'A double victory,' Jericho says, as Jim comes in and shakes Archie's hand.

'Well done, man,' Jim says. It's not Archie's first time over here on the track of the pirate ships.

After the quiet evening when Martha and Milton ate alone, tonight the table is crowded and the talk noisy. There's laughter, and

Bili standing up to make her point, and Archie with a guitar. It's their last night with the television crew, and they are celebrating. After the meal, Jim sets up a screen so the cameramen can show their footage.

Milton clucks gloomily as he watches the old men speak of the oil-palm plantations they've seen in other parts of the country. Jim recognises where the camera is as it tracks along a river bounded by forest. An elder leads the way to the border between the village and the hunting grounds. He points to medicinal plants and names the butterflies that cross the camera's path. In a village, another elder lists the work they did to stop the logging, and the women show the sewing machines and the hats they made. An old woman tells of the dreams she had before they knew of the loggers, and she's having them again. It's fishing boats now, she says, pointing out to the still water of the bay, but the loggers will come again. There have been sightings of trees weeping blood for sap.

'We won,' Bili says on camera, giving a lucid account of the legal issues. In another scene, the villagers dance in celebration, and she and Jericho sit with the elders.

'No victory is conclusive,' Milton says as Jim opens a bottle of champagne. 'Never was, never is.'

Watching with them, Martha finds herself drifting into the memory of Leonard's film. She'd watched every screening of *The Mountain* during that wet week of his visit in 1973. She'd slipped into work-shops and seminars and, as soon as Leonard left, she shut herself in her room at the library, took out a clean sheet of paper and wrote 'The Mountain' at the top.

She wrote each day for a week, and when Laedi took the girls out to Milton at the river, she spent a weekend alone on their platform – Pete was in the Sepik – and wrote on. Rika came and read for a while and still she said nothing, though it was of her on the mountain that Martha wrote. When she finished, she put it in a drawer and did nothing with it until after she and Pete returned to Sydney and she'd published *Colonial Travellers*. It was 1982 when she showed it to a publisher. 'No one's interested in Papua now it's independent,' he said. 'Besides, your view is surely romantic. Isn't the place depressed and disaffected?' So she put it away in a folder, and it was only after her lunch with Jericho that she went back to it. What came to her as she read was the surrealists' remark about Oceania arousing covetousness in them. Covetousness. What a strong word. An 'irresistible need to possess', Breton called it.

When *Colonial Travellers* was published with a small print run to respectful, if muted, reviews, Leonard wrote her a kind letter. Maybe he meant it, or maybe he saw that it was important to her, the fruit of long labour, and also that it was disappointing. Not something to let pass without comment. It fell far short of the hope she'd set out with, which was to give expression to their paradoxical relationship to New Guinea and therefore, maybe, to her own. To give words to a place and a time that had changed the course of her life. To *possess* them. She came nowhere near. Worse, really – because the story she told had passed its moment. Ten years earlier, even five, an audience of her generation might have responded to their adventures, but by the time the book was published, six years after independence, no one wanted to encounter a 'jolly crowd of natives'. Everything had changed: language, sensibility, politics.

Her travellers didn't talk of covetousness. They were lured by *dreams* – of a Pacific imagined from Europe, all tall palms and blue skies. Dreams of steamships and rescue from the damp cities of their birth. Confident dreams that could win large audiences – of jungles and cannibals; dreams that landed them in a house above a harbour with shutters and cool walls and a servant standing at the ready.

At dinner that evening one of the Germans from the film crew told her it was 'passion' that brought him to the Pacific on a 'mission' to alert his country – in fact, the whole world – to the perfidy of illegal logging. He was a serious man with intelligent eyes. Martha liked him, and when he said he'd take something back with him that would be more than the film, more than the experience – something *indelible* – she nodded. Yes, she knew that feeling.

Sitting there, half watching the footage from Collingwood Bay, she sees the link she'd missed, the uncomfortable truth that connects her to her travellers, and then to now. We used a different language, she thinks as she watches this other film, but were we so different, all of us who came with 'dreams of things longed for' and hearts to be unlocked? The fact that we rewrapped our dreams as gifts and offered them in the spirit of service, or dressed as Research, or Art, or Film, doesn't make them any less potent, or greedy, or blind. Weren't our dreams also driven by some hidden something inside ourselves? Our own covetousness. Our own lack of ground, our dissatisfactions with where we came from. Our emptiness, perhaps.

When the footage ends, Jim rolls down the screen and they all move back to the cool of the veranda. The talk returns to the man with an interest in logging and fishing boats. When he heard that Archie and Bili were both in Collingwood Bay, he arrived in a helicopter at the small township where Archie was based. Bili had seen this man in court and knew he was ruthless. She and Archie walked to meet him with the elders, and the news they'd received from her office that morning: the injunction against the pirate boats with their winches and freezer units had been granted by the court. The man spat on the ground. 'Whore-lawyer. No husband, no children. What kind of woman are you?' He stood there with his security guards, threatening the elders that he'd win yet.

'You be careful, girl,' Milton says, and Bili pats his arm. She's had worse than that, she tells him.

Undeterred, he presses on with cautionary tales about accidents that befall those working to document the loggers and record the illegal movements of bulldozers and sawmills. One goes over a ravine, another into a river torrent, another disappears without trace.

Bili shrugs, she knows these stories. She drinks another bottle of Coke and says she's safe because she's visible. 'It's harder to kill a lawyer from the capital.'

'No, it's not,' Milton says. 'Car accident. *Raskol* hold-up. A robbery turned violent. A snake through a vent in the wall.'

'A snake?' Bili says, looking up sharply.

When Martha and Milton get up to go to their rooms, it's almost midnight. They leave Jericho rolling a joint and Bili leaning against him with her eyes closed. Archie is playing his guitar.

'She should take more care,' Milton says.

'Is it true about the snake and the vents?' Martha asks.

'Could be. I read about it somewhere. Africa, I think.' He pauses, with a mischievous nudge. 'Bili doesn't like snakes. Never has. Don't you remember?'

Martha doesn't, and laughs. 'Good try,' she says. Over at the bar, Archie is singing 'The House of the Rising Sun'. 'They must be stoned,' she says, and takes the path towards her hut and the solace of a mosquito net.

THE NEXT MORNING, THE SKY IS A CLEAR DOME OVER THE MOUNTAINS and Martha is on the terrace in time to see the first tendrils of sun reach the other side of the fjord. The large girths of the trees turn a theatrical orange, the rocks shine beneath tumbling vegetation. Below, on the water, all is calm. There is a whole day before the plane arrives with Laedi and Leonard, and she is up, determined to spend some part of it with Jericho.

Archie arrives on the terrace with his coffee. Milton, he says, is inside eating sausages and eggs. He looks across the fjord at the great old trees, lit gold, clinging to the edges of the fjord. Past the cyclone zone that leaves the peninsula ridge tops a grassy green, it's forest all the way to the perfect cone of a small volcano, which Archie tells Martha is called *Komoya*. He's come to find Jericho for an early swim, and when Jericho ambles onto the terrace with a blurry smile, Martha feels a kick of dismay. She doesn't smile when he stretches and says good morning, but she does when he tells her that in Tahiti, Matisse said the light was like 'plunging your eye into a gold globlet'. He ran out of sketch paper in a matter of days, and the island had to be scoured for more.

Martha watches as they go off down the path. At the bend, Jericho turns and waves, and she leans over the railing of the terrace to see them on the wharf. They stand there for a while, talking, and then Archie climbs down the ladder into the water and swims out, kicking a silver trail in the morning water. She watches as Jericho puts on his goggles and follows, down the steps, another trail of silver in the dark water. In the goblet light, something swells in her – forgiveness? acceptance? pleasure? – and why would it not? The days she waited for him and the girls at the international school are still vivid to her, standing on the grass at the bottom of the hill with the other mothers, watching him come out of his classroom and run down the walkways to find her. When he wrapped his arms around her, it was a blessing. The girls, too. For those two years she had every reason to believe that new sorts of families could be created in the new life they were making. And as with any family, the children let them exist up on the busy surface of daily meanings. Down below, unspoken injuries might have kept a steady pulse, but they rarely rippled to the surface. She sighs. They were young enough to hold fear at bay, to plunge into the golden goblet, and now all she wants, she says to herself in a plaintive bleat, is some time with Jericho. Today. Alone. Before Leonard and Laedi arrive, before they go to the village, before the memorial for Aaron. She wants to hear his account of the mountain and how it is with Bili, and what he is going to do now that the future is upon him. She wants to feel the air between them before they stand at Aaron's grave. If there is a grave. She doesn't even know that.

When Bili appears from Jim's office, where she's been on the phone to Moresby, Martha can tell from the briskness of her walk that it's going to be a day of interruptions.

'Do you want to come to the *haus sik*?' Bili asks. 'I wouldn't mind your opinion.'

So Martha goes with her to see the young man who came in on the dinghy with them and was carried up the hill on a stretcher. At the small hospital along the point past the school, he lies curled tight by a pain that has his breath coming sharp and shallow. He's running a fever, hot to the touch, and when he's persuaded to turn on his back, there's a growth like a hard mango extending up under the left side of his ribcage. His spleen, the Highland doctor says. He needs to go to Popondetta, or, better still, to Moresby. But the old man who's come with him rejects the idea. Gnarled and implacable, he's crouched beside the bed. With an insistence matched by the set of his jaw, he says that the ill boy – not much more than seventeen, by the look of him – must go instead to the point at the far western edge of the fjords where the traditional medicine man lives.

Bili reasons with him, but it's not reason that's at issue. She says she'll cover the expenses and the old man can go with him. No, he says, he will not have his charge leave these waters. When the doctor tells him to listen to Bili, he raises himself to deliver a torrent of vernacular in the language of the patient, who's in such pain he doesn't register the angry words that fly in the air above him.

'I suppose it's what happens when you're caught between two cultures,' Martha says when they leave. 'Two epochs.'

'Does that mean we take the worst from each?' Bili snaps.

It's easy enough for you, she says to Martha, living in Sydney, to buy the liberal version. Easy enough to say that all these cultural manifestations are equally valid, equally important. It's another form of racism to say it's fine if a young man dies for a cultural belief that wilfully prefers witchcraft over medical science. Is that what Martha wants? For us to say, fine, you go on believing the world is flat and the stars are made from the souls of dead ancestors and we'll say you're just as right as anyone else, and in the meantime those who have good hospitals will reap the rewards of your ignorance and make off with your resources. There are powerful forces ready to take advantage of the lie, she says, and if Martha hadn't known Bili as a child, she might have crumpled under the force of her words, which come out something like this as they leave the *haus sik* and propel them back along the path to the township.

'If we're not to become another post-colonial casualty, *more of a post-colonial casualty*,' Bili says to drive home her point, 'we have to *discriminate*.'

Then she quietens, and they walk on more slowly. She puts her arm across Martha's shoulder and looks at her with an expression that is half sigh, half smile. 'In any case,' she says, 'this business with the boy has more to do with a land dispute than with sorcery. Magic's useful in a power struggle, it's a potent accusation.'

'You still gave him a hundred kina for the dinghy to Spear Point,' Martha says, and Bili laughs. Sort of.

*

Outside the councillor's house they find Jericho and Milton under a tree, at a table of bush planks. They are sitting with an assortment of men Martha doesn't recognise. Archie is mixing coffee and sugar and powdered milk. He pours hot water from a blackened kettle and passes round the cups. The councillor is asking Archie about the fishing boats. He doesn't want them back, anywhere near the fjords, and nor do the elders, who are here at his house to prepare their reception for Laedi. They want to ask a minister of government what it means that the pirate fishing boats can go against clan laws and *gavman* laws all at the same time.

The government, the councillor says, is like a big bird, a bird that comes from somewhere else. It's not a bird that knows this land, and when it comes time to lay its eggs, the bird can't get a grip on the earth – it doesn't know how to grip this soil, doesn't know mountain, or fjord, or swamp; it knows nothing of where to put an egg. So when the eggs come, they lie *nabaut, nabaut*, some in grassland where they are taken by bad men, *raskol* men, who make off with them. Some land in the forest and when the chick pecks its way out, it doesn't know where it is. Or people from the village find it on their way to a garden, and they take it home to their village, and it grows there like a large and stupid child, knocking things over and cutting the wrong wood, planting the wrong seed. It sets up quarrels amongst the clans when no one can agree what to do with this big, clumsy creature.

Milton claps and takes the councillor by the hand, saying, 'Good one, good one true.' He tells him that long ago, before independence, when he, the councillor, was a small boy, they used to say much the same. 'My old friend here, she knows,' he says, gesturing to Martha, and the councillor nods sagely when she agrees that, yes, that's what we used to say. Sort of.

'We thought drama would do it,' Milton says. 'Plays and books and poetry. But, just like the big bird, we had the wrong roots. There were no roots down into the village.'

'That's harsh,' Martha says. 'There were roots, maybe not deep roots, but roots all the same.'

'Shallow roots are no good if they don't hold the tree,' Milton says, and Martha feels the metaphor slip away from her. The tree that is sheltering them from the morning sun casts an imperturbable shadow.

From the other side of the table, Jericho is watching Martha. Her face is pink with the exertion of the conversation, which has returned to the welcome the councillor is planning for Laedi, and the gateway they've built at the top of the runway. The women will decorate it with flowers when the sun starts its slide down the sky; the plane gets in late, leaving just enough time to get back over the mountains before dark.

It's true that Jericho has been in the present. The present is proving a good place to be, with Bili taking him back into her bed. Not that there was a bed in Collingwood Bay, just sleeping mats next to each other. There were nights when Jericho couldn't sleep for thinking about the elders who were facing the same problem he encountered on the mountain: of satisfying the new needs while safeguarding the old. 'It's not your job,' Bili says, awake beside him. 'It's the government's. That's why Laedi stays in.' It's a western conceit that we can solve this individually. *The saviour complex.* She turns on her mat and goes back to sleep. There were nights when Jericho stood at the edge of the bay watching the moon track across the water, thinking of the bark-cloth that was sewn into hats, and Hector determined there would be no sewing machines on the mountain.

Under the tree outside the councillor's house, the heat is building up like the clouds that billow on the horizon. They are soft and round, like clusters of breasts. They could be a sculpture by Louise Bourgeois. Rika photographed her when Jericho was a child. It kept her away. He'd hoped that a memorial for Aaron might bring her back. He'd hoped that if Leonard came, she might too. To see her here at the fjords, that was his wish; to hear her tell what happened the day Aaron drowned. Maybe then he could lay the past to rest.

Leonard has given him the outline, but when he asks for more, he says it's Rika's story to tell, not his, and anyway he wasn't there. Aaron had a heart attack in the water, and afterwards there was a disturbance. *A cross-cultural misunderstanding.* That may have been the case, but it doesn't explain an enmity of decades between friends from the same culture, friends who'd once been as close as sisters. He looks at Martha. She was there that day, with Rika, she saw it all.

What he wants is a narrative, and clarity of detail. Rika keeps the archive, as she calls it; she's never barred him from that. *Look at the photographs. They'll tell you.* When he was at university, reading Proust, he'd told her that on their own photographs were like raw incidents from life, memory without thought. Like negatives, that's what Proust said, they needed to be held to the light, 'developed' by the intellect. By Rika's narrating voice.

'If you're reading Proust,' Rika had said, 'you should know something about the errors of the senses.'

Back in the present, Jericho has lost all track of what's going on around him at the table. Milton is laughing. Laughing! His shoulders are going up and down with the surprise of it. He has his hand on Martha's shoulder, and she's laughing too. It's hard to imagine the two of them young, though he's seen them often enough in photos. They were so thin, and their hair so long. Milton's grew out in a wide halo that caught the light. Martha's was rather stringy. Now it's cut short, like Rika's. The brown has faded to a silvery gold. With the help of a hairdresser, he supposes. Milton's is cropped short, greying. Their faces are creased with lines that seem at that moment to be all smiles. They have turned to look along the path, and when Jericho follows their gaze, there is Wilkie coming towards them. He has one of his sons with him, and Martha is on her feet, calling out, shaking the boy's hand, saying he looks just as Wilkie did when he was at school in Hohola. The boy has a ukulele with him and is looking across to a stand of trees where a string band is setting up to practise. Wilkie gestures across to the boys, calling them to come and meet the visitors.

Wilkie has an elder's pendant over his sports shirt. He has canoed up to see Jericho, as they'd arranged. He tells him they've cleared a space around the grave, cut back the bush that has grown around it. A new cross has been made and the grave marked with clam shells. They will sleep in Wilkie's guesthouse, where there are six beds, each with a mattress and windows that open to the fjords. He's come to buy coffee and milk from the trade store, rice to go with the fish and cray they will cook for the feast to honour Laedi, who is a minister now, he says as if maybe Jericho didn't know. The feast to remember Aaron. He gives Jericho a copy of the agenda he's drawn up for their meeting, everything set out for the ceremony at the village.

Among the boys from the string band is one with an air of confidence that borders on arrogance. He's wearing a sharp black T-shirt with the name of an Australian band. He is Jacob's son, Lance. 'His lastborn,' Wilkie says.

The smile Lance gives might be the smile of a prince, and Wilkie says something sharp to him in their language. The boy recomposes his face and retreats with the band, back to the trees, where they start playing. They will play, Wilkie says, to welcome Laedi when she comes off the plane. The councillor will give a speech, for Leonard too, he says, Jericho's father, long known to his village, but not yet seen, except by Wilkie, long ago when he was in Moresby for school.

'Big trouble, that boy,' Milton says to Martha as they watch Lance with his guitar and his fine voice. 'He was expelled from his school in Brisbane for dealing drugs. Jacob isn't letting him back to Moresby until he's learned humility and the ways of the village. He's here without money, working in the gardens, learning to be a man.' By the look of him, it could take some time. Lance's hip movements have become exaggerated with the arrival of a group of girls. 'Just like his father, eh?' Milton says, smiling at Martha. 'Remember?'

Yes, she remembers. She's not sure what Milton is remembering, and she doesn't ask.

When the sun is hot overhead and they go back into the resort, back to the wicker chairs and the fans, Martha is reconciled to the interrupted face of another day. So it comes as a surprise when Jericho appears with his goggles later in the afternoon and asks Martha if she'd like to go down to the wharf for a swim. It's a good time of day to swim, he says, and if she doesn't have goggles, which she doesn't, they can borrow a mask and snorkel from Jim. 'I'll take you along the edge of the reef,' he says.

Swimming in these fjords had not been among her considerations. That was not a past to be reawakened. A refusal is on its way up from her belly, when she realises that Jericho's invitation is made only to her. 'Thank you,' she says. 'Why not?'

She sees, or thinks she sees, a look pass between him and Bili, who has taken a chair opposite Milton; a slight nod of her head.

ON THE WAY DOWN THE HILL JERICHO POINTS TO THE CLOUDS THAT are billowing out on the horizon.

'Did you see them this morning?' he asks. 'They were like breasts. Or a sculpture by Louise Bourgeois.'

Martha laughs at such odd, incongruous remark, and then she realises it's his way of bringing Rika onto the path with them. 'I've seen Rika's portraits of her,' she says. 'I've got the *Artists Series.*'

'Did you know that she went to some of her Sunday salons when she was in New York?'

No, Martha didn't know that. But she did know that Leonard met her husband, the art historian Robert Goldwater, and she's read his *Primitivism in Modern Art.*

'Did Robert Goldwater ever come here?' she asks. 'To New Guinea?'

'No,' Jericho says, matter-of-fact.

'He became a *leading authority,*' Martha says, her voice incredulous. 'He became the director of the Rockefeller Collection, and he never came here?'

'He went to Africa,' Jericho says, as if that will help, and asks if she knows Bourgeois' early *Personnages*, the tall wooden beings she made on the roof of the building where they lived in Manhattan, vertical creations she moved around in groups. 'When I first saw them,' he says, 'those tall vertical sculptures with carved faces, I thought of the Asmat spirit figures Michael Rockefeller collected.'

Martha has only seen the *Personnages* in reproduction. 'More like vertical slit drums, the ones I remember,' she says.

'Don't you love the way this place works its way into the western imagination? The way you encounter it in the strangest places.'

400

'It's rarely acknowledged. Even in the case of Louise Bourgeois.'

'Still, it's there in us in ways we don't know,' Jericho says. 'Rika has one of her *Paddle Women*. Bronze and wood. Did you know?'

She didn't know, and envy gives a sharp kick. Rika's done well for herself during these years of silence.

The water is silky clear. They climb down the ladder from the wharf and Martha follows Jericho past the damage that was done by the building of the wharf. Chunks of coral have been blasted off to make way for the pylons, and the reef beneath the wooden platform is littered with rusting cables, soft-drink cans. But the mess doesn't spread much past the wharf, and then they are swimming along the silvery rim of reef that extends, cuticle-like, a few metres out from the cliff before the drop into deep water. Bright squadrons of fish flash past, just as Martha remembers. Brilliant blue starfish and fat sea cucumbers lie on reef ledges that are bleached a disappointing white with only occasional blooms of colour. Warming waters, Jericho says. Long, thin strands of an elegant weed wave upwards in a graceful plume. Jericho dives down to take a closer look and when he comes back up and his head bursts through into the air, he says that the weed grows so slowly, this one could be older than he is.

'How do you know that?' Martha doubts that it's true. Jericho's no expert on reefs.

'Archie told me,' he says, and they swim on, until the cliff begins its slope towards the fingertip point where the grass of the airstrip meets the water.

Above them, trees grow out over the fjord, vines loop from their branches in a rich fringe, a kind of celestial conservatory; among the ferns and mosses that cover the rock face are clusters of tiny orchids. Being there with Jericho, languid in the water, is, for Martha, an unexpected moment of grace. Buoyed by the salty water, protected by Jericho's presence and the soft sounds of birds in the trees – *wee-ip, wee-ip* – her pulse doesn't change its beat when a large mackerel cruises the line of the reef below them. Mar-ve-llous. That's how Rika used to say it, and it is. *Marvellous*. A marvel.

On their way back towards the wharf, Jericho comes to the surface with a clamshell.

'I've always wanted to do that,' he says, shaking water from his hair and grinning. He looks at the shell proudly, small though it is, then kicks his way back down to deposit it on a convenient ledge. Watching him, grief surges through Martha. A pure, sad grief loosened from anger. Yes, she thinks, it's this silky water that is our madeleine, this and the pattern of light passing through it, tiny bubbles from a diving body.

'In the dinghy yesterday,' Jericho says when they return to the wharf and sit like sea creatures that have come out to warm themselves in the late rays of the sun, 'I was thinking about Michael Rockefeller drowning over in West Papua when he was collecting those Asmat poles, back in the sixties, and his sister in the helicopter looking for him. I was imagining what would have been in his mind as he tried to make it to shore. How easy it'd be for a canoe to be swept out to sea. He had a small motor but it was drenched when they capsized in a rip from the Eilanden river. In our dinghy, even without a river mouth, I could see from the currents that it'd be a hard swim.'

'Did you think you'd capsize?'

'No, not in a dinghy. Though now you come to mention it, I did check out the life jackets.'

'Were there any?'

'Two ancient yellow things that wouldn't have passed an inspection.'

'Jericho!' she says. 'Please be careful.'

'We weren't in danger.'

'No one thinks they are. If they did there wouldn't be any drownings. Danger doesn't declare itself.'

'Like Aaron.'

'Yes,' she says. 'Exactly.'

He looks her straight in the eye. 'What happened?' he asks.

THE MASSY GREEN

 'IT WAS A CLEAR DAY, LIKE THIS,' MARTHA BEGINS. SHE can feel Jericho's eyes on her. Across the fjord there's a wisp of smoke rising through the trees from a village; in the distance, the mountains are clear against the sky. The day she must return to was clear like this, a benign day. From the shore the sea was calm and glittery, with soft clouds billowing on the horizon.

'We were in the village,' she says. 'As you know, we went down with the canoes after the New Year celebrations. Jacob was with us, which made it easier; Angel too. And on the station with people in from everywhere and the dancing and the races, the greasy pole and the speeches, all seemed well. But when we returned to the village and Jacob and Angel recrossed the fjord for the climb to his village, I could feel that something had changed, and it wasn't only that Rika and Aaron now slept in the guesthouse. Rika didn't go to *afa* Noah's house, or to Aita's. You and Bili did, and Aaron, of course. But Rika, no. There was a strange kind of static in the emotional air, as if a storm was brewing, quite at odds with the sky and the flat water.'

'Why wasn't Laedi there? If Bili was there, why not her? Why just you?'

'Hasn't Laedi told you that?'

'She said she was in the Highlands.'

'She was with Simbaikan, for the celebrations there. Bili was meant to go with her, but she didn't want to be parted from you. She refused. Not just refused, but *refused*.' Martha lifts her arms in a gesture that says *what can you do with a girl like that*. 'I was there by fluke really. Another pair of hands.' There's no laughter now. Her lips purse. 'Useful Martha. That was me.'

'And Pete? Where was he?'

'In Sydney. His mother had had a stroke. A bad one. We'd probably have had to leave Moresby anyway.' But that's not how she feels about it. In her mind it has always been Aaron's death that ended those years which remain, despite it all, and all that she's come to think, bathed in gold. A tarnished gold, maybe, but still, gold is gold.

'So,' she says, returning to the story. 'It was a clear afternoon, our third in the village, when Aaron went out with the canoes. You and Bili were playing with the children in the water, jumping from that tree with branches hanging out over the water – you must remember.'

Jericho thinks of the photo in Laedi's house, of him and Bili with water below and a shimmering wall of green behind. Around it he has concocted something that he doubts is memory. Ominous. That's the feeling, the sensation of the photo.

'Bili had to coax you out along one of the lower branches. You were timid, a mountain child, not yet sure enough about the salt-water to drop into it from up there. You sat on the branch for a long time, bracing yourself with your skinny arms, refusing to jump. Then suddenly you let go and plopped in. It took us by surprise and we missed it. All we saw was that it'd happened. Rika had the Leica with her on the mat, but her mind and her attention was with Naomi. She'd come to sit with us, which meant a lot to Rika. Most of the women were keeping away. They weren't hostile. Just distant. We might have been tourists for all anyone would have known. So Naomi coming to sit with us, it was good. Rika had always felt closest to her, they called each other *gháto*, cousin, or sister-friend – you know what it means. Rika was trying to explain that her condition of infertility was not as Angel had described. Nothing had been drilled up into her, but the notion of a metal coil being inserted into her made no more sense to Naomi than it would to a woman in the suburbs of Sydney if you told her that the spirits of babies really do gather by a particular spring to wait for their mothers to sing them into the womb. I could see that the further Rika went down this track, the worse it'd get, but when I tried to stop her, she snapped at me. That's when you jumped. As if you knew to save her. Rika leaped for the camera in time to catch you shaking the water from your hair, and blowing it out of your mouth. All the kids cheered, but Bili couldn't get you back into the tree for a repeat performance. So you were on the mat with us when Naomi was on her feet, seconds before Rika or I heard the shouts and the conch from the canoes. "They're coming in," she said.

'Looking out towards the horizon, we could see nothing, a smudge perhaps, far out in the calm shine of the sea, but the crying had begun, quiet at first, a rumbling sort of whisper gathering pace as the women and the old men came running to the edge of the fjord. *Cry! Cry loudly! Oh unhappiness.*

'"Aaron," Rika said. "It's Aaron," and though no one broke through the lament with information, and though I said, "We don't know that, Rika," we did. We knew. I don't know how, but we knew before we saw. Before the canoes came in. The sky was very blue, and Aaron's skin was grey. The faces of the men on the canoes were grim.'

At that moment everything was vivid, without subtlety. Stark. *Oh unhappiness!* Jericho and Bili screamed. That is what Martha remembers. An animal noise, registering death. All around them women were keening, their wails rising in shock and grief. *Aaron, brother, do not leave us!* Only Rika didn't cry. She gasped. Her breath came in gasps, and then she crumpled, her knees literally folding beneath her as if all strength had gone from them.

'That happens, you know,' Martha says, turning to look at Jericho. 'Knees give and legs collapse. I never knew it till then, but it's true, they do.'

Her eyes are bright with tears, though nothing spills over. Listening to her voice, the grit of emotion in it, Jericho is barely breathing. Everything inside him is intent and still.

'When the body came ashore,' Martha continues, 'and was laid on the grass, she went to it like the widows you see in old photos, on hands and knees. Leaning over Aaron as he lay there on the grass, grey, sodden, *dead*. Then the sound came.'

Martha doesn't have words for the terrible sound of a woman who registers the cold and the stiffening of the body that once curved around her in love. *Nanda kómbo*, my lover, my body-self, husband-love. Or for the voices all around, rising in lament: *ai, ai. Mother of the ground!*

'You were crying,' she says, taking Jericho's hand into hers, 'and Bili was screaming, and all around the women were pleading, *Do not leave us. Oh beloved! Do not leave us.* I pulled you and Bili towards me, and you strained away towards each other, and it was Bili who covered your face. For months, years, still even now sometimes, I dream of that moment. Bili with her hands over your eyes, and her mouth wide and open, taking in every detail. That's what I remember. That I didn't cover her eyes. And leaning back, or forward, I'm not sure, until the world was spinning and everything went black and red and I too was on the ground with the crying and the wailing.'

She doesn't tell Jericho that with that swooning sensation came the thought: *it's over*. More than a thought, a conviction, raw knowledge. Something was over. Everything, all of it, *over*.

But right then, in the village, the drama of Aaron's death was just beginning. Aita was calling into his ear, 'Come back, sister's boy! Come back!' The women had brought a mat for the body. The men lifted it gently, feet towards the ocean, and carried it to Noah's house for the women to wash and wrap. The cousin-sisters climbed the steps behind, his uncle's children and children's wives. 'You leave us poor and alone! Come back!' Rika stumbled after them, following the body to the house. Noah stood at the bottom of the steps and would not let her pass. Aita stood at the top. '*Ai, ai*,' she called. '*Káe*. Evil day. This is the work of *káe*! Sorcery!'

'That's when Rika screamed, a bellowing, raging scream. As the widow she should have taken her place at the dead man's head, first amongst the mourners. She screamed. Dulcie hit her, other women too, with rolled mats and bark-cloth, and though it was mourning custom, and though they called out to her to be strong, though they called *aya* to her, the *aya* she could never be, she hit back at them. She hissed and lashed and kicked. Naomi managed to get her in a grapple, a kind of weird embrace, then she and I pulled her, *dragged* her, back to where we'd been, across the green, under the tree.'

There are no words, no sequence, to describe Rika howling *no, no, no*, and Naomi trying to calm her, and being shaken off, and Rika's face swollen, saliva dripping in long strands from her mouth, mucous from her nose. Her running forward, zig-zagging towards Noah's house, and Naomi running after her, and the two of them back on the ground. And then, clear as day, *aya* Aita standing at the steps to the house, a praetorian guard. 'My mother took him from the womb. She wrapped the placenta. Oh evil hands, evil day. He leaves us for the town. The order is broken. Mother ground, we all weep to you.'

'Do you remember nothing from that day?' Martha asks Jericho.

'Nothing other than colour. Green, that terrible green.'

'Nothing else?'

'The one image I have, and I don't know if it's from that day or another, is of Rika – I think it's of Rika and not Janape – lying still and turned from me. I touch her, and there's no response. I touch her, and she's cold.'

'Do you remember Jacob coming?'

'No. I don't think so.'

'Not at all?' Martha is surprised, though she has reason to be relieved that on this his memory is partial. Even now, even here, there are some things she doesn't want known. She tries to imagine, sometimes, what would have happened if Jacob hadn't been there, up at the high village, if he hadn't come with the men as soon as the news was shouted up the ridge. He was in the gardens where they were planting vanilla. It can't have been long, an hour, maybe two, before he arrived, but for Martha, waiting for him that afternoon, it might have been eternity. Time indeed stood still. Everything stood still, a great breath taken in with the shock, and at the same time nothing stayed still long enough to be comprehended. Except Aaron's body, which lay dead and cold in Noah's house, a *corpse* with its knees loosened so he could walk.

All Martha can tell Jericho with certainty is that Jacob was in the village before dark. She watched him cross the fjord. He was fast and accurate. All those years of canoeing to school, she supposed. He came ashore, came to her, right up close, first, before anything else, before going to Noah, to the body. She leaned in towards him and grief hit like an aftershock, and it was then, weeping in the release of his presence, that she understood how afraid she was. Badly, seriously afraid.

'*Kâe*,' she said. 'They're saying it was sorcery.' *Kâe*. The word had clanged at her like the toll of a bell.

'Where are the children?' he asked.

'With the others. With Naomi.'

Why weren't they with her? Why hadn't she gathered them to her? Another memory that returns to her at night, and that she does not tell Jericho.

'Stay here,' Jacob had said, but she didn't want to let him go. She clung to him, held on to his arms. Even after all these years, it's humiliating to recall Jacob taking her arms, peeling her away from him. 'Stay here,' he said. 'Stay with Rika.' Anyway, it has no bearing on the story Jericho needs to know. That's what she thinks, sitting under the shade-cloth at the side of the wharf, his hand in hers. It is late in the afternoon. The same time of day. A canoe pulls up. A man comes over and talks to Jericho. They hear voices in the trade store, and Jericho walks over to buy two cans of Coca-Cola. Martha drinks one down for the first time in perhaps thirty years.

'Shall I go on?' she asks.

He nods. Smiles. It's as if they're on a marathon, though his pulse has quietened.

'When Jacob got to the village,' Martha continues, 'Rika was in the guesthouse. I don't remember how she got there. She'd been there for a while, inside the house, scrabbling through Aaron's pack, making noises that weren't words, grunting like an animal. She took off all her clothes and pulled on his. The shirt he'd worn the day before, a pair of shorts that slipped down low over her hips. She made a knot at the waist. He'd been lean when he was young – you've seen the photos – and in memory he's still a size that could exchange clothes with Rika. But afterwards, when we looked back through the photos, we could see how large he'd grown. When we lined them up, six months by six months, there it was, that deadly layer of fat under the skin. You know the diagnosis; well, it was only a supposition as there wasn't an autopsy. A silent heart attack, the result of undiagnosed diabetes.'

'Is that what you think?'

'Yes, I suppose it is. Don't you?'

He shrugs, and his face creases with the impossibility of knowing. Somehow, today, the diagnosis seems less important. 'What happened out on the reef?' he asks. 'Did Jacob say?'

'Yes. Of course. The men, who'd been on the canoe, told him. They'd been fishing, and Aaron had been swimming off the edge of the reef. There were strange currents along that drop, but the tide wasn't turning and none of the others felt a tug that could pull a man down. There was nothing exceptional about any of it until they saw that Aaron wasn't rising from a dive. He was folded over, suspended beneath them. They moved fast, as they would, pulling him up, lifting him into the canoe, a dead weight, though Aaron was gasping, moving, a twitch, nothing more, a last gasp for breath before his spirit fell out through his arse. His eyes rolled back, then centred themselves, stared ahead. Blank, open. Dead.'

'That's pretty much what Leonard says. Except for the bit about the spirit falling out of his arse. Where does that come from?

'I don't know. Jacob, I suppose.'

'Is that who Leonard would have got the story from?'

'Or from me. I don't know. I don't remember. It sort of came to be the official story.'

'Do you think it happened like that?'

'I've always supposed so. Something like that. There wasn't a mark, or a sea snake, nothing anyone saw. They wouldn't have killed him.'

Jericho gives a shocked sort of a laugh. 'I wasn't thinking that,' he said. 'It's just that it's so neat. So precise.'

'Maybe Wilkie will know. One of the younger men who were out there that day.'

'Wilkie says it was an accident, that's all. He was full of apology this afternoon, as if somehow it was the village's fault. Says it was the old people. They didn't understand.'

'It wasn't only old people. If you mean what happened that night. When they turned against Rika. What does Leonard say about that?'

'Not much. There was a *disturbance*, and the kiap came for us. Not much more than that. Anthropological stuff about how easily cultures can misunderstand each other. Examples, but nothing specific when it comes to Rika. And she's so closed down on it, I can't ask her.'

'Have you tried?'

'I did, a few years ago. She became angry, then silent and reproachful. The whole thing was so awful I haven't gone near it since.' He sighs, a long exhale of breath held in. He wants a narrative to dress the wound. It's what he's always wanted, and here he is, with Martha beside him on the wharf. 'Will you tell me?' he asks, though in another part of his mind he is struck by the beauty of the sky, its *immediacy*, its light, yellow over the mountains to the west.

'I can try,' she says. 'But you know how it is. With something like this, you have to make sense of it, and over the years you think of it differently. I mean, you give different meanings to it. And then things shift a bit. Anyway, the night was confused.'

From Martha's face Jericho has an inkling of how it must have been for Rika. How very bad.

'Jacob went over to Noah's,' Martha says. 'He left us in the guest-house. It was dark. We didn't have a lamp until he returned. Rika was lying on the floor, completely still. We heard the women from the high village arrive. Their cries echoed over the fjord and joined the wailing that got louder and louder, more and more awful, with each next arrival. The news spread fast. Voices were calling out in the dark, and young men were banging saucepans to drive out the angry spirits that are drawn to a death.'

Oh unhappiness! He has left us poor and alone! Oh unhappiness! The calling cries that came to her in dreams for years, and woke her up. *Ai! Ai!*

'From the door, I could see movement on Noah's platform, shadows moving in the lamplight, and the crowd gathering outside. When Jacob came over with a small hurricane lamp for us, I sat outside on the steps with him. And, yes, he said, emotion was running high; and, yes, they did think it was due to Rika, this death. Or if not to her, as her, then to the order that was broken because of her. No one saw a snake on the reef. Jacob had looked at the body and there was no puncture wound. They didn't accept his suggestion of a heart attack or a stroke. He told them that it happened in Moresby sometimes, to men working in the government, hard work, some of them die suddenly, just like Aaron. He had names to give them, but, no, it was due to the broken order, to the bad spirits that had declared themselves in the strange, improbable story of Rika's infertility. They knew it from the tear that dropped from Aaron's dead eye when they spoke her name. *Kaé.*

'"You must understand," Jacob said to me, talking softly as if he was protecting Rika, didn't want her to hear. She was inside, lying there, without movement, or sound. He'd been in, he'd spoken to her, roused her enough that she turned and leaned against him. He took her face in his hands, said something, I don't know what – I was at the door. Then she gave a shuddering sort of a sob and turned back to the wall. He stayed with her a few minutes, then came back out to me. He said I had to understand that in their world, *in this world*, it had disturbed the ancestors as well as the living to see Aaron lost to the clan and the gardens and the fertile women. They'd let him go to the new order of government and town, they'd expected knowledge and power to come to them, and instead, this.

'Of course they were angry,' Martha says. 'Why would they not be?'

'And from Rika's point of view, why wouldn't she be?' Jericho says.

'Jacob couldn't get her to understand that it wasn't her. Not her personally. She was a symbol. That's what Jacob said. I *think* that's what Jacob said, and she hated it just as much.'

Something surges through Jericho – understanding, sympathy, sorrow, he isn't sure. Unexpected tenderness softens the anger of years, as Martha describes Rika moaning, crawling around the floor, gulping at the air, until she subsided back into silence.

'Jacob called across to Angel, and she came. Naomi too.' Martha's voice is steady and calm. 'They brought you and Bili. I've blamed Angel for a lot of it. She told the women things about Rika she shouldn't have told. Damaging things. But there she was, with your hand in hers, sweet and kind. You and Bili loved her. She sat beside me, stroking my arm. Naomi touched Rika's head, *gháto*, and you went to Rika, your small arms tight around her neck. For you, there was response. She wrapped herself around you and wept, great coursing tears wetting your face until you struggled against her and Bili shouted at her to let you go, hitting at her, a small tornado, and when Rika still didn't let you go, she bit her arm. Oh, she was angry.'

'She still is. When she thinks about it, which she doesn't much, she's angry.'

'With Rika?'

'Yes. With Rika.'

'Why, do you know?' Martha asks. Now it's she who wants detail, not a blurry outline.

'She felt abandoned – you know how she is. She'd loved Rika, right from the start – or that's the story – and Rika abandoned her. Pushed her away, and kept me. That's what Laedi says.'

Martha doesn't want to admit to her own anger. She doesn't describe freeing the child Jericho, the *sobbing* child Jericho, from Rika's grip. She doesn't describe Rika hitting her – hard enough that she had bruises the next day. She doesn't describe Rika spitting out her name, accusing her of *being there. Always being there.* What kind of an accusation was that? The unfairness of it, when she was there because Rika had *asked* her to be there.

Martha has lapsed into silence. She doesn't want Jericho to hear in her voice that she is aggrieved, still, after all this time. Besides, she doesn't have the words to describe the long night while Jacob sat smoking in the doorway to the guesthouse. Outside, small fires were burning as people arrived from other villages. The wailing and the crying rose and fell, rose and fell.

'You know,' she says to Jericho, 'I sometimes rerun that night as if it were an entirely different film. In it we leave the guesthouse and walk over to Aita and the women. We confront them with our anger, our grief, and refuse this terrible, frightening separation. In that film, Rika and I sit among them, call out *aya*, and let our grief be absorbed into theirs. In this film, she holds Aaron's head in her lap and anoints it.'

Jericho knows the impulse to reorder the pieces. How many nights has he lain awake in his flat in Shoreditch re-spooling his life? And before that in beds going back all the way to when he was a schoolboy in Oxford. If Janape hadn't died. If Bili wasn't so proud and would come to London. If Rika had told him what happened, all of it, exactly. When Martha describes her crawling on the floor, rocking and moaning, he can visualise the woman cast low. She looks like Rika, the Rika of photos, but she is not the Rika he knows.

'Strange, the things we remember,' Martha says. 'Naomi gave you and Bili some pawpaw, and Bili left a piece of it for Rika. It sat there most of the night while she lay beside it, and eventually I ate it.'

'Bili remembers a man in a black cape attacking Rika. His teeth were sunk in her neck, and she was crying.'

Martha knows exactly what that was, and when. It wasn't at the guesthouse in the village. It was afterwards, two days later, at the government station, before they left. She had Bili by the hand when she opened the door of the room where Rika was sleeping, and there they were. Jacob and Rika. Her head was back, tears coursing down her face, crazed with grief, clinging to Jacob, clinging to life. He was kissing her throat, and she was arched towards him, her hands pressed low on his back. When she saw Bili and Martha at the door with fruit and a thermos of tea, she jolted back, pushed him away. 'You,' she said to Martha. 'It's always you.'

So, Martha thinks, Bili doesn't remember. Martha's long wondered. She lets herself agree with Jericho that, yes, somehow a vampire movie has got mixed up in it. Odd, the ways of the mind.

'So how did it end?' Jericho asks.

'Late in the night, I heard someone come up onto the steps, the low exchange of voices. Then someone else arrived. Jacob called inside for paper, a pen. I took them out, and recognised two young men from the top village, boys really, who'd been to school in Moresby. They greeted me. "Do not be afraid," they said. "The village, they are sad, that's all. We take a message to the kiap." One of Aaron's uncles came over from the house where the women were maintaining their lament. More low voices, talking in language. And then the sound of a canoe leaving. From the door I saw it glide into the fjord, paddling westwards, up this way, towards the station. The moon cast shadows that added to the sense of ghostly movement swirling around the house where Aaron's body was. A wind had got up, and the tops of the palms were swaying.

'I must have slept, though I don't remember that I did. Or Rika. Maybe it was more like a trance-state that we were awoken from. It was dawn and something was bumping against the walls of the house. That's what woke us. You and Bili were sitting up, eyes wide open. Jacob pulled the door tight. Through a small gap in the plaited wall, I could see people on the grass outside the house, there was an eerie quietness about them. Because we were inside, I'm not sure of anything. I've come to see that fear makes its own images. It divides friend from friend, skin from skin. It was as if every corner of that room held a demon, and even now I can't say how many were of our own imagining.'

Jericho is nodding and Martha leans towards him, maternal, a hand on his leg. 'Are you okay?' she asks.

'Fine,' he says, and he is. 'Keep going.' His breathing is strong and even. The tap, tap, tap of anxiety that came down the hill from the resort with him, that swam out into the fjord with him, has gone.

'Whatever it was that hauled us from sleep,' Martha says, 'had put Rika on alert. For the first time in all those hours she was focused and attentive. She held you close, and I held Bili. We were silent, all of us.

'Jacob was outside on the grass in front of the guesthouse. "Listen," he said. Then Noah; I recognised the voice. "He was a great orator. He raised our name. He is gone. Why?" Then other voices – some placating, some hostile, a range from grief to anger, a howl from *aya* Aita. Then Jacob's voice.'

Again Martha is silent. Looking at her, Jericho can see how painful this tumble into memory has been. For her, more than for him, oddly. As she's talked, as she's taken him back to that day so long obscured with not-knowing, he's felt a lightening somewhere inside him as her words have merged with his own submerged remembering. Right then he can see Bili standing on the rocks beside the water, eight years old again. She is wearing red shorts. They are as clear to him as if she were standing there in front of him. He knows it's just an image forming in his mind, probably not memory at all – or a memory from some other place, some other time. He laughs.

'What?' Martha asks.

'Just the strangeness of memory. So vivid. I've had Bili down here on the wharf, in front of us, right here. Eight years old and in red shorts.'

Martha laughs too. A short, sad laugh.

'How long did it go on like that?' Jericho asks.

'With us trapped inside?'

Martha didn't know. An hour? Maybe more. The sun was still low in the sky, early in its journey out of the ocean, when the dinghy arrived. The mangroves at the end of the point made perfect silhouettes against a pink and orange sky, and somewhere in her mind she registered again the beauty of the place.

The dinghy swung in close to the rocks and cut its engine. The kiap jumped ashore with two station policemen. He shook Noah's hand, conferred with Jacob, went onto the platform to see the body and pay his respects to the women. With Jacob standing beside him, he spoke to the crowd. He said he'd leave the police to make a report, and, heaping injury upon injury, he asked – he ruled – that the burial was to be delayed. Jacob would stay with the village, and he, the kiap, would take Rika to the station and ring to Moresby, speak to the chief minister.

Martha relays these details in a calm, even voice. Jericho already knows most of them from Leonard. The mechanics of how they left the village.

'I opened the door of the house and bright light fell across the floor. You two children stepped out into a golden morning with me. Matisse's goblet,' she says with a sigh. 'I could smell the smoke of wood-fires and knew this was the last food that anyone would eat before the burial. The kiap took you children, handed you into the dinghy.

'I went back for Rika. She was hunched down on the floor with Aaron's singlet held to her face. I couldn't lift her, couldn't persuade her to lift herself. Jacob came and together we got her onto her feet and into the doorway. "Better if you walk alone," Jacob said, and she did. Like a sleepwalker, she walked down the steps and through the crowd that she had tried so hard to regard as family and clan. She walked to the edge of the water where the dinghy waited. The kiap put out his hand to help her across the rocks but she turned and walked back. She walked up to Naomi, who was streaming tears, and took both her hands. She went to Dulcie. Dulcie nodded, and she too put out her hand. And last to Aita. Aita looked her straight in the eye. "*Ai*," she said. "Go! You go!"

'That,' Martha says, 'is what happened. That is how we left the village.'

On the wharf, thirty years has spooled back, and for Jericho, as well as for Martha, that distant day is more vivid than the men smoking in the door of the trade store. When a canoe slides in, it takes an effort of reason and will to comprehend that it is not *aya* Aita sitting on the platform with the wives of her sons. Then, for a moment, Martha thinks it is Naomi, now an *aya*, come with a letter for Rika. But no. Jericho stands up and walks across to help the old woman onto the wharf. She tells him the name of her village and gestures across the fjord. She has a swollen, bloodied ankle, from a fall in the garden, and when she adjusts the cloth that is wrapped around her foot, he sees it is a recent wound.

The sun is dipping towards the mountains. The sky is streaky. The injured woman and her daughters with their babies begin the steep climb up the hill to the *haus sik*.

'You know,' Martha says, 'I hadn't thought of this until right now, but do you think that Rika's still bound to him? That their spirits are still trapped in each other? That's why she won't talk?'

'What a thought,' Jericho says, though it's not what he thinks. Laedi says Martha is a romantic, always has been. It may be illogical after all these years of pining for Bili, but he doesn't believe spirits get trapped in each other, or that true love takes only one form.

He is feeling something altogether different, and it's a radical shift of sensation. He's always assumed it's narration he needs: interpretation, explanation. And yet, as Martha gives it to him, he knows from the tone of her voice when she keeps a detail to herself, and he finds to his surprise that it does not matter. What she gives him reminds him of something he should have known all along, and did: it is form, and contour, the shape things make in space, the absences that are left between them that matter. Not the detail. Or even the narrating voice. Not only. If he had been able to see what Rika had shown him – *it's all there in the photos* – maybe he could have spared Martha the hard work of remembering. She is tired. He can see the effort that will be required to climb the hill. He takes her arm.

When they stop to regain their breath at the bend, they hear the plane with Leonard and Laedi on board circling out over the reef before coming in to land.

'Don't hurry,' Jericho says. 'It'll take them ages to get through the welcome that's planned.'

So Martha takes the chance while still alone with Jericho, and edges up to the question she's been wanting to ask.

'You and Bili are looking good,' she says. 'Happy, even.'

Jericho grins. 'Did you know that Louise Bourgeois said that in marrying Robert Goldwater she married her mother?'

'Is that what you're doing with Bili?'

'I haven't proposed, if that's what you mean. I'm moving carefully, but I think she's coming round to the idea that we can live in two places.'

Martha is surprised. 'You mean she'd leave here?'

'Not for long, she wouldn't. It's her ground, this place, and it's what makes her solid, like the earth, all the way through. That must be mother-longing, mustn't it? Loving that in her enough to contemplating living some of the time here?'

'Do you remember Janape?' Martha asks, still with her arm in his.

'All I remember,' he says, 'is a kind of deep, rooted-down, *absolute* feeling.'

'Does she have a face?'

'Only in photos, and they are Rika's, not mine. For me, Janape is a sensation, something I once knew and can no longer describe.'

Right then, there on the path, it is enough, complete in itself, an internal space made ready for the future.

EPILOGUE

Lunch with Jacob, 2006

IN MORESBY, MARTHA HAS LUNCH WITH JACOB. SHE HAS THREE DAYS in town, that's all, and on the second she rings. She is answered by a secretarial voice, polite and guarded. She gives her name.

'What shall I tell him it's in relation to?'

Martha is tempted to say *the past*. 'A personal call,' she says.

'Just a minute, please.'

A click, then music comes on the line. A Pacific string band. Then Jacob's voice.

'Martha. What a charming surprise.'

Martha doubts that it's a surprise.

When it comes to lunch – on the top floor of the hotel that looks over the airstrip to the mountains – it's clear he knows she'd been at the memorial for Aaron. If he is offended not to have been asked, he doesn't show it. How evenly he speaks. It's hard to get away, he says, as if that were explanation enough.

Everything about him is suave. His hair is greying at the temples. His shirt is expensive, his tie subdued. He's grown a little plump, but he has the gait of a younger man. His eyes seem less hooded, less veiled.

'So how was it?' he asks.

'Good,' she says. 'Jericho spoke. He's another orator. He talked about Aaron as one father and Leonard as the other and how Rika had loved the fjords, and the part Aaron played in bringing independence, and now this new generation and another one coming, more children at school, we are one again. One of Naomi's daughters spoke and said it was her mother's wish to see Rika at the fjords before she died. Ask her to come, she said. *Aya Rika*. Everyone cried and you'd never have known any of it happened.'

Jacob laughs. 'We're a tactful people.'

'Sometimes,' Martha says. 'I met Lance. His string band played. Handsome boy.' She watches Jacob's face, which remains as smooth as an actor's.

The waiters are attentive. While Jacob chooses the wine, she looks out at the view across to the mountains, which have not yet disappeared behind cloud. The sky is hazy, their outline indistinct, a high barrier the colour of a bruise.

'So,' Jacob says. 'Tell me how you are. I was sad, very sad, to hear of Pete's death. A good man.'

'He was.' Her answer is bright, disingenuous. This isn't what she wants to discuss, and she's beginning to think it was a mistake coming here to meet Jacob, this charming stranger who might be entertaining a client. As he talks, of his business, and his other children – two boys who are doing well, two girls who are married already – the young Jacob who has lived in her memory all these years evaporates, and Martha is sad, a little cross, and maybe that is what makes her ask about Rika, even though she knows he can't see her, or Wana, surely, would have said.

'Do you ever hear from Rika?' Martha asks.

'Yes,' Jacob says. 'Quite often.'

'You do? Do you *see* her?'

'When I'm in Europe or New York. Yes. Always.' He laughs at the surprise on her face. 'Why the surprise? You saw us that day.'

'But . . .'

'You thought it was a one-off? The black man taking advantage of the distressed white woman.'

Martha blushes.

'The Marabar Caves,' Jacob says.

'That's not fair.' Martha is angry. 'I never thought you were forcing yourself on her. I saw. I saw that you weren't. I thought it was her way of not going under. *I understood.*' The back of her neck is hot. She breathes in, looks down, composes herself. '*Besides,*' she says, shocked that he could think otherwise, 'I've never told anyone. Not one person.'

'That's what I tell Rika.'

'Does she think . . .?'

'She doesn't know. But the whole time is a very bad memory. She feels exposed by it.'

'She sees you.'

'That's different.'

'Why?'

'Because I was never one of the good ones. Like all of you were, on the side of everything good. Sometimes those people are hard for those of us who are not always so good. Who live in the world as it is.'

Martha's face is scalding. 'Is that why she hates me? Because I'm good?'

'Martha, Martha. She doesn't hate you. I told you, she just doesn't want to be reminded.'

'Don't you remind her?'

'She can talk to me.'

'She could talk to me once.'

'She was young. She thinks she talked too freely.'

'Are you lovers?'

Jacob leans back in his chair and laughs. Calls the waiter. 'You're the one who reads the novels.'

'What does that mean?'

'Martha.' The waiter pours her another glass of wine. She is unaccountably close to tears. For all these years, the successful Rika has been like a character from a different film. Martha has followed her from afar, but mostly she exists in some other reality. It's not a comfortable solution, but she's used to it.

'Tell me about Jericho,' Jacob says. His voice is kind. 'I've told him he should have lunch with me.'

'He's well. I think it's been good, this return. Not easy, but on the whole good. You know Leonard is here?'

Jacob nods.

'Well, they're about to go to the mountain. There's talk of a *bisnis* with the bark-cloth.'

'So I hear.'

'How?' she asks. 'You seem to know everything.'

He bows his head, an ironic modesty. 'They should be careful,' he says.

'Why?'

'Many's the white man I've seen go in with good intentions, but, as you know, Martha, you put money into the villages and it sets off a chain reaction. I've seen it go wrong too often.'

'It worked in the fjords. Those villages are looking good. Wilkie's guesthouse. It's gorgeous. All the kids are at school. And he even told me they have introduced *gender equity*. That's what he said.'

Jacob laughs. 'He's another who reads too much. But it's true, those villages are good. Very good. So they should be, the work I've put in. But there are others not so far away where the situation isn't good. I wonder sometimes if I got it right. I can't do it for every village. I tried with seed funding for vanilla, but without me there supervising, some of the villages spent the money and didn't plant. They're a mess. The young men go. The elders lose authority. The usual story.'

'No gender equity there.'

He shakes his head. 'On the contrary.'

'And Angel? How is she?'

'I'm a good husband to her.'

'And Rika?'

'A very good husband,' he says, and stands up to shake the hand of a man who's come in with an Australian guest.

'Will Leonard and Jericho be okay on the mountain?' Martha asks when the hand-shaking ends. 'Jericho was stopped on the road coming down last time.'

'I heard.'

'Can't you prevent it?'

He leans back and laughs again. 'How do you think I can do that? Police the boys on the road. I'm not fool enough to walk up there at this age.' He pats his stomach. 'How fit is Leonard?'

'He seems okay. He swam across the fjord.'

Jacob shrugs. 'Tell Jericho to come and have lunch with me.'

423

'He won't.'

'Because of Bili?'

'Probably.'

'She's a fool, that girl. Always was, even as a child.'

'She's brave and she's strong,' Martha says.

'Doesn't stop her being a fool.'

'She won that Collingwood Bay case against you.'

'She'd have done better to settle. It'll come back, and it'll come back in a worse form.'

'But they won.'

'Win on the rules and the rules are changed.'

'And you think that's okay?'

'No, I don't think that's okay. That's why I wanted her to settle.'

'That's not what she says.'

'I told you, she's a fool. Can't see past the battle she's in. She fights for it all and won't compromise.'

'Isn't that a strength in a compromised world? To stand up for what's right?'

Jacob laughs. 'There you are,' he says. 'I told you you were one of the good ones.' He smiles, changes tack. 'Is Jericho going to stay here?'

'His job starts again in a few months.' She's not going to tell Jacob their business.

'He should take her to London.'

This time it's Martha who laughs. 'You wish, ha! Get rid of the opposition!'

He shakes his head. 'Not what I was thinking at all. Dessert?'

Martha pats her own stomach. 'Better not,' she says, and manages not to be dissuaded. Coffee is enough. Coffee and one black chocolate.

'Lance,' Martha says. 'I heard he was expelled. Drugs. That must be a worry.'

'He was a late child. Angel's last baby. She spoiled him.'

'Her fault?'

'No. Too much ease. Boys his age forget what was won, they forget the villages. They take wealth for granted.'

'I thought the entitlement of the young was a western problem.'

'He's a western boy. That's why I sent him back to the village.' Martha sees a shadow cross his face – pain perhaps, or disappointment. Regret. She doesn't know.

The shadow passes and Jacob smiles, putting his napkin on the table. 'There's one thing you can tell me,' he says before he asks for the bill. 'Did Bili realise what she saw that day? At the station?'

'No.' Martha smiles. 'She thought there was a man in a cape biting Rika's neck. She thinks a vampire movie has got entangled in her memory. She thought it was at the fjords. That night.'

'Ah.' For the first time over lunch, Jacob's face is serious. 'Rika will be pleased. It's one thing she needs to know.'

'I hope she knows I've not said anything. Not to anyone.'

'Yes, she realises. But it doesn't make the betrayal less.'

'Betrayal? How was it a betrayal?' Was *being there* betrayal? Seeing, what? Her vulnerability? Her derangement? The episode with Jacob?

'Everything was a betrayal.' Jacob opens his hands in a gesture of query. 'How does one know anyone's mind? Especially a western mind. I put a lot of it down to growing up at the end of the war and her mother dying. Rika sees things in terms of betrayal.'

'Not Aaron?'

'Yes. Him too.'

'But they were so close. So bound together.'

Jacob makes an equivocal gesture with his head. 'In the end he couldn't give her what she wanted.'

'Nor she him,' Martha says, and then, 'Do any of us?'

'Depends how much we ask for.'

'What does she ask of you?'

'Not much. A bridge, that's all.'

A bridge? What sort of bridge? To the past, Martha supposes, and in her mind she sees a Japanese bridge over a pond. She transforms it into a bush bridge over a Highland river, and it morphs into a bridge over the lily pond in Monet's garden. She laughs. She's glad she's had this lunch, glad to see Jacob. Glad for her own bridge: that's what it's been, this return. A bridge, not a reckoning.

'Do you think she'll come back? For Naomi?'

'She might for Jericho.'

'And for you?'

Jacob laughs his cultivated laugh, and his heavy lids slide down, veiling his eyes as he pays the bill.

'It's been good to see you, Martha,' he says, as they stand up to go. 'Very good.'

'Will you look out for Jericho?' she asks, taking his arm.

'For you, Martha, yes. I will if I can. But you know, it's an unpredictable place here. No one controls it. Not all of it.'

'I love him,' Martha says.

'I know. Rika does too.'

'So you'll look after him for her?'

'For both of you. If I can.'

As they leave the terrace to go down in the lift to where Jacob's car is waiting, they stand for a moment and look out over the airstrip. The mountains have disappeared. All there is to see is a row of round, green hills, and below them on the tarmac the plane for Australia taxiing out for take-off.

ACKNOWLEDGEMENTS

The Mountain is a novel. It is not a work of history, ethnography or anthropology. However, in writing about a place as rich and complex as Papua New Guinea, I have drawn on the work of historians, linguists and anthropologists, in an attempt to situate the fictional characters and events in a world that shares salient features of history and experience with a real place and real groups of people. In so far as I have achieved this, it is due to wide reading and consultation, and to the generosity of many people, both in Papua New Guinea and in Australia. What I have made of it all, remains, of course, the view of a white outsider, and misreadings are entirely my own.

The book began with four images I have carried in my mind for many years. So my first thanks go to Russell Soaba for the image of the bird of paradise destined to vanish into 'the massy green' in his poem 'Naked Thoughts' (1978); to Gary Kildea for the image of the mimic with a 'camera' at the edge of the frame in his film *Trobriand Cricket*; to Tony Deklin for the story of the large bird of government causing confusion by laying its eggs in all the wrong places, which appears in his unpublished typescript 'Is there a Melanesian way? Conceptualising the fundamentals of the Melanesian dream of development in the 21st century'; and to the Ömie women chiefs, or *duvahe*, who told me the story of the old woman who carries the sun and the moon in her string bag, and allowed me to carry it away to tell in *The Mountain*.

The lines from Elizabeth Bishop's 'Questions of Travel', which appear as the epigraph to Book One, are used with permission of Farrar, Straus and Giroux, LLC.

The lines from Russell Soaba's 'Naked Thoughts', which appear as the epigraph to Book Two, are used with permission of the Institute of Papua New Guinea Studies. My further thanks go to Russell Soaba for allowing me to give the image of the 'massy green' to the fictional Milton.

In Papua New Guinea my thanks go to the Korafe people of the fjords, who have shown me kindness and patience over many visits. In particular, thanks to Joseph Daubi, Gerald and Euphemia Masevaki, Jackson and Pamela Borime, Gladston Aguba, his sisters, and their mother, *aya* Gillian.. While the fjords of *The Mountain* could not have been imagined without the fjords of the Korafe, they remain a place of fiction peopled by fictional characters, including Aaron and Jacob.

The same is true of the mountain, which took root in my imagination after a visit to Ömie in 2004. While I owe thanks to all who welcomed us, and especially the *duvahe*, as well as my dear friend Pauline Rose Hago, the mountain of *The Mountain* is fictional. There have been no ethnographic filmmakers in Ömie, and no Jericho.

The Ömie are, however, fine bark-cloth artists. Their work is held in many galleries, including the National Gallery of Australia, the National Gallery of Victoria and the Queensland Art Gallery. I thank curators Maud Page at the QAG, and Judith Ryan and Sana Balai at the NGV for their support and assistance. I also thank David Baker, who introduced me to Ömie. Tragically, he died suddenly in November 2009, just days before the opening of *Wisdom of the Mountain: Art of Ömie* at the National Gallery of Victoria. He is remembered well by the people of Ömie.

Brennan King, as manager of Ömie Artists, has been an invaluable source of assistance and support. The Ömie icons that appear at the head of each chapter of *The Mountain* are used with permission of Ömie Artists and the Ömie chiefs. Copyright remains with Ömie Artists.

In Port Moresby, I owe thanks to Sir Mekere and Lady Roslyn Morauta, and to Daisy Taylor for their support, hospitality and advice. And to Marion Jacka for her invaluable wisdom and experience.

At the University of Papua New Guinea, I thank my fellow writers Steven Winduo, Regis Tove Stella, for many hours of conversation, and of course Russell Soaba. As well as for everything else, I thank him for his careful reading of the manuscript, and for correcting my *Tok Pisin*.

In her capacity as director of the Environmental Law Centre, Port Moresby, Annie Kajir spoke to me of her experiences as an environmental lawyer, including the story of the woman who showed Annie her land after it had been clear felled – an incident loaned to Bili. She also spoke about forestry and logging in Collingwood Bay, as did Lester Seri of his time at Conservation Melanesia. I thank them both, and also Mary Boni of the PNG Ecoforestry Forum. The case between the Collingwood Bay landowners and defendants, PNG Registrar of Lands Titles, PNG Forestry Authority, Keroro Development Corporation Ltd and Deegold (PNG) Ltd, was heard in the National Court of PNG in May 2002. The court ruled in favour of the landowners. The account of this case given to me by John Wesley Vaso, a Maisin elder from Uiaku village in Collingwood Bay, has been invaluable in coming to understand something of the experience of finding one's land and heritage threatened. Bili's fictional case in *The Mountain* has points in common with this matter. John Wesley Vaso's account can be seen on www.drusillamodjeska.com, along with The Maisin Declaration, and developments since 2002. I also thank John Vaso Wesley for translating Milton's fictional song.

At Tufi I thank Simon Tewson, who was manager of the Tufi Dive Resort from 2005–10, and also Sharon Tewson.

In Sydney, first and foremost I thank Michael Monsell Davis for letting me read his diaries from his twenty-five years in Papua New Guinea, many of them at the University of Papua New Guinea, and for numerous conversations over many years. These diaries and his support have been invaluable. I also thank Dr Ruth Fink Latukefu for her interest in this book, and for loaning me research material from the eighteen years she and her late husband, Dr Sione Latukefu, spent at the University of Papua New Guinea. She loaned me copies of *UPNG News* and *Nilaidat*, the student newspaper, to add to my own.

I owe thanks to the late Ulli Beier, Georgina Beier, Donald Denoon and Ruth Cholai. Peter Trist has been an unfailing source of support and information. I am grateful to him, and to Nora Vagi Brasch and William Takaku for the sharpness of their memories, some of which can be found in Peter Trist and William Takaku, 'Living Legends, Dying Stages', *Meanjin on PNG*, Vol. 62, No. 3, 2003. William Takaku's death in January 2011 is another grievous loss.

It should be noted that the character of Aaron makes fictional history by his appointment to the university in 1968. In the non-fictional world, the first PNG academic staff were appointed, like the fictional Wana, in the early 1970s. A conference on the history of Melanesia, the Second Waigani Seminar, was held at the University of Papua New Guinea, 30 May to 5 June 1968. But there was no paper on the bird of paradise trade. For Aaron's research I drew on work done much later by Pamela Swadling, and published in her *Plumes From Paradise*, Papua New Guinea National Museum in association with Robert Brown and Associates, Queensland, 1996.

The *Surrealist Map of the World* first appeared in the Belgian magazine *Variétés* in 1929; the lines quoted from André Breton were first published in *Océanie*, 1948; '*amour fou*' is Breton's phrase; the lines from Paul Eluard were first published in *cahiers d'art* in 1936. The speech in which Labor Prime Minister Gough Whitlam spoke of Australia being 'no longer willing to be the ruler of a colony' was given in Port Moresby on 18 February 1973.

Captain John Moresby published an account of his *Discoveries and Surveys in New Guinea and the D'entrecasteaux Islands* in London in 1876. Charles Lyne, the *Sydney Morning Herald* correspondent in 1884 published his *Account of the establishment of the British Protectorate over the southern shore of New Guinea* in London 1885.

Paul Ham, *Kokoda*, HarperCollins, 2004, an excellent history of the Kokoda campaign, tells of the missionary mending his deck-chair when the Japanese warships appeared off the north coast of Papua. Howard Tilse's poem 'Fuzzy Wuzzy' was first published in *The Musings of a Moresby Mouse: Papuan Poems*, Barker's Bookstore, Brisbane, 1944.

James Baldwin's *Another Country* was first published in 1962, *The Fire Next Time* in 1963.

Anthropologist Elisabetta Gnecchi-Ruscone worked with the Korafe in the late 1980s. I am grateful for the opportunity to read her PhD thesis, 'Power or Paradise? Korafe Christianity and Korafe Magic' published by ANU in 1991. Her essay 'Parallel journeys in Korafe women's laments' appears in *Journal de la Société des Océanistes* 124(1), 21–32.

C. A. W. Monckton's account of his encounter with Giwi, as he called him, appears in *Some Experiences of a New Guinea Resident Magistrate*, John Lane, The Bodley Head, 1921. I am also grateful to Jan Hasselberg for sharing his research on Jiwu, as Giwi is called by his descendants, and to the Royal Anthropological Institute in London for showing me Captain F. R. Barton's photographs of the early government settlement at Cape Nelson, some of which can be seen on www.drusillamodjeska.com.

For answering medical questions, I am grateful to Dr Liz Rickman, Dr Susan Pendlebury, Dr John Daniels and Dr Charlotte Hespe. For answering legal questions, I thank Paul Blackett SC. For advice on the practicalities and complexities of ethnographic film, I thank Bob Connolly, Gary Kildea, Patsy Asch, Les McLaren and Annie Stivens. *The Decisive Moment* is, of course, the title of Henri Cartier-Bresson's influential photobook of 1952.

Hilary McPhee and Liz Jacka both read drafts, and their responses have been invaluable. I thank them both, and doubt that I could have finished the novel without them. Patsy Asch read with an eye to photography and ethnographic film, for which I am most grateful. Jeremy Steele has read various versions at various times, and has remained patient, for which I thank him. My sister Jane Victoria Bentley, and my niece Amy Bentley Cochrane both read the manuscript, as did Virginia Heywood and Susan Hampton, and their support has made all the difference. As has the support of all my family, both in England and Australia.

At Random House Australia, I thank Nikki Christer and Catherine Hill for her excellent editing.

A fellowship from the Australian Research Council made possible the research that underpins this novel. I am very grateful for this support. However the views expressed in *The Mountain* are mine and not necessarily those of the Australian Research Council.

For further notes on sources, please see www.drusillamodjeska. com.